THE GRANDFATHER PARADOX

Book I

A Clash of Ages

A novel
by
Stephen H Garrity

THE GRANDFATHER PARADOX

Book I: A Clash of Ages

Book II: Time Trap

Book III: Some Other Time

Book IV: The Wrong Side of Time

Book V: A Violation of Causality

For more information concerning the author and his works, please visit his website at **www.shgarrity.com**.

This is a book of fiction. All the characters and events portrayed in this book are either products of the author's imagination or are used fictitiously.

ISBN: 978-0-9952315-0-4

This book is dedicated to my wife, Colette, and to my children, Carina and Matthew, for a lifetime of encouragement, support and eternal patience.

A special thanks to Jeannette Giesbrecht for her editing and invaluable input into this novel.

HISTORY OF THE GRANDFATHER PARADOX

What began as a hand scribbled short story, somehow, incredibly, became a four decade literary adventure as epic as the story itself. In 1977, I saw a movie called *The Emigrants*, chronicling Swedish emigration to America in the late 1840's. I immediately embraced the saga as a great setting for an accidental time traveller. The following morning, I had completed a short story called *The Time Warp.*

From the onset, I was determined to avoid the typical time travel clichés of time machines, mad scientists, and especially having to go back in time to correct history. Time travel would be through a naturally occurring and unforgiving phenomenon. I extensively researched scientific studies on time travel, developing a realistic-as-possible science tailored to the needs of my book. The historical settings were just as meticulously studied, relying heavily on diaries of people who actually lived through similar adventures as a prime source and giving a personal touch that conventional research would miss. I read many books written in the 1800's to get a feel of speech, expressions, attitudes and dialogue spoken during that era. The one constant that stood out was the strength and reliance of their faith.

Between 1978 and 1982, the first full length version, *A Slide in Time*, took shape. In 1986, with my Apple 64 computer, I completed a massive 310,000 word saga entitled *The Wizard Blew His Horn*. My writing had matured dramatically, and armed with endless ideas, boundless expectations for my writing, I had high hopes. Then, in 1989, raising two young children and overburdened with too many commitments, I careened into a decade-long writing hiatus.

About 1998, I crawled back into the writing mode, brushed off and revamped *The Wizard Blew His Horn*. I got an editor/agent, and after four years of work, the final rejection notice sent a message to pursue other writing endeavours. After moving from Montreal to Kelowna, my new romantic thriller, *Sweet Obsession*, won the 2007 grand prize of the Mount Arrowsmith Novel Writing Contest, and immediately sought a literary agent. After the last of the rejections—one was so malicious it was as if I had run over her dog—I turned back to *The Wizard Blew His Horn*, completely re-imagining both the story and the main characters, and capitulated about not altering the timeline. Replete with a secret military mission, treachery, sudden plot turns, mystery, cinema friendly pyrotechnics, a forbidden romance, and a whole new set of characters to love and hate, I re-named it *The Grandfather Paradox*, and committed to pursue a five volume series, incorporating two planned but never written sequels.

Then the unimaginable happened. I strayed to other interests and became completely disconnected from my writing. Once in a while, I had short bursts of inspiration, but then lost it again. Three years after our 2012 move to Edmonton, I had an awakening, re-discovering the passion and sustained thrill of writing I hadn't experienced since the 1980's. In nine months of thrilling keyboard adventures, I completed the three book epic and finalized Book I; *A Clash of Ages*, for publication in August 2016. With Books II & III completed and pending final review, and Book IV well underway, I'm finally on the cusp of fulfilling my life-long quest.

I hope you enjoy the story as much as I enjoyed writing it.

Stephen H Garrity
July 2016.

In historical events, great men—so called—are but the labels that serve to give a name to an event and like labels, they have least possible connection with the event itself. Every action of theirs, that seems to them an act of their own free will, is in an historical sense not free at all, but in bondage to the whole course of previous history and predestined from all eternity.

Leo Nikolaevich Tolstoi (1869)

PROLOGUE

APRIL 28, 1848
A DAY'S SAIL PAST THE ENGLISH CHANNEL

Swaying with the ship's motions, the four steerage lanterns cast an amber glow on the young woman walking towards the deck hatch, her shadows dancing against the canvas partitions like wayward spirits. Tiptoeing around some clutter, she timed her footfalls to match the corkscrew roll of the ship. Most below were still sleeping, though the steerage was never a quiet place, even in the dead of night. She climbed the steep staircase to the main deck.

Though aboard ship for just one week, Alvina-Kristina Gabrielsson had already learned to detest the sea. No one forewarned her that over one hundred souls would be competing for the space intended for just eighty, or of the rank food, foul water, the vermin, the stench, and nothing, absolutely nothing, prepared her for the complete absence of privacy that stripped her soul naked of its dignity.

She stepped into the fresh air and the gloom of the predawn. Even above on the decks, the sea confined her world to just nine short steps from side to side, thirty-five bow to stern. The waves, wide and broad, rocked the deck as she stumbled to the starboard bulwarks. She clung to the ratlines while fending off the cold, huddling within her white shawl as her blond braids flapped angrily in the stiff wind. High above, the tiers of canvas were full, belled against the velvet of the awakening sky, swollen hard like metal breastplates. Beyond the ship's wake, the sun glowed just below a horizon of liquid brass. A crescent moon and the morning star waltzed together above the dawning sea.

Her eyes, wide and very blue, sparkled with fresh tears while lamenting over her beloved home in Sweden. Her husband had dragged her away to sea, taking her far away from everything familiar and dear for the promise of a better life in America. She lost all she ever loved—her father, brother, sisters, and most painfully, the mortal remains of her firstborn. Their cattle, barn, and nine acres of barley had once been home, but home no longer. Now other feet trod the fields and tilled the soil. The floorboards of her house sang to some other's footfalls.

This deep and aching sadness was as if her heart had been torn from her bosom. She convinced herself she carried a greater anguish than Cain when God exiled him to the Land of Nod—and she felt just as vanquished. She knew her husband would be angry if she stayed above deck much longer. It wasn't fair he must tend care to the new baby while she cried of homesickness. She stole just a few more moments to compose herself. The remaining stars yielded their ancient fires to the encroaching dawn. The birth of the new day seemed so calming.

Her breath staggered. A green fireball burst from the sky—but this was no shooting star, for it remained without motion. It hovered at the exact point where the sea met the northern sky, shining so brilliantly its reflection sparkled upon the waves. Her china-blue eyes, wide in stunned disbelief, watched as tentacles of emerald lightning reached out from the orb, menacing the air and water surrounding it. She couldn't hear any thunder, just an uncanny silence while the glittering green fireball spat sparks into the predawn.

It exploded! A blinding spit of light lit the northern sky, and from it, a shockwave of liquid green flames shot across the summit of the waves. She gasped, paralyzed, unable to breathe. It was going to strike the ship! Her fingers tightened around the bulwark, gouging into the weathered wood and she hunched down. At an exhilarating speed, the shockwave dashed by with a perfect silence.

The instant the green radiance struck the ship, her entire world lost its motion. The vessel ceased its downward fall as if colliding into a wall. Falling off balance, she grasped the ratlines to pull herself upright. The waves stilled—the ship held firm within a frozen sea. The wind ceased to blow and her braids dropped to her sides. The voices on the decks and the wash of the sea lost all of their sounds. She turned and saw that everyone else was motionless like marble statues. The smoke from the galley stove lay frozen against the sky as fine frost on glass. With an expression of grotesque terror and a dawning realization, she accepted that death must have consumed her.

But dead people don't breathe or have beating hearts. Her mortal body breathed in great swallows and gasps while her heartbeat thudded in her chest with angry fists. This was something other than death, and she wished the ship had the courtesy to stop its motion in a level stance, for it settled pitched down listing to port, which made standing difficult. She needed to put her hands back to the bulwark to remain upright.

"Hello?" Her voice still worked. In the entire world, was her voice to be the only one spoken, the only sound to fill the air? *How long was she to endure such a lonely fate?*

She became aware of an itching—a sensation of scurrying ants covering her hands. She glanced down, slowly, fearful of what she may find. Tiny snakes of the green energy were slithering along her fingers and the back of her hands! Alvina-Kristina shook her hands free from the bulwark, fluttering them in a frantic effort to shake off the static.

They wouldn't come off. She decided to scream. No one was to hear her, and she could do so as loud as she pleased, without fear of shame. She screamed like a demon as she shook and flung her hands about. The effort was wasted. She stopped screaming and extended her glowing hands before her. The tiny snakes faded away and just a few moments later, they were gone, leaving a mist of static shimmering from her fingers. The emerald radiance vaporized with a flash and her fingertips stung as if she had jammed them in a closing door.

Her world returned to life. The ship resumed its ride down into the wave. The wind again tugged at her braids. Voices from the decks resumed their chatter. The ship's sudden motion tripped Alvina-Kristina backward and she clutched onto the ratlines as she spun with her feet off the deck. When she caught her footing, she looked about to find all was calm. The ship with her 108 emigrants continued to shoulder through the long, broad waves as if absolutely nothing transpired.

She glanced around to see if anyone else may have taken notice. Most of the passengers were still below with just a few women lined up for the galley stove. The sailors appeared to be going about their normal business. Everything existed as it should be—except for herself. Her confusion grew into a sick, thudding headache and she tried to pretend it never happened—that it was some kind of waking dream.

Something beyond herself pulled her eyes back to where she first saw the green fireball. At first, there was nothing but the tranquil purple-black waters. A moment later, a faint orange glow appeared while a stain of black smoke rolled skyward. A terrible realization became clear. A column of smoke at sea could only be caused by a ship on fire. *A ship in grave peril!*

She searched the decks for a crewman, spotting the boatswain near the galleyhouse—a young sailor liked by the passengers. She gathered her skirt and with her fingers still biting with pain, moved towards him. Her legs were uncertain and she stumbled on the pitching deck as if she had drunk too much wine.

How she hated the sea.

"Mister Olsson, I see smoke!" She struggled with her breath. "I believe there might be a ship afire."

He followed her outstretched arm, searched a moment, then his eyes locked onto the tendril of black smoke. His expression twisted as it veered from scepticism to one of alarm. He summoned the ship's master.

Stepping out of his cabin, Captain Olof Liedberg shrugged into his black coat. A short, well-fed man with straggling brown hair and a trimmed black beard, tugged his cap and waved over the first mate. They waded through the passengers who were filing out of the steerage, the mate carrying his towering bulk behind his captain and the boatswain like a man-of-war among sloops. The captain extended the telescope, and swaying to the motion of the ship, adjusted the brass tubes. When the glass was in focus, he held it on the twist of smoke, appraising the magnified and inverted scene the optics presented. His expression was set, his rigid eyes curious.

"You possess a marvellous power of sight, Alvina-Kristina Gabrielsson of Kisa. A ship afire it is!" With lungs of leather, he hailed orders to change course for the burning ship. From the decks to high in the masts, the ship erupted with activity. The captain returned his eye to the spyglass, his mouth set firm.

The young woman tapped the captain's arm. She had the look of a frightened child. "Just before I saw the burning ship . . ."

"Yes?" the captain asked. His mild eyes glowed in a weatherworn face. She stood considerably taller and he had to look up.

"I saw a green ball of fire that when exploded made my eyes quite ache with its brightness. The ocean and atmosphere were felt to be full of electricity. Some," she lowered her voice to a hush, "went on my hands."

The captain chuckled, amused and somewhat enchanted by her charms. "Do not make your mind uneasy, my dear. That is simply a manifestation of St. Elmo's fire."

"Nothing could have startled me more completely." She didn't dare mention the world losing its motion. He would think her quite mad.

He smiled as he placed his hand gently on her shoulder. "It is not an uncommon thing at sea." He put the telescope back to his eye. The woman could sense the captain also saw something uncommon. Something uncommon for both a land dweller and a man of the sea: Something so uncommon he was unwilling to speak of it. Neither was willing to speak of the uncommon.

The vivid fires of the sun rose from its berth beyond the distant waves, blushing the towers of canvas and setting fire to the glimmering wave crests. The light played backward and forward over the woman's face as the long, early morning shadows of sail, rigging and ratlines followed the motion of the ship. A conflict between the wind, sea and the ship heightened into a sharp struggle. The captain countered with orders roaring into the shrouds as the stubborn wind yielded into acquiescence, like a woman's resistance giving way in her lover's arms. Alvina-Kristina knew from the creaking of the timbers, the particular heave of the ship, that the wind was holding steady. She felt the ship pick up its stride in the water.

Disaster struck.

A brilliant flash burst from the burning ship. Some seconds later, a roar thundered across the waves to give voice to the blast. The ship was gone. All gone. Standing with the captain, boatswain and the first mate, Alvina-Kristina uttered an inhaling sort of scream.

"Thirteen seconds elapsed between the explosion and its report," Captain Liedberg said, his low voice grave. "Therefore, the imperilled vessel remains precisely two and a half miles from our own."

"It must have been carrying munitions to explode with such fury," the boatswain said.

"We can ascertain, Mr. Olsson, if not the cause which has occasioned the catastrophe, at least the terrible effect it produced."

"May their souls be with God," Alvina-Kristina whispered, her voice jagged with pain.

"No sense in attempting a rescue now," the first mate said.

The captain collapsed the telescope with a sharp click. "Fortunately, Mr. Rödin, it is I who is in command and not you! We will continue on. Humanity commands us."

A few minutes of dreadful silence ensued—a flash of light! Using a mirror to reflect the sun, desperate survivors sent one flash after another to guide the ship to their rescue. A chorus of excitement erupted from the decks and into the towering shrouds as the ship adjusted its course.

One of the reflections seared into Alvina-Kristina's eyes, so intense it blinded her. Her legs gave way, and clinging to the bulwark, she collapsed to her knees. Wavering in a realm of darkness, a cold dread overwhelmed her like a black wind. She sensed herself drifting into a place where no one else could follow. Another of those foreboding messages consumed her that too often came to her without warning or invitation—surreal, mesmerizing, enchanting—but never wrong. It spoke to her in utter silence and yet with a deafening roar.

A great evil will soon be amongst you.

Something awful, something dreadful, was in the making.

Eight survivors will be brought aboard. The jackals will bring terror and tyranny, misery and cruelty, violence and anguish.

Death.

This ship was too tiny to offer the crew and passengers sanctuary from their horrors.

As the black mists of her vision drifted away, the premonition whispered its final message. *One of the eight is not among the wolves . . .* and she knew, at that moment, her simple existence would never again be the same.

PART I

MINE IS YESTERDAY, I KNOW TOMORROW

Book of the Dead (3500 BC)

CHAPTER 1

AUGUST 6, 2016
CAPE LOOKOUT STATE PARK, OREGON

Perched at the edge of the cliff with the steady roar of the surf pounding the beach 100 feet below, Jennifer Burke calibrated her ultrahigh frequency magnetometer. She returned to a portable camping table, sat in a folding chair, glanced at her laptop and was pleased with the readings.

She, along with the other four members of the crew, had set up their field lab at the northern tip of a peninsula. A heavily wooded spot concealed them within the soft shadows of the overcast day.

Through a tight gap in the foliage, she watched Professor Fleming assist two of the other students, Bob Scranton and Stuart Roberts, to mount the video camera on a tripod. It was a beast of a camera with a telescopic lens perhaps powerful enough to bring out features on Mars. In his early forties, the professor packed a significant waistline and fought to catch his breath from the hike and set-up. He took off his beige canvas hat to wipe his forehead with a sleeve.

Sitting beside her, Russell 'Cosmo' Wynn, a curly black-haired sophomore, activated the transmitter linking three custom-made buoys to their laptops. He wore a Los Angeles Dodgers baseball cap backwards, and thinking the rugged look enhanced his masculinity, hadn't shaved in about four days. There were four other laptops monitoring the live feed from the cameras along with various other instrumentation, including the buoys deployed five miles from shore triangulated a hundred yards apart.

"We're live, Professor. All three buoys transmitting," Cosmo reported with a wide smile as Fleming joined them.

"Hopefully, this time the radio reception won't be too adversely compromised by the event," Fleming said through his British accent.

"The buoys are grounded with anchors which should negate the radio interference," Jennifer said. Brushing her fingers through her short, sassy brown hair, she noted Fleming consulting his watch every thirty seconds or so and wished he would calm down—but they were right in the middle of a tourist trap, on a Saturday no less. All it would take would be one yahoo wandering right into their operation. Or worse, a park ranger. Their cover story—should they be forced to explain their field lab—was that they were studying whales.

Bob Scranton and Stuart Roberts followed the professor to the table. Scranton stood at an average five-nine, but Roberts, lanky and towering at six-five, made Scranton appear much shorter than his actual height. Scranton possessed uncannily small ears, concealed by his long blond hair, looking like a six year-old's ears grafted on a full-grown man.

Almost worthy of a tease, they could feel the tension shake out of Fleming's body. "We cannot bring any attention to ourselves. Once the event has concluded, we lay low in town until it is dark enough to retrieve the buoys."

"You hear that, Cosmo?" Jennifer said while typing on her keyboard. "Don't bring any attention to yourself."

"I'm not, Muffins. You're the one smashing your fingers against the keyboard. You can probably hear it from the beach."

She continued to pound the keyboard like she would an old-fashioned Underwood typewriter. "You're the attention seeker wearing Daisy Duke shorts."

He looked at her with a kind of lost expression. "Daisy who?"

"Oh, my Lord! From that old show—*The Dukes of Hazzard*. Daisy Duke wore cut-off jeans so short it was indecent."

"Oh." He looked unimpressed as he did his own typing—with significantly less noise than Jennifer. "It's obvious, Muffins, that I have a more cerebrally enhanced taste in television entertainment."

She slapped the table. "You're wearing girly shorts!"

"They're three inches above my knees."

"My point. Look at Scranton's shorts."

Scranton's cargo shorts fell to his mid-shins. "Those aren't shorts."

Cosmo stood up. "Real shorts, real legs, real tan, real man—and tattoo free." He sat back down, resuming his study of the data streaming from the three buoys.

"You could use those ridiculous shorts for hot yoga. I'm surprised no one has beaten—"

Cosmo jerked forward, dragged his chair over the dirt and roots closer to the table, closing nose to nose with the monitor. "Uh-oh."

"What do you mean by *uh-oh*?" Roberts asked.

Cosmo said nothing. No one moved. No one spoke.

"*Uh-oh* is something bad, isn't it?" Roberts said.

The tension ratched up a notch with Cosmo's silence. He keyed a command to the laptop controlling the buoys. One set of the four measurements displayed a series of undulating lines. One data set peaked significantly while another became agitated.

"What does *uh-oh* mean?" Roberts' mind binging on his internal fears overshadowed his mounting frustration of not getting a reply. Jennifer looked over to Cosmo's computer, trying to understand what the *uh-oh* inferred.

Cosmo licked his lips and looked at the professor. "We have company!"

"Company! What kind of company?" Fleming asked.

"Some kind of boat."

Fleming leaned closer to the monitors. "Who?"

"We'll find out in a minute." Cosmo controlled the large video camera with a joystick and panned to the right. "There—a yacht."

"Oooooh, richie-richies," Jennifer said. "Nice boat."

"At least it's not military," Fleming said, relieved. "Do you think they are just passing through?"

Scranton leaned over Cosmo's shoulder. "Goddammit! They're at the precise distance from shore to the center of the zone. Dead center! No chance in hell is this coincidental."

"What if they see the buoys?" Roberts asked. "They'll know we're here."

The professor glanced at some switches on the table. "Mr. Scranton, prepare to scuttle the buoys. But only do so if it is apparent they have been discovered."

"I think we should play it safe and scuttle them now," Roberts said.

"Chill, dude," Cosmo said. "They're gray, have a low profile, and are hard to see."

"Good thing we designed them to be scuttled," Jennifer said.

"We can never be too careful." Fleming stuffed an unlit pipe in his mouth.

"Those aren't cheap and we'll lose the data," she added.

"No, they were not inexpensive, Miss Burke. Losing the data would be an even greater loss."

Scranton and Roberts grabbed some cameras and binoculars and made their way to the edge of the cliff to watch the boat, Scranton muttering profanities the entire way.

"How much time remaining until the event?" Fleming asked.

"Twenty-three minutes and . . . mark, 10 seconds," Cosmo replied.

"That's loads of time," Jennifer said. "We'll find out soon enough if they are passing through or decide to stick around."

The camera stopped panning. The image of the yacht was sharp and steady. "That's a Canadian flag it's flying," Cosmo noted.

"Canadians?" Fleming said, a little perplexed.

"No one in their right mind would deliberately go into the zone at time zero," Jennifer said. "I really think that they're at the wrong place at the wrong time."

"If they're in the zone at time zero, Muffins, they'll be a lot more than in the wrong place at the wrong time," Cosmo said, holding a trace of a laugh.

* * * * *

Bowlegged and hunched, Tom Trasler tried to counter the sway of *The Salty Dog*'s aft deck while pressing the BlackBerry tighter against his right ear, a finger plugging the opposite.

"Drop twenty-eight thousand on the counteroffer and . . ." He was losing the reception. The thirty-three year-old pressed the device tighter against his ear. "Sally, Sally, I can't hear you. Sonuvabitch, I lost her!" The phone went dead, with just classic Beatles beating out of a boombox filling the silence of the terminated conversation. Tom nearly squeezed the circuits from the BlackBerry while redialling the office.

Though the ride over the waves was a little too rough for Carol Parker's liking, Tom's thirty year-old wife matched the rhythm of the seas without spilling a drop of her brandy. “I told you to get an iPhone,” she said.

The dour look Tom returned was well worth the tease. The wind blew his brown shoulder-length hair across his face while he redialled three times, still not getting through.

“Why now? Why? Why?” Tom shook the phone.

Tall with wavy black hair, Carol flaunted her figure with a tight beige pantsuit unzipped to the level of an overloaded bra. She wore a pale, yet photogenic complexion that held no sibling resemblance to Ralph, her sandy-haired half-brother piloting the yacht. She took another sip of brandy. The gem on her wedding finger—a boulder of a diamond flanked by a smaller pair on each side worth a year’s common wages—clinked against the glass.

“Isn’t he supposed to be on vacation?” Alice Cousineau said, brushing her short auburn hair from her eyes and finishing with a giggle. The nineteen year-old spoke with a mild French Canadian accent. She was young, yes, but had no wide-eyed innocence about her.

“This is vacation for him.” Carol smiled tolerantly and took another sip of brandy while relaxing on the aft deck’s couch not far from where Alice sat. It was overcast, windy yet agreeably warm. Though Tom wore a jacket, Alice, barely five-foot and 90 pounds wet, was more than comfortable in her yellow tube top. She never forgave God for making her look like a pre-adolescent boy, though the short haircut was her own doing.

“Come on, Trasler, chill and have a drink.” Charlie Mason, on the opposite side as Carol and Alice, held a list resulting from the excess of alcohol consumed, not the choppy seas. A towering carrot-topped twenty-two year-old with a matching full beard, he was the company’s IT specialist for the big meeting in Long Beach, but also the target of a surreptitious attempt by Tom and Carol to set him up with Alice. To say the set-up didn’t work out would be like saying that the maiden voyage of the Titanic went a tiny bit awry.

Carol pursed her ruby painted lips into a sensually enticing pout at Tom and patted the space next to her.

“Come on, sit and relax, Tom.”

The soured look she got back from Tom was not what she strove for, though exactly what she anticipated.

"This dead zone is about to cost me a two million dollar deal and you expect me to relax?" Still in denial over Montreal relocating to Washington, Tom tugged his prized Expos baseball cap and leapt up the ladder to the flying bridge. "Take us closer to shore, Ralphy. Hurry!"

Ralph, a thirty-nine year-old man of average displacement with a broad, clean-shaven and unremarkable face, put his hand in the small of his back and grimaced as his spine cracked. He glanced at the GPS, looked up to Tom's six-foot-one level, and gave him a sharp look.

"We're on vacation—including you."

"We're on a business trip, Ralphy."

"Not until we arrive in Long Beach. Until then, we're on vacation. Mellow."

Tom lost the friendliness in his eyes. "I'll mellow when I close the deal."

Ralph toasted the world with a potent Bacardi and Coke and drank. He took a deep drag of his cigarette, smiling as continued to drink, thoroughly enjoying Tom's torment.

Tom's deep brown eyes were venom as he thumped down the ladder. Once on deck, he jabbed his finger at Carol as if she was to blame, the look he gave her screamed profanities. Dressed in jeans and a blue polo shirt that were woefully under-classed by his Prada leather jacket, he continued to scrutinize the BlackBerry for the all-important signal. He could feel his frustration creep into cold panic.

"Forget it, Trasler, come and have a drink," Charlie said, holding up a 40-ounce bottle of vodka, more empty than full. Alice noticed Tom's fixated eyes on the bottle, homing in on it like a missile's targeting lock. She was rough when she snatched it from Charlie and took it inside the galley.

"What was that all about?" Charlie asked as Alice returned.

Alice sat back down and crossed her legs above the knees. She was all legs with blue jean cut-offs so high they might be panties. She boasted a perfect tan. "Tom doesn't drink."

"But he drank last night."

"He's allowed a glass of brandy when he smokes his cigars," Carol said. "Once a week, under supervision, and that's it."

Tom didn't appreciate Carol's response. Not so much as what was said, but her tone of voice. He was tempted to counter about the thirty or so pounds she ought to lose, but getting cut off from sex for at least a couple of weeks wasn't worth it.

Charlie threw Alice a harsh look, still bitter at her less than delicate rejection of him. There was no subtle brush-off. She delivered an outright get-the-hell-out-of-my-life rant, then turned against Tom and Carol for the ill-conceived set-up with another overdone tirade. The mood remained toxic.

The Beatles degraded into half static, like a radio station drifting while driving under some high-tension power lines, except the music played from the boombox's internal drive.

They all exchanged unsettled expressions as Tom gave up trying to fix the issue and turned it off. He bent over the flame of his lighter to light a cigarette. He took a couple of deep drags to quell his anxieties, all the while keeping a sharp eye on the BlackBerry for a flicker of life.

As if something was dragging him away in a trance, Tom's eyes drifted from the phone. Not because he gave up hope of reacquiring a signal, but because of a creeping awareness of a low buzzsaw sound. What alarmed him was the realization that this sound had been in the background for quite some time and he just took notice of it now.

* * * * *

Cosmo looked at the countdown clock on his screen. He changed his voice to low and steady. "This is Apollo Launch Control; we are at T-minus—"

Jennifer slapped his bare leg above the knee with a resounding smack. "Will you stop that!"

"You're too wound up, Muffins."

"I agree with Jennifer," Scranton said, returning from the lookout. "You're no Jack King." Cosmo laughed and the two exchanged a fist bump.

"Like, I'm supposed to know who Jack King is?" Jennifer said.

"Ya," Cosmo said, Scranton nodding in agreement.

"Jack King, the legend—indeed," Fleming said, his eyes twinkling as he added to the tease. They could see Jennifer tense up; the way her hands clawed like a prehistoric carnivore got them all chuckling.

She muttered something unintelligible and resumed her attack on her keyboard. She stopped typing with a lurch. "Oh, you've got to be kidding me!" Jennifer gasped on her words. "Professor, big trouble!"

Fleming's pipe, still unlit, froze in his mouth. After the initial shock, he withdrew it. "What is it?"

"We have more company. A helicopter."

"Who?"

"Uncle Sam," Cosmo reported. His tone, along with the look he gave, was dour to say the least.

"Bloody hell!"

"Are you certain it's military?" Jennifer asked Cosmo.

"It's an army Chinook helicopter."

"Anyone but the military," Fleming said. "This is distressing."

"What are they up to?" Jennifer asked. The worry tightened around her words, squeezing them.

"You can be sure it's nothing good," Cosmo replied.

"First the yacht and now the military," Jennifer said. "Just how many others know about this? I thought it was just us!"

"I think we should abort," Roberts said.

"And miss this?" Cosmo said. "Dude, this is Hollywood!"

"Cosmo, there's one thing about watching a Hollywood movie and another being a disposable character in it," Jennifer said.

"You're not the disposable character, Jennifer. Plucky comic relief, maybe."

"How can you joke at a time like this?"

Fleming glanced at the image feed of the Chinook displayed on one of the laptops. "Please, Mr. Wynn. Focus. Note the probes mounted on the fuselage." Fleming clamped his pipe back in his mouth.

Cosmo controlled another of the video cameras to track it. "They have a bigger budget than us."

"Indeed." Fleming lit his pipe, smouldering with a previous bowl's embers. He glanced at Stuart Roberts standing at the edge of the cliff, following the Chinook with his binoculars. "Be assured, Mr. Roberts, if we see the military taking notice of the buoys, they shall be immediately scuttled and we flee in great haste." He faced Jennifer. "How's the transmission from the buoys?"

"Signal is compromised by about 60%, but as predicted, the anchors are doing their job acting as a ground. We're just about twenty minutes from the event. My guess is that those on the boat are pretty much in a full radio blackout by now."

"And their electronics going to shit," Cosmo said.

"Language, Mr. Wynn!"

* * * * *

Above the ambient noises of the boat, Tom tuned into the whup-whup-whup of the helicopter off their port bow, flying at an altitude of three hundred feet about a half-mile ahead. It headed west—perpendicular to their due south course. Tom wiped the hair from his face and tightened his Expos cap. He looked at Carol in an absent, distracted sort of way as if she had something to do with it.

"Ralph!" Carol indicated the approaching helicopter with a nod of her head, her hair a fountain of black as it trailed to leeward. "What is going on?"

She directed the question at Ralph with good reason. Still wearing his old army jacket, he had served in the Canadian Army for eighteen years. Easing the chrome-plated throttle, he slowed *The Salty Dog* to quarter speed. Ralph stood and stretched a kink from his back. He recognized it as a CH-47 Chinook—an army transport helicopter.

"A Chinook. Bloody loud bastards to fly in," Ralph said.

The Chinook veered abruptly, now headed directly towards the yacht. The whup-whup-whup of the dual rotors beat the air like war drums.

Tom lifted a hand to his forehead. "I don't believe this." He slipped the BlackBerry into its belt holster and stood still, swaying against the ship's motion. "They're coming right for us, Ralphy. Why?"

"No idea."

Carol hunched forward, her legs pressed together while she sipped her brandy in short, incremental shots.

Ralph eased the throttle to a quiet purr.

"He has no idea why the helicopter changed course and decided to intercept us. Lovely," Carol said, splashing another shot into her mouth.

Tom leapt up the chrome ladder to join his brother-in-law on the flying bridge. He took a sharp drag on his cigarette. "Why are they intercepting us?"

A steady eyed man with features that at first appeared severe, hard, but when Ralph flashed a smile at Tom, everything changed. "Don't worry, we're not doing anything wrong."

"Then why are they coming after us?" Carol asked from below.

Ralph looked down at his half-sister. "That's an army Chinook transport helicopter, not a gunship."

Carol gulped a mouthful of her brandy. "Whatever the hell it is, it's intercepting us, Ralphy!"

Ralph turned up the radio to see if the helicopter was trying to call them. Dry static filled every channel, and he looked at Tom with a deadpan stare. "That's odd."

"What do you mean by *that's odd*? Ralph, it's obvious those assholes are jamming our radio!"

"Keep calm."

"Keep calm when those Cro-Magnons are about to take us out?"

The Chinook, now less than three hundred feet ahead, stopped her forward motion. It hovered with the downwash of the propellers beating mists from the water while the cockpit windows stared menacingly at them.

"That looks like a warning not to get any closer," Tom stammered.

"You've got that right." Ralph pulled the throttle into neutral and the yacht bobbed as it drifted over the waves.

"Closer to what?" Carol asked. "What is it they don't want us to get any closer to?"

Ralph lowered the binoculars. "Get in the dink and head to shore. I'll pick you up after."

Carol looked at the back of the ship to the tender hanging from its davits. "In these waves in that tiny thing? Nope, I don't think so."

Ralph looked at her with disconcerting eyes. "Your choice."

Carol mouthed something profane but did not speak it.

"Look at all those weird antennas and sensors sticking from the fuselage," Tom noted.

"Why aren't we leaving?" Alice asked. No one responded.

Ralph studied the Chinook through his binoculars and offered Tom a static no-comment. Tom scurried down the ladder. "It's probably on some kind of classified mission and we just happened to show up at the wrong time."

"Come on, Tom. What kind of classified mission can they possibly do five miles off their own coast?" Carol asked.

Tom hooked a thumb at the Chinook. "They're not here for a social.

That, and they're jamming our radios, and I very seriously think we should split—like right now!"

* * * * *

Cosmo sat back with his arms crossed, grinning at the monitor. "Uncle Sam is displeased." The yacht continued to drift over the waves. The Chinook moved south then a little east. Its movements were sharp, aggressive. "Look at them freaking out over each other. Is this great or what?"

"It's great if you like drama," Jennifer said.

"Do you like drama?"

"No. I prefer comedies. This isn't a comedy."

"Where is the helicopter in relation to the zone, Miss Burke?" Fleming asked.

"They're looking for the zone but can't quite locate it," Jennifer replied. "There's a lot of indecision going on. They've gone in and out a few times."

"They should have deployed three buoys in the zone like we did," Cosmo added with a tidy boast. "We know exactly where it is."

"In situ and with all of that equipment, they must have readings." The professor's mind whirled with too many thoughts. "I would think they should pick up our buoys. They are beginning to glow with static."

The helicopter was on the move again, the yacht still drifting. "The helicopter is back in the ellipse, but slightly off center," Jennifer reported. "But they seem to be sticking around this time."

"The yacht's location?" Fleming asked.

"Thirty-two meters outside the zone," Cosmo reported.

"What's that in feet?" Jennifer asked.

"No clue, Muffins."

"I hate being called that and I hate metric. It's so un-American."

"Scientists use metric, Muffins. Get with it."

Fleming puffed a couple of smoke bombs from the pipe. "I want a sterile field lab. Only discuss the event, nothing else. Is that understood?" Neither said a word or even gave a gesture to acknowledge the command, but they understood plainly enough. "Time to the event?"

"Just over eighteen-and-a-half minutes," Cosmo replied.

"The helicopter has been in the zone long enough that the temporal static should commence." Fleming withdrew his pipe to lean in closer to the monitor. "There."

"Green or red?" Jennifer asked.

Cosmo waited a moment and flashed a smile. "Green!"

"A negative event." Fleming gave his pipe a couple of sharp puffs. "As predicted. Excellent."

"We're good," Cosmo said, a wide grin creasing his stubbled face. "Are we good?" he asked Jennifer.

"We're amazing!" The two high-fived.

* * * * *

A faint glow appeared from beneath the Chinook's fuselage, resonating in a green-blue radiance. Tom licked his lips that suddenly turned dry. Carol opened up her camera case and bent over, switching lenses when she noticed Charlie staring at her.

"Definitely not a good idea to stare down my top. Especially when my father is your boss." She locked the telephoto lens in place. "IT guys are a dime a dozen these days."

Charlie yanked his eyes from her, his face flushed, and reached for his own camera case.

"You flaunt it, expect a guy to look," Alice said critically.

"When boobs are big like mine, they get flaunted whether you try or not. Something you couldn't possibly understand."

Alice rolled her tongue inside her mouth while Tom glared at Carol with a sharp reproach. Carol took aim at the Chinook and the camera clicked away.

"What the hell are you doing?" Tom's voice shrieked in a high octave of panic. "It's bad enough that we're seeing whatever crazy shit they're up to, but they'll lock us up forever if you photograph them!"

She dismissed him with demeaning kind of wave she'd use in a bar to brush off some drunken redneck. She supported the Nikon by its telephoto lens while the camera whirled away. Charlie snapped off a picture with his Polaroid. A blue-gray film whirled from the camera. Carol glanced obliquely at him between taking frames.

"I can't believe you were even able to find film for that antique," Carol said and resumed taking shots.

Charlie stared at the blue-gray emulsion slowly coming to life. "I belong to a Polaroid club. A lot of people love these cameras and I've got tons of film." His voice slurred from the excess of screwdrivers.

"I can't fathom why. The quality's crap. Besides, there's new insta-matic cameras out there a lot better than that piece of garbage."

"Polaroids are still the best way to get an instant print."

"Prints? They're sooooo passé."

Charlie, drunk and feeling intimidated, put his camera away. He continued to watch the print develop. The helicopter was a distant, blurry spec and he frisbeed the wasted print over the side.

Alice became transfixed on the Chinook's fuselage as the glow increased in intensity. "I think we should leave," she said to Tom.

"What do you think I've been saying?"

"Ralph isn't about to leave," Carol said, still taking frame after frame.

"He's your brother, you tell him."

"Half-brother. Don't push it." Carol stopped taking pictures and looked up to Ralph. "Ralphy, we're leaving right now!"

"You really want to miss this?" Ralph wasn't about to leave.

"Yes, I want to miss this!" Tom said while Alice motioned for his cigarette. She sucked a huge toke off it and handed it back.

The emerald glow on the helicopter brightened and spat sparks into the air. Tom leapt up the ladder. The breath shot out of him. "Sonu-vabitch, Ralphy, look!" His voice was hoarse with terror, awe, or both.

A thunderbolt of emerald voltage zapped the water with the intensity of a giant death ray. Ralph didn't reply. An odd look settled on his face. Not one of fear, but of childlike wonder. The glow pulsating on the helicopter resonated in a three or four second cycle while thunderbolts sizzled into the rotors, dissipating with violent explosions, casting a brilliant verdant reflection across the waves. The perfect silence of the explosions was downright creepy. Something releasing so much energy should at least have the courtesy to make some kind of scary-as-shit sound.

* * * * *

"The temporal static is discharging off the rotors." Cosmo's excite-ment remained unhidden while the others took the event far less lightly.

"Barely any TS on our buoys. I wonder why?" Jennifer asked.

"They are mostly submerged, Miss Burke," Fleming explained.

"If those dudes don't leave the zone soon, they're going on a long trip," Cosmo said, grinning.

"That's nothing to smile about, Cosmo. Peoples' lives are at stake," Jennifer said with disdain, just short of contempt.

"Indeed, Mr. Wynn. The situation is very grave and is not to be trivialized." Fleming took a tobacco pouch and put a pinch in the pipe's bowl. That's when he noticed just how much his hands were trembling.

* * * * *

The thunderbolts shot off the Chinook into the sea like an alien invasion. The emerald lightning wasn't a flash, but a long, steady discharge. The water did not react to the voltage—no vapour, no waves, no disturbance and still no sound. Within the electrical mayhem, the Chinook commenced a descent.

"Is this great or what?" Carol said to Tom, keeping her eye pressed against the viewfinder. She squeezed off frame after frame.

"Great?" Tom's voice rose to a decibel past full-fledged hysterical. "I thought you wanted to leave?"

"I changed my mind," Carol said as her camera whirled away.

"How can you just change your mind?"

"It's a girl thing."

Yes, it was a visual extravaganza, but this wasn't Le Cirque de Soleil. This was just a little too far over on the Darth Vader side of the entertainment genre for Tom's liking. The Chinook continued to descend with the downwash from the rotors beating the water into a mist thick as fog. The static flared up brilliantly with a massive surge of voltage. A new sound could be heard, like someone feeding metal sheets into a tree chipper—the kind of noise that didn't sound like something good was about to happen next. With a cannon shot, black smoke belched from the port engine. The starboard engine roared to compensate, going from full throttle—then to nothing at all. It didn't shudder, fade, or stall—it was an instantaneous shutdown. The Chinook careened into a sharp right bank and dropped.

Ralph jolted to his feet. "She's going down!"

Crawling with the parasitic static, both of the Chinook's rear engines exploded. The blast had a thud felt inside the body causing the ears to pop. The rear pylon tore off while the aft loading hatch spun in the air like someone tossing a playing card. The brilliance of the explosion lit the overcast day, blushing the white hull of the yacht within an ivory fan spreading across the gray waters. Hissing with black smoke, the fuselage cartwheeled while a meteor shower of flaming debris rained down on the water, creating leaping feathers of spray, some striking close to the yacht.

Ralph sucked in his breath. Tom's hands clutched a handhold, his biceps swelled while something within him thrilled. Carol froze her finger on the shutter. Frame after frame whirled with automatic weapon-fire rapidity. Charlie screamed like a girl and covered his eyes. Alice watched with her hand moving towards her throat, her mahogany eyes open wide.

The Chinook's cadaver slammed into the water face first, performed a slow-motion somersault, and came to a rest upside-down. The aft pylon, concealed in sputtering flame and smoke, hit the water a second later. A scarf of black smoke boiled out of the tossing gray waters, marking the spot.

"Sonuvabitch, Ralphy," Tom hushed in a low, awed voice.

CHAPTER 2

Twenty seconds following the explosion, the muffled roar of the blast rolled over the waves to reach Fleming's team.

"Oh my Lord!" Jennifer could hear the alarms shouting from the others. She chewed off a fingernail, not even conscious of doing so.

"This is a calamity," Fleming acknowledged.

"What caused it to explode?" Cosmo asked. Panic strangled his voice and this was no longer any fun.

"We don't know," Fleming said. "Remain calm."

"Remain calm?"

* * * * *

The tip of Ralph's cigarette trembled, creating jitters of smoke. He puffed in and out without inhaling while staring at the severed fuselage floating upside-down with a fog of smoke sighing from the blasted open rear-loading door. The Chinook appeared stable on the water, at least for the moment, while filaments of emerald static continued to sparkle across the wreckage. Off to the forward starboard side, a rotor blade probed lamely out of the water.

The expression on Tom's face was one of drugged horror. He stared at the wreck for a few seconds, waiting for the moment to become real.

"I got the entire thing," Carol said, appearing oblivious to the loss of life she documented. Charlie stood trembling while Alice lamented over the families back home who just lost a loved one. Tom's cigarette dangled loosely, then he tightened his lips to suck in an enormous drag.

Tears were stealing down Alice's face when she tried to call 911.

"Phone's dead."

"So it wasn't the helicopter jamming our signals," Tom concluded.

"Then what's causing it?" Carol asked. The tension grew like tightening a tourniquet. Though Carol lost the enthusiasm, she continued to photograph the wreck, accepting it as a grim duty to perform.

"Hang tight!" Ralph rammed the throttle forward. The yacht heaved out of the water and banked hard to the right.

"Sonuvabitch, Ralph, don't go anywhere near that wreck!" Tom's words rushed out in a strangled shout.

"Are you insane?" Carol shrieked.

"We're going in!"

"It might be radioactive, you idiot!" Carol yelled, straining her voice to its limits.

"Come on, Ralphy, let's get the hell out of here!" Tom pleaded.

"Got to see if anyone's alive."

"Ralph!" Carol screamed in frenzy. "Turn around before we get killed!"

"Will all of you shut up!" Ralph raised his voice to a frightening pitch. "We have a legal and moral obligation to assist a vessel in distress. Like it or not, we're going in!"

* * * * *

"Professor!" Cosmo called. "The yacht's rescuing the Chinook!"

Fleming motioned with his hand for Cosmo to lower his voice, while he, Roberts and Scranton edged closer to look at the video streaming on Cosmo's laptop.

Jennifer chewed on another fingernail. "The rescue will bring the yacht almost dead center of the zone."

"How much time?" Fleming asked.

So unnerved, it took Jennifer a moment to find the right screen. She spat out the chewed fingernail. "Fifteen minutes, twenty-six seconds. Those poor people!"

Cosmo licked his lips. "Come on, dudes, get out of there."

* * * * *

Ralph eased the throttle to a troll and aligned the boat for its final approach. The emerald aura had rebounded since the crash and continued to envelope the smouldering wreck. The equipment bolted to the fuselage looked like featureless gray spheres of various sizes and shapes, so unusual, it gave it the appearance of a crashed UFO. One of the two long sensor booms bobbed through the waves.

"Tom, get on the nose. Once we're close enough, tie the boat to one of the helicopter's wheels. Give me—"

"I'm not going anywhere near that freaky green stuff."

"Lasso it then, and give me a few feet of slack. Use a bowline and don't blow it like the last time. Remember? The rabbit goes up the hole, around the tree, once, not twice and—"

"And goes down the goddamn hole. I know, I know."

"Ralph, you idiot, there's no way anyone's still alive!" Carol shouted. "I've had it with you!"

Carol balled her fists and her body shook with the roaring words. "Open your eyes and look at this freaky electrical glow!"

"That radiation could be lethal," Alice added.

"Ya," Tom said, on his third attempt with the bowline.

"Alice's right," Charlie stammered.

Ralph tapped the ash from his cigarette, took a final drag and flicked it overboard. He let out a smoky sigh, letting his head hang in front of him for a moment while searching for just the right means of persuasion. "I need thirty seconds to find out if anyone's alive. If no one is, we hightail out of here. Okay?"

Only because Ralph's promise came in a blessedly reasonable tone of voice did Carol even contemplate accepting the proposal. "Fine," she conceded. "Thirty seconds in there, not a second more."

Ralph arrived at the nose of the yacht to join Tom. He untied Tom's granny knot and without a word of critique, replaced it with a bowline. The air was quiet except for the wind whistling through the frayed metal of the wreck. They tried to see inside for signs of life, but an acrid veil of grimy smoke obscured the interior. A few lights flickered from inside, the odd filament of the green voltage, then vague shadows. They heard no movement, only a beeping alarm.

Tom cleared his throat and with pleading eyes, turned to Ralph. "No one's alive. Let's go."

"I'm going in."

"Are you nuts? It's full of freaky radiation and it's about to sink."

"And the stench coming from it is disgusting," Carol added.

"If anyone survived, they'll need help getting out. Come on."

Tom's eyes bugged. "What do you mean, come on?"

"I can't rescue anyone alone."

"This is your rescue, man, not mine. I'm not setting a foot in there with that freaky green stuff."

Ralph looked deep into the shadows of the Chinook. "We're not going to leave those poor bastards in there to die."

"This is a soldier thing, right?"

"Damn right. We never leave our own behind."

Tom stared into the entrance of the Chinook, its wasted shell stirring in the troughs. It was as if the helicopter's hatch was an entrance into Hell. He did not want to go in there.

With a lock of his sandy hair escaping from under the brim of his black skipper's hat, Ralph stooped within the Chinook's entrance. Despite the glow of the emerald radiance covering the walls, the ceiling, conduits, floor, and inner confines of the Chinook, it had so far spared Ralph. "Look, Tom, the green stuff isn't touching me and I don't feel a thing."

Tom sighed in resignation, tugged his Expos cap and breathed in some courage. He handed Carol his leather jacket and BlackBerry, and reluctantly, clambered off *The Salty Dog's* nose. With a little acrobatics, he made it to the loading ramp entrance. The rear pylon, severed from the blast, would have been directly above the ceiling at the aft end of the fuselage. Now upside-down, water flooded through the jagged fissure. Walking on the submerged cabin ceiling, each step was blind, slow, searching for secure footage among the conduits, light fixtures and wires. Ralph probed the flashlight's beam into the smoky shadows, lighting a dismal glow on a cluster of harnessed corpses, dangling from their flight seats.

"Sonuvabitch!" Tom grunted, stunned by the bloody shambles. "Jesus, Ralph, there's only a red bone where the head's supposed to be—and it's a woman!"

"Don't stare at the bodies, Tom."

"This is horrible!"

Tom wasn't about to go any further, content to watch Ralph forge deeper into the shadows. Ralph probed ahead with the flashlight. Despite the crash, some of the equipment still returned data. A dull background glow of the green static shimmered inside, but nothing close to what they saw on the exterior of the craft. Upholstered blue swivel chairs, with their dead technicians strapped into them, faced port, which in their upside-down orientation, appeared on their right side. Ralph ducked past a dozen or so crates strapped down on the floor. One huge crate—dark gray, featureless and with large hoses snaking from it— stood out from all the others. Heat radiated from it. A lot of it.

"Come on, Tom."

"I'll wait here. If you need help, then I'll come."

"Move it!"

Tom's mind recoiled as he waded deeper through the shadows and he knew that somewhere, a woman's head lurked unseen in the water. The water rose past his shins to his thigh. The bodies surrounding him in the acrid smoke and gloom swayed like cattle carcasses in a slaughterhouse cooler. The acrid smell and stench of burnt flesh, more than anything else, was about to set him off into some kind of lunatic delirium. Tom saw it as a wild dream—he had wandered into Hell—and he knew that so long as he lived, he would always carry this moment with him.

The multicoloured glow of computer monitors continued to glimmer within the fog of smoke. The scorched displays revealed numerous graphics and a heck of a lot of math. One of the stations had an insistent beeping alarm, trying to reach the deaf ears of its lifeless technician with a warning that came too late. The dead soldiers were wearing khaki flight suits. Tom made the mistake of gazing into the face of one in his early thirties, his nametag identifying him as Arbing. The dead man's eyes peered through their mask of gore—dazed and unknowing. Tom seemed to feel the gaze of Arbing linger on him. His face branded into Tom's memory while he tried to depersonalize this tragedy. He recoiled when the arm of another swaying body brushed by his face.

The Chinook shifted with a groan of stressed metal. The incline grew steeper and Tom found himself sliding rather than wading. He picked up speed to keep up with Ralph, not knowing if what he felt was terror, exhilaration, or some unholy blend of the two. Clinging onto a flight seat occupied by a mangled corpse, Tom forged ahead. Ralph flashed the cone of light to a bulkhead about two-thirds of the way into the fuselage. The water lapped against a metal door, bent out of shape from the blast.

They continued to dodge the swaying bodies as the water swirled around their stomachs.

"The bulkhead might have protected others from the blast," Ralph speculated. The explosion wrenched the door inside the frame. Ralph pocketed the flashlight and pulled on the door. It held tight. "Give me a hand, Tom."

The Chinook lurched into another drop, like a stumble down a staircase. A fresh wave flushed through the cabin as the water level rose to their sternums. They glanced at each other for support, to find a new confidence. Tom gouged the tips of his fingers into a gap in the door seal and yanked, but mostly floating, he had no footing for leverage. He reached deeper into the dark water and found a door handle. He put a foot to the wall, floating and face up, heaved with his full effort. The door lurched three inches.

A hand reached from the behind the door! Shouts and screams exploded, trying to open it further. The water continued to rise and the panic behind the door was extreme. Tom and Ralph double-teamed, managing to heave the door open another inch. It was heavily insulated with a blue, rubber-like material that gave off a rank smell like fresh epoxy glue. Another heave, another inch. A collage of other hands appeared—female, black male, a tiny pair that might belong to a boy. They were all pressing against the twisted door, the shoving and heaving holding a rhythm while desperate shouts urged more effort. The door burst open as if someone released a locking bolt.

A captain in his late forties plunged through, spitting out water and gasping for air. His nametag visible just above the waterline identified him as Anderson. He removed his flight helmet, revealing close-cropped hair that once been blond but was turning gray. He glowed with enough of the green static to be a source of illumination.

"Another thirty seconds and we would have drowned. Thank you and thank you, Lord." He moved forward, gasping at the morbid sight of his dead crewmates. A woman, wearing a green flight helmet, dazed with a bloodied face, struggled to keep her head above water as Tom and Ralph floated her through. A corporal in his forties, barely the size of a twelve year-old, followed. His bulky flight helmet over his small face and wire-rimmed glasses reminded Tom of Rick Moranis playing Lord Dark Helmet in *Spaceballs*. He emerged with absolutely no expression on his face. Once he had a foothold, he waded towards the back to a functioning workstation, ducking past a swaying corpse to study the data streaming through a monitor.

A colonel in his early fifties floated through. If Ted Rood was thankful for Tom and Ralph saving their lives, his pale blue eyes, cold as tempered steel, gave no indication of it. The spurts of his breath came out strong and fast. He glanced at his dead crew.

"Christ Almighty."

He helped out Jackson, a black thirty-something lieutenant who wore a thin, tidy moustache like a modern day Errol Flynn. On the razor's edge of panic, he splashed his arms through the water. Gasping for breath, his eyes were desperate.

"We've gotta get out of here, Chief. We have less than fifteen minutes!"

"Calm down, Tyrone."

"We have thirteen minutes, twenty-four seconds," said the tiny corporal at the workstation. He showed no concern whatsoever as he keyed commands on the upside-down keyboard. He tossed the arm of a dead soldier out of his way with the same emotion as flicking away a bothersome fly.

"Thirteen minutes to what?" Tom asked.

"Until the implosion," the black soldier wheezed, still out of breath.

"Whoa!" Tom's voice elevated with raw fear. "What's he talking about? What's an implosion?"

"Put a lid on it, Lieutenant," the colonel ordered.

Tom didn't accept the non-reply. "What the hell's an implosion?" No response. "That's the opposite of an explosion, isn't it?"

"Nothing you need to be concerned about," the colonel replied. He teamed up with Ralph to pull out a sixth survivor—a completely submerged young soldier. He hissed out his breath, caught another and after a couple of deep heaves, breathed like nothing at all transpired.

"Wally's dead," he said with a thick Latino accent. "Not much need for a pilot anyways." He glimmered in the gloom like a mirage, shrugged off his green flight helmet and dropped it into the water.

"Where you from?" Anderson asked.

"Victoria, BC," Ralph replied.

"Dear God, you're not Americans?" His accent was pure down east

Yankee.

"Canadians," Ralph said. His tone was borderline apology.

Anderson noticed Ralph's jacket. "Army?"

Ralph flashed a brief smile. "Canadian Army—retired."

The colonel turned to Ralph. "All right, soldier," Rood slapped his shoulder—a soldier-to-soldier respect, "let's get aboard that yacht of yours."

Tom made an interesting observation, though nearly imperceptible chest deep in the water, was of how Ralph's body stiffened as if he was about to stand to attention. Only the salute was missing. Ralph transformed back into the soldier—eager to show those Americans the metal a Canadian soldier was made of.

Rood stared at his dead crew, tight lipped, shaking his head. The woman's hand clawed as she clutched it before her mouth. Tom followed her line of sight and wasn't certain if the mangled heap was a man or a woman. Her grief betrayed they had been close.

"What's going to happen in thirteen minutes?" Tom pressed. He and Ralph were still unaffected by the green radiance, but all the others were lit like human glow sticks.

"Classified." The colonel's eyes were moving everywhere, tabulating the destruction. His face twisted in a terrible cramp of concentration. He grabbed the black soldier's arm. "Secure the field equipment."

"You're not serious?" The black soldier's eyes filled with amazed disbelief while a grin twitched Captain Anderson's lips.

"We can still save the mission."

"With what, Chief?" Jackson asked in a loud, desperate way. "We're dead in the water and more than half the crew is dead!"

"I'm ordering an ERAP onto the yacht, people. Move it!"

The female soldier, Sharon Bodmar, collapsed and slipped beneath the water. Ralph heaved her up, struggling to support her. Blood flowed across her entire face.

"Get her to safety," Rood ordered. "We'll be out in a few minutes."

"What's an ERAP?" Tom asked.

"**E**mergency **R**esponse **A**ction **P**lan. Now get her out."

"On our boat? What does that mean for us?"

"This bird will be on the bottom of the ocean in a few minutes. I don't intend to go down with my ship. Move it!"

"Come on, Tom," Ralph said.

Bodmar wore corporal stripes, stood at five-foot-three and appeared to be in her forties. She hooked her arm around Tom's neck while he held her tightly. "We're dead center of the implosion zone," she said. Her tone held so much terror Tom could feel his bones cringe.

"We're exactly where we're supposed to be, Sharon," Colonel Rood said, smiling without humour.

"Better shut off the boat's engine," the tiny man said. He glanced at an upside-down monitor, still trying to keep the dead technician's arm out of his way. His voice was indifferent: Giving the facts, nothing more.

"Shut it off?" Ralph asked.

"The same energy source that caused our helicopter to explode will also blow up your boat."

"Jesus," Ralph hushed.

"What happened, Silver?" Anderson asked the tiny corporal interpreting the data.

"The TREP caused an instability within the fuel or engines, not certain yet."

"I thought the dampers were supposed to protect us from any TREP?" Rood asked.

"Dampers didn't work."

"Christ, that's an understatement," Rood said.

"What the hell is a TREP?" Tom asked.

Sharon Bodmar offered the reply that didn't please Rood. "It's an acronym—**T**achyon **R**esidual **E**mission **P**henomena."

"Thanks. As if I'm supposed to know what that's all supposed to mean."

"You asked."

Silver glanced at Ralph. "The explosive effect of the event was completely unexpected. A couple more minutes in the zone and your boat will have absorbed enough of the magnetic resonance to start glowing the way we were. Better hurry and shut it down."

Tom had no idea what an implosion zone was, but it definitely did not sound like a good place to be in. They plowed against the water, not an easy climb against a sharp list. They clawed their way out while he and Ralph double-teamed Sharon Bodmar. With Carol and Alice assisting, they pulled Bodmar onto the nose of the yacht. Blood splashed from her forehead in big raindrops onto *The Salty Dog's* white deck.

Ralph scrambled to the flying bridge to kill the idling engine. Tom crawled and sat on his haunches, dazed in shock. Carol continued to document the evacuation from the Chinook, not even bothering to ask Tom if he was okay. Charlie observed the drama from the flying bridge, a safe vantage point to ensure he remained nothing more than a non-participant. Alice, who got a small first aid kit, pried the flight helmet off Bodmar, revealing thick tied-up strawberry-blond hair streaked with a few lines of gray. She put a gauze pad over the wound and wrapped the white medicine tape around her head like a headband.

"Nothing too serious." Alice gave a reassuring smile and patted her shoulder.

Bodmar grasped Alice's wrist so tight it hurt. "We need to get out of here!"

Alice tapped Tom's shoulder to snap him out of his morose daze. "What's going on?"

"Something about us being inside an implosion zone. They're not talking about it. Top secret!"

Carol lowered the camera, all at once afraid. The fear lines sat on her face as if she aged thirty years.

Anderson's appearance from the Chinook's hatch redirected their focus. He carried large cases, the same type of heavy-duty cases used to transport sensitive audio-video equipment. Ralph returned from the flying bridge and gave Anderson a hand. Tom glanced at the feverish activity and decided it best not to piss off the military by being a dead-weight. The explosion had stained most of the cases in soot, some took a hit and another was completely destroyed.

* * * * *

"They have survivors," Jennifer reported with a *woo-hoo* cheer.

"Thank God," Roberts said.

"They still have ten minutes to get out," Scranton said.

Jennifer exhaled some of the stress from her body. "Loads of time."

"You will be surprised just how quickly ten minutes can expire," Fleming cautioned.

"They're unloading equipment off the helicopter onto the ship," Cosmo said, seeing a clutter of crates on the nose with a lot of activity happening on its deck. "I count six survivors."

All survivors were on the nose of the boat, stacking and sorting the crates.

"Professor, why aren't they leaving?" Jennifer asked.

"I fear it is not their intent," Fleming said.

"They're going through the event deliberately?" Scranton asked. His voice sounded a lot calmer than he felt. Fleming puffed on his pipe, sucking so hard they could hear the fire eat into the tobacco.

"But why?" Jennifer asked. "That's . . . Oh my Lord!"

"Take a great big guess, Muffins. It's the military. I can guarantee they're up to no-good."

"*No-good*? Cosmo, do you have any idea what *no-good* means?"

Cosmo stared with a death row look at the monitor.

Fleming found his bearded cheeks ballooning while releasing an extended smoky breath. "He knows, Miss Burke. He knows."

* * * * *

Sharon Bodmar looked resigned. Not scared, just resigned. "Well, I hope you didn't have any big dinner plans for tonight."

Tom grunted while grabbing a crate. "I'd be really happy if everyone would stop talking in goddamn riddles and just tell us what the hell is going on!"

Twenty-two cases and crates from the Chinook cluttered the nose of the ship; many damaged, some heavily, most stained or charred, one splattered with human gore like a grotesque expressional art piece. The huge gray crate took the full effort of four of them to lift to the deck. The temperature radiating from it was so intense they could see silver heat lines hissing from the empty hose rings like a dragon's breath.

"What is that?" Tom asked. He got no reply. "Why is it so hot?"

"Ya, it's hot," Anderson cautioned.

Rood joined Rodriguez standing on the rim of the Chinook's rear loading bay. "Anything left?"

Rodriguez gave a long, slow shake with just the trace of a smile. A private in his early twenties, not so tall but thick in the shoulders and chest, was short on speech, shorter on social niceties. His face seemed far too soft for a trained killer, possessing some feminine qualities. Put a wig, make-up, a stuffed bra and a dress on him, and he'd be a knockout.

Colonel Rood stared into the shadows of the Chinook. He snapped a salute to his fallen command. When he turned to get onto the ship, Tom saw the pain lines on the man's face. He never imagined Colonel Rood could spill tears, but he was awfully close to doing just that. With a wicked looking dagger designed for the specific purpose of carving up human beings, Rodriguez severed the nylon rope binding the ship to the fallen Chinook. He and Rood climbed to the yacht. A flash and a muffled explosion came from the front of the fuselage.

"Why scuttle it?" Tom asked.

"A lot of valuable data aboard as well as my people," Rood replied. "Need to make sure they're not going anywhere."

"It's not exactly about to fly away," Tom said. Rood's vacuous stare gave Tom a jolt of terror. The realization occurred to him that he wished they had left the crew in the Chinook to drown, that things would have worked out much better if they had.

Colonel Rood's eyes, far from empty, were too full. They were the most desperate eyes Tom had ever seen. Barely medium height and thin-shouldered, Colonel Rood had the physique of a career accountant, not of a soldier. Yet something about him was disconcerting. He didn't come across as a spit and polish officer—there was a rogue element in him. You could see some of it in his eyes, sense it in the way he had command over his subordinates.

The helicopter gained weight with water, taking only a half-minute to nose down and vanish. Alice wrapped her arms around Tom, stunned by the trembling pounding out of his body. Both stared at the core of bubbles foaming up, marking the location where the Chinook disappeared.

"It was awful in there . . . all those dead people."

Alice countered Tom's trauma with a caress and a gentle kiss on the lips.

"Will you stop kissing my husband!" Carol shouted with a brief but pointed look. Alice had been pursuing Tom years before she was legal, and even after his marriage six months ago, Alice still refused to give up.

Too much in shock, Tom didn't give a damn about who kissed him, just that it was exactly what he needed.

"Okay, I'm getting data," Jack Silver said, hunched over a laptop hooked into a router connected to other pieces of equipment. He had a narrow, clean-shaven face, curiously thin lips, and short black hair with a natural wave running through it. Though his face was small, he had a cartoonish full-size Jimmy Durante honker.

"For the last time, what's going on?" Tom demanded.

"Where am I not making myself clear?" Rood was losing patience with Tom in a serious way. "It's classified, top secret, hush-hush. Understood?"

"We know it's top secret, dammit!" Tom said. "I need to know what we're up against." Rood refused to reply. "We've got women in the goddamn boat, for Chrissakes!" Still no response, just unpleasant gestures working the lines of Rood's mouth. Ralph just stood there, looking uneasy, not willing to counter the will of a commissioned officer of the United States military.

Rood glanced up to the sky, then faced Tom head-on. "We're observing a natural phenomenon."

"All this fuss over a simple natural phenomenon?" Tom asked.

"In about seven minutes, you'll get to see just how unsimple a natural phenomenon can be."

Tom had heard enough. "We're outta here!" He lurched for the flying bridge.

"Stop right there," Rood said. "I have just commandeered your ship."

"In case you haven't noticed, man, this is a Canadian boat. You damn Americans have no authority!" Tom arrived at the flying bridge to turn over the engine.

Rodriguez pulled a nine-millimetre Colt from his holster. "I have this authority."

Carol gasped when Rodriguez pulled back the gun's slide with a sick, impersonal sound.

"Rood!" Ralph shrieked a plea.

Rood did nothing.

Rodriguez took aim at Tom's head.

Tom didn't see anything else but the gun. Not the man holding it, just the barrel of the gun, the black orifice of its opening staring at him.

Rodriguez fired.

CHAPTER 3

Just as Rodriguez pulled the trigger, Rood's hand slapped him underneath his arm. Tom collapsed below the dash for cover. Charlie, just two feet from Tom, made a series of choked grunts not quite rising to the level of a full scream. For a nightmare second, Carol thought Rodriguez killed Tom. The slap of the waves against the ship hushed the leaden silence.

"Sonuvabitch!" Tom clutched his hammering chest, seeking reassurance he was still alive. "Are you out of your goddamn mind?"

"Trasler!" Rood barked a guttural yell. "Stand up."

Tom's ashen face rose above the dash in a slow moonrise. He raised his hands and stared at the weapon held irritably by Rodriguez. Although no longer aimed at him, it waved about with a lot of aggression.

"Look at me when I talk to you," Rood demanded. Tom took his eyes off the gun to Rood's face. It was not a pleasant thing to see. "I don't know how to break it to you, so I'll explain it Barney-style. This isn't a high school football game. It involves the highest echelon of national security. Now, the next time you step out of line, I'll personally blow your guts out. I've had a goddamn hard afternoon, here, and don't you make it any worse. Do you understand me, Barney?"

"Ya, I get it."

"You saved our hairy arses, now I'm going to save yours." Rood's voice dropped to low and steady. "If you turn on the engine, the same goddamn thing that blew our bird out of the sky will blow us out of the water. Simple as that. Now, if you don't behave yourself, Rodriguez will tear you a splendid new asshole with that blade of his. Are you with me?"

"Yes, sir."

"Good boy. Stay put."

Tom stayed put.

Rood took Rodriguez's hand and eased the Colt into its holster. Rood looked over to Silver. "What are our chances of continuing the mission?"

"We have no option but to continue with it, Chief. We're trapped."

"That's not what I asked."

"If this boat has a two hundred kilometre range—excellent."

Rood turned to Ralph.

"Two hundred clicks, easy." Ralph gave an eager tone to his response. *My name is Private Parker and I can play with the big boys.*

Rood's crew wasn't entirely enthusiastic, but resigned themselves to continue their mission—whatever it may be. "We have secured all the equipment and supplies," Silver said, "but the library took a hit. Worse, the extraction equipment is completely destroyed."

"You certain about the extraction equipment?"

"Nothing left." Anderson pointed to a mangled heap of casing and gutted electronics lying dead on the deck.

"Won't we be having fun," Bodmar said with a dose of cynicism.

"We lost Brent Arbing, the key mission specialist, not to mention the rest of the crew who didn't make it," Anderson said. Every time Tom heard him speak, his accent reminded him of Bobby Kennedy. "We needed the extraction equipment."

"Crucial but not essential and no one promised success would be easy."

Tom could detect no strain in Rood's voice. It held imperative but no fear. Whatever else Rood might be, he had a cool head and right now, that's what they needed. Tom, however, heard enough of the exchange to know they were about to witness something of an extremely sensitive nature. *Top secret, classified, hush-hush, the highest echelons of national security.* He tried to imagine what kind of interrogation army intelligence would put them through, wondering if the military would ever let them go free.

Rood pulled out a walkie-talkie modified to transmit through the electronic interference. "Colonel Nolan, do you read?" Rood's face flashed into a smile. "Silver, Rodriguez, Anderson, Bodmar, Jackson and I are safe aboard the Canadian yacht along with the field equipment. Only the extraction equipment was destroyed. Yes, sir, we lost the rest of the crew. We have ascertained there is no safe exit out of the zone and are preparing to continue with the mission aboard the yacht. There's five Canadian nationals with no option other than to remain with us." After another brief silence, a triumphant grin crawled through his features. "Thank you, sir." He holstered the walkie-talkie. "Five minutes, forty seconds to go, people. Deploy the field equipment."

All of the American soldiers gleamed with an aura of green static. "How come you guys are glowing but not us?" Carol asked.

"We've been in the zone longer," Rood replied, pausing a moment to observe his crew setting up the equipment. "You'll be glowing soon enough. Don't worry, it's harmless. All of you in the back." Rood shot a quick glance at Charlie before focusing back on Tom. "You, too, Barney." He gestured to his eyes and pointed at Tom, giving him the *I'll-be-watching-you* gesture. Rood nodded at Rodriguez. "Make sure they behave." He looked back at Tom. "No warnings."

Charlie Mason worried Rood the most. He was the poster boy for losers. He wore a pair of white shoes with touches of red, blue and silver shock absorbers that might have looked really cute on a seven year-old. He wore denim shorts falling halfway down his powder-white shins with oddly little leg hair for a man. He constantly pulled up his wide leather belt because his beer belly was considerably bigger than his butt, and his jumbo-sized Daft Punk T-shirt billowed on him like the Pillsbury Doughboy. He was a big boy, not coping well and it's the panicky types that will always screw things up. That was a lot of bulk behind a panic attack, something he knew Rodriguez would have to be careful with.

Carol threw a glance over her shoulder at Rodriguez, the same leery look you'd give to a pit bull who you know damn well would maul you if it ever got off its leash. Tom followed Charlie down from the flying bridge. Still unnerved after having a weapon fired at him, Tom felt nauseous, his heart was beating like a jackhammer, and he walked in short, awkward shuffles.

"Take them with us?" Anderson asked Rood, like going on a hot date with the girlfriend's homely friend tagging along type of irritation. "Put them in the yacht's tender and get them out of the zone."

"I considered all the options. No choice. They've seen too much to let them go in the tender and at this point, we may need the extra bodies."

"Who's going to tell them?" Jackson asked, with the slightest of smiles.

"I'll break it to them only when it's necessary. I want to monitor the event, people. You know your jobs, let's move it."

Alice held out her hand. The green energy glowed off them just as Rood forewarned. "How do I look?" she asked Tom.

"Enlightened?" Tom said and laughed.

She forced a grin but the worry was too deeply rooted in her eyes for the smile to be real.

"How about enchanted?" he teased.

"I'll settle for angelic!"

A strike of green-fire flashed, hitting the boat with a tremendous shudder. Tom locked eyes with Alice. His eyes told her that in the next instant, almighty hell was about to be unleashed.

Hell was unleashed in the form of a fireball, twisting, writhing with a gush of flame bursting through the aft deck. Ralph exploded into the air like a man blown out of a circus cannon, slamming against the cabin wall. He screamed in a heap next to the entrance to the galley, his body resembling a twisted swastika. As debris rained down, an inferno raged.

Knocked flat to the port corner, Rodriguez lay trapped by the flames. Blood flowed from his forehead and he shook reality back into his head. The blastwave blew Alice and Carol clear over the side. The Nikon flew from Carol's hands into the water while she lunged for the yacht's railing, kicking in the water in the attempt to climb back in. One finger at a time, she lost her grip. As her fingers slid over the railing, her wedding ring slipped off, falling to the carpet. With a gasp of fear, she splashed into the cool gray waters.

* * * * *

"Oh my Lord!" Jennifer fought off the temptation to cover her eyes. All the others gasped a wide spectrum of profanities.

"Poor dudes are toast," Cosmo said.

"This is a calamity," Fleming acknowledged.

A plume of black smoke rose off the ship.

"What made it explode?" Jennifer asked Fleming. She forced the words out and still they were frail.

The professor resigned himself for the worst. His voice reflected the horror of watching people going to their deaths. "The same phenomena that caused the helicopter to explode, Miss Burke."

"I see two of the girls in the water." Jennifer's voice was a whisper. She touched their image on the screen with her fingertips. "Those poor souls." She went to chew another fingernail, except there were none left to gnaw on.

"Time left?" Fleming asked.

Cosmo grasped the edge of the table, never taking his eyes off the monitor. "Three minutes, twenty seconds."

Jennifer, on the precipice of tears, said, "Three minutes and twenty seconds to—oh Lord, this is awful!"

* * * * *

Rood, up front on the nose when the blast hit, had fallen over a piece of equipment and his ribs hurt like the devil. He crawled up, careful not to make things any worse. With a stiff torso, he pivoted slowly to Jackson. "You're a praying man, Tyrone?"

"You know I am, Chief."

"Then pray to the Father Almighty to get our hairy arses out of the dragon's den they're in. Will you do that, Tyrone?"

"Consider it done."

Ralph screamed against the cabin wall. This was no hit-the-thumb-with-the-hammer pain—this was goddamn blitzkrieg agony. Tom broke free from the terror-induced paralysis and shook Charlie out of his stupor. "Get lifejackets to the girls, I'll get Ralph."

Charlie dashed inside the cabin, hauled out three life jackets and without losing a step, lunged with a screaming belly flop into the water. The way he did it reminded Tom of the Cowardly Lion leaping through the window in the Wizard of Oz's castle. Carol and Alice took the life jackets and helped each other put them on.

Tom dragged Ralph into the galley, away from the baking heat and toxic smoke. Ralph's right shoulder, lacerated and bleeding, had something sticking out of it. Rodriguez dove into the water and moved from the port to starboard side that was relatively undamaged from the blast and fire. He glanced at Alice and Carol, struggling to get into their lifejackets, and he determined, for the moment at least, they were safer in the water and out of the way. It took just seconds for him to crawl back into the yacht. He wiped the blood from his face with a towel and dropped it to the floor. Rodriguez's blood on the towel glowed with the green static like florescent paint.

Ralph curled in a fetal position as the pain in his right shoulder mauled him like talons. Tom eyed the yacht's tender for a quick escape, though undamaged, the portside fire blocked access to the davits on the right. Both dazed, Carol and Alice managed to get into their life jackets and bobbed atop the waves while Charlie swam further out. The excruciating heat from the fire forced Tom to seek sanctuary in the galley. Fuelled by diesel fuel and the fiberglass fabric of the ship itself, the blackened orange-red flames towered eight feet.

Inside the galley, the smoke alarm went off like a banshee. *No kidding.* Tom found a pot and clubbed the smoke alarm off the ceiling. It still shrieked, right through his ears and into his teeth. He tossed it into the flames where after wailing in agony for a good ten seconds, it finally shut up.

Rodriguez hurried his way to the nose of the ship. Rood still clutched his ribs from the fall.

"You okay, Chief?"

"I'm good. What's with the fire?"

"Out of control."

Rood looked over at Silver, hunched over his laptop. "Jack, how much time?"

"Two minutes, thirty-eight seconds."

Rood stared at Rodriguez with a look so severe that it spoke louder than any words could convey. "I need ten more minutes. Twenty would be a bonus."

"I'll need help. Parker's injured."

"How bad?"

"Not good, Chief."

"Christ." Rood looked over to Anderson and Jackson, who were keeping the large magnetometer steady. It resembled a relic moon experiment from the Apollo era with three long arms, a pair of small rabbit ears with a diameter of over five feet. "Tyrone, go help. We need minimum ten minutes. No matter what it takes, make it happen."

The two made their way aft.

"TREP should hit us any second," Silver said.

"TREP without dampers," Bodmar said, "won't this be fun." Bodmar huddled over another laptop, though hurt and unnerved, she had settled in to do her job. "Here it comes."

"People, you know the routine. Be careful," Rood said.

The deck's rumbling had nothing to do with the fire. Tom looked down at his feet, and like standing on an illuminated glass floor, the deck itself glowed. Parts of it grew brighter when long, indistinct forms outshone the background. Serpent-like charges emerged right out the fabric of the deck, as if they crawled out of a hidden snake pit. They darted in wild abandon across the decks in complete silence. Some were massive; an inch in diameter and six feet long, green, glittering and so vibrant that anything next to them cast a shadow.

Emerald voltage slithered up his leg to the thigh of Tom's blue jeans and he shrieked when it vanished inside his body head first, looking like a carnivore burrowing into his flesh. Within seconds, all on board glowed in radiant brilliance. Tom wiggled his fingers and were numb—*when had it turned so cold?* Ralph watched in sedated horror as two more of the huge discharges drilled into Tom's torso and leg.

Ralph fought back the pain that his body wanted so desperately to scream out. "Are you all right, Tom?"

"I'm not sure," he replied tentatively while gazing at his torso. There were no marks, but his entire insides were tingling. "I feel like a spark plug."

"You look like one, too."

"Are you certain this is harmless?"

"That's what they said."

"It doesn't feel harmless."

Jackson and Rodriguez, after exhausting the galley's small fire extinguisher, had resorted to buckets of water with limited effect. The snaking discharges interfered with their fight against the fire; they sidestepped around them like kids playing dodgeball.

"What about the three in the water?" Jackson asked Rodriguez.

"They're no bother in the water," Rodriguez replied.

Jackson thought the three in the water should get back onto the ship, but shrugged off the thought and continued to fight the fire.

"We're stuck," Tom offered grimly, "on fire and right in the middle of this goddamn implosion zone. Trapped!"

"Sorry, Tom. I thought I was doing the right thing."

Tom knew Ralph did the right thing, but his earlier sentiment was bang on that they'd have been better off had they left Rood's crew to drown. It was a terribly selfish, immoral thought, and yet Tom felt no guilt. That was the harsh reality of the matter.

"Check on the girls, Tom."

Tom, for a malicious moment, thought Ralph got exactly what he deserved, and for a fleeting instant, was actually glad about his pain. Carol and Alice, within the security of their bright orange lifejackets, bobbed thirty feet away on the wave crests while Charlie swam further out in a due-south course. Tom had no idea what possessed him to choose south when the coast was east, but that was one determined swim.

"Abandon ship, Tom," Carol said. "We're safe in the water. There's no electricity."

Except for a faint aurora borealis hovering above their heads, they were free of the static that had become so thick that those on board looked angelic. Jackson and Rodriguez, two gleaming ghouls in some kind of afterlife dance around a sacrificial pyre, were too preoccupied fighting the fire to notice Tom and Ralph, offering an opportunity to escape. Tom felt another long serpent bite into his ankle, the surge of energy seeping right up into his kneecap and felt it was about to disassemble on him.

"I'll get Ralph, but he's hurt bad," Tom said.

"Just get him and hurry!" Carol pleaded.

Beyond the three in the water, the green radiance glittered on the water's surface in a well-defined oval. Outside of it, everything appeared normal, unaffected; just the rambling waves rolling under the paste-coloured sky. They were marginally off-center in the implosion oval. The maximum radius was the length of a football field and they were on their own 35-yard line. They could still swim out to the safety of the waters beyond the zone.

"You guys, start swimming that way." He pointed due south—*okay, Charlie knew where he was going.* "Go, I'll catch up."

Resembling a marionette with half its strings tangled, Ralph stumbled to his feet. He clutched onto the ladder leading to the flying bridge, barely able to hang on. Tom knew Ralph wasn't going to make it into the water.

"Colonel Nolan has arrived to watch our grand exit!" A satisfied grin stretched the smile lines in Colonel Rood's face. Another Chinook, staying well clear, orbited the zone. Rood stood at attention on the nose of the yacht and snapped off a salute at it so crisp it sparkled with static like fairy's dust. He retained the salute, a long steady bon voyage. Rood felt dizzy with the thrill. He knew all along what to expect—he trained a year for this—and here he was now, experiencing something he never expected to see in his lifetime. Life couldn't get any better.

"Watch it, Chief," Anderson warned. Rood shuffled a couple steps to his left just in time to avoid a radiant snake attack. Bodmar leapt from her laptop to avoid one as well. For whatever reason, they didn't harass Jack Silver, as if he possessed the power of repellence.

"One minute," Silver reported.

Directly overhead, a mass of fiery crimson churned though the clouds. The enflamed sky reflected against the sea in a lurid glow as it spread across the low-level cloud deck. Ralph stared spellbound at the sky, loose-jawed and mouth gaping. Tom struggled to get the lifejacket on him. Ralph folded and a gruesome howl wrenched from his body.

"Just go, Tom."

"Not without you, Ralph. I'll hold you in the water."

"Go, damn you!"

Like Silver, the glittering serpents were not bothering Ralph, but streamed towards Tom like a piranha attack.

"Sonuvabitch, this is bugging me." He tried to kick one away, all in vain as it vanished inside his foot. His entire leg sustained an electrical jolt, deep and intense. He flailed off balance with only his grip on the railing keeping him upright. "Come on, Ralphy, let's get the hell off the boat!"

"I'm done—just go!"

A high-pitched whine peeled through the air, cutting short their dispute. It held its tone pure while it picked up in intensity, becoming musical, singing a flawless C note, beautiful and sweet to the ears, like the song of an angel's trumpet.

"The implosion." Tom's expression changed from fear then to nothing at all—like a man under sentence.

Carol got caught in Tom's death stare and felt a sinking terror that seemed preordained, like watching someone trapped in a burning house with no hope of escape. She looked back at Tom with wild, staring eyes.

"I love you, Tom!"

"I love you, too!" Alice said through a sob.

Tom's heart plummeted. They had just given him a final farewell. A *see you on the other side* kind of farewell. He opened his mouth to tell them that he loved them both, but rammed by a massive discharge, his words seized in his throat as if they had locked with rust.

"Twenty seconds," Silver reported. His voice held absolutely no emotion.

Rood's face didn't change—it held the same look of childlike awe—but his heartbeat kicked up a couple of notches. "Goddamn, this is fun!" With his hands on his hips, eyes sparkling, he watched Nolan's helicopter hover four hundred meters distance. The orbiting Chinook lost its motion, becoming a still photograph frozen in the sky.

Silver continued his emotionless countdown. "Fifteen seconds." He was no Jack King.

Tom embraced Carol with a final, longing look. She was deep inside the oval, but free of the static. She and Alice huddled together as they watched the blood-red sky above while Charlie continued to swim with big, heavy splashes. He wasn't going to make it out in time. Tom grasped the chrome deck railing and could feel more of the discharges creeping into his legs, could sense them flowing deep inside his limbs right into his chest, certain it was going to kill him.

The sea around them shone with a flaming glow while above churned the Armageddon that burned with a crimson glare. The vermilion plasma-like vapours spun in a counter-clockwise motion, growing rapidly until the conflagration engulfed all of the heavens. Tom had to squint to see the flaming clouds, nearly too brilliant to look at, like a late afternoon sun in a humid sky. Piercing and sweet, the trumpet's song increased its volume, building up to a climax.

Carol floated below the sky, blood red with the radiant mass looming above them in Biblical splendour, just like the Four Horsemen of the Apocalypse—the harbingers of the final judgement. She let out a terrified shout, rising to a shrill scream. The trumpet peaked, deafening their senses. In perfect symphony with the trumpet blast, the flamed sky glowed from crimson to liquid gold to searing white, all within the space of a heartbeat.

Tom felt himself screaming. Raw panic amplified by every fear of death he had ever possessed. It wasn't just the fear of dying—it was much worse than that—*the fear of what may lie beyond.*

Everything went silent.

* * * * *

The data flatlined. Jennifer glanced past the monitor to the sea. A puff of rolling smoke was all that remained. Without a source, the drifting smoke column dissipated into the wind. The second Chinook continued to orbit the zone a few hundred yards from the epicenter. Other than that, it was just the sea. An empty sea. A gust of wind blew through the clearing, the leaves flapping in the breeze like a distant applause.

Cosmo stared at the inert readings on his monitor. "Elvis has left the building."

CHAPTER 4

The mouthpiece of Fleming's pipe nearly shattered. He unclamped his teeth and withdrew it. His heartbeat was nowhere near control. "Our buoys?"

It took a long moment for Cosmo to make the reply. His voice was listless, just like his eyes. "The signal is back at full strength, all readings nominal."

"Like nothing has happened," Jennifer said. "Except so much has happened. Those poor people."

A period of extreme quiet remained within the group as their thoughts were on those who had been taken into another temporal realm. The wind hushed through the leaves, creating a white noise that helped mask the stress.

Traversing through a temporal event was like playing Russian roulette, except that five of the six of the chambers were loaded. The exit path could dump you in the middle of the ocean, on the highest mountain, in the middle of a Siberian winter, an Antarctic ice sheet, the most barren desert, and only dumb luck would put you where it's safe. The team didn't know the location of the exit path, just something in the neighbourhood of a century and a half into the past. Jennifer could not help but imagine what they were going through right now, especially those in the water. She tried to paint a picture in her mind and yet tried not to. She was in shock. They all were.

It was like a sneak attack. The monitors lit up, data exploded from nothing into pounding bar graphs, twisted horizontal lines, bell curves arcing and waning, zeros turning into complex equations and two alarms screaming like air raid sirens.

"Whoa!" Cosmo jerked forward, face-to-face with the monitor. He gave a couple of quick breaths, ballooning his stubbled cheeks. "Another temporal event!"

"That's impossible," Jennifer said.

His hand gave a couple of karate chops in front of the monitor. "This is crazy!"

"How?" Fleming asked.

Cosmo's tongue crept into the corner of his mouth. "A secondary temporal event. Three separate spikes!"

"It's against the laws of physics, Cosmo," Jennifer said. She remained calm and refused to be deceived by what had to be faulty readings.

"Are you certain of this?" Fleming asked.

"Got to be equipment failure," Roberts said.

"Yup," Jennifer agreed.

Scranton, licking his lips, grasped both sides of the monitor in a death grip, his eyes shifting with wild abandon across the screen. His head snapped to his right and he looked directly into Fleming's lake-blue eyes. "It's not an equipment failure."

"Three spikes? That—can't—be—real!" Jennifer's fingers spread wide and she thrust her hands downward as if she was trying to levitate. "Impossible!"

Cosmo's heart hammered crazily. "This is real, confirmed, same data from all three buoys, flux gate magnetometer going apeshit, three massive temporal spikes—amazing!"

"My equipment is picking up the same thing," Roberts reported. He shook his head. Just like Jennifer, he concluded it couldn't be real. But it was happening right before his eyes.

Jennifer shook her head. "It doesn't make any sense. If it doesn't make sense, it's not what it seems."

Cosmo's heart felt like fists hammering inside of him trying to get out. "Okay, short-lived, very massive, over, it's done, finished. Far out!" He puffed out a breath, blowing a fallen leaf right off the table.

"Okay, I got it," Jennifer said, as if she just figured out a magician's card trick. "We had capacitors in the buoys to collect the temporal static. They probably reacted and set off the temporal event like a bomb. Three buoys, three events, case closed."

Scranton looked at the data transmitted by the buoys. “Capacitors are stable. Not sure they collected anything, but it wasn’t them.”

“Let’s not come into any inane conclusions here,” Jennifer said.

A haze of bewilderment blanked Robert’s narrow face. “I thought we had all this all figured out.”

“This is still a new science,” Fleming cautioned.

ABOARD THE SALTY DOG

The emerald static exploded outward from the yacht like exercised spirits. It skittered across the waves in every direction, soaring past the horizon. An awkward moment of transition passed from the mid-afternoon electromagnetic mayhem to the tranquil backdrop of a sea brushed by the frail light of the pre-dawn. The ship was uncertain with her new surroundings. It rolled sharply to port, its bow reared up, and rolled to over to starboard until she recovered her sea legs. The comforting sea noises arrived to greet them, giving a reassurance like an old love.

The warm July breeze turned into a cold wind, fresh and steady, blowing in from the southeast, sweeping the sea into high, broad ridges. Low in the east, the morning star lay suspended above a shimmering crimson scarf draped across the distant sea rim. The crescent moon stared down at them, casting an ivory sheen upon the roving wave crests.

His anticipation of death so absolute, that for a long moment, Tom remained convinced he was still in the process of dying. His lips stretched across his teeth like the grin of a corpse, staring at the dark, brooding sea with unblinking eyes. After a shuddering gasp, his mind grappled with the possibility he wasn’t about to die.

He gazed over his shoulder. Just the faintest trace of discharges slithered on the deck, until they popped into oblivion like insects zapped in an electronic bug killer. He glanced at Ralph, the two soldiers and over to the fire consuming the port corner. The heat of it was strong on his shoulders and burned with a noxious smell. Jackson and Rodriguez stood motionless between the fire and the galley, neither paying attention to the inferno. The smoke bent with the wind, billowing into a clear sky with no trace of the smoke burning prior to the white void. The fire released a brand new smoke plume to the winds.

“Ralph?” Tom said in a hush. A standing-around-the-open-casket hush. A long silence drifted by.

Ralph replied like a man awakening from a deep sleep. "I'm here, Tom." He clung onto the ladder leading to the flying bridge. Blood oozed down his arm to his wrist and dripped onto the splintered deck.

Tom looked ahead, then snapped his head left, right, he glanced aft and lurched past Jackson and Rodriguez, and stared off the port side. He looked ahead. He rushed back to Ralph.

"I don't see the girls or Charlie!"

The pain drew Ralph around the ladder, wrapping his arms around it like a lover. "Whatever happened to us, didn't affect them in the water. You should have jumped in and joined them when you had the chance."

"No man left behind, right?"

"You're such a goddamn hero."

Another extended moment of silence passed while Tom tried to make sense of what happened, of where they were. Tom looked back at Rodriguez and Jackson. Neither showed panic in their eyes, rather, an awed wonderment. Both were inside their own utopias, not interacting with the other, the fire at the moment inconsequential. Their faces reassured Tom, if just for a moment, that they were not facing imminent mortal danger. He made a quick assessment of the ship. The sea had breached the waterline at the back port corner. They would drown before burning to death.

"That was something, wasn't it?" Ralph said.

"Something! You call this something? I hate goddamn clichés, Ralphy, but look around, Toto; we're not in Kansas anymore!"

Ralph's eyes squinted when the impossible became reality. "Jesus, you're right. No sign of land, different time of day and it's a lot colder."

"A hell of a lot colder." The hiss of the fire and the splash of waves against the hull were the only sounds for a drawn out minute. Jackson had a giddy expression on his face. Tom tapped him on the shoulder. "Where the hell are we?"

Jackson shrugged, his eyes concealing a momentous secret and he wasn't about to talk.

"Classified, right?"

"You got that right."

Tom cut a sharp glance at Rodriguez. Blood still flowed from his right forehead. He put some chewing gum in his mouth, and it was apparent he also wasn't in a conversing frame of mind.

"I'm going to see Rood."

Tom's first couple of steps were lurching and unsure until he found his footing. The waves were much larger to what they had off Oregon, making walking an adventure. Panic rose in Tom's throat like bile as he thought about the question, somehow more scared of the asking than of the answer. Silver and Bodmar huddled over their laptops, Anderson worked with the magnetometer, with its three large arms spread out and two smaller ones spinning on top looking like a cheap Hollywood prop. Rood took in the new surroundings, standing with his hands on his hips, balancing against the high, broad waves, also wearing a giddy look of triumph.

Tom went right up to Rood and encroached his personal space. "What the hell happened to us?"

"Calm down, Barney."

"Calm down? We just got teleported like goddamn Captain Kirk and you expect me to calm down?"

"We'll confirm our situation in a couple of minutes," Silver said. "Stop disturbing us."

"How's the boat?" Rood asked.

"Burning and sinking and Ralph's hurt bad and my wife and friends are missing. What the hell just happened?"

Rood's breath seized. "What do you mean; your wife and friends are missing?"

"They were in the water! They said they weren't affected by that electricity stuff."

Rood exchanged a brief but pointed look at first Sharon Bodmar and then Jack Silver. Both held poker faces.

"When we know, you'll know," Rood said.

"You must have some kind of general idea?"

Rood's face remained unresponsive.

"How about a wild guess?"

Bodmar glanced at Tom, shaking her head with a kind of dismal finality—the look of a doctor about to tell her patient he was terminal. Her look made Tom's guts free fall. She turned her attention back to her computer, positioning herself to avoid Tom's eye-to-eye intrusions.

"What about my wife and friends?"

"They're fine, now shut up!" Rood said.

"What about Ralph? He's hurt bad."

"I suppose I should check on him."

Without any conversation between the two, they made their way to the aft deck. Rood, still stiff from the fall, walked with his arms tight at his side. Rodriguez and Jackson resumed fighting the fire.

"Twenty minutes?" Rood asked.

"Doing our best, Chief," Jackson said.

Rood knew they'd have to start packing up a lot sooner than twenty minutes. Evac would take four minutes—he was aware of that. He pried opened Ralph's army jacket. "You took a good hunk of metal, there, Parker. A few inches lower and it would have been good night."

Ralph hissed from the pain of Rood's brief exploration. "Any of you by chance a surgeon?"

"Bodmar has a good bedside manner—she'll have a look at it. Get inside and lie down."

Ralph remained put as if spot-welded to the ladder.

CAPE LOOKOUT STATE PARK, OREGON

"I've triangulated the location of the new event, Professor," Cosmo said. "A hundred and fifty meters ahead of us and a hundred to the south."

"What's that in feet?" Jennifer asked. All of them glanced at her and shrugged an *I don't know,* though they did. She puffed a snort through her nose. "Who's the idiot that invented metric anyways?"

"Someone who wasn't daddy's little rich girl from Pasadena," Scranton said.

Jennifer jerked her gaze away from Scranton and put her attention back to the monitor.

"I would have expected the secondary event to be in the same zone as the primary," Fleming said. A trace of scepticism could be detected in his voice as well.

"Now it makes even less sense!" Jennifer said.

The team tore themselves from their equipment and brushed through the branches to the edge of the cliff. There were three people in the water bunched together, all in bright orange lifejackets within swimming distance from shore. Unquestionably the same three from the yacht.

"Oh my Lord!" Jennifer said.

"Told you, Jennifer, that it wasn't an equipment failure," Scranton said.

"Once again Jennifer, you were wrong," Roberts said.

"Excuse me?" Jennifer issued a glove-slapping-across-the-face challenge. "The data clearly showed that they passed through the event horizon."

Fleming puffed on his pipe, sending up a miniature mushroom cloud of smoke. "This is extraordinary."

Jennifer looked at the three in the water with an uneasy fascination. *They went through the event, the data will conclusively prove that they did, but what power or force could have brought them back? And why not inside the primary zone?* Her mind tabulated all the possibilities and she gave up. The explanation lay concealed in the data and she would have to be patient until they deconstructed the phenomena—which still made absolutely no sense.

"They were hurled out the zone. How?" Cosmo asked.

"They weren't hurled out of the zone," Jennifer said. "They passed through the temporal event. Then somehow, they were regurgitated back."

"A dozen seconds after the primary event, no less," Cosmo said.

"It was like they went through the singularity, but found the door locked at the other end, and forced back," Scranton said, offering a rudimentary explanation.

"Maybe because they were in the water?" Roberts asked.

"Maybe that's it. This was our first event over water," Cosmo said.

"It will all make perfect sense once we better understand the mechanisms of its forces," Fleming said. "We only know the effect of the phenomena—we are entirely ignorant of the cause. That is our quest."

People gathered at the surf, first alerted by the helicopter crash then the smoke from the burning yacht. The crowd coalesced along the shore while someone in a small boat sped to pick up the three.

Two military helicopters swooped low overhead.

"We better take to the woods," Cosmo said.

"Agreed. Scuttle the buoys and pack up," Fleming ordered. They dashed to the table cluttered with their equipment. A squirrel nibbled on some snacks Roberts had left and dashed away as they approached. Bob

Scranton flicked three switches one after another. This opened valves in their buoys, and within seconds, all three stopped transmitting.

"All buoys successfully scuttled, Professor."

"Let's hope the military doesn't discover them with the helicopter wreckage," Roberts said.

"We must assume that they will, Mr. Roberts," Fleming said, all the time grinning, but the grin never touched his eyes.

Roberts forced his words through a sandpaper throat. "That will betray our presence!"

"Indeed, Mr. Roberts, it most certainly will. They will not be pleased that others not only know of the temporal phenomena, but witnessed their clandestine expedition to the ages."

"They're going to come after us, won't they?" Roberts stammered.

"Difficult, Mr. Roberts, if they don't know who we are."

Jennifer blew an exasperated raspberry at him. "We didn't exactly leave a name and address on our buoys asking them to return to sender."

"What about the three in the water?" Scranton said, more suggestion than question. He pulled plugs out of the equipment and stuffed battery packs into sports bags. "I'd love to get some readings off of them."

"The military will be all over them in minutes," Roberts cautioned.

"We'll just be another face in the crowd, Stuart," Jennifer said, not quite able to keep the annoyance out of her voice.

Fleming took some thoughtful puffs with his pipe. "Mr. Wynn, grab a camera and the portable flux gate sensor. Take pictures of the three and try to get close enough to take a measurement."

"I'm on it, Professor," Cosmo replied.

"Be discrete and do not—I repeat—do not communicate with them. We'll meet you on the main road just past the entrance."

ABOARD THE SALTY DOG

Jackson and Rodriguez were getting the upper hand on the fire, but with an appreciable list, water continued to lap over the port corner, and every subsequent wave pushed deeper into the boat. Rood glanced at the ship's tender still harnessed in the davits. One side had a light gray smoke stain, but it appeared undamaged.

Tom froze. His face turned white as if he had seen death. "The moon, man! The moon!"

Ralph, clinging onto the ladder, made no effort to look at the moon. "What about the moon?"

"What about the moon? It's a waning crescent, that's what!"

"So?"

"So? So? Last evening, it was just a sliver, about a two or three day-old moon. Now it's . . . the exact opposite phase!" He ticked the days off his fingers. "Twenty-five or twenty-six days old."

"So the phase of the moon is twenty-six days old. What's the big deal?"

"Twenty-six days less a three-day-old moon equals twenty-three days." His voice rose in panic. "That means we're twenty-three days later than we were just five minutes ago!"

"Are you sure it's the Earth's moon?"

Tom choked and shot another quick look at the moon, reassuring himself that it was indeed Earth's. Despite the mauling pain, Ralph managed to chuckle.

"You asshole, Ralph. You freaked me out of my goddamn mind!" Ralph continued to laugh. "What the hell's so funny?"

"Imagine if it wasn't the Earth's moon? Then where would we be?"

"Look at me, Ralphy. How do you explain over three weeks of missing time and teleported to God knows where?" Tom turned to Rood. The colonel seemed amused at the exchange. "Screw this classified nonsense. I want to know what's happened to us and to my wife and Alice and Charlie!"

Rood twitched a brief grin. "You already figured it out. We passed through a temporal singularity."

An overwhelming sense of dread swept through Tom. He shook his head in an effort to resist the horrible truth. *Time travel! The military brass will never let him or Ralph go. Were they to be locked up forever, or have their brains blown out to keep them quiet?* Then a new realization came to him, bright as day and red with panic. Tom's eyes moved to Rood's face. They were the solemn eyes of a frightened child.

"How much time?"

"I'm impressed that you were balls on accurate that there would be a twenty-three day difference between the moon's phases—assuming it was the minimum time going forward. But that supposition was incorrect. We're still reviewing the data, but we should be in the year 1848. April 28th, to be precise."

Confusion, fear, panic, heartache—all of it combined into an explosive blast of dread. Tom's mind grappled in the face of such an impossible statement. A leaden silence drifted by while Tom gazed in sedated horror at Rood.

"Are you saying we just time travelled over a century and a half into the past?" Tom asked, the breath chopping out of him.

"One hundred and sixty-eight years just off the British coast." Jackson spoke with so much excitement he stumbled over his words and exchanged a hearty fist bump with Rodriguez.

"What the hell are we doing one hundred and sixty-eight years back in time off the British coast? You did this deliberately!"

"Obviously, Barney, we passed through the temporal zone deliberately." Rood's eyes turned very dark. "The why is none of your concern."

Tom shook his head the way people do when refuting impossible words that have stunned them past the point of disbelief. He stood there, motionless, looking at Rood like someone waiting for the punchline of a really bad joke.

"Your lovely time machine has a reverse button, I presume?"

"No time machine. Mother Nature provided the ride."

"She'll provide a ride back home?"

"It's my intent to return home. If we stick to our itinerary, best case scenario is that we'll be back nine weeks before we even left—May 23rd 2016."

"Then what?" Tom's fingers wiped the cold sweat off his forehead. "Our boat will be missing."

"We'll have nine weeks to work out a cover-up." Rood smiled and winked at Tom, who wasn't smiling.

"Will the military let us go on our own merry way after all we've seen?"

"We'll make an arrangement." Rood's face showed no emotion, but he held sincerity in his words. "You did save our hairy arses. We owe you that much."

"When do we make the return trip?" Tom asked.

"Assuming everything goes perfect, just over two years."

“Two years!” Tom shrieked. “Stuck in the eighteen forties for two goddamn years?”

“We have no control over the temporal events or the locations. We simply traverse through them. The return implosion will occur on May 19th, 1850, on the Queen Charlotte Islands. That’s in British Columbia just south of the Alaskan panhandle. That’s best case and shortest duration option we have. There are two other opportunities, the third after three and a half years. After that, we’re looking into multiple jumps to make it home—and those get messy.”

Tom shuffled to an intact couch on the starboard side. He collapsed into it, his legs giving way like he had just finished a marathon. He glanced at Rodriguez and Jackson fighting the fire, thankful the wind carried the smoke away from them. He looked up to Rood.

“Okay, so what’s the itinerary?”

“We’ll have to cross the Atlantic then make our way first to Texas, and then after, to San Francisco right during the height of the gold rush, then onto the Queen Charlotte Islands for the trip home. Goddamn, this is going to be fun!”

“Ya, a splendid time is guaranteed for all.” Tom’s shock transformed into panic, yet in a perverse way, felt an underlining feeling of primeval excitement.

“How far away are we from the British coast?” Ralph asked, still clinging onto the ladder.

“At most, a couple hundred clicks from the Welsh coast, perhaps closer,” Rood replied. “We have a couple of large dinghies and will have the gulf current at our back. All we have to do is proceed northeast.”

CHAPTER 5

The sky slowly bloomed into daylight. The widening wedge of light tossed an amber fan across the ridged sea. With a burst, the sun soared free from the sea, the warmth of its fiery breath whispering away the cold of the predawn.

Bodmar took her first close look at Ralph's wound. She carried two pieces that made up her medical equipment. The first was a battlefield surgical kit, the second stocked with dozens of medicine vials.

"There's a piece of metal in there, all right," Bodmar said. "The waves are far too rough for me to do a surgical procedure so we'll have to wait until we arrive on shore. I can only give something for the pain, the bleeding and to prevent infection." She gave Ralph a shot, treated the wound with a cauterising sponge and applied a compress. Ralph heard a thump and splash accompanied by a lot of profanity, but Tom managed to avoid the flames to get the white fiberglass boat down. He secured it to the starboard side and loaded it with their luggage. Jackson and Rodriguez continued to fight the fire, buying as much time as possible. The water breeched the inside of the galley and the ship could be felt losing its stability.

Rood peered over Bodmar's shoulder at her screen, trying to read some of the data. "Where's Trasler's wife and friends?"

Bodmar glanced up at Rood. "All three passed through the event."

Rood said nothing, but the realization of what happened to the three electrocuted Anderson's guts. "Then they're dead."

Silver adjusted his round glasses. "At this time of year, they would have succumbed to hyperthermia within 15 minutes."

"We should be able to pick up their TREP?" Rood asked.

"Only if they were within ten clicks, which is the maximum range of our equipment," Bodmar said. "The way the exit path works, they could be as far away as a hundred."

"Check to see if you can find anything."

"I'm trying to secure the data, Chief," Bodmar protested.

"Do it!"

Bodmar gave him a look bordering on insubordination while Silver configured the equipment to begin a search.

Rood scanned the horizon—just in case. "Trasler and Parker are not to be informed of this, understood? As far as either are concerned, the three didn't pass through and were rescued by Nolan's Chinook."

"Wait a minute . . . wait a minute. Believe it or not, I do have a temporal signature," Bodmar announced.

"The three in the water?"

"No, just one—a single entity. Very faint."

"I see it, too," Silver said. "That's just over five kilometres to the southeast."

"It's not the same frequency that the three in the water would have carried. This is different," Bodmar said.

"What could it be?" Rood asked.

"No idea."

"Wait, this is odd," Silver said. "It's the signature of an exit flash."

"Exit flash?" Rood peered over Bodmar's shoulder to take a closer look. "By the nailed hands of the Christ, that's a ship!"

"Inanimate objects don't absorb TREP at that wavelength," Bodmar pointed out.

"But people on her decks do. The TREP explodes outward during our egress. Someone on board, bless their hairy little arse, got absorbed with some exit path TREP."

Bodmar wore a tidy little smirk. "Someone on board that ship got a tiny little fright."

"Tiny?" Anderson chuckled at the thought.

Rood stood up, winked at Anderson and patted him on the shoulder. "Pack up." Rood stumbled over the pitching deck to the aft end. The waves crested the entire aft corner and flowed into the fire itself, yet it still burned vigorously.

Jackson threw another bucket at the fire when Rood arrived. "Chief, I think we're good for another 20 minutes."

"Let it burn," Rood said.

"Let it burn?" Jackson objected. "We just worked our asses off to buy you twenty minutes!"

"There's a ship less than five clicks away. Let them see the smoke and wait for a rescue."

"A ship?" Tom stepped out of the galley with a couple of suitcases.

"That's right. Once we're certain they've seen the smoke and are on their way, we'll have to scuttle the yacht."

Tom pointed inside the galley. "Nice big propane tank inside. Filled just before we left Victoria."

"Thanks, Carlos." Rood nodded to the galley and Rodriguez passed through.

Tom kept his look fixed on Rood. "What about our clothes?"

"We've got a complete 19th century wardrobe for fourteen. We're down to eight, so lots to spare." Rood smiled at Jackson. "Good praying."

"Don't thank me, sir." Jackson pointed up.

Tom climbed to the flying bridge, Rood following. He took the binoculars and saw the three masts of tanned sail rising majestically above a sliver of a black hull. He passed the binoculars to Rood. The colonel's stern face broke into a broad smile, his teeth flashed in the awakening dawn.

"They're coming this way. Goddamn, this is going to be fun!"

"Ya, a real lark." Tom went back to the deck to finish loading their tiny boat. Rood returned to the ship's nose to deploy their inflatable rafts, each equipped with an outboard motor and three tanks of fuel. They deployed the second inflatable strictly for their cargo. Tom helped Ralph into the tender, difficult with the heavy list that raised their side, and all at once, Ralph found himself competing for space with a mountain of luggage.

Tom took a last look when he found Carol's wedding ring lying on the damaged floor. He picked it up and held it. His chest heaved as he fought back a sob. Two years without her, yet, he had some solace that she wouldn't have to wait for him. If Rood's assurances were correct that their return would predate their actual departure, he'd be there to greet her, to place the ring back on her finger. The ring became his focus to make it through all this. He put it into the pocket of his jeans and glanced down at his own wedding band, giving him the hell or high water resolve to see this through. He released the moorings and with the second pull, started the outboard motor. They moved across the monstrous waves like an out of control rollercoaster. They joined the six military personnel huddled in their dinghy.

"Rodriguez put an explosive next to the galley's propane tank," Rood said. "Let's get some distance."

The blast rent the air. The ship tore apart while a blizzard of shattered wreckage snowed down. A white puff belched into the air, replacing the black smoke, then nothing further discharged into the deep blue sky. The yacht's bow slipped into the waves, the chunk of stern followed shortly after. With the exception of scattered flotsam, no trace whatsoever of the yacht remained.

Tom glanced at Ralph. Somehow, they both burst out laughing. It was all that they had left to do. Tom rummaged through his luggage, his travelling bag and frisked the pockets of his leather jacket.

"My BlackBerry!"

"What about your BlackBerry?"

"I lost it!"

"Now you're really screwed."

"It's the pictures I lost, Ralph. Pictures of Carol. Now I have nothing of her."

"Charlie took some Polaroids, Tom. Check his luggage when we have the chance."

Tom remembered taking those shots and felt an enormous relief. They redirected their attention to the approaching ship. It possessed a certain majesty that could not but be admired. The absence of mechanics, the perfect silence and the motion of the ship propelled only by the winds.

"Hard to believe we colonized the planet in those things," Tom said.

"Whatever happens, Tom, you and I have to stick together."

Tom gave Ralph an overhead handshake, the two extending the clasp, drawing strength from the other. Tom released Ralph's hand and stared hard at the ship.

"The way this day's going, that's probably a pirate ship."

"Bring it on if they are!" Rodriguez said, and gave a smile of eager fighting lust.

Tom slowed the motor to a fast troll, maintaining just enough speed to navigate the towering waves. They had little to do but wait for the rescue and somehow the waiting seemed the hardest part to get through. Tom glanced at Rood and his crew. Bodmar kept lamenting about the dead crewmates left behind, specifically a woman named Janice. Jackson and Anderson were fighting off the grief and horror of losing their dead mates. They trained together for the better part of a year where they forged close friendships, and apparently in Bodmar's situation, more than just friends. But friendships aside, the discussions highlighted that these lost people were to have been key components to the mission's success.

What mission? Why are we here? What is so important about 1848 anyways?

* * * * *

Cosmo took a digital SLR, backtracked off the peninsula, took the path to the beach and could see the boat returning with the three. The crowd swelled as they got closer to shore and he wiggled through. More helicopters flew overhead, and out of sight, one could be heard landing.

He had to work fast.

All three getting out of the boat were cold, shivering and wore dazed, lost looks. Cosmo wondered what exactly they knew, had seen, and how were they hurled out of the zone? He experienced a temporal ride first-hand, and remembered how damn scared he had been, so he related to their fears. He snapped off some frames. One of the women, a tall chunky girl with raven-black hair in a beige pantsuit with huge knockers, looked lost and afraid. The other girl, much calmer, had a yellow tube top and cut-off jeans. Now Cosmo understood what Daisy Duke shorts were all about and resented Jennifer's tease. Nonetheless, her legs were thin and delicious. A tall fellow with bright orange hair and full beard was the most panicky of the three.

The sky filled with additional military helicopters, a whole variety of them. The crowd grew to a pilgrimage and he had no choice but to bull-doze through, receiving some harsh comments. He slipped the ultrahigh frequency fluxgate sensor from the camera case. It possessed the same shape and size as a cardboard tube of an empty paper towel roll. When he got within a couple of feet of the three, he recorded a reading on each.

Soldiers invaded the beach in a flat out charge, some armed to the teeth. Cosmo bolted and never looked back. He ducked into the bush, found a trail and ran to the campground, arriving at the main road leading away from the park. Bob Scranton tooted a horn, coming out of a small pullover and with the car still rolling, Cosmo dove in head first. Scranton squealed away just as a column of police cars, roof lights blazing, shot past heading for the cape.

He opened the camera case and read the device's readings. "They're off scale. All three of them!"

"Are you shitting me?"

"Language, Mr. Scranton!"

"Cute?" Roberts asked.

Cosmo grinned and held his hands in front of his chest, indicating big breasts.

Jennifer gave him a good whack in the arm, and Scranton and Roberts exchanged some lewd laughter as they turned onto the highway. They continued towards Salem, encountering additional squad cars screaming towards the cape.

* * * * *

Rodriguez didn't say a word the entire time Bodmar stitched up his forehead. He never flinched, not a flicker, even when the rocking of the dinghy threw off Bodmar's aim that would have made any other man scream death cries.

Tom glanced at the box of alcohol he rescued at Ralph's bequest. Rood told him to rip off the labels since they may have their brew dates displayed. He just finished doing the Bacardi when he came to an unopened bottle of vodka. It seemed to speak to him with a fond *hello, old friend. Long time no see.* He fought off the urge to swallow some courage. Perhaps he'd have a couple of shots after the rescue. He glanced at the bottle like a long lost love.

Goddamn alcoholic.

That's what he was—what he'd always be. He didn't give a rat's ass if he drank the entire bottle or the consequences if he did. He needed to reinforce his courage to step aboard the ship. *1848, for Chrissakes.* His life had ended, he was reborn, starting a brand new life and that vodka looked like a gourmet dinner for a starving man.

Goddamn alcoholic.

He picked at the label. Just as the seductive voice inside his head insisting he needed a drink, *just goddamn had to*, was finally vanquished, he finished ripping off all the labels. Rood waved him over. Bringing their boats side by side, Bodmar tossed Tom a bundle of clothing.

"Long-johns?" he complained.

"Briefs are a twentieth century innovation," Bodmar replied pointedly. "They've never seen elastic waistbands on underwear, on socks or nylon stockings for that matter."

"Don't tell me—I need garter belts for my socks?"

"You're catching on."

"Lovely."

"No bras either and don't even talk to me about feminine protection. What shoe size are you?"

"Eleven and a half." She rummaged through a case and tossed him a pair of ankle-high black leather shoes. The clothes looked well used. At least they wouldn't look like they just stepped out of a department store changing room. Tom received a green calico shirt, brown trousers and suspenders that took an effort in the tiny boat to put on and adjust.

"These clothes represent a significant downgrade to my social status," Tom complained.

"Welcome to your new life," Bodmar said.

"You're not married to a millionaire's daughter in this life," Ralph said. "I'm in the same boat, so enough with the whining."

Leaving Ralph's T-shirt on so not to disturb the wound, Tom helped him into his class-deficient attire. Rood and Anderson dressed in dark-blue military uniforms. They were double-breasted frockcoats with fourteen large buttons on the front and three on the split cuffs. Their rank insignia displayed on the shoulders, with silver borders denoting infantry. Rood maintained his rank of colonel, with an embroidered gold eagle within the strap border while Anderson elevated himself to major with the insignia's gold oak leaves. Their trousers were light blue with a white stripe and crowned themselves with wheel caps of dark blue wool. They looked like puffed up sailor hats with small brims, nothing at all like those cool-looking Civil War caps Tom anticipated. Bodmar wore a red cotton dress. She, too, wasn't immune to the downgrading of her social status, but Tom noted she was a tough little thing, likely raised in a working class family. She pulled her strawberry blond hair into a tight chignon.

Rodriguez and Jackson dressed much like Tom and Ralph. Silver was the exception, decked out in a brown suit, including a cravat and a collar he attached separately. The speed in which he got dressed showed he had a good deal of practice assembling nineteenth century attire.

"Nothing in your luggage comes out in public," Rood cautioned.

"That's a no-brainer," Tom replied, still struggling to get the right suspender to match the left.

"Shouldn't have let him bring any," Anderson said.

"Always keep your options open," Rood countered. Tom, in a rare moment, agreed with the colonel. Rood's voice raised a pitch. "Here's the rundown of the rules."

"Rules?" Tom asked with a skewed grin. "Time traveller rules?"

"Precisely, Barney."

"Scared we're going to change history?"

Rood gestured his hand to Silver for the reply. "We exist in an environment which we call a benign violation of causality, which does not permit paradox."

"You can't change history," Rood translated in plain English.

"What if I tried to save Abe Lincoln's life?"

"Something would prevent you from doing it," Silver said. "I'm certain that you have heard of The Grandfather Paradox of causality violation theory?"

"I'm afraid not."

"You are presently in 1848 and happen to meet your great grandfather, and you shoot him dead. Since you killed your ancestor prior to him conceiving the required offspring to ensure your birth, you cannot be born, therefore never able to travel back in time to kill your ancestor—hence the entire event could not have taken place."

"I'm confused," Ralph said.

"What Silver is trying to explain," Rood said, "is when you approached your ancestor with the gun, because of the intervention of the chronology protection conjuncture mechanism, he survives his wounds, or, he shoots first and kills you. The Novikov self-consistency conjecture asserts that the only possible timelines are those entirely self-consistent—so anything a time traveller does in the past must have been part of history all along, and, the time traveller is powerless to prevent the trip back in time from happening. You're a prime example, Trasler. It's your destiny to go back in time. You could have done nothing to prevent it from happening. History would have changed had you not."

"In the long and short of it, your great grandfather survives so you can be conceived to go back in time to try to unsuccessfully kill him," Silver said.

". . . Okay." Ralph's face turned into a blank mask.

"And the moral of the story, Mr. Parker?" Silver asked.

"I can't change history?"

"Respect your elders." Both Rood and Silver chuckled with Silver continuing. "Simply put, the Feynman quantum probability amplitude for inconsistent histories for closed timelike world lines vanishes exactly."

"Whoa!" Ralph said.

Rood smiled patiently. "You lose your own free will to create a paradox when you travel to your past. History will be unchanged because your travel from the future to the past has already occurred prior to your departure. If that wasn't the case, then any macroscopic object traveling back through time would inevitably create paradoxes where cause and effect break down."

"We can't change history because we've already been part of history before we were sent into the past?" Tom paraphrased, beginning to get a grasp of the science.

"Exactly," Silver said. "Whatever you will be doing during the next two years, had already transpired prior to your extraction from 2016. This is why these natural occurring traversable wormholes permit travel to the past utilizing the chronology protection conjuncture mechanism. Hence, any travel to the past is within a benign violation of causality where paradox is prohibited. A violation of causality is impossible. We are active participants, but our actions have already been pre-ordained."

"Okay, time traveller rules, 201: You can't change history. So how come no one has ever recorded one of these over the entire course of human history? The CIA hasn't been around that long to cover it up," Tom said.

Anderson offered the answer. "Over 85% of implosions aren't strong enough to create a temporal wormhole. You would barely notice a thing inside one of those weaker events. Being highly magnetic, they are attracted to the magnetic poles and most occur in the sparsely populated far north and Antarctica. The kind powerful enough to have over a century of temporal displacement, such as the one we passed through, represents less than one percent of all impacts and the area is relatively small. Furthermore, a displaced person would have to survive the egress point and chances are quite low for anyone to talk about it later on. Birds and animals have the sense to leave the area, as most people do. This is why you won't find a temporally displaced polar bear in Australia, for instance."

"An event occurred in downtown Vitebsk, a town in Belarus in the then Soviet Union, in 1966," Rood said. "Not enough for a temporal extraction, but scared the bejappers out of the population. Dismissed as a freak weather event and a few UFO reports. That's the only recorded hit in a major city and they had no clue as to what happened."

"So you're not here to change history, right?"

"What did I tell you?" Rood's voice became a deep growl and Tom got the point.

"So what about the rules?" Tom continued. "Like *Star Trek's* Prime Directive?"

"You got it," Anderson replied. "You can't deliberately try to change history because you'll fail and you can't tell anyone that we're from the future or about the history you know."

"I think they'd lock us up in an asylum if we tried."

"In this day and age?" Rood grinned. "An asylum would be getting off easy."

The ship looked lovely enough out there, with her tanned sails set against the rich blue, braced sharp on her starboard tack. It was, regardless of their impossible predicament, a remarkable sight to behold. Tom leaned forward, struggled with Carol's suitcase and extracted a vanity mirror with a white plastic frame, a foot wide and nine inches high. "I want to make sure that the ship can find us," Tom explained. "They'll be asking a lot of questions if we start chasing after them with our outboard engines."

"Good point," Rood said.

Tom ricocheted the sun at the ship. He tossed a sharp look at Colonel Rood. "Any idea what's happening to Carol, Alice and Charlie?"

"Safe and sound. You two have already returned from the past and are right at their sides."

AUGUST 6, 2016

The wooden cabin had that stuffy smell of old buildings. A Cape Lookout State Park ranger stood by the door while two soldiers escorted Carol, Alice and Charlie inside. All were still in their wet clothes and offered seats. They were hard, wooden chairs. Carol sat on the left, Alice in the middle and Charlie on the right. Carol wore a wide, starry look on her face.

The military officer excused the park ranger and closed the door, flanked by the soldiers who escorted them. They stared into nothing, it seemed. One of them carried a short, compact assault carbine, efficient looking and ugly. They wore the cold looks of men who looked as if they never learned to smile.

The officer sat behind the desk. He held the rank of major with green camouflage fatigues. Mastracchio was in his early forties, fair complexion with a receding hairline. He slid a rack of park literature to the side of the desk to get a full view of the three. He settled his soft blue eyes onto Carol.

"Again, I offer my deepest condolences on your loss. I understand your grief."

"My husband and brother are dead," Carol sobbed. "You have no idea of my grief!"

CHAPTER 6

"I want to call my father."

Mastracchio looked at Carol, who seemed to miss the point that she was the detainee. "You made three calls already, including your father, and my commanding officer, Colonel Nolan, to say the least, is displeased."

"I have my rights."

"Right now, you have nothing."

"Excuse me, Major. Did you not take a vow to protect the Constitution of the United States of America?"

"Of course."

"I have rights as guaranteed by that constitution. You're in violation."

"I am protecting the constitution of the United States of America, to ensure there is no violation of our national security."

"By law, the military cannot make an arrest on US soil."

"You were exposed to an electromagnetic burst and we are awaiting a medical specialist to evaluate you. In the meantime, we'll kill some time by having a nice chat. Furthermore, we have an FBI agent on site that can take you in should we choose to do so. We know the law. Nice try."

Charlie trembled in his seat, but Alice was the calmest of the three, sitting with a bland expression. Alice noticed one of the guards ogling over her and tugged the yellow tube top higher above the swell of her breasts.

"The public already knows an army helicopter went down," the major continued, holding the line of a cover-up already in progress, "and we need to get control of the situation quickly. In this day and age of social media, it doesn't take long. In a nutshell, you will have a brief medical examination, processed and released, but at Colonel Nolan's discretion."

"We're Canadian citizens and you can't hold us and we have rights," Carol bit back.

"One last time. You intruded into a classified military operation. You're foreign nationals. Your brother was a retired Canadian soldier who may have been under orders to spy on us. You three may have been part of an espionage team."

"All we were trying to do was to save lives," Alice said, her voice became harsher than she intended. She wanted to cooperate, tell them what they wanted to make this as painless as possible, but Carol was going out of her way to make it painful and long.

Mastracchio faced Carol. "Your brother and husband perished trying to save the lives of United States service personnel." The major's voice dropped to low and fatherly. "This is not a sacrifice that we take lightly, but understand this involves a highly classified operation testing countermeasures equipment. Now, we are in a state park packed with tourists asking too many questions, and already there are Facebook postings of the event."

"Countermeasures testing within view of a tourist trap, on a Saturday, no less?" Carol scoffed. "That's a good one."

The major avoided Carol's eyes, putting his attention to his paperwork. "We eventually have to tie in your boating mishap to the helicopter accident. But it's not that simple. As I said, you have been exposed to a unique form of electromagnetic contamination. It's not harmful, at least in the short term. We have a specialist en route who will extract it out of you."

"Extract?" Carol asked, her right eyebrow soaring. "Why doesn't that sound pleasant?"

The wry smile the major returned dried the spit in her mouth.

* * * * *

With the ship's main sails furled, she glided through the water more from forward inertia than from the wind. High atop its three masts, sailors climbed the crisscrossing shrouds, waiting for their captain's next command. Closer, closer it came.

A fully rigged ship, she possessed a black hull just over a hundred feet long and twenty-five feet at its beam. A tradition dating back to the days of pirates, a white stripe with phoney painted-on gunports ran along the hull to give the illusion that the ship was armed. Close to a hundred passengers swarmed the three decks, intrigued by the rescue. A babble of voices came from the decks, with one roaring voice booming far above the rest. The crew dropped a rope ladder over the starboard side at amid-ships.

Tom slipped the outboard engine below the waves. Next, he dunked the fuel tank, letting it fill with water before releasing it. With braced feet and a locked back, he took to the oars. His back muscles swelled as the oars thrust through the waves, the full effort to quell his shock more than to hold the course.

Ralph's voice, though dreadfully weak from his injuries, still held an air of excitement. "Once we get aboard, be careful and keep a close eye on our luggage. The last thing we want is to be the center of attention."

"You're staring at me like it's my intent."

"You have a pretty good track record in that regard."

Tom glanced at the ship, his enthusiasm far below Ralph's. "It's not exactly the Queen Mary."

Ralph squinted his eyes against the sun's glare. "No, it sure the hell isn't."

* * * * *

It wasn't the actual waiting for the commanding officer that had become unbearable, it was the silence. The two guards stood aside the doors, inert, motionless, almost like the ceremonial guards you'd find at Buckingham Palace—but not quite. Their eyes shifted from time to time, looking at the three, specifically at the women. A squat tugboat of a man with a crew cut, beret and a bulldog face, seemed to have a thing for Alice. The other, a black fellow with a body builder physique, was handsome despite a scar running down the right side of his face.

A colonel barged into the room. He imposed his body on the space surrounding him like an invasion. Each step was an assault on the air he walked through. Cliff Nolan's ridged shoulders floated above a lean tapered waist, towering over six-foot-three in his green camouflage fatigues with thick army-issue footwear. He was thirty-eight with jet-black hair sliced with a tight side part. He glanced at Mastracchio and the two guards, and they all left. With heavy strides felt through the floorboards, he squeezed between the three detainees and the desk. Carol backed her chair off a good foot, Charlie and Alice followed suit to give some breathing space from the colonel. His eyes were the palest of hazel, carefully moving about, reading, cataloguing the three.

"You're a very attractive woman," he said to Carol. "I could stare at you all day long." His eyes slipped off her face to her chest. "Fake?"

Carol zipped her one-piece pantsuit to her chin, returning a sour smile. "The real McCoy."

Nolan gave each a long, steady look. Both Carol and Alice felt his eyes roam over their breasts, licking over them like a tongue drooling with slime.

He glanced at Alice's yellow tube top. "Don't even try to convince me those are real."

Her expression didn't flinch—just like those ceremonial guards at Buckingham Palace.

"My name is Colonel Cliff Nolan. I appreciate the sacrifice of Tom Trasler and Ralph Parker giving their lives in an attempt to save the men and women under my command. This great feat of bravery will not be covered up or dismissed." His voice carried a low, steady monotone. "However, there is a process of due diligence to ensure that the security of the United States of America has not been compromised. I need to understand exactly what you have seen and exactly what you know."

Colonel Nolan's hazel eyes settled over each face. Carol Parker expressed defiance and pure loathing. Alice Cousineau was wary, careful, the most composed of the three. Charlie Mason exhibited outright terror. His lips, particularly his jaw, trembled constantly. He was incapable of direct eye contact.

Carol was the recipient of the first question. "Why were you there?"

"We had an appointment with a shipping company based out of Long Beach. Ralph and I work for our family-owned company, Northstar Navigation. Ralph was trying to secure the traffic from Long Beach into Canada. I'm the custom specialist and I would have been in charge of the cross-border paperwork. We took the yacht as the company's president wanted to be wined and dined at sea. Charlie is the IT guy who came along to discuss electronic interfacing with their computers. Tom and Alice came along for the ride."

"Who went inside the helicopter?"

Carol responded. "Ralph and Tom."

"No one else?"

"You got a hearing problem, mister?"

Nolan's eyebrows soared at her boldness, his face animated, even amused. "Did any of you speak to the crew?"

"Yes," Alice replied, trying to intercept Carol and her acidic temperament.

Nolan moved right before Alice, lowering his face to the same level as hers. He grabbed her by the chin. She batted his hand away before he even knew she had swung. *Nice reflexes,* and he admired her youthful spunk. He stood to his full height, hands on his hips as he stared down. The girl was calm, too calm, leaving him a little unnerved.

She rolled her deep brown eyes at him and her voice, smooth as silk, had an incredibly sexy French accent. "We kept demanding an explanation, but all we got was a no-comment classified reply. Then they commandeered the ship at gunpoint."

"Gunpoint?" Nolan asked, a little startled.

Alice wiped her face from some spittle. "Do you always have to spit when you talk?"

"I do not spit when I talk!" Nolan's eyes flared and his fists balled.

"Boy, is that not the first time that's been complained about." Alice did this big roll of the eyes in deliberate theatrics.

"Answer the question."

She again wiped her face and made an exaggerated gesture of flinging the goop off her hand. "Anyone got an umbrella?"

"Answer the question!"

"Okay, I'll settle for a rainsuit." Nolan recoiled to strike her so Alice rushed her reply. "The Hispanic guy fired a shot and nearly killed Tom."

"We just saved his sorry ass and that's the thanks we got!" Carol shot back.

Nolan looked a little shell-shocked at the defiance and loathing they confronted him with. He settled his calculating cold look onto Charlie. "How did you get so close to shore?"

Nothing came out but a grunt.

Carol challenged his gaze unflinchingly. "There was all this green electricity and the sky went all red and the next thing we know, we're swimming distance from shore."

"Three hundred and seventy feet, precisely," Nolan said.

"Then gonzo!" Carol said. "Our boat—vanished into thin air!"

"It's gonzo because it exploded and sank," Nolan said. "The effect you went through caused you to blank out. You drifted to shore unconscious. It has that effect on everyone."

"We blanked out?" Carol's face and tone was overdosing on cynicism.

"You blanked out."

"I guess I blanked out." Carol understood their little game. She blanked out. They all did.

* * * * *

Tom dug into a traveling bag, pulled out Ralph's skipper hat and shook out the wrinkles. "Here, it'll help you look more distinguished."

Ralph clamped the black cap tight over his head. "Thanks, Tom. I thought I'd lost it."

The bowsprit crawled by and Tom gazed up at the starboard-side bulwarks, lined with dozens of curious passengers staring down at them. These were people who died of old age perhaps a century before his birth. It was downright haunting, like staring at lost spirits trapped between the living and the afterlife.

Tom cupped his hands and raised his voice an extra pitch. "Ahoy! Captain Parker is injured and requires assistance." Voices were returned, but in a foreign language. "Dammit, Ralph. They're not English."

"What do you mean, they're not English?"

"Just what I said."

"They've got to be English or we're screwed."

Tom turned to Rood, who worked up a sweat trying to catch up. "They're not English."

"No kidding, Barney," Rood replied, breathing heavily from the paddling. "They're flying a Swedish flag."

"That will explain it," Tom said to Ralph.

The ship's hull continued to creep ahead in total silence. Tom held his position, waiting to catch the dangling rope ladder. With his hair blowing across his face, he cupped his hands and shouted upward.

"Does anyone speak English?"

After a bit of a bustle, a short man with a trimmed beard and dressed in a black coat with double-breasted buttons, leaned over the railing. Straggling brown hair fluttered in the breeze. "I am Captain Olof Liedberg, at your service." The English spoken to them betrayed just a trace of a Swedish accent superimposed over a British inflection.

"There, English," Tom said. He looked up to the Swedish captain. "Captain Parker is injured and needs help getting aboard."

"Grab a hold of the ladder, kind sir, and I shall dispatch assistance."

Ralph's frown changed into something like a smile. "Tom, this Captain Parker bit—"

"You were the skipper of the yacht, right?"

"Someone at the wheel of a pleasure craft and a ship's captain are not even in the same league."

"Ya, but they'll take better care of you if they think you're a captain, right?"

"They sure the hell won't take good care of me once they find out I'm impostering a ship's master!"

Tom steadied the ladder while the first sailor climbed down.

"I have dispatched Mr. Rödin, my first mate, who has two strong arms, which, I can tell you, are not to be despised onboard a ship, and which I now have the honour of putting at the service of Captain Parker."

The height and the build of the mate did not deny the captain's pretensions to his strength. He plucked Ralph from the tender with as much effort as scooping up a toddler. Ralph clung to his neck of warm granite. A gasp of pain hissed from Ralph's lips while the mate carried him up the ladder and planted him on deck. With some visible apprehension, Ralph met the crowd, face by face, his eyes gratefully embracing them all for the rescue.

Tom passed up the heaps of luggage. The case of liquor went first. "Careful!" Tom called. "There's booze in there. You know—spirits." He cocked his thumb towards his mouth. The entire crew caught on, cheering and urging the sailor in Swedish to be careful, threatening him if he was not. A chain of sailors passed up the case and the luggage followed. Ralph's suitcase went first, one of Charlie's suitcases, two of Carol's, Alice's, Tom's bright blue nylon backpack, three small traveling bags, and last, Charlie's second suitcase, vacated of most of its belongings to become a carrying case for his boombox. He gave the tiny boat a farewell and cast it away. Without the ballast, it bobbed like a cork over the ridged back of the sea.

Rood's crew trailed fifty feet back, putting their full effort in catching up, hindered by the drag of the second dinghy carrying their crates. Tom began the long climb up the ladder. He swayed precariously, paused from time to time to steady himself and to catch his wits, then continued with short, tentative spurts. The seas were heaving the ship up and down, side to side, the motion oscillating the ladder like a pendulum. It was a terrifying climb. Just as he reached the bulwark rail, something made him pause. He stared at the faces of the crew and passengers. He had arrived at the point of transition from his world into theirs. He took a quick breath of courage, and stepped into the nineteenth century.

* * * * *

The colonel coaxed a grin through a tight jaw. He took an iPhone off the desk and held it before Carol's face. "This yours?"

"Yup, except that it got ruined in the water. I made the calls with someone else's phone."

Nolan slapped the phone on the desk, straddled the wooden chair backwards, crossed his arms on the backrest then leaned into her. "How did you just happen to have the number for the Canadian consulate? Hmmmm?"

"Hello, Einstein!" She tapped her finger to her temple in the stupid gesture. "It's called smart phones that connect to the net and do a Google search. In this paranoid country, that's the first call you make."

"Paranoid?"

"Homeland Security makes the Gestapo look like a knitting club. I'm amazed how Americans have so willingly given up so many sacred freedoms out of government manipulated fear."

"Have care of what you say about America. Be very careful with your words." His looks were cryogenic. "I have no use for Canadians."

She gave him a defiant little smile. "Canada is everything that the founders of the United States wanted America to be."

"I should slap your face."

Carol's eyes met his head on in a dare. "My father is a personal friend of the Canadian Prime Minister, who is a golfing buddy of your Commander-in-Chief. You're the one who has to be very goddamn careful. My guess is that the Prime Minster is having a chat with his golfing buddy right about now."

Alice glanced at Carol, trying to have some kind of eye contact to tell her to shut the hell up, but asking Carol to shut up was like asking the wind not to blow.

"The Canadian prime minister is a minor league waterboy compared to the Commander-in-Chief. But let's get right down to the nitty-gritty, shall we?"

"Nitty-gritty? As why you insist on spitting on people's faces when you talk?"

"Is that your alternative to water boarding?" Alice added for the kill.

For a moment, Rood's face went idiotic with surprise at their boldness. Then it filled in with crimson rage. "Your boat arrived at the exact moment and the exact coordinates of our test. Don't tell me that was a coincidence!"

Alice and Carol didn't flinch at the question, but it unnerved Charlie. Nolan pounced in front of him. "Why were you there?"

"We told you, it . . . it was a business trip. I'm just the IT guy for Northstar Navigation. I didn't do anything! Please let me go!"

Nolan grabbed his copper-haired face, scrunching his lips, making him look like a goldfish. "What were you doing on the boat?"

"I . . . I was supposed to meet with the customer to talk about computer stuff. Then Tom and Carol tried to set me up with Alice."

"You and her?" Nolan chuckled a ball of phlegm from his throat.

"I still haven't forgiven them," Alice said.

"Okay . . ." Nolan turned to Alice. "You're so nice and calm—that comes from training. You were there deliberately. Who's backing you?"

Alice rolled her eyes. "I wasn't involved in the business part of it. It was supposed to have been a pleasure cruise, that's it. I've known Tom my entire life and now he's dead. I'm not calm, you bastard!"

"You related?"

"Tom was my next door neighbour."

"Big age difference?"

"He was my babysitter."

"And he married this miserable broad with the great big tits. How does that make you feel?"

Alice rolled her tongue inside her mouth and stared straight ahead.

There were some seriously hard feelings there.

"Answer the question."

"As you Americans are so fond of saying—I'm taking the fifth."

"You assholes killed my brother and my husband," Carol said. "You have no right to treat us like this!"

Nolan would love nothing more than to slap her senseless. Carol read the look perfectly, knowing she'd strike right back. She knew her life would be far more bearable if she could.

"Why do you hate me so much?"

"We rescued six of your crew. The thanks we got? My husband and brother are dead and the result of their ultimate sacrifice? You bastards detaining us like we're the Islamic State!"

"I don't want to appear insensitive," Nolan gave the slightest trace of a smirk, "but for someone who has just lost a husband and a brother, you haven't spilled a single tear. Big inheritance?"

Carol jolted and Nolan jerked backed a step. Had the man in the gray suit and canary tie not entered, she may have actually attacked him. The civilian, a white thirty-something gentleman, obviously held authority over Nolan. He glanced briefly at the three then motioned Nolan to come to the door. He whispered something. Nolan looked at Carol one last time and gave her a final, furious glance.

"We're not through."

She could tell she'd be seeing him sooner than later, and her eyes tracked him out of the cabin like some guided missile from hell. Mastracchio and the guards came back in.

* * * * *

Captain Liedberg issued his orders with a natural bullhorn of a voice. His crew stood next to the rope ladder, preparing to assist Rood and his crew. Tom steadied Ralph against the motion of the ship. The cold wind penetrated through his new clothes and he regretted packing his leather jacket. His shoes were too large, weren't at all comfortable and he wriggled his feet in the empty spaces, seeking a better fit. The pants were not fitting well either and adjusting the suspenders only made things worse, giving himself a ridiculous looking wedgie. Tom sucked in his breath and could feel his hands tremble. Not a soul on board, not even Ralph, knew how frightened he was. *1848! Here he was, within the verses of history, trapped within its pages.*

The captain approached, gazed at Tom's shoulder length hair with disapproval, then stared directly into his eyes. "Mister . . .?"

"Trasler, Tom Trasler." The captain held out a hand and Tom took it, each gauging the other's grip. Both firm and cordial. "I've got to tell you something, Captain." He closed in to whisper the words. "We're not with the five men and the woman."

"I do not understand."

"We were trying to rescue them, and then our own ship was destroyed."

"How many souls lost?"

All at once, Tom lost his composure. He choked out a sob.

Ralph replied. His voice cracked a little. "Three, including his wife, who was my sister."

"May the God of mercy have had pity on the souls of the lost." Turning to Tom, the captain looked with compassion into the inner depths of Tom's brown eyes, circled with the white of shock. "You poor, unhappy fellow. Even in your misfortune, you must thank Providence for your own deliverance. It was only by the mercy of Him that we happened to come upon your catastrophe." He turned his attention to Ralph. "Describe to me the extent of your injuries."

"I took a piece of metal in my shoulder from the explosion on my ship."

"My sailmaker will tend to it. He has an excellent hand with needle and thread."

"I'm certain he does," Ralph said. "However, the woman with us, she has medical training and she'll—"

"A woman tending to your wound. Certainly not!"

Ralph winked at the captain. "She's good."

Liedberg's eyes bored into Ralph, the doubt still strong. "I have laudanum for the discomfort, Captain Parker."

"That won't be necessary. We have our own medicine." In fact, the shot Bodmar gave him had done wonders for the pain.

"Perhaps it is best if you repose." Liedberg pointed to a bench against the side of the faded green galleyhouse. Tom led Ralph there where he collapsed.

"It's going to take awhile to adjust to their mind-set, Tom," Ralph whispered followed with a painful chuckle.

"It's going to take them a lot longer for them to adjust to ours."

"You got that right!"

The emigrants watched them with intense fascination. They reminded Tom of a herd of cattle. They had that same curious gaze. Sharon Bodmar, the first of the six soldiers to climb aboard, had a large blood stained dressing wrapped around her forehead.

"Miss Sharon Bodmar," she introduced herself. The captain returned her a tidy bow.

Liedberg took notice of Anderson's uncommon short hair when he stepped aboard. "Major Anderson, US Army, at your service." The two shook hands. Anderson looked at the crowd, smiling tentatively at them.

The next aboard caused a gasp, a blend of shock, amazement, revulsion and curiosity. Liedberg's face soured when Tyrone Jackson stepped aboard. Tom and Ralph both grinned as they watched intently.

"Tyrone Jackson. Thank you, sir." Jackson offered his hand to the captain. The captain returned his hand after much hesitation.

There was a varied reaction with passengers. Most had never seen an African American; many never knew blacks existed at all. A few cringed into the crowd, one little girl shrieked in terror and cried, another giggled, and the laughter irked Jackson far more than the crying.

Silver was next. He stood two inches below Liedberg's five-foot-six height.

Neither offered their hand to the other. No introductions either.

Rood and Rodriguez, still in the dinghy, teamed up with the crew to rope the equipment aboard. It took the full effort of six men to hoist the large, hot crate to the main deck. The soldiers crated the outboard engine long before they arrived at the ship, but the crew and passengers alike marvelled at the two gray dinghies floating next to the ship. Rood and Rodriguez, dangling on the ladder, deflated both. The sailors heaved them up with ropes. They flopped onto the deck like dead squids. Rood and Rodriguez finally arrived on deck. Rood's ribs were still tender from the fall and all the lifting left him exhausted.

"At your service, gentlemen," Liedberg said, offering his hand to Rood.

"My name is Colonel Theodore Rood, United States Army." He accepted the captain's hand, hard and calloused, shaking it vigorously.

"Welcome aboard the *Margaretha*. I am Captain Olof Liedberg."

"This is Carlos Rodriguez." Rodriguez gave a tidy little bow. "We thank you for the rescue, Captain."

"How many souls of your vessel were lost?"

"Eight of my people."

"May their souls be with God. Let us pray for those whom we have lost."

"The time for prayer, Captain, was before their deaths. Prayer cannot help them now."

"I have learned that Captain Parker and Mister Trasler's ship was conducting a rescue of your own when a great calamity struck?"

"That is correct. It was a very unfortunate tragedy."

"A greater tragedy was thus avoided by your deliverance." The captain turned to crowd of onlookers. "This was once a proud ship of commerce," Liedberg said, more an apology than explanation. He spoke with so much force, Rood backed up a step to spare his ears from permanent hearing loss. "Now, well . . . you can see that they have converted my beloved vessel into an emigrant ship." Hoards of children ran unchecked while mothers confined infants within their warm embrace. "I have never been so cursed with so many children. Devil take the captain if this ship isn't a nursery!"

"You are taking these people to America?" Rood asked.

"Indeed I am, Colonel Rood. I am in great perplexity as to why these tillers-of-dirt must travel thousands of miles to till another patch of soil. Dirt is dirt."

The passengers competed for a better view as if it was some kind of circus freak sideshow. Typically, the men were clad in wadmal jackets with a handful wearing suits. They wore gray caps or wide brimmed hats with a wide assortment of leather shoes, knee high boots, while others clunked about with sabots. The women, wrapped within their woollen shawls, tied up or braided their hair due to the brisk winds. Most wore plain homespun dresses, but three women stood out with a fashion statement a cut above the others.

The *Margaretha* possessed three decks. The main deck, where they presently stood, measured a length of fifty feet and a width of twenty-five. A sliding deck hatch was sandwiched between the pair of steps leading to the forecastle deck. Unbattened with only a box-like frame around it, someone could, with very little effort, fall through into the steerage. Some open space led to the mainmast, six feet further aft stood a green galleyhouse, with the ship's white lifeboat perched upside-down on top of it. Behind it, another deck hatch. The captain and mates' cabins were situated aft, the crew's quarters inside the forecastle.

The forecastle deck, the smallest of the three decks, highlighted the capstan with the foremast three feet from the rear edge. The mizzenmast and the ship's teak wheel, manned by the helmsman, occupied the poop deck. Over their heads, tanned pyramids of sail reached up, up, up, as if trying to touch the cotton ball clouds moving swiftly across the blue of the morning sky.

Liedberg turned his attention to Ralph, slouched on the bench against the green galleyhouse. He was listing in distress. "Captain Parker, we need to tend to your wounds."

Ralph was wondering just how goddamn long it would take for someone to take care of his misery. "Thank you, sir."

"But first, you must meet the one who first sighted your burning vessel. The one whom you have contracted a great debt of gratitude."

"After we get this hunk of metal out of my shoulder, sir, I'd be very much delighted to."

"One must not be impolite, Captain Parker. She is a lovely creature."

Ralph fought through the pain and forced a twisted smile. "How lovely?"

Liedberg, speaking Swedish, called his first mate. "Mr. Rödin, where is the Gabrielsson woman?" The big mate glanced about, then pointed into the crowd. "You there, come forward. The fortunate souls whom you have given deliverance from a watery grave would like to offer their gratitude."

With much apprehension, the woman, a striking blonde in her early twenties, passed through the crowd. Holding a bundled infant, she stood just a couple inches shorter than Tom's six-one. A white woollen shawl framed her softly rounded face and her long braids nearly reached her waist. Her face was of a light, unblemished complexion, features perhaps a little too plain, but otherwise very pretty. An unbuttoned black jacket with large side pockets reached her thighs. A long green dress concealed her feet. She handed the infant to her husband, revealing her full figure for the men to admire. Her striking eyes, cerulean-blue, were wide and round and she was definitely sensual—the type of woman most men dream of.

Ralph struggled to his feet and stood next to Tom. His brows arched while he openly admired her breasts, cramped inside the homespun dress. Dark thoughts caroused through his mind.

He leaned towards Tom and whispered, "Nice century."

Tom didn't—rather couldn't—respond. A power beyond himself seized his eyes from their line of sight, coupling with the woman's. The primeval fear residing in her eyes was so striking they impaled Tom to the deck the way a collector pins a butterfly specimen to a board. Carefully cataloguing the eight strangers, she shifted from one to the other. She was not willing to offer a smile, not even a tentative one.

"They are North Americans and cannot speak our tongue. Say your name slowly," Liedberg asked.

She forced a swallow to release the paralysis from her mouth. "Alvina-Kristina Gabrielsson." She looked down to Liedberg's level. Her voice found a new intensity. "They are from North America?"

"That is correct."

She scrutinized Tom the way she would a slave on an auction block. "Do many North Americans have such long hair?"

"Some of the frontiersmen, I understand, have long unkempt hair. The Indians—the godless savages who are murdering innocent settlers—some of them have hair as long as their women."

"What is wrong with that man? The dark one."

"He is a man from the continent of Africa."

"The skin and hair . . . is it a disease?"

"No. God in His holy wisdom created him that way."

"Are they dangerous?"

"In their native habitat, his fellow creatures are in the lowest scale of humanity. However, this man is a civilized Christian and lives in America."

"Are there many such men in America?"

"Most are slaves in the south."

"Slaves?" she gasped.

"Slaves, yes."

"We are travelling this great distance to a country that enslaves their fellow men?"

"It is only permitted in the South and only with his kind. It is prohibited to enslave those of the white race. You will be going to the northern regions of the United States where there is no slavery. Say something to them in English."

"My English is deficient—please do not ask me to shame myself."

The captain turned to the eight. "This young lady has some command of the English tongue, but is too shy to speak it."

Ralph continued to rip her clothes off with his eyes. "I want her, Captain!" His eyes locked directly onto her breasts with no attempt to conceal his target. The woman may not wish to speak the English language, but she certainly understood Ralph. She snapped her unbuttoned jacket shut, gave Ralph a look of murderous intent then knifed through the crowd, muttering her disgust at his perversions.

"Hey, doll, come back!"

"You have all the tact of a bulldozer, man."

"That's a woman, Tom."

"She is a married woman, Captain Parker," Liedberg rebuked. His tone held a stern warning.

"Didn't you notice something freaky about her eyes?" Tom hushed. "She reminded me of your kooky Aunt Clara."

Ralph grunted when he sat back down on the galleyhouse bench. He struggled to balance himself against the harsh ride of the ship. "I couldn't even tell you what colour her eyes were, Tom."

"You can be a real asshole, sometimes, Ralphy."

"Ya, whatever."

Tom felt his mind tugged right out of his skull. Carol, Alice and Charlie exploded into his thoughts like a psychic bomb. He sensed they were in trouble, big trouble. He didn't know how he knew, but accepted the knowing. Despite Rood's earlier assurances they would be safe, that he'd be there to greet them after the army rescued them, he sensed the danger.

* * * * *

A stern-faced blond soldier in her mid thirties, average in height and build with green camouflage fatigues, entered the cabin. She clewed her hair into a bun emphasizing her high hairline and she wore thick, black glasses. She had a pale-complexioned face, a pleasantly dimpled chin and an overbite made her two front teeth appear like a chipmunk's. The heat gave her face a waxy sheen that made her look ill. Her motion was not graceful, and a first impression might conclude she would be a terrible dance partner.

Her name was Captain Lucy Lewis—US Army. She had a PhD in quantum physics, could fly Black Hawk helicopters and was the US Army's lead scientist on the temporal phenomena. She carried a case, that by the way it tugged her shoulder, didn't look too light.

Carol nearly wet herself when she pulled the contraption out from the case. Shaped like a fireplace billows with handles cut in the sides, three small metallic-blue prongs stuck from the end in a triangle pattern.

"You mentioned you had political contacts," Mastracchio said as he glared unkindly at Carol. Her black hair fell over one eye, concealing it, the other looked at Mastracchio with chilly indifference. "We have confirmation that your father is on his way aboard a chartered aircraft with a Canadian government official. The speed this was carried out ought to make me suspicious," he smiled at Carol, but the smile was chilling, "if I was a man of a suspicious nature."

Charlie's chest heaved with relief. Carol smiled in a vengeful, satisfied way while Alice was too busy staring at the woman holding the alien death-ray device. Lucy Lewis stared above the contraption, grinning at the three like a sadistic mad scientist.

"What's that horrible thing you're holding?" Alice asked.

"We call it an extraction device," Lucy Lewis said. "I designed it myself."

The extraction device whirled to life with a high-pitched whine, sounding like a dentist's drill, that sent ice shivers down Alice's spine. The woman pressed some yellow buttons, looked at the display while adjusting the settings. "I need to inject this into your buttocks to extract the magnetic contamination you have absorbed, which is the least painful area on your body to do so."

"All three of you, on your knees and drop your pants," Mastracchio ordered.

"Charlie," Carol glared at him with twin howitzers, "if I see you turned on or even glancing at me, you'll be carried out as a eunuch. Understood?"

Charlie understood. He understood very well and he wasn't turned on.

No, it was much worse than that. It was very much the opposite.

Lucy Lewis brought over a wooden chair. Alice put her head and chest on the seat of the chair and clutched onto the back legs. Lucy Lewis snapped on a pair of latex gloves, swabbed Alice's right butt cheek with an alcohol wipe, and gave her a shot. She waited for about ninety seconds then pinched.

"Feel anything?"

"Nothing."

She covered the cheek with a slimy blue grease. "Hold tight," she said. Lucy Lewis had a Deep South accent she tried to conceal or in the very least minimise, but every now and then, a couple of unfiltered words leaked out with a heavy drawl. Alice didn't feel the three metal needles jab a half-inch into her, but her butt cheeks certainly knew all about it. They squeezed tightly together while the sound of the contraption made her want to scream. It produced an accelerating miniature motorcycle kind of buzz. She could feel the extremities of her body turn cold—her toes and fingertips tingled until a dull frostbite ache rendered them numb. Alice became faint and struggled drawing a breath. When the buzzing stopped, her hands lost their grip on the chair legs. She flopped off the chair and lay half-naked on the floor with absolutely no dignity.

Her butt drooled blood from the three triangle-shaped entry points. Lucy Lewis wiped and bandaged them and slipped her underwear and shorts back on. Alice, still stomach down, broke out into a sweat. Her feet twitched, she felt sick while her butt cheeks trembled like a Richter 8 seismic disturbance. She needed to pee and wasn't certain if she could hold it. She hadn't felt this godawful since her first and last attempt at hot yoga.

"Does that magnetic stuff really have to come out?" Carol asked, staring at the extraction device, then to Alice lying prostrate on the hard wooden floor with her little ass vibrating like an out-of-control floor sander.

"Trust me when I say that you really don't want to be walking around with it," Lucy Lewis replied with a wink.

Charlie was next, followed by Carol. When the nausea had passed, the woman left. Throughout the ordeal, they heard helicopters come and go like a war zone. They were pronounced quite fit by a uniformed doctor. A man in a black suit with a thin black tie arrived, sitting at the desk, he laid out three sets of paperwork. He seemed a little too stereotypical for Carol's liking and she concluded they dressed him that way just for effect. A guard assisted Carol to her feet. She walked in short, unsteady shuffles and slumped into the chair before the desk. The painkiller gave her the sensation of listing over to one side when she wasn't.

"Read the security oath and sign it," the nameless man in black said. He wasn't a patient man, didn't expect her to read the entire document, and seemed incredibly pissed-off that she did. "We will be issuing a press release shortly, confirming that a Chinook helicopter went down while conducting classified countermeasures experiments. During rescue operations by a Canadian yacht, fumes from the helicopter's leaking fuel ignited, destroying the ship, instantly killing Ralph Parker and Thomas Trasler. We are still searching for their bodies. Essentially, you are promising not to talk about the incident to anyone. Not to your parents, lover, best friend, shrink, parish priest, certainly not the press. Not even to your pet cat. Not amongst yourselves. There will be harsh consequences if you so much as daydream about this. Understood?"

"Yup. Open my big mouth and bad things will happen, I get it," Carol said.

"Don't think by residing outside the United States that you are in any way immune should the oath be violated." His tombstone look pretty much conveyed the consequences. Carol signed the document in three separate places. Her signature was significantly larger than the space allocated for it.

Charlie and Alice signed their copies with much less fine print review. Welling tears doused the fire in Carol's eyes and her anger gave way to grief. She suffered the worst loss and would have to face Tom's mother and sister. Her mother would be the hardest, having to tell her that her son had died. It took nine soldiers and one FBI agent to escort them to the local airport, where her father and a gentleman from Canadian External Affairs waited. She fell into the comforting embrace of her dad's arms. The sobbing threatening all afternoon finally arrived with a cloudburst. She leaned deeper into the warmth of her father's love, and wept.

CHAPTER 7

APRIL 28, 1848

Rood offered the captain a thin slice of a grin. "What is your destination, sir?"

"New York."

Rood's flawless dental work flashed. "That's perfect."

"Captain Liedberg, how long until we arrive in New York?" Tom asked.

"This ship will arrive no sooner than six weeks, perhaps as long as ten."

"What?" Tom shrieked. "Six weeks!"

"Perhaps ten. I do not have dominion over the winds or the currents, Mr. Trasler, I simply navigate through them. However, you needn't be concerned. It must be acknowledged that the number of passengers is already beyond the means of this vessel. I will promptly turn the *Margaretha* about and drop you off at Liverpool."

"We have adequate supplies, Captain," Rood countered carefully.

"Let us reason cooly, Colonel Rood. We are presently thirty souls in excess of this ship's capacity. So many that the peasants have chased the rats from their holes. Regrettably, another eight is completely beyond our means."

"Captain, with all due respects, my business is critical to the interests of the United States. I need to get to New York without delay." Rood spoke with too much confrontation in his voice, and prudently changed his tone to one of collaboration. "You will be amply rewarded."

"Colonel, you will distress me much if you persist in speaking thus!" Liedberg placed his hand near the large crate and didn't have to touch it to feel the heat. "What is this contrivance?"

Rood's anger leaked through his fabricated smile, annoyed he even had to explain anything. "It has a small source of plutonium. It's harmless."

"I am very much ignorant of plutonium, Colonel Rood, but I confess that this harmless piece of equipment is causing my mind much uneasiness."

"It's designed to be water cooled," Rood replied. His impatience was audible. "Once we're settled, we'll hook hoses to it, drag one in the water and it will be cooled down very quickly."

The captain was still unnerved by the crate, but other matters were more pressing. A series of commands shot from the deck and echoed through the shrouds. Moments later, the main course flapped with a thunderclap and grabbed hold of the wind. The *Margaretha* picked-up her stride as she turned east towards Liverpool.

Tom took a few steps back, coming across the aft deck steerage hatch. He winced from the pungent odour rising from it. "Nasty!" He waved his hand in an exaggerated gesture of blowing the smell away from him. "What stinks down there?"

The captain's lips locked in a snarl. "Tillers-of-dirt."

"They actually live down there, in that stench?"

"I beg of you to have my assurances, Mr. Trasler, that sundries and pig iron are my cargos of preference. However, until you disembark in Liverpool, you shall also be installed below."

"You're kidding? Where that stink is coming from? I'll barf!"

"The tillers-of-dirt do not mind and you will soon get accustomed to the foul air and the company of their vermin."

"What precisely do you mean by . . . vermin?"

"Lice. A nuisance, perhaps, but harmless."

"What do you mean, harmless? They're the carrier of—"

"Silence! It has been decided."

"Well . . . well, what about poor Ralph?"

"Captain Parker? He is a ship's master and will be accorded the honour duly his. He shall be installed in the second-mate's cabin."

"Well isn't that just fine." Tom's face puckered with contempt and mauled Ralph with his eyes. "So much for sticking together, eh? You up here, nice and cozy. And me? Stuck in the stinking hold of the ship!"

After the soldiers finished squeezing the dinghies into their containers, and stacked their crates for storage in the hold, Rood turned towards his crew. "I need to convince the captain that it's in his best interests to keep us aboard."

"This ship is completely inadequate," Silver protested.

"We're on a ship, already destined for New York, people. We can clean it up or have it cleaned up, but we're not going to Liverpool. That will cost us weeks."

"That was part of our original itinerary," Bodmar said, also leery of Rood's intentions. "Get to Liverpool and book first class cabins on an American packet."

"Don't argue with me, Sharon." Rood's eyes were direct and challenging. "We're already on a ship destined for the exact port we require and we are going to sail with her right to New York."

"I object," Silver said. "This ship is a converted merchantman and has not a single cabin for passengers. That would mean staying below with those disgusting peasants, or worse, right in the ship's hold."

"It stinks like high-heaven down there," Tom said. "You can smell the stench from up here."

"We need an isolated space to set-up our equipment," Anderson added quietly.

Rood's face showed reluctant compromise. "Let's go below and have a look. Oh, Sharon, take that hunk of metal out of Parker's shoulder before the sailmaker gets any silly ideas."

All Tom wanted was to find a toilet and have something to eat and drink. His bladder was about to burst but he couldn't find a single toilet stall on board. He loitered about the decks while the captain and Bodmar attended to Ralph. He felt desperate to find a refuge from the passengers and crew who pestered him about the rescue in a language he didn't understand.

The insane events of the last few hours drained him to such an extent that his entire body, specifically his hands, trembled constantly. He just needed some time alone to try to cope with his incomprehensible predicament, but there would be no sanctuary aboard this tiny, overcrowded ship.

He was beyond desperate for the bottle of vodka.

Tom noticed Liedberg strolling on the main deck, carefully scrutinizing his command, inspecting and listening to the shrouds. An endless network of lines, spars, stays, backstays, lists and buntlines were required to work in precise concert for the canvas to lock a grip on the wind. A trained ear could hear this symphony of the sea as the wind whistled through the shrouds to conduct the sails and rigging into a majestic waltz. Liedberg zigzagged through the passengers mingling on the main deck to reach the aft starboard steps. He sat down on the fourth of the nine stairs leading to the poop deck, focusing his attention on the young maidens mingling on the deck.

Anxious for an update on Ralph, Tom stumbled against the roll of the ship until he passed the mainmast on the starboard side, where he slowed to smirk at a passenger, tied to the ratlines by the ankles and wrists some ten feet up. For some unknown reason, the man, dressed in a chequered suit, tight pants and fancy shoes, climbed the ratlines. As a consequence for violating the crew's exclusive domain, the first mate punished him to set an example to the other passengers.

Tom sat next to Liedberg. "How long is that poor bastard going to remain tied to the ratlines?"

"Until I am convinced Axel Lennartsson fully understands that the ship's sacred rules are not to be flagrantly disregarded."

With a trembling child's voice, Tom asked, "How's Ralph?"

"The woman extracted the metal from his wound and she has pronounced him quite out of danger. Regrettably, she cannot assure he will ever attain full use of his arm again."

Tom wanted to hear better news, but he held up hope there would be no permanent damage. The growl from his gut turned into a howl. By his clock, suppertime was just about due, but the last stragglers were still preparing breakfast and it became obvious he would have to wait until lunch. He also thought about the bottle of vodka again. Unfortunately, the captain took the box of liquor directly into his cabin for *safekeeping.* His bladder screamed profanities, but he didn't have the nerve to ask where the toilets were located. He was curious about what the facilities would be like. *Had they invented urinals yet?* He noticed the captain scrutinizing the women.

Tom pointed towards Alvina-Kristina Gabrielsson. "There's the chick Ralph likes so much."

"Chick? Is that what you young villains call them these days?" Liedberg coughed out a coarse chuckle. The object of their admiration was washing clothes in a tiny wooden tub with other women and young girls.

Tom leaned into Liedberg and spoke with a whisper. "She gives me the creeps."

The captain's voice dropped to a mere hush. "There have been some whispers among the passengers concerning the Gabrielsson woman. One old woman called her the *Enchanted One*, seeming as if gifted with a sort of second sight, so often did events justify her predictions."

"Sonuvabitch, that's just what I need. Another goddamn Aunt Clara."

"Excuse me?"

"My wife's Aunt Clara possessed a similar gift. The kook is a big-shot psychic celebrity. Drove me crazy."

"I take no mind of such foolery."

They were quiet, each drifting within their own contemplations.

Rising like a goddess from the aft steerage hatch, a woman of singular beauty appeared on deck. She wore a lavish lavender dress with a tight, pointed bodice with the soft curve of her breasts just visible from the low neckline. Long skirts flowed about her feet while her shoulder-length hair appeared as bleached platinum in the bright sun. Holding her head high and shoulders squared, she angled her face to the wind and smoothed her hair over the top of her head. Cradling a tiny wicker basket and a cooking pot, and glancing neither right nor left, she joined a line-up of nine other women waiting for their turn at the cooking grate, situated inside the galleyhouse.

A smile lit Tom's face. "Hubba-hubba!" Tom nudged Liedberg in the ribs. "Is that a first-class babe or what?"

"That is the loathsome whore, Carina Svensson, from Kritianstad County."

"She's a prostitute?"

"Indeed."

"Good for her!"

"Gossip informs me she recently returned to her birthplace after whoring in Marseilles for five years. Her family had long declared her dead and her mother threw her off the land. So, she is emigrating, too."

"What a gorgeous woman."

"I confess to also subscribe to that opinion. She is endowed by nature with her richest gifts of beauty."

"How much, you know . . . ?"

"Any attempt to solicit her pleasures will be futile. I must be obliged to give council to you, Mr. Trasler, to free you of the burden of such a hopeless aspiration. I offered her a good coin, favours even, to share my berth. All for naught."

"How much did you offer?"

The captain huffed. "Forty shillings. That is nearly a full riksdaler!"

"What's a ricks-dollar?"

"Eight and forty shillings to a riksdaler. It takes two and a half to equal one dollar."

"That's like offering her two bits for a—"

"Yes, and despite the generosity of my offer, I have been rebuked!"

Hearing the prostitute speak to one of the other women in line, she sounded refined and exotic. Everything about her was exotic. Her skin was pale. Not the shade of pale that is milk-white and unhealthy looking, but creamy and vigorous, so without flaw, she appeared as delicate as a porcelain doll. With her high cheekbones and platinum hair, she might have been a fashion model in Tom's time. She stood in the line-up like a diva.

An obese woman yelled at her. Carina Svensson refused to respond. The verbal assault intensified. Carina Svensson gave not so much as a twitch of a reaction. The uppercut struck her below the chin. Completely unexpected, Carina Svensson's head snapped back, she staggered half-dazed, tripped over the box-like perimeter of the hatch, falling straight down.

Tom cringed as he heard two thuds and a crash. "Now, that's what you call a fallen woman."

"All aboard detest the whore," the captain said, very much amused. "Especially that unsightly sow, whose husband shared an acquaintance with Carina Svensson's bed."

"Her husband was one of Carina Svensson's customers?"

"So gossip informs me."

Tom's eyes ignited with a thought. "Wait a minute. If Carina Svensson whored in Marseilles for five years, then I assume she must speak French."

"I would assume she would speak the French tongue. Do you speak it?"

"I'm from Montréal and am fluently bilingual. I do believe Mademoiselle Svensson requires the assistance of a gentleman."

"You are very noble, but it is wasted gallantry, Mister Trasler."

Tom winked. "Just watch *Don Juan Trasler* in action."

"This should prove to be of splendid entertainment!"

Tom paused halfway down the nine steerage steps, arranged more like a stepladder than staircase, to gasp for air. It reminded him of stepping into the men's room just after someone laid waste to the toilet, but it wasn't from one person, but dozens. Their living room, dining room and bedroom were all inside one huge men's room with scores of backed up toilets.

Once his eyes adjusted to the gloom, the steerage unveiled itself to be nothing more than a crudely adapted hold the width of the ship and the length of the main deck. There was so little clearance that the top of his head brushed against the overhead beams. Four lanterns ran the length of the aisle, but presently unlit, the only source of illumination filtered through the two overhead deck hatches. Two-tiered bunks lined both sides. Canvas partitions divided the steerage into a single men's section, a single woman's and a family section. He saw a scattering of food boards but no proper place to eat. It was anything but quiet. Babies were crying, kids screamed at one another while a heated altercation raged between two women that someone really ought to put an end to.

A chattering mob surrounded Carina Svensson. She laid face down to the right of the stairs, propped up with her right forearm, shaking the haze from her head. Tom knelt on one knee at her side.

"Can I help you?" He spoke French with his low, soothing voice that he knew women liked. Carina's pale blue eyes met Tom with a candour that took him by surprise. "Nothing broken?" She made no effort to reply, or even acknowledge him. *"Parlez-vous français?"* Still no response.

He offered her a hand. She ignored the gesture, staggered up on her own and clutched the soiled steps for support. Still wavering, not entirely present in reality, she smoothed her lavender dress and brushed off some dirt. Her hair spilled wildly about with one strand stuck to an incredibly erogenous lower lip. She brushed out the knots in her hair with her slender fingers, shook away the last of the mists from her head, and picked up her basket. Her white-blond hair cascaded around her shoulders as she turned her back to him without so much of a flicker of appreciation. She limped up the steps to rejoin the line-up for the galley stove.

Tom heard rumbles of disgust and realized he gave the impression of trying to make a proposition for Carina Svensson's services. He tugged a loose suspender, still trying to match it with the other when the crowd about him cleared enough for him to see Rood and Silver at the forward end. Silver held a handkerchief tightly against his mouth and nose.

Tom passed through the family section, following the four-foot wide center aisle, dodging a clutter of crates, barrels, boxes, and even garbage. Old, cut-up canvas sails lined the aisle for privacy. The berths, positioned so the passengers lay in the direction of the ship, generally feet forward, had top and bottom bunks. One hundred and eight passengers made up the manifest while the steerage was rated for eighty. He passed a cluster of emigrants who were in poor health, particularly a twelve year-old girl who looked in really rough shape. He accelerated past them and dodged his way through the clutter until he caught up to Rood and Silver. They stood just before the partition leading to the single men's section.

"Bare minimum would be four berths," Silver said, his voice muffled by the cotton handkerchief stuffed against his nose. "The most stable spot would be amidships."

"We would need two bulkheads amidships and there aren't enough raw materials." Rood pointed to the berth next to them. "We can make use of the wood from the berths we dismantle. It would be far more secure."

"This is disgusting down here," Tom said, with his puckered face doing the rest of the complaining.

Silver turned to face Tom, the handkerchief pressing even tighter against his plus-sized nose that would make a proboscis monkey jealous. "Concentration camps were not much worse than this. All that's missing are the Nazis."

Tom knew they were coveting the berths. "I thought we were going back to Liverpool?"

"The timeline was already tight," Rood said, his voice low. "With half our crew gone, including the principle mission specialist, we'll need all the extra time we can muster." Tom saw that Silver believed the ship completely unsuitable for their needs, but since resigned to Rood's resolve.

"The merchantmen of this era are not designed for emigrants," Silver explained. "Most are like this wretched tub—modified with a deck above the cargo hold for passengers, hence called the 'tweendecks. This stench is not just from the passengers. There are also the fumes of the organic decay of the ship's hull, rotting planks and caulking. On top of that, there's the bilge water and the stink of present and past cargos. With no ventilation facilities other than the two deck hatches, this steerage is a recipe ripe for a plague, and with all these canvas partitions, a firetrap. I've already seen several who are gravely infirm."

"Ya, I saw them, too," Tom said.

"How many passengers have to be displaced?" Rood asked Silver.

"Twenty-four, minimum."

"Let's have a chat with the captain and convince him it's in his best interests to keep us aboard."

There was something in the underlying intent of Rood's words that caused Tom's stomach to knot. When he arrived on deck, Sharon Bodmar trotted towards the others of her team guarding their equipment.

"What's going on?" Tom asked, keeping pace with her.

"Something really nasty is about to hit the proverbial fan."

Rood showed up with Silver. He snapped a sharp look at Tom. "You want to get back home, Barney. Yes or no?"

"Of course," Tom replied.

Rood handed Tom a black leather army holster. "Put it on."

Tom hesitated for three heavy heartbeats then handed back the holster. "They hang mutineers in this day and age, do they not?"

Rood refused the holster and stared at Tom in a sharp and frightening way. "I'm going to say this to you just once and only because you clearly don't know your asshole from your peehole. If you're not with us, you're against us, and if you are against us, you'll die in this century. Decide now."

A dull anger came to Tom. He couldn't find the words.

"On the same page, are we? Are we saluting the same flag? Pissing in the same latrine?"

"Yes! Yes, goddamn, you."

Rood put his lips so close to Tom's ear, it was almost a kiss. "If you so much as waver in your loyalties towards me, I'll put a round in the back of your head."

Tom felt his gut tighten and sink, stranding his stomach about a foot from where it had been. He peered inside the holster. It resembled a contemporary revolver, yet was a modern weapon with cartridges. His fingers trembled so wildly he had difficulty buckling the holster to his waist.

"Stay here. Silver and I will do the talking." Rood adjusted his cap, nodded to Anderson who went aft, then to Rodriguez to guard the fore-castle deck. Rood tugged his uniform's jacket, brushed off a wrinkle and walked against the heavy roll of the ship towards the captain.

Liedberg noticed Rodriguez, then Anderson, and his eyes darkened when he saw the holsters. "Colonel Rood, what is the meaning of this?"

"I wish to state, Captain, that I will never put into question that you are the sole authority of this vessel. However, our mission is too critical to the interests of my government and cannot—and will not—be compromised. I require the use of the assets of this vessel and crew to reach New York without delay."

"In my cabin." Liedberg led Rood and Silver, shutting the door just short of a slam. A lattice of window work offered a panoramic view of the ship's wake, slightly warped by the glass' imperfections. The daylight gleamed through, revealing a spartan cabin with just a stand-up wardrobe, a berth, and a table just big enough to sit four for dinner. "Are you threatening my command?"

"Never, you are and will always remain the captain. I simply expect that you will accommodate the needs of United States military personnel during a time of national emergency."

"What is this emergency?"

"A lot bigger than you and I, Captain. That's all I dare say."

"What you are saying is that though I remain captain, you none-the-less will have authority over my command?"

"We will have a relationship as if I have chartered your vessel for hire."

Liedberg stared at Rood, his hatred unveiled. "This is nothing less than an act of piracy."

"Captain, should you not cooperate, I will file a report that you refused to accommodate the United States military during a time of national crisis, which will result in the impoundment of your vessel upon its arrival in an American port. Now, we both want to get to New York as soon as possible. There is no conflict here. Don't turn it into one. You'll fight a battle that you cannot possibly win. On the other hand," Rood flashed one of those big PR smiles, "this can be a very profitable business arrangement." Rood plunked down a gray sack possessing the particular clink only gold coins can produce. "You will be very well compensated."

Liedberg met Rood's eyes with a dark challenge. He opened the bag, jiggled the gold coins and listened to their music. He tightened the strings and placed it on the table in a way that indicated he had not accepted the bribe, but acknowledged to Rood that he had his attention.

"My government will give you thanks, Captain. You can be either rewarded, or punished. That is entirely up to you."

Compromise began to replace anger. "As I already declared, we are overcrowded. There are no tolerable quarters available for you and crew."

"Mister Jack Silver has assessed our requirements. You shall carry out his recommendations as if they were my own."

Silver adjusted his wire-rimmed glasses. "It is obvious that this old ship was never designed to carry passengers, and the steerage is a crude makeshift contrivance. There is no ventilation below. There is an infestation of lice and there are six people who are already gravely infirm. We will make modifications to make the steerage more bearable for our people. First, I will require the forward four berths, two per side. We will create a bulkhead separating our cabin from the general steerage with a door. We have the hardware for a secure locking mechanism."

"What of the souls we displace from the berths?"

Silver again adjusted his glasses. "Your longboat can accommodate eighteen."

The world hung still. When Liedberg found his voice, it was a blend of a scream and a whisper. "You are a madman!"

"Captain Bligh was put to sea in a longboat and navigated 3600 miles in just under two months to East Timor with the loss of but one man. We are less than two days from the coast. The currents and the winds will be at their backs and they will not be menaced by cannibals."

"The passengers will revolt!"

"Then I suggest you find a way to placate them."

"I will compensate you for the lost fares," Rood said. "This will allow you to give the displaced passengers a refund with a little extra for the inconvenience."

A silence developed between them that became very awkward, in a real sense, unbearable. "I alone will decide who is to be cast adrift." Liedberg's voice wavered, the next words drawn out—a strong man close to weeping. "O, divine Providence, sacred author of all things. Forgive me for what I am about to do!"

Eight of Liedberg's crew emerged from the rear cabins with muskets, single shot pistols and revolvers. Brandishing a blackjack, the first mate, Lars Göran Rödin, accompanied the captain with four armed men to below the decks. Liedberg selected the unfortunate men, including the man in the chequered suit just released from the ratlines.

He offered no explanation, just that they were to carry all the personal belongings, money and valuables they could carry. Their faces had a lost, starry look, like prisoners taken away to face a firing squad. Anderson and Rodriguez overlooked the main deck from the aft and fore decks, while Jackson, Bodmar and Tom remained by the luggage. Anderson looked a little frightened, but Rodriguez remained perfectly still, chewing gum while his eyes gazed around in quick little tics.

A taste of hot despair rose in Tom's throat as he thought of what he was a part of.

Once all the selected men arrived on deck, the crew battened down the steerage hatches. A rumbling of protest rose from the depths. Liedberg gathered the men. Every single man from the steerage had been selected, as well as three young married men without children, splitting them from their wives.

He took off his cap and asked forgiveness for what was about to be done. He ordered calm, *for the sake of your lives,* he pleaded, *do not contest this.* Then he told them. Bewilderment quickly turned into anger, but the captain maintained a sense of cold calm. *Go with the grace of God and in two days safely wash upon the British shores.* He refunded their passage, and as Rood offered, extra for board and travel to Liverpool.

Liedberg crossed each name from the passenger manifest. The second-mate, Polman, gave them two weeks rations. One of his men volunteered to go with them, a seaman in his late twenties who knew Liverpool. One of his best. Two of the passengers were fishermen, capable sailors, who were reassuring the others of a safe journey.

Taken off the galley, they lowered the boat into the water. One by one, they climbed down the rope ladder. It killed Tom to see the faces, particularly the eyes of those set adrift. The forlorn expressions so haunting, that pain, starting at his temples, swept down through his chest, twisting his insides until he wanted to scream.

The captain offered a brief prayer.

Two pairs of oars flashed in the sky, and with a mournful chant directing the strokes through the water, the boat turned east. Just the oars driving through the water, the creak of their oarlocks and a mournful chant whispered through the silence. No protests, no prayers, no hymns. Just silent, desperate hope.

The rear deck hatch still battened down, Liedberg unlocked the forward hatch and descended into the steerage. A rumble of outrage exploded from below. Liedberg returned to the main deck and battened down the forward hatch to let the masses settle down.

It was a superb execution of crowd control from start to finish.

CHAPTER 8

A smile curled Jack Silver's thin lips. "We'll let the peasants calm themselves and then begin the alterations."

"What exactly are we going to alter?" Tom asked.

"You needn't be concerned," Silver replied. "You won't be staying with us."

Tom's jaw worked silently for a moment before he spoke. "Then where the hell am I going to stay?"

Silver moved his shoulders a little—not quite a shrug. "That's your concern with the captain."

"What happened to *if I'm with you or against you*? I put on the holster and the passengers saw me support you guys. They hate me!"

Rood stuck his hands into his pockets. "We'll be setting up a field lab. Our activities are far too sensitive to have you about."

"What difference will it make? I'll be seeing whatever you're up to once we reach shore, for like, the next two years."

Rood gave him a look low on patience and even less on sympathy. "We huddled and decided that our activities will not be involving you. We brought along a significant quantity of replicated cash and coin, as well as gold and gems. We originally budgeted for a crew of fourteen, so we have funds to spare. We'll give you enough to cover your needs for the next two years. Part of our training was learning contemporary skills to supplement our income with employment, so if you don't find work, don't splurge your funds on whores. We'll set up a rendezvous point in San Francisco for the spring of 1850."

Tom's upper lip trembled. "What are we supposed to do for the next two years?"

"Trasler, most people would give their right arm for this opportunity. Whether you appreciate it or not is one thing, but you are going to have the mother of all adventures, and experience with your own eyes the mid-nineteenth century."

"That's what museums are for. I hate museums!"

Liedberg released the passengers from the steerage a handful at a time until he could gauge their mood. They had been stunned into disbelief, outrage, but mostly fear at the presence of armed American soldiers. Tom walked up to Liedberg, who was chatting with a cluster of passengers. The captain gave reassurances to the frightened faces, possessing a remarkable skill of persuasion. He explained to the passengers that anything but their full collaboration with the soldiers would be disastrous.

Tom met Liedberg's dark looks head on. "So far, the villain has succeeded in his wicked design. Once ashore, I will see that you are named along with Colonel Rood in this despicable act of piracy. You'll be hanged along with the rest of your blackguards!"

Tom closed in to whisper. "They took over our ship as well, at gun-point, and Rodriguez fired a shot at me. Then just before all this happened, Rood told me I had to cooperate or he'd shoot me in the back of the head."

Liedberg took a long time to react. "Come with me."

They went to second-mate Polman's cabin. It was a tiny, cramped closet. Ralph lay in the tiny berth, shirtless, with just a loose draping of linen covering his wound. His chest rose and fell with an erratic rhythm, struggling with each breath. His eyes couldn't find Tom, just yellow slits with sweat flowing off his face in rivers.

"Hey, Tom." His voice was a mere whisper.

"You don't look so good."

"Don't worry about me, Tom. Got a bit of a fever. The captain insisted I take some of his laudanum."

"Did you get a good high off it?"

Ralph chuckled. "Nothing like your convoluted past would be able to relate to."

"Bodmar said you might not have full use of your arm."

"Hopefully, once we get back home," he cracked a frail smile. "You know what I mean." He could feel the tension in the room. "What's up?"

"Rood put seventeen men and a crewman into the ship's lifeboat and cast them off," Tom said. "Just to make room so that our pals can have their own private suite in the steerage."

Ralph took care with his words and he replied cautiously. "We're only a day or two off the Welsh coast. They should make it to shore and the weather looks fair."

"Captain Parker, I must know the truth. On your oath as a gentleman, do you confirm that you and your vessel fell into the power of Rood's blackguards?"

"Yes, at gunpoint. It was cooperating or getting shot."

Liedberg gave a look of immense relief. "It seems to me that those ruffians have no right to any pity, which we ought to rid the ship of them as soon as possible."

Ralph replied quickly and with urgency. "This is an elite military force with weapons far advanced of yours. All of them are trained soldiers, even the woman. If you attack them, they'll kill you all."

The revelation sobered Liedberg from his rage. "I confess, gentlemen, that under the influence of violent excitement, I am prey to a thousand reckless thoughts."

"For the sake of us all, just let it ride out," Ralph begged.

"At this point, it makes no difference," Tom said. "He and his crew want to get to New York as fast as possible. Once we get to shore, then you can go to the authorities."

"And I shall."

Tom looked deep into the captain's agitated eyes. "I was told by Colonel Rood that I am not permitted to be berthed with them."

"Then I shall have you installed below."

"It's not going to be pleasant down there. The passengers despise me."

"Indeed, they do, Mr. Trasler."

"Sune Gabrielsson, I have begged you to come to me for an important reason," Liedberg started, while Alvina-Kristina stood next to her husband with her child cradled in her arms. A couple of years older than Alvina-Kristina, Sune was a tall, strong man with a shock of blond hair spilling beneath his wide-brimmed hat. A quick glance at their wardrobe ranked them in the lower echelons of the emigrants' wealth scale. "I understand your wife has some command of the English language?"

"She does."

It irked Alvina-Kristina the captain didn't ask the question directly to her. "My mother was English, but her eyes closed upon the light of this world when I was but twelve. It has been many years since I have spoken it."

"Your mother was English?" The revelation startled Liedberg.

"Yes, she accompanied her husband to Sweden. He was a merchant and died in our town of the measles. My father met her shortly after and they were wed."

"It is fortunate you can speak the language of your new country. However, as you are the only one below who can speak the English tongue," Liedberg rubbed his bearded jaw, then his voice boomed, "you shall board that man, Thomas Trasler."

Alvina-Kristina gave her husband a sharp tug on his shirtsleeve. "Sune! Do something. I should be very miserable and unhappy!"

"He was armed and a participant of the piracy," Sune said with a hoarse growl.

"The American soldiers commandeered his vessel with force then destroyed it," Liedberg said just above a whisper. "The horrible result cost his wife and two dear friends their lives and this unfortunate gentleman, despite his burden of great sorrow, is forced to cooperate with the soldiers under the menace of death."

The mood placated at that revelation.

"Where is he to sleep?" Sune asked. "My brother, his wife and three children are below. My beloved wife, her sister, our infant and I share the top berth. Nine of us where there is room intended for only four and yet you wish to add a tenth?"

"I have to find places for nine others removed from the forward berths, Mr. Gabrielsson. You are not the only family to be inconvenienced by a stranger. I have three young women separated from their husbands."

"To have that long-haired heathen, who is not of the Lutheran faith, share the same bed as my wife and her virgin sister is an outrage! How can you reconcile this atrocity to your conscience?"

Alvina-Kristina's eyes flared, bold and filled with unconcealed contempt. "They are the most disagreeable creatures I have ever encountered!"

"Mr. Gabrielsson, I have hostile military men who have all but seized control of my ship. Thus, I have anxieties which are far too great to have unease because you and your wife and her virgin sister must share the sheets with this unfortunate man."

"For the sake of their dignity, I beg of you. My beloved wife needs to nurse Edvard. Must she expose her naked bosom to his eyes?"

"I will have Polman give you a sheet of canvas and rope that will keep his eyes cloaked from your wife's nursing breast and her virgin sister. I will also see to it that you will receive additional food rations."

"Why not put him with that wretched whore?"

"You cannot fail to know that his reputation would be ruined."

"I'm certain he wouldn't mind," Sune said, a little too lewdly for the captain's current state of agitation.

"Mr. Gabrielsson, since you oblige me to speak more plainly, then I shall say this plainly. If I have an obstinate crewman—or passenger—I have them lashed and condemned to the chains. As master of the ship, I command you to install that man, Thomas Trasler, into your berth, or face the consequence which I have thus described!"

The captain stomped away. Sune and Alvina-Kristina stood dazed and the baby cried, as if it too was protesting. While the captain lectured Tom regarding the ship's strict and extensive rules, Alvina-Kristina spoke to her husband concerning her fears.

"I know you do not approve when I speak of such things, husband, but I have not been deceived in my forebodings. Right from the moment I saw their vessel in distress, I perceived a dreadful peril."

"Of what sort?"

"The soldiers are a great, evil menace and will bring misery upon us. Even Thomas Trasler, though not one of the soldiers, has in his possession a terrible hidden truth."

"Are you certain of this?"

"Yes, it is something for which I have no doubt."

"A secret? Of what sort?"

She couldn't speak the entire truth to Sune, especially those seconds when the world lost its motion—he would declare her quite mad. "I am in great perplexity, but . . . it is something so profound that he cannot speak it."

"What can we do?"

"We must penetrate his secret, Sune. For the sake of our lives, we must!"

"Then we must do so with patience. Do not let us press him to tell us his history, lest we expose ourselves to danger."

"This secret is of too much consequence to be allowed to remain long unsettled."

"Then we must seek an opportune time, with stealth, to reveal this concealed truth. Then take whatever action is required to preserve our souls."

As they waited for their guest, Alvina-Kristina lamented fondly of the friendly trees and tussock-filled meadows where she once played as a child. She departed a home where she knew every creaking plank, the way the icy winter wind would hush across the roof. She would never see her father, brother and sisters again, or dear childhood friends. She wanted to wail and cry, hate and hurt her husband for creating so much pain. She wanted to go back home and fall into the embrace of all those who she loved so dear. She felt nothing but regret when he told her about the emigration. At first, she protested, but a wife must submit to her husband's will, and after her firstborn, Johannes, died, she lost her resolve and capitulated to her husband's dreams. The conditions aboard the ship were more deplorable than her worst nightmare could have ever conjured. Now these vile soldiers invaded their ship like jackals and imposed against all decency to care for one of the heathens, who would be sleeping in their very bed.

"Well," Tom said as he arrived, all too aware their heated exchange with Liedberg concerned him—and he didn't blame them one bit. "Let's go below, shall we?"

Alvina-Kristina and Sune remained silent but the baby was quite vocal. They turned their back on Tom and descended the steerage steps. Burdened with the large boombox concealed in Charlie's suitcase, three handbags and the dark-blue backpack on his shoulders, Tom followed the Gabrielssons to their berth.

The lair of the prostitute dominated the aisle behind the main mast. Ostracized by the passengers, Carina Svensson's enormous coffin-sized chest became her makeshift bed, roped to the mainmast and circled with a sheet of canvas for privacy. Ironically, she was the only one on board with private quarters and the arrangement suited her just fine. She stood by the perimeter of canvas, looking quite respectable in her lovely lavender dress and stared, clearly amused, as Tom followed the Gabrielssons like an unhappy shadow.

A couple of berths past Carina's enclosure, Tom and his new hosts arrived at their starboard side bunk. The canvas privacy curtain hung on a rope much like a shower curtain. Sune moved it aside to reveal the rough-hewn berths. Another family sat on the lower berth, waiting for the introductions.

Jonas Gabrielsson, Alvina-Kristina's brother-law, was a handsome, husky fellow in his early thirties. His wife Catharina, a striking woman in a pretty dress, towered barefoot at six-two with blond hair and nice facial lines. Tom noted that her breasts were so enormous, that if she turned around suddenly, and he was struck by them, he would be killed instantly. They had three children; Stina-Sophia, 11, Carl-Johan, 9 and Johanna, 6.

Johanna giggled when she saw Tom. Looking down, she greeted him with a pair of big round eyes, gleaming powder-blue orbs, and a lit smile. He gave her a little wave with his fingers and she smiled delightfully back. The last introduction was Alvina-Kristina's sister, Selma-Olivia Eriksson, a sixteen year-old, fresh-faced girl who had just crossed the threshold into womanhood. She greeted Tom with complete indifference.

Alvina-Kristina patted the top bunk. "Tis is our bed't." Though her accent was brutal, Tom managed to understand her. He also had no difficulty picking up the malice in her tone.

"So you do speak English," he said as an acknowledgement, not a question.

"Joost a leeh-tel."

"Your English is quite good." She didn't expect the compliment and Tom saw her appreciation. "So where do I sleep?" She patted the upper berth. "Okay, and you and your husband are below?"

She shook her head and pointed to Sune and her baby, then patted the top bunk. "And Selma-Olivia."

"Are you serious? Four of us and your baby?"

Each bunk measured six-foot square with just 26 inches from the top berth to the ceiling, worse—the mattresses were made of prickly straw. A six-inch high edge ran the length of the bunk to prevent people from toppling out during rough seas. Planks of wood separated their bunk from their neighbours. Tom tossed his hands in the air in disgust. Sune hung a dirty sheet of canvas on a line to segregate Tom from the family.

"Behold, *The Walls of Jericho!*" Tom proclaimed. He received blank looks in return. "Okay, Cro-Magnons, let me explain. There was this old Clark Gable movie called *It Happened One Night* and he strung up a blanket between him and this young woman and called it *The Walls of Jericho* so the dirty deed wouldn't happen." More looks of the dead. "Anyways, not to worry, *it's not going to happen any night!*"

Jonas lifted the bottom mattress, as well as the rough planks it rested, to reveal a storage area a foot and a half in height. Tom placed the first item of his luggage when a gargantuan rat touched eyes with him. Its pointy nose squinted, then scurried away with its stubbled-haired tail waving a tidy little goodbye.

Tom shrieked like a child. "Sonuvabitch! Did you see the size of that mother?" Still gathering his wits, and cautiously verifying there were no other creatures lurking in ambush, Tom stuffed the rest of his luggage in, joining three chests and a couple of burlap bags. Their remaining luggage would be stowed in the lower hold.

Tom planted his fists on his hips and gazed irritably about. "Okay, guys, here's the scoop. I haven't peed in hours and my back teeth are floating. So where's the men's room around here?" They stared at him with blank-eyed expressions. "Come on, guys. You know, toilet stalls, water closets, whatever they're called these days." He turned to Alvina-Kristina. "I have to pee." She shook her head, still not understanding. He gestured quite crudely and made some disgusting sound effects that quite explicitly revealed his needs. He heard some gasps of disgust from the females, though young Carl-Johan chuckled crudely. The boy handed Tom a stained wooden bucket with a thick iron handle.

"Very cute. Seriously, where's the men's room?"

"You use this," Alvina-Kristina said.

There was a bloody long pause.

"You're goddamn serious, aren't you?" Judging by the unmistakable stains and odour, that was indeed the toilet—and she was very goddamn serious. He felt a rising tide of panic rushing so fast it was about to blow his head off his shoulders. "Where's the toilet paper?" Nothing but blank looks. Catharina, interpreting Tom's gestures, handed him a stained rag. His mind dissolved into a boiling caldron of black panic. His face paled and his toes shrank inside his oversized shoes. His face drew down into a rictus of terror while his eyes grew into huge white rimmed spheres. "Toilet paper, man, there's gotta be rolls of toilet paper!"

"Feeling better?"

Ralph reached up and grasped Tom's hand. His grip was dreadfully weak. "I'll be fine."

"Why does Rood call me Barney?"

"He's just being a jerk. So Liedberg put you with the babe with the great love bubbles who spotted our burning ship?"

"As a matter of fact, he did," Tom said, released Ralph's hand, scowled, and planted his fists on his hips. "You'll be pleased to know that I'm forced to sleep in the same bed as her."

"Forced? You lucky bastard."

"And as an extra bonus, her sixteen year-old sister as well."

"Get the hell out!"

"Don't get too excited. The captain gave me the riot act concerning the women's virtues. If I see even just one of them in their underclothes, I get chained. One complaint from the women about me, I get chained. Our good buddy, Colonel Rood, even gave Liedberg his blessing to discipline me any way he sees fit. So I'll be sleeping against the hull, next to Alvina-Kristina's husband, with the women on the opposite side along with the baby. Five of us, with just over a foot of bed space apiece. Spending six to ten weeks cuddling another man every night doesn't exactly fit into my criteria of having a cool time. Then we get to share the berth with all these goddamn rats. Big mothers with tails this long. Lice! Did I mention the lice infestation? And the food situation? You wouldn't believe the gruel I had for lunch. Gagged on every bite."

Ralph responded to Tom's rant with a dead silence. Tom took two sharp breaths and continued.

"Then I finally got to use the men's room. Yes, Ralphy, let's have a chat about this absolutely charming love boat. There are no men's rooms aboard this tub! Not a single stall! These Cro-Magnons' idea of a toilet is a splinter-infested bucket. So I had to crap like a dog over this bucket while the boat was heaving all over the goddamn place. Let's talk about the toilet paper situation on this delightful ship . . . there is no toilet paper! That's beyond disgusting! How can they not have any toilet paper? It's common sense. What's wrong with these people? Ralph, get me the hell out of the steerage or I'll be certifiable within a week!"

Ralph's expression remained unchanged throughout Tom's tirade. His voice slurred from the cocktail of Bodmar's painkillers and the captain's laudanum. "I really don't pity you and I can think of a lot of things worse than having to crap like a dog for a few weeks. And get over your infantile homophobia. Now get out. See me when you're in a more mature frame of mind." Tom stood there, swaying against the roll of the ship, feeling ostracized. First it was Rood, now his own brother-in-law. "Get out and shut up with the complaining."

By late afternoon, Tom felt the effects of jetlag, since by his clock it would have been about 2:00 AM. He felt a resigned dread about his situation, but the guilt of forcing those poor bastards off the ship was driving him to within the hailing distance of madness.

Rood called him over. "Settled in?" The look Tom gave Rood was somewhat less than felicitous. "Come below."

Tom followed Rood through the aft hatch. Since all the single men had been cast off, and the single women billeted with families, there were no longer any divisions in the steerage. Walking through the cluttered aisle, women clutched their children as they slipped behind the canvas curtains lining the aisle. They went to the forward steerage where Rodriguez stood guard with a disguised 9mm semi-automatic rifle resembling a percussion-capped musket. They had stripped the four sets of berths, the wood laid out by size. The nails and bolts collected in a bucket. Their luggage and crates were stacked in the far corner.

Bodmar, still wrapped with a dressing around her head, stared at Tom, and for the first time since he met her, she had a smile. "What's with the wedgie?"

"Wardrobe malfunction!"

It took about a second for her to adjust the suspenders and Tom finally felt a semblance of comfort and a restoration of his dignity.

"I hear you're berthed with a couple of women," Jack Silver queried.

"Sure, with a two hundred pound barrier of man-flesh between them and myself."

"Who's the teenage girl?"

"Selma-Olivia. Alvina-Kristina's kid sister."

"She's very pretty."

"What sixteen year-old girl isn't?" Tom was a little harsh.

"I guess you're going to get to see them in their night clothes. Perhaps less."

"I don't exactly think any of them will be wearing Victoria's Secret lingerie."

Rood chuckled. "I suppose not."

"Tell me what she's like in her nightclothes," Silver pressed.

"The sixteen year-old?"

Silver's lips, oddly small, thin and white like a fish, twitched expectantly. "Selma-Olivia, yes."

Tom shivered away his disgust and helped move the giant crate to the starboard side just behind the spot where they would build the bulkhead wall. Anderson pulled out a power drill with a two-inch bit and drilled a hole through the hull just underneath a deck beam. Rood assembled a large hose, twinned into an intake and outtake with a nine-inch long brass head. They passed twenty feet of it through the drill hole, sealing the hole with the brass ring. Anderson connected the hose to the big crate. He drilled a second, larger hole for the intake hose to draw in fresh air to the unit.

Silver pressed a few buttons on the control panel, watched the readout on the unit's screen, and then pressed a big red switch. They heard a grinding, the hose shimmied as water sucked into it. A deep hiss came from the inner guts of the crate, making the hoses tremble so violently Tom was certain they were going to shake free from the clamps.

"What's going on?"

"That's our central station," Silver said. It contains a power supply, air filter, climate control, stove, microwave, cooler and water distiller."

"Powered by plutonium?"

"Yes, a radioisotope thermoelectric generator."

"Uhhhhh . . . Isn't that what NASA uses to power some of its spacecraft?"

"Yes, when solar panels are impractical, such as the outer solar system. There is a worldwide shortage of this fuel. We are fortunate to have it."

Tom's eyes bounced back and forth between the crate and Silver. "That's radioactive."

"It's very well shielded and is very hot," Silver said. "So we use water to cool it. The steam produces an additional source of power and is expelled through the hose. Because seawater is saline, it will build up salt deposits if we don't flush it. So it has a water distiller to purge the system when required."

"It generates an excess of 20 litres of drinking water a day," Bodmar mentioned while she and Silver made some adjustments to the controls.

"When you have a taste of what the passengers are forced to drink, you'll soon thank us for your rations," Rood said. "They fill water right out of a local river near port, and put them in whatever containers they have handy, even those that transported tobacco on the outbound voyage. A pig would object to what they're forced to drink and I'm surprised that so many of these poor bastards manage to survive the voyage. We have enough that I can give you a little extra to appease your hosts."

"Sounds good because the reception I've gotten so far hasn't exactly been stellar." Tom stared at the equipment. There were computers everywhere. "Got any games or movies?"

"Yes," Bodmar replied. "Lots."

"I have an amazing porn collection," Silver said. "As well as horror and Steven Seagal films."

"All right! When can I book some time?"

"That's a negative," Rood replied.

"Negative? Come on, Colonel. I won't be seeing my wife for over two years, at least let me watch some dirty movies."

"I said that's a negative."

"Come on, there's squat to do. I'm already bored out of my mind."

"Sorry, Barney. You're going to have to entertain yourself—the old fashioned way!"

Tom stomped off, found a spot on the forecastle deck and clung onto the ratlines, staring at the endless sea before him. He watched the sun kiss the distant horizon with a blood-red sundown. He never felt so alone in his life. The passengers detested him, the American soldiers wanted nothing to do with him and even Ralph was being anal. The end of his first day in the nineteenth century, and he concluded that Hollywood and the romantics gave this century a far more glamorous portrayal than it deserved.

PART II

THE PAST IS LIKE A FUNERAL GONE BY. THE FUTURE COMES LIKE AN UNWANTED GUEST

Edmund Gosse (1849 – 1928)

CHAPTER 9

AUGUST 9, 2016
PASADENA, CALIFORNIA

Horatio Fleming eased into his chair and puffed on his pipe with slow, deliberate care. He and his team of young students had made one of the most significant discoveries in the history of scientific pursuit. *Time travel through a naturally occurring singularity.* They had learned how to predict the time and location of the events, the power and polarity, but the cause of the temporal wormholes, the actual physics involved, remained a daunting mystery.

A moral dilemma confronted Fleming. Temporal mobility, forward or backward, carried implications so profound that their discovery and ongoing research must remain within a shroud of utmost secrecy. *If so, then what was the purpose of their research? Where was it going to lead them? What if their knowledge fell into the wrong hands?* In so many ways, he regretted the discovery that had led him and his students on a dangerous road with no destination.

THIRTEEN MONTHS EARLIER
NORTHWEST TERRITORIES, CANADA

Jennifer Burke reached the rocky plateau first. She held what resembled an oversized walkie-talkie with long, twin aerials protruding eight feet at a twenty-degree angle from the other. She swept the nearly featureless gray box side to side in slow, broad strokes.

"Professor Fleming!" she called. "This is it—the epicenter."

He and the three other students finally caught up to her, all with backpacks bulging with specialized equipment, the value of each exceeding the average household income severalfold.

Fleming slipped off the backpack and swept away the mosquitoes with his beige hat. Stuart Roberts breathed with a deep wheezing sound and knew he'd have to get serious about quitting smoking. With a specially modified metal detector, he panned the suspect area; a rocky plateau the size of a couple of football fields laid side-by-side.

Stuart Roberts glanced at Fleming. "It's clean, Professor." He turned to Jennifer, staring with complete defiance. "There's nothing here."

"Don't argue with me, Stuart," Jennifer said. "Right here. It's hot."

"There has to be something below the subsurface," Bob Scranton mused, stuffing his hands in his vest pockets. "Some kind of object to explain these readings."

"There's zilch," Roberts said.

"I still say it's a buried UFO," Russell Wynn said, convinced a buried alien craft created the exotic magnetic anomaly.

"Will you stop it!" Jennifer stomped a foot. "It's not a UFO."

"Klingons for sure," Russell persisted.

"With their cloaking device still activated?" Jennifer added with a twisted grin.

"You're catching on, Jen."

"My friends call me Jen. You call me Jennifer."

"You have friends?"

"You two, please stop the squabbling!" Fleming said. He turned to Stuart Roberts, staring with a lost, if not disbelieving, look. "A magnetic anomaly requires a source to create these magnetic readings."

"But there's nothing here."

"There must be something, Mr. Roberts."

"Whoa!" Russell Wynn jolted with the words. "My EPD just picked up all kinds of crazy readings. You said that your colleague first noticed energetic particles, then picked up the magnetic anomaly?"

"Correct."

"I can't explain what I'm reading, but it's correlating with the magnetic readings Jennifer picked up. They're not energetic particles I can identify, but whatever it is, it's increasing in strength."

Fleming's colleague, from the Applied Physics Laboratory of John Hopkins University, was investigating unexplained readings from a European spacecraft's EPD—the **E**nergetic **P**articles **D**etector—and its magnetometer, leading them to this site. Fleming's equipment—the most sensitive for analysing energetic particles and magnetic fields available anywhere—ought to shed light on the mystery. The findings so far just muddled the puzzle.

"It is not a magnetism with which we are familiar," Fleming explained. "This is very exotic." He turned to Russell who just smacked his arm, taking out four mosquitoes with a single swat. "Mr. Wynn, I believe we are observing an energy force we have not encountered in the field before. The readings have increased three and a half fold since the initial orbital survey."

"Yes, and of extraterrestrial origins." It wouldn't be so annoying had Russell been joking.

"This is odd. My readings seem to peak at an ultrahigh magnetic frequency," Jennifer Burke observed. "I'm only picking up a fraction that's out there. Whatever it is, it's not conventional magnetism that we're equipped for."

"What do you mean—ultrahigh magnetism?" Bob Scranton asked.

"It's like a dog's hearing. If my readings were sound waves, most would be too high for the human ear to perceive, but a dog can hear it. Our equipment is like a human's ear, it's only able to pick up the standard magnetic spectrum. Most of this is beyond the normal range of magnetic fields as we understand them."

"What you're describing doesn't exist," Roberts said.

Jennifer's eyes flared. "I didn't say it wasn't weird, but it exists!"

"All we can do is to collect data to determine precisely what we are observing," Fleming said. "I suggest we set up camp and wait."

"Wait for what, professor?" Jennifer asked.

"Both the magnetic and EPD readings continue to increase. We must wait and find out what Mother Nature—or the Klingon Empire—has in store for us."

They waited precisely twenty-seven hours and seventeen minutes. They could hear it before seeing it. A cry came from beyond the distant hills. It grew in depth, low and hollow; an elongated wail. A throated shriek from thousands of terrified voices haunted the air around them. The sound chilled Fleming's blood into ice.

Then they saw it.

The horizon clouded as scores of beating wings shot from the trees as if dynamited out of them. United in terror, every species of feathered creature combined their voices into a single, depraved shout. The shock-wave of terror encircled the plain, contracting in on them. Aside from the frenzied birds, nothing else was out of the ordinary. No wind, force, sight or sound, blast or evil menace of any kind could explain what panicked the birds. It was as if an invisible club swept across the landscape battering every tree dweller into the air, leaving the trees untouched. Something out there created the panic, something unseen—and it was closing in on them.

Stuart Roberts stared at the incoming wave of madly beating wings with a kind of sedated paralysis.

"This is so radical," Russell said.

Scranton considered the option for a moment. No, he was too far gone to puke.

Jennifer brushed her short hair away from her temples and felt an odd sense of exhilaration mingled with a hollow pain in the middle of her gut. "Okay, this isn't good!"

Fleming looked at the readings on Russell's energetic particles detector, fixated by the data. "The readings just doubled."

Roberts looked over to the professor for reassurance. "Professor?"

"It's just the unknown, Mr. Roberts."

The sound made Jennifer's flesh crawl. "The unknown is scaring the crap out of me!"

"It's just the buried Klingon ship engaging its warp drive, Jennifer."

A drowsy terror steeling through his veins, Fleming gave Russell a look of darkly brilliant doubt, and for a moment, seriously considered an extraterrestrial intelligence. He wasn't thinking so much of a Klingon Bird of Prey, something more in line with the black monolith in *2001: A Space Odyssey.*

Scranton gave himself three breaths to get the panic out of his voice. "The proton magnetometer shows nothing. The wireless equipment in the magnetic zone has also stopped transmitting. I'm getting no signal at all from them."

Roberts shook his head wildly, his eyes capital Os of terror. "It's coming right for us!"

Scranton put his attention back to the birds. He shook his head, giving the vaguely frightened look of a man who wanted to back slowly out of a room.

"Stay calm, people," Fleming said, sucking rapid puffs on a dead pipe.

"Stay calm?" Russell replied with a stutter.

Jennifer's breath seized in her throat and cold panic took over. She closed her eyes, hunched forward like walking into a blizzard and covered her head with her arms.

When it arrived, there was no sensation. The air remained unchanged, just the beating of wings from the few remaining birds. The feeling of terror and awe was distorted by their internal perceptions.

"Professor?" Stuart Roberts hushed, all six-foot-four of him hunched in a statuesque, awkward pose, still anticipating an impact.

With several false starts, Fleming's mind reassembled. "Is everyone fine?" He slowly looked about. The birds coalesced into several flocks, all fleeing the area. Jennifer picked up her magnetic detector and swept the area. With her fingers trembling uncontrollably, it was hard work.

"Was that far freakin' out or what?" Russell laughed a nervous giggle.

Jennifer shrieked. "Professor, Professor!" The tips of her twin antennas sparkled with a deep emerald glow. She took an involuntary step backward, opened her mouth to scream, then clamped it shut. Moments later, serpentine discharges slithered up and down the shafts, spreading to the unit itself. She dropped it. All $42,000 of the unit struck the rocky ground. The static saturated all their equipment, even the backpacks. In just moments, the electrical serpents slithered on the ground like angry rattlesnakes. The area of activity appeared confined to a specific ellipse, leaving part of the plateau unaffected. Their campsite of tents outside the zone were spared.

As if hunted by a great and awful predator, small animals scurried out of the zone with the same terror as the birds fleeing the trees. Something bad, something very, very bad, was in the making.

"Everybody out!" Fleming roared. Scranton went to get some of the equipment they had set up. The ellipse containing the magnetic anomaly zone became a glowing emerald cauldron. The ellipse's border had a diffused edge, but its center shone as if a brilliant spotlight lit the earth from beneath. "Leave it. It will do its job on its own, now everyone out!"

They dodged the glittering snakes past the boundary to the unaffected area of the plateau, like walking through a door into another world. Whatever weird science lit up the inside could not be detected on the outside. There were all safely outside—except for one. Russell Wynn—on the inside—continued to take readings.

"Mr. Wynn, get out!" Fleming roared with a desperate plea.

"Okay, I'm fine. I don't feel a thing!"

"Out, goddamn you!" That was the first time anyone heard the professor swear.

Bob Scranton, mystified when the dials went to zero when he stepped outside the ellipse, took two steps back inside—the readings were off scale.

"Wow, this has a very pronounced border, Professor."

"Please stay on our side of the border, Mr. Scranton."

Scranton obeyed, but Russell Wynn remained deep inside, staring into the sky. "The sky's on fire!" Russell's face bled a crimson glow, the source invisible to those standing outside the zone.

"Get out!" Fleming shouted. All of them were yelling at Russell to get out. Russell Wynn didn't get out. Rather, he moved closer to the epicentre, struck dumb by dreadful curiosity. The emerald static spread on the trees and bushes like an infestation. As Cosmo stood, the electrical charges streamed towards him, crawling up his legs and vanishing inside of him.

Fleming, in complete panic now, continued to shout and plead. "Get out, damn you!" All of them pleaded, yelling at the fool to get out. He wasn't about to get out, and no one was about to take the risk to go in and drag him out.

Something odd, strange and musical rose from the maelstrom. It started as a distant whine, increasing into a spectacular blast of a magnificent trumpet. Russell stood dead center amongst thousands of emerald filaments slithering on the ground, some creeping on his legs like living entities. He stood in perfect splendour, hypnotized by the sky, a broad smile of wonderment as the trumpet blasted its song in a haunting C note. It built up—a great final note in some epic musical score—

then it was gone. The green static vanished with a brilliant flash. It was all gone. And Russell Wynn was gone.

A smooth, serene silence and a whisper of wind blew across the plateau.

Jennifer's face turned pale as window glass. "Russell got beamed up!"

In the privacy of Fleming's skull, everything fell apart.

Nothing could be said. They were all trying to absorb their inexplicable loss. *How were they going to explain Russell's disappearance? What do they tell the authorities? To his next of kin? How do they explain six figures of missing equipment?*

"Professor, look!" Stuart Roberts pointed to the route from the road. A solitary figure approached them.

"Is that Russ?" Scranton asked.

"It can't be," Jennifer said with a whisper. But it had to be. It was Russell! He had an afro the size of a supernova and wore different clothing. His jeans were baggy and torn. His plaid jacket was a tattered rag. His face, though gaunt with a hollow concentration camp look, had a broad, wide smile.

"That is indeed Mr. Wynn!" Fleming stumbled towards the edge of the rocky ridge. He looked back over his shoulder at the empty spot where Russell Wynn vanished just moments before, then back to this new Russell. Professor Fleming looked as if hypnotist just snapped him out of a deep trance.

"Don't worry, Professor, I recovered all of the equipment. It's in my pick-up truck."

Jennifer's voice drifted down to Russell, small but perfectly audible in the wilderness calm. "What happened to you?"

Russell smiled broadly. "After the Horn of Gabriel sounded, I found myself in New Mexico."

"How did you get back so fast?"

"Jennifer, I materialized in New Mexico nineteen months ago!"

* * * * *

Fleming's team observed three additional temporal events, each study completed with greater sophistication as they consolidated their knowledge leading up to the massive Oregon event. Though water does not retain a temporal signature, they inferred the location through residual traces detected along the shoreline. Extensively studied with new equipment specifically modified for this new science, they were just beginning to analyse the terabytes of data they reaped.

A new danger arose since the last event—the presence of the United States military. Not only were they aware of the phenomena, but intentionally dispatched a crew into the maelstrom, taking with them two Canadians. This development was ominous to say the least. The Canadian yacht's arrival was just as perplexing. *Were they there by accident or by intent?*

Fleming and his crew huddled in front of the 50" TV screen reviewing their latest encounter with nature's greatest mystery. Scranton, the video guru, had contrast-enhanced, motion-stabilized and sharpened the high definition image.

"Here's the yacht," Jennifer said.

"This coincides with the data that the yacht was at the exact distance from shore as the temporal event," Roberts said.

"Proving they were there deliberately," Scranton added.

The Chinook entered the scene, engaging the standoff with the Canadian yacht, its explosion and crash. "The yacht seemed content to observe the developments, waiting for it to land." Fleming observed.

"The helicopter can land on water?" Jennifer asked.

"Chinooks are specifically designed for water landings—for special ops," Cosmo explained. "That's why it was still floating after the crash."

"The military was there with intent to pass through," Fleming said. "The role of the yacht remains to be determined. It is clear they arrived uninvited."

"Something fishy is going on with the secondary temporal event," Jennifer said.

"Fishy?" Cosmo said with a cynical jab. "That jargon sounds so scientific. I'm so glad your parents are getting their money's worth out of your education."

Her response carried a rigid, mechanical voice. "Sorry. The secondary event is an unexplained anomaly—just like you."

"Ha-ha."

Jennifer jerked her gaze away from Cosmo and faced Fleming. "The data clearly shows that Carol Parker, Alice Cousineau and Charles

Mason passed through the temporal event. Their temporal signature matches the yacht's. There's no doubt that they passed through the singularity's event horizon."

Roberts wasn't convinced. "They were mostly submerged. The water may have acted as a ground."

"The ship was also partially submerged, dude," Cosmo said. "Jennifer was right, something fishy transpired with the three." Cosmo's eyes bugged.

"What?" Jennifer asked.

"Did I just admit that you were right?"

"Yes, you did. And you said *fishy*."

"There's a first for everything," Scranton said.

Roberts got up and wrote on a wall calendar at the current date—*Cosmo agrees with Jennifer.*

Jennifer looked into Fleming's lake-blue eyes. "I can understand if they were hurled out instantly, but twelve seconds after the event? Come on, guys, something isn't right, that's all."

"Twelve point six seconds, Muffins."

"Whatever."

"Get your facts right."

A flush of anger as intense as it was brief flashed in Jennifer's face.

"The indisputable fact was that the yacht showed up at the precise moment, at the exact location, of the temporal event," Fleming said.

"Neither was expecting to be blown to pieces," Scranton added.

"Indeed not," Fleming agreed.

"We need to speak to our three survivors," Roberts said.

Fleming shook his head. "Out of the question. The press and social media are all over this. The military will be undoubtedly keeping a close eye on them. Our curiosity might be observed by military agents and our presence betrayed."

"I've been watching the Canadian news," Jennifer said. "The three we saw plucked from the water seemed pretty scared."

"Muffins, it is scary. When I passed through my time warp, I wet my pants all down the right side."

"Right side?" Roberts said through a laugh. "At least we know which side you park your minivan."

"Hummer, dude."

"Over share!" Jennifer shrieked.

"Please, Mr. Wynn."

"I wish we knew what year they went to," Scranton mused.

"More than one hundred and twenty years, less than two hundred. We need to observe more of these events to improve our estimates," Fleming said.

"Your source still has no idea of what these magnetic anomalies are?" Roberts asked.

"No. He simply has some unexplained data from a European satellite. We may have to bring him into the loop."

"We can't let the university know of the results, either. They did finance the first expedition, did they not?" Jennifer asked.

"Yes," Fleming replied. "I have never falsified a report more than that one. I paid for the last four events out of my own pocket. To continue the research, we will require completely redesigned equipment. The three buoys were of no small expense."

"How are we going to get funding, then?" Cosmo asked.

Fleming smiled. It wasn't a happy smile. "Let me worry about funding, Mr. Wynn. I know you are all planning to go back to school shortly. I'd like to know how many of you are willing to stay on full time."

"With the military poking around as well? If they find out we recorded them travelling to the past—we're dead," Roberts cautioned. "Sorry. I'm going back to school. It's a lot safer than being shot in the head."

"They sent a crew deliberately back in time and we must find out what they are up to," Fleming said.

"So . . . we're self-appointed time cops now?" Jennifer said with a jab of cynicism.

"The quest for knowledge is why we are all dedicated to learning science, is it not?" Fleming challenged. "Temporal mechanics is indeed the holy grail of quantum physics."

"There is no way we can share our knowledge," Jennifer reminded the professor.

Stuart Roberts laughed. "She has a point. We can't exactly submit our findings for peer review or publish them in *Nature Magazine*."

"What are we going to do with the knowledge if we can't share it?" Bob Scranton asked.

"Bob's right," Jennifer said. "Where is all our research leading to, and what are we going to do with this knowledge? If we don't have an end-game, there's no point to all this."

"And dangerous," Roberts said.

"I'll take the semester off," Cosmo said. "This is bigger than all of us. I found out the hard way that we're dealing with temporal wormholes, and I know we just can't stop the research because we might be scared where it's leading to, or because the military might find out about us. The professor is right—this is the holy grail of quantum physics and I feel very privileged to be part of this team."

Jennifer pondered Cosmo's words. She agreed with him, but she was not in any position to give up her studies. "I can't tell my father I'm taking a semester or two off. He'll freak out all over me. Last year, we did it part-time, but it was too hard mixing this and our studies. It's one or the other for me."

"I have enough credentials that I can write to the dean to get you a leave of absence, Miss Burke. They permit these things if the research is directly correlated to your studies."

"Your credentials will mean squat to my father. I can only offer my help during my spare time, which will be limited."

"Is your father abusive?" Cosmo asked.

"None of your business."

"You just answered my question."

"He's not exactly abusive, he's . . . dominant."

"And you are what? Twelve years-old?"

"Cosmo, my home life is none of your damn business."

"You don't even live at home," Cosmo countered.

"I need time to think about this," Scranton said. "I'm really nervous about the army being involved."

"Exactly," Roberts echoed.

"We still have some time before the fall semester," Fleming said, concerned about losing his team. "I believe we can still accomplish most of the research without any of you needing to sacrifice a term. In the meantime, we must ensure that the military has completed their salvage operations. Then we will be returning to the site."

"Why?" Jennifer asked.

"To go fishing, Miss Burke."

"Fishing?"

"Yes, fishing. We need to see if our three buoys are still there and if so, recover them. If they are missing, then we know the military has them and they will know they are not alone in the pursuit of this knowledge."

"They'll be looking for us, won't they?" Roberts said.

APRIL 30, 1848

For two days, the *Margaretha* rode hard over hill-sized waves, sliding in toughs so deep that the wave crests surrounded her like towering mountain peaks. Beneath a canopy of cold, lurking clouds, Tom sought refuge at amidships, the most stable part of the ship, hoping for relief from his seasickness. He sat half-slouched on the deck planking, leaning against the bulwark, shivering off the cold while cramps mauled his insides.

Through strands of sodden hair grappled across a face that hadn't been in the presence of a razor since he came aboard, he saw the approach of a pair of black leather boots. They were stepping unhindered along the heaving deck with no greater effort than if the ship had been laid up in drydock.

"I know precisely what you are thinking, Mr. Trasler," Liedberg said and chuckled, "that the world ought never to have been created, specifically the watery part. You are hardly alone in that sentiment. Many of the passengers are cursing Christopher Columbus for discovering America. Do not despair—it will not be much longer until you find your sealegs."

"I don't mind a bit, Captain. I'm feeling so wretched that I've gotten over my nicotine fits and I don't even want to think about tobacco."

"I have tobacco, Trasler, should you wish to purchase some."

"No need. I've been trying to quit smoking for years." He glared at the captain unkindly. "This is one hellova way to quit."

"You have not been coping well since you have been brought aboard."

"You worry about keeping this ship on course, Captain—I'll navigate myself out of my own doldrums, thank you."

Liedberg stood to Tom's left and leaned his forearms against the bulwark. Towering pinnacles of white crested ridges continued to menace the tiny ship as if it was a toy to abuse. A child ran shrieking by, brushing against Liedberg's trousers while a parent pursued the tot.

"Avast, young scoundrel—or it will be a flogging and the chains!" he bellowed in Swedish, then turned back to Tom. "Those brats have nothing to occupy themselves. They are restless and tiresome and they constantly mimic my walk. Pity me, Trasler!"

"You do have a distinguished walk, sir."

"I detest it when they do it right behind me."

"I noticed that you were slightly irate when you smacked that adorable seven year-old child right across his face."

"Well deserved. One does not mimic the master of the ship!"

Tom cleared the hair from his face and gazed at the passengers. Thirty or so who had their sealegs congregated in small groups. Children seemed to have adapted the best, many of them enjoying the wild ride. A pack of farmers clustered in one group. The men huddled in gray wadmal clothes and their women wrapped in shawls to fend off the damp cold. Runny-nosed children ran, shrieking unsupervised on deck, playing and rolling with the ship's ride.

"They're simple, ignorant people, Captain."

"I beg to differ, Mr. Trasler. The cost per adult for passage is 150 riksdalers, then perhaps another 50 to get them through the voyage and to their final destination. To afford such a fare, they had to have been landowners or expended their entire savings or inheritances, specifically those bringing large families. Most are tillers-of-dirt, but others," he glanced at another group who were far better attired than the farmers, "are well-to-do merchants. They are on this ship with all their worldly possessions. Most are consigned to the unenviable duty to build new homes out of the wilderness and nay but the Gabrielsson woman speaks the English tongue. They are beginning their lives anew, such as you. Do not be proud, Mr. Trasler. You have much in common with them."

One of the men on the main deck stumbled over a coil of rope and fell, grunting as he got up, clutching his arm. He glared at the captain, his eyes blaming him.

"Must I hold your hand as you walk across the deck?" Liedberg bellowed, then turned back to Tom in English. "I've noticed you have established a good-humoured acquaintance with the Gabrielsson woman and the other who is heavy with child."

Tom's belched up some empty air. "Alvina-Kristina appreciates me for the fresh water I'm getting from Rood, and she's really determined to rediscover her English and sees that I might have some value after all. The pregnant girl—her name is Anne-Sophie—has an English tutorial and I've been giving her, Alvina-Kristina and her kid sister, Selma-Olivia, lessons."

"Capital, jolly, Mr. Trasler! Teaching the English tongue to the tillers-of-dirt would be a splendid diversion. You could content yourself and teach them all."

"Whoa! All of them?"

"It would be most splendid."

"Teaching them to read, write and speak?"

"Most already have rudimentary reading skills. Swedish church law states that the clergy must instruct the children how to read so they can observe the holy laws and commandments with their own eyes. In the very least, so they can learn Luther's Small Catechism by heart."

"What's in it for me?"

"You are sleeping in their berth and consuming their food. They associate you with the soldiers and thus despise you, Mr. Trasler. This would be a grand opportunity to redeem yourself."

"All right. I'll give it a try, but only because I'm bored to tears. But I'll need your assistance to motivate them to attend my classes."

"God grant it. They will be commanded to do so by decree of the master of the ship. They will be occupied at last from the grievous daily drudgery, and we shall go on from this moment splendidly!"

It was known as *The Office*. An inauspicious name considering the dear price in human toll it cost. The American soldiers converted the expropriated berths to a self-contained living quarters and laboratory including its own ventilation and water supply. Twenty-five feet at its width, the length fourteen. With the exception of Rood's, their bunks and the central station were on the starboard side, the equipment laid out on the port side. LED lights provided the illumination. The collapsible desks and chairs were made of lightweight materials. Except for Rodriguez, content to sketch a drawing with a pad and artist's pencil, the soldiers huddled around Jack Silver and his computer.

"The library's fried," Silver said.

"Goddammit!" Rood was full of rage—sick and useless rage at the damaged equipment, which symbolized this sorry, busted-up operation.

"Nothing at all?"

"Nothing is salvageable," Silver said.

"And the passenger manifest?" Rood asked hopefully. "Any matches in the remaining history files?"

"No," Silver replied. "What we know is that most of these emigrants are following Peter Cassel, an emigration pioneer from Kisa, who emigrated three years ago and set-up a colony in Jefferson County, Iowa. There are two groups—most are from Östergötland, the balance from a southern province known as Småland. This is the first wave of Swedish emigration. That's all I can find."

"So there is no way to confirm that this ship will arrive safely in New York?" Rood asked Silver.

"None."

The ship pitched inside a trough and Silver clutched onto his chair as they dropped like a mad elevator. Anderson held Silver's chair in place. Located at the front of the steerage, they had to endure the full up and down motion of the ship.

"Going to lose it again?" Rood asked.

Silver flung off the chair, hunched over a plastic pail on all fours and retched up a barf.

Rood turned to face Bodmar, who stood behind them, clutching onto a ceiling beam for support. "I've given him enough Dimenhydrinate to placate the entire ship."

"So we're operating completely blind," Rood said.

"If we don't know who is to live, or who will die, this makes every action we take a gamble," Bodmar cautioned. "If fate has determined they will die another day, then that adversary will be invincible. Careful how you choose your enemies."

Rood nodded grimly.

AUGUST 12, 2016

THE WEST ISLAND OF MONTREAL, QUEBEC

Ralph Parker's wishes to be interned at The Field of Honour, a Montreal suburb's military cemetery, with an armed forces send-off, would be respected as much as possible without an actual body to bury. They surrounded the coffin, draped in a Canadian flag. Friends and family placed mementos, childhood toys, notes and cards inside the casket.

Over sixty presided over the graveside ceremony, with a few reporters off in the distance. Other uninvited guests stood watching, and they weren't reporters. Past twenty or so rows of markers, another funeral took place—a veteran of World War II. Lots of grandkids there. Some great grandkids, too.

Carol clutched onto Alice's hand while her father stood with her mother, heavily sedated with a cocktail of pills to get her through this. It was not a parent's place to bury a son. They attended Tom's memorial two days earlier, a much simpler affair at his mother's home that drained Carol to such an extent she had no idea how she was going to cope through another.

While the bagpipes played *Amazing Grace*, the tears trickled down Carol's cheeks, but the playing of *The Last Post* wrenched the sobs right out of her. While the casket eased into the ground, they tossed poppies on top, mercifully ending the ceremony.

They would spend the rest of the afternoon at her aunt's who lived just down the road. Carol took a deep breath. Her hair, ruined by the humidity, drooped down her black dress that showed too much leg and cleavage for a funeral, but in this heat, she didn't care. Once the wake had concluded, Carol intended to find a bar—she wasn't choosy which one—to get shitfaced drunk and she didn't care how bad the next morning's hangover was going to be.

As the Parkers had moved from Montreal to Victoria the previous year, Aunt Clara offered to host the wake in her Dorval home, located in a predominantly English speaking suburb of Montreal. In her fifties, she had long dyed blond hair, thin rather than thick with a side part and no bangs. Her long flowing dress and scarves looked as if she pilfered them from a 60's flower-child exhibit. She didn't shave her legs and wore hiking boots. Carol had never seen Aunt Clara without an enormous pair of dark sunglasses, even at night. A local psychic celebrity, the relatives considered Aunt Clara an embarrassment to the family.

The house's air-conditioning woefully inadequate for this heat wave, Carol sat in the dining room chair, flapping the skirt of her dress to cool off her legs. Aunt Clara passed her tea to the unsuspecting guests. When the cups were empty, she would snatch them and conduct a tea reading, with or without the guests' consent.

Only two of Ralph's military buddies remained. Both handsome—*bordering on dashing* Carol thought—and striking in their military uniforms. She noticed that other than family, the two soldiers were the only friends attending. None of Ralph's childhood friends were here. How sad.

Todd Perkins, an old friend of Carol's father, clutched one of her hands, clammy with the heat. "How did you get that scar over your eye?"

"I've had it a while," Carol said, trying to dismiss the conversation.

"I've never noticed it before."

"All this stress brought out all of my defects." She offered a follow-up grin. "I usually do a better job in dusting it up but in this heat . . ." and she gave him another grin exactly the same as before, like an echo.

"Our prayers are with you."

"Thanks, Todd."

Carol's father, Glenn, seemed very composed for a man at his stepson's wake. It was no secret that he had a strained relationship with Ralph. It had been this way since the day his mother introduced the two. Ralph, then seven, had still not recovered from his father's sudden death just five months prior, and it was all downhill between the two from there. Glenn adopted Ralph, and with Dinkler as his birth name, Ralph had no motivation to change back to it. Ralph joined the military as an act of rebellion, and only after his retirement a couple of years ago, did Glenn and Ralph begin to have a relationship that entertained any civility at all. Ralph used his logistics experience from the military and had been in charge of Northstar Navigation's ground freight division. His performance was lacklustre to say the least, but Glenn put up with him in an attempt to unify the family.

Tall and athletic with short-cropped white hair and a radiant smile over a clipped, white moustache, Glenn Parker held onto his good looks well into his sixties. Carol's kid brother, Jim, spent most of the time supporting their mother. Exceptionally tall and attractive, Jim noticed Alice sitting quietly in a wooden dining room chair. She wore a lost, dazed look. Her short auburn hair looked casually unkempt—giving the impression of having hurriedly dressed after a shower. A thin shine of perspiration broke out on the back of her neck and it wasn't all from the heat. Fluently bilingual, Jim spoke to Alice in French.

"Are those actually breasts?"

"You're the fourth person to ask in the last twenty minutes." She smiled patiently. "I was fed up of looking like a fourteen year-old."

"Well, it's added a few years in a very good way," Jim said and laughed, as much as one can laugh at a wake without being inappropriate. "You holding out?"

"Tom's memorial was really tough on me. I've known him all my life. I didn't know Ralph too well." She glanced at Carol, chatting with someone, who by appearances and deep affection, must have been an old family friend. Her face fought through the grief, putting on a brave façade. "Poor Carol."

Jim nodded. "This whole ordeal has really aged her. Don't tell her I said this, but she looks just awful. I hope she can recover." Jim patted her leg just above the knee and excused himself.

Alice finished her tea, trying to avoid any further discussions concerning her recently acquired boobs. Since her return from the tragedy, she had been going to church and sought spiritual counselling from her parish priest, and yet no one talked about her new spiritual enlightenment. *Nope. Just the new boobs.*

"Hello, dear."

Aunt Clara filled the spare seat next to her. Aunt Clara's hands seemed to be filled with ammonia coolant when she grabbed Alice's wet, clammy hand. Her long fingers with their knobby joints and apple-red nail polish curled around Alice's hand. They were bony and hard, and so cold that Alice's skin ached from their touch. Despite living in Montreal her entire life, Aunt Clara didn't speak a word of French, nor did she ever have the inclination to learn the language. She thought no ill of the indigenous Francophone population—she simply had no interest in learning the language. She spoke slowly, just above a whisper.

"What really happened to Tom?"

Alice, very carefully, turned and faced those black glasses, seeing her reflection in the lenses. "You know that I can't discuss it."

Aunt Clara glanced into Alice's teacup. Alice countered by tilting it away from Aunt Clara's line of sight. "I can sense Tom's presence."

"Really?" Alice said, trying to mask as much of her irritation as she could. She really wasn't in the mood for this kook.

"But not Ralph's." Aunt Clara said it in a bland out-of-body tone that gave Alice the willies.

Aunt Clara snatched Alice's hand, tilting the cup to see the formation of the tea leaves. It only took an instant. She sat straight for a time, not saying anything. Alice sat stiffly, perspiration tricking down her sides and front to her brand new cleavage, waiting for this nutcase to say what she had to say. Alice could faintly see her eyes through the sunglasses. They were wide-open, moony spheres.

"You are going into hiding from those who would do you grave harm. You hold a great secret for which they seek."

"Please, don't pry." Alice's voice was tight, her French accent more pronounced.

"There is one other great truth that you and Carol are trying to conceal." Aunt Clara's face held no expression. At first, she spoke with a monotone, then her face twisted, and she wreathed her words from her cherry lips with a scream. "You both have blood on your hands!"

The murmured chats in the room shut off like someone muting the TV volume with the remote.

"If you will excuse me." Alice got out the chair.

"Carol carries the greatest shame." Aunt Clara stood up. Her arm raised into a long, skinny stick as she pointed at Carol. She issued the incredible accusation with a raised and revolted voice. "You have the guilt of the spilled blood of your own flesh and blood. Ralph perished by your hand!"

Carol's fingers clawed as she covered her mouth.

Glenn Parker escorted Aunt Clara to the kitchen for a scolding. If it weren't for the fact they were in Aunt Clara's home, he'd have booted her out.

The following day, Carol, fighting a monumental hangover, bade farewell to Alice. They headed in different directions, both ensuring they would be disappearing off the map.

MAY 2, 1848

"How's our invalid this afternoon?" Tom stepped into Ralph's cramped cabin and found Bodmar dressing his wound.

"Fine, Tom."

"The infection gave me a scare." Bodmar flashed a relief smile at Tom. She was fit and lithe and looked like she could handle herself quite well in a barroom brawl. “We’ve finally got it under control.”

Tom turned to eye Ralph. “Got some gruel for you.”

“What’s on today’s menu?”

“Barley mush and salted herring.”

“Oh, joy.”

“Ralphy, the extent of my menu the last four days has been rice, pea soup, sweet soup, barley mush, salted mutton, salted cod, salted pork and anything else that could possibly be salted. Oh, since they aren’t baking bread on board, they gave me a biscuit that nearly cracked my molar. Catharina showed me how to let it sit in tea for half a day, that’s right, half a day, until it was soft enough that I could gnaw on it like a goddamn dog on a bone. So here is your delectable barley mush and salted herring.”

“You make it sound so appetising.”

Tom’s teeth flashed a coy grin. “Don’t forget to give thanks to the Almighty.”

“I can’t promise I’ll finish it.”

“You need to get your strength up. Eat,” Bodmar ordered.

Ralph turned sharply to Tom. “You should have taken food from *The Salty Dog’s* galley.”

“I did. Three boxes of Kraft Dinner.”

“You’re kidding me, right?”

“Hey, I know my priorities. Saving it for a special occasion, though.”

“You don’t have any spare MREs?” Ralph pleaded to Bodmar.

“Very little. Even we are supplementing our MREs with the ship’s fare.”

“I see you found your shaving kit,” Ralph said to Tom, freshly shaven for the first time since coming aboard.

“Ya, but what happens when our disposable razors run out?”

“We do it the old fashioned way,” Ralph said.

“Have you seen the old fashioned way?” Tom said and glowered. “On a heaving ship, one slip and you’re decapitated.”

“Hence the bearded sailor,” Ralph said.

“I imagine the straight razor is an acquired art,” Bodmar said. “This is why women didn’t shave their underarms and legs until the invention of the safety razor at about the end of The Great War.”

“Whoa! Hang on a second.” Tom drew in a ragged, terrified breath and then coughed it out in a series of bursts. "None of these women shave their armpits?"

"Nope."

"No, no, no, no, seriously."

"Hairy armpits. Suck it up."

"All of them?"

"All of them."

Tom leapt out of the tiny cabin and stared at the women. Alvina-Kristina acknowledged him, also looked a little curious as to why he looked so aghast. With jerking steps, he stumbled back into the cabin. "There's no way Alvina-Kristina has hairy armpits!"

"Hairy armpits, hairy legs and definitely no Brazilian wax."

"Carina Svensson?"

She nodded, wearing a rueful little smile as Tom's face paled appreciably.

"I hope to God you shave?"

"When in Rome . . ."

A shiver careened down Tom's spine with so much violence that it nearly threw out his back.

AUGUST 13, 2016
NEAR CAPE LOOKOUT STATE PARK, OREGON

Henry Mitchell looked far too young to be the civilian overseer of the military-led project. His good looks conspired to take away the credibility of his credentials, which were many. Neither the temporal project nor the team had a name or label. Names and labels leave traces.

He found Lucy Lewis next to the salvage ship's crane in her fatigues with her hair clewed up and nearly out of sight beneath her cap. Fair skin was her curse and her face glowed with a sunburn. The barge with the wreckage of the Chinook floated next to the salvage ship's starboard side. The Chinook's fuselage lay sprawled half on its side, mostly intact, while its blown off rear pylon lay in a mangled heap. Scattered next to it lay bits and pieces of scrap metal, rotor blades and broken off sensors and equipment. The wind's whistling through the wreckage had a haunting effect, as if the ghosts of his crew still remained at their posts. The smell permeating from the wreck, that oily blend of scorched metal and burnt combustibles, caused Henry's insides to veer over in the wrong direction. The deck rolled over the waves just a little more than Henry's stomach appreciated, and with the two-fronted attack to his guts, he was about to lose his $39.00 lunch.

"These guys are good," Lucy said. Her eyes sparkled when he touched her arm in a greeting. "Were here in three days, cleaned up the wreckage in four. Just picking up scraps now. We'll be done by the end of the day and will be heading out."

"How you holding out?" She grabbed his hand tightly, not willing to let go. His tanned arms goosefleshed, exposed by a poor decision to wear a short-sleeved business shirt, and his black tie flapped out of control in the wind, wondering why it was brought along.

"I don't like ships."

"That's not the issue. You trained with this crew for a year. More than half didn't survive."

"Honestly, I didn't expect to see most of them again. I just didn't expect them to die before the event." The pain eked out traces of her repressed southern drawl.

Henry grinned painfully. "I handpicked each one."

"The food sucks on this ship," she said, changing the topic.

"I'll take you to a fancy restaurant."

"I think I might need a little more than a fancy dinner to get over this. That and a change of wardrobe." She followed up with a smile, but a smile filled with pain.

He touched her captain's rank patch, located right where her cleavage lurked beneath. "That can be arranged."

"I don't like this uniform. I prefer the desert camouflage scheme."

"Doesn't matter what colour they are, they all look like pyjamas." The type of smile she gave Henry told him that his words were borderline blasphemy. "I bought you a new dress. It's in the car waiting for you."

Her eyes pooled with tears, but she managed to compose herself after a deep breath. "We let our people down, Henry. We never tested aircraft in a temporal zone. I can't help but blame myself for that."

"I'm the man in charge, Lucy. Ya, we failed eight of them in the worst possible way."

"Figured out what caused the explosion?"

"No. The helicopter's turbines were obviously running, but the yacht shut its engine shortly after they rescued the six. So it wasn't running and blew up regardless. The yacht had a tender with a small outboard, Rood's crew had two motorized dinghies. They didn't explode."

"The engines that exploded were hot. The others that hadn't run were cold and didn't explode."

"That's all we've got to work with. Not only that, but the force of the explosion is about fifteen times more powerful than a catastrophic engine failure could have produced on its own. So the TREP reacted with a hot engine, fuel, or both and amplified the explosion into something far worse." Henry couldn't help but be drawn to Chinook's twisted carcass and could almost hear the death screams of its crew.

"What have we found about the five Canadians?"

Henry shrugged. "We're still working on background checks on them, but so far no flags indicating they were anything other than tourists at the wrong place at the wrong time."

"They were at the exact right spot at the exact right moment. That's not just a flag, Henry, it's a great big red one. We shouldn't have let the Canadians go as fast as we did."

Henri gave her a look expressing his sentiments quite clearly. "I was overruled—very quickly."

"The three Canadians just didn't take advantage of political contacts at the highest level. Her father organized a charter with a government official in three hours. That's called a premeditated get-a-way, Henry!"

"There was a lot of pressure to release them. Keeping them would have put more attention to the secret ops. The longer we held them, a lot more questions were going to be asked about what we were doing, especially within our own military establishment. Even Mastracchio, who first interviewed them, is asking questions beyond his level of clearance. A lot of others are asking a lot of questions about a counter-measures mission that no one, even at the highest levels, knew about."

"We should have come up with some excuse to keep them for twenty-four hours at least."

"We have the extraction data, and we're watching them 24/7. They can't go for a leak without us knowing about it."

"Ralph Parker? Eighteen years in the Canadian military."

"We're in contact with our Canadian counterparts. We're doing a deep background check on him—on all of them. We're talking cell phone records, emails, internet searches, everything. But it will take time. If we need to pick them up, our Canadian friends have given us their assurances of full cooperation."

"I'd prefer to bypass Canadian intelligence. It could compromise our own security. No one outside our immediate group should conduct any kind of investigation."

"I'll take that into consideration."

"Consideration? Three of them didn't pass through, Henry. Our data says they did. Our models said they did. From their location relative to the yacht, all three should have exited in the ocean a hundred and ten kilometers from the boat—and died within half an hour from exposure. They shouldn't be alive, and they shouldn't be here. But they are—and that simply defies science."

"It's a science that's still new, Lucy. If we knew everything, we wouldn't have lost eight of our best."

CHAPTER 10

MAY 2, 1848

A cluster of passengers congregated around the aft hatch, idling away the time. Others stood, sat or lay down, occupying just about every available inch of deck space. Wives sat on their husbands' knees, children nested in their mother or fathers' arms. Sometimes the men would share a jug of brännvin—a home-stilled moonshine.

Liedberg detested the human swarm infesting his decks. It hindered free movement of his crew and often delayed them carrying out their assignments. A sudden, edgy shuffle of passengers distracted Liedberg, a result of two of the soldiers coming on deck.

They carried a contraption that caught everyone's attention. Rodriguez held a glittering chrome pole seven feet long, while atop it gleamed a black cylinder capped with a rounded dome of seven inches diameter. Rodriguez held the unit straight up while Rood plugged a wire into the base of the pole, then studied the display screen on a small control box.

Whatever Rood was up to, it took less than a half minute. Rodriguez collapsed the telescopic pole, Rood wound up the cable and the two disappeared back into the office. Shortly after, Rood rose from the depths like a medieval gargoyle. Still in his uniform and cap, along with his black leather holster, he held a letter sized sheet in his hands.

"Captain, may I see you in your cabin?"

Liedberg gestured for Rood to follow him and they entered the cabin. Rood lowered the paper to Liedberg's desk. "I've calculated our present position and outlined the course that would take best advantage of prevailing currents. This should shave off significant time off our route." He didn't give so much as a gesture of a goodbye.

Liedberg closed his door and countered the heavy sway of the ship with a natural instinct, and stared at the sheet of paper. Displayed on a full colour chart, the position of the ship was exact to his own. However, the proposed course was significantly further south than the one he plotted. Rood possessed far superior navigational aids and Liedberg decided to follow the colonel's directive. Not out of fear of being insubordinate to Rood's will, but mostly out of professional curiosity.

He brought his chair to his desk, pulled out his log and brought it up to date. After, he shrugged into his redingote, tugged his cap into place, and went to the helmsman with the new heading.

The sun crawled from its slumber and greeted the crew with its blood-red eye. Tom had a dismal night's sleep. Sleep could never be adequate with the crushing confines of his bed and the other 91 passengers' non-stop gibberish and the never-ending chorus of crying babies. The official wakeup at 7:00 AM roused them out of their berths, but there were always the early birds who wanted to be first in line at the galleyhouse for the cooking privileges. Just after first light, the men left the enclosure.

Once Sune, Alvina-Kristina and Selma-Olivia were off the bed, Tom crawled down the coarse wooden ladder. He stretched a kink from his back that even the sonuvabitch in the crow's nest must have heard. He followed Sune, Jonas and Carl-Johan through the canvas divider to wait in the aisle. While Alvina-Kristina nursed the baby, Catharina, Selma-Olivia, Stina-Sophia and Johanna got dressed.

Before going on deck, Catharina read from a prayer book—a different prayer for the morning, lunch and evening. She had expectations the entire clan would be attendance for the prayer reading, which no one dared to defy. Tom did so even though he didn't understand a word.

Emerging on deck wearing his 19th century clothes, Tom breathed in the fresh sea air. It would take him fifteen minutes for his sinuses to recuperate from the stench below. The sails were full and pregnant, heaving the ship over the broad swells. The timbers creaked in tune with the roar of the canvas, the whistling of the shrouds and the spray washing over the forecastle deck brought all the sounds together like a grand symphony. The ship hauled a good speed this morning.

A boisterous row of women stood in line for the galleyhouse. The ship's cook took his time cooking for the crew specifically to irritate the women and he enjoyed the confrontations immensely. Once the cook finished, came the arduous wait for each family's cook to prepare their meal and this always stretched the patience of those waiting. The frustration often exploded whenever someone fussed too long and especially if they spilled water on the fire, snuffing it out. Often, the weaker women got bullied off the stove before finishing.

After breakfast, a rotation of all males tidied up the steerage, swept the floor and threw out the garbage. The enforcement of this practice was poor, as people left spoiled food and garbage in corners or under bunks, often infested with worms. This attracted rats that competed viciously with one another for scraps.

Tom used Anne-Sophie's English tutorial to help him prepare the lessons. Written for the Swedish speaker, Alvina-Kristina assisted Tom and they worked closely on the first lesson, which would be an introduction to the English alphabet. Alvina-Kristina struggled with certain sounds, and Tom decided he would start with the *thhh* sound.

"Say it again," Tom said to Alvina-Kristina.

"Gooh-da night, Mooder." She stomped her foot. "I hate my accent!"

"Break the words apart first. Just say Gooooo,"

"Goooo . . . t'his is silly."

Tom glared at her. "Goooood night."

She huffed and gave it another try. "Gooo-ood night. Goot night." She was frustrated and had the potential to have quite the temper. "Goooh-duh night, Mooder."

"Muh-thhhh-errr," Tom said, and he got her eyes flaring back at him at an unsettling point blank range. "Try saying water."

"Wooh-ter."

"Wah, wah, wah – ter, ter, ter. Wah-ter."

"Wah . . . wah-ter."

"All right!" He motioned a high five and she stared at him, her eyes blank, looking at the hand suspended in mid-air wondering what that was all about. She returned to the tutorial and Tom abandoned the high five.

"Spoooon, ffffffork, kuh-nife-ah," she said.

"Nife," said Tom. "The K is silent."

She slammed her foot to the planking, so hard it must have hurt. "Why is t'he K silent?"

"God knows." She looked at him as if he were to blame. "Hey, I didn't invent the words, I just speak them!"

Alvina-Kristina spent much of the day idling about the decks, the steerage, waiting in line for the cooking grate and tending to the baby, all the while working on her pronunciations. Half the time she stuck her tongue stuck in between her teeth, doing a *thhh–thhh–thhh* sound like an out of control toddler playing with its first kazoo—all day long. It drove Tom stark craving mad. Shortly before supper, Tom took her aside.

"Alvina, okay, you're making excellent progress, but you've been doing this all day and I've had enough of it!"

"Mineh-soooh-ta."

"Minnesota," Tom said. "You don't have to sing when you speak."

"Minny-soota. It doesn't sound goot that way."

"It's an improvement."

"My seeh-ster is a wergin."

"Wergin? What's a wergin?"

"A wooh-man who has not been wit'h a man."

"Virgin. Virgin, good God, I can't believe you actually said that. Okay, my sister is definitely *not a virgin*."

"Is she married?"

"No."

"And she is *not a wergen?"*

"Vuh-vuh-vuh virgin. No. Not for a long time."

"Before she was married? T'hat's a terrible sin!"

"You speak well when you're preaching." Tom's face went sullen. "To think that sonuvabitch was my best friend."

She looked appalled but said nothing. Tom could tell she wanted to say a lot—and none of it good. "Virrrr-gin."

"You got it," Tom grinned. "I'm not a *wergen* either."

"At your old age-ed, I hope not."

"Old *age-ed?"*

"You are tirty-tree."

"Thirty-three."

"Thu-thu-thu-thirty-thhhhhh-ree. Thirty-three."

"And that's not old!"

The next day at two bells of the forenoon watch—Nine AM for the landlubbers—Tom ambled up to the capstan. With a lot of reluctance, the passengers migrated towards him. With Liedberg acting as interpreter, Tom divided his new students into four groups. Carina Svensson created a commotion when she arrived. The passengers didn't want her in their class. After a few heated exchanges, Liedberg excused Carina from taking the lessons, which suited her just fine. Each class would be an hour. Tom would have three classes in the morning and the fourth after lunch. Selma-Olivia took care of baby Edvard while Alvina-Kristina stood next to Tom with Anne-Sophie's tutorial as his official helper and translator. She was just as terrified as Tom.

The students snuggled from the bitterly cold wind in coats, shawls, blankets, and a couple had sheepskins. Alvina-Kristina wore a black coat while Tom huddled in his leather jacket. He spent three days preparing for class and he felt he needed another week. *What had he gotten himself into?* Leaning against the capstan, Tom cleared his throat and started with the basic ABCs, since the English and Swedish letters had different sounds.

As he taught, there were murmurs of conversations, kids ran about, their parents chasing them or just letting them do as they pleased. Two women chatted away as if they were at a social. The second, third and fourth classes were just as chaotic. Ralph sat on the top step leading to the aft deck smoking a cigarette. Tom, wrung out, sat beside him, looking like he had just completed a triathlon.

"You have to take command, Tom." Ralph took a deep drag of his cigarette. "You let the peasants run wild. Take a stick and start whacking them if they're not paying attention."

Tom offered Ralph a dour look, his shoulder-length hair fluttering across his face. "Ya, right."

Ralph chuckled. "Tom, it's not the new millennium. They're not about to hire a lawyer or call the cops if you whack a kid for not paying attention. Remember what year we're in, Tom; it's 1848, and harsh discipline is expected and they'll respect you for it. You have to show them whose class it is."

They were quiet for a time. It was sunny but cold and the wind had a fierce bite to it. Tom huddled deeper in his coat. Ralph put his full attention to the cigarette. With a finite supply, he had cut back to two or three a day, which he savoured like a fine wine.

"All the women wearing scarves looks like we're on a boatful of damn Muslims," Ralph noted.

"It's because it's windy on deck, that, and people covered their heads in this time period—just like a lot of Muslim women still do."

"I noticed that Snuggle Pups is your personal helper."

"Alvina-Kristina comes and goes, though. Edvard fusses, she needs to change or feed him. She's a mom first, assistant second."

"She's hot."

"Her face is too plain for me to get excited about."

Ralph drew on the cigarette so deeply Tom could hear the fire eat into it. "What do you mean, too plain?"

"Unphotogenic. Take Carol for example. Her lines are sharp around the cheek and jaw. Alvina-Kristina's pretty, but not photogenic."

Ralph found her on the deck with Catharina. She held the baby while her long braids flapped in the stiff wind. "Ya, I see your point."

"Carina Svensson, now she's hot."

"Flat as a board, Tom."

"Ahhhh, breasts or nothing, eh?"

"You got that right," Ralph said. "Alvina-Kristina's sister-in-law is one hell of a woman, isn't she?"

"She is," Tom acknowledged.

"Damn, that girl's tall."

"Barefoot a good inch taller than me."

"I can't get over the cannonballs on that woman." Tom wouldn't get drawn into Ralph's lewd girly game and refused to comment. Anne-Sophie noticed Tom sitting with Ralph and flashed him a kind of special smile. "That pregnant woman has a bit of a crush on you."

"I wouldn't call it a crush," Tom said. "I'm using her English tutorial and she's very helpful giving me a hand in preparing the classes."

"Tom, she's crazy over you. You can tell just by the way her eyes light up when you're with her. Go for it."

"The captain will have me flogged and chained if I do anything with the women. I have been duly warned. Besides, she's in her second trimester."

"Damage already done, Tom. No risk."

"Cool it with the women, Ralph. I'm married to your sister, so stop with the trash talk."

Ralph took a heavy drag of the cigarette, held it in and puffed the smoke out of his mouth like a gunshot.

Johanna and Stina-Sophia came laughing from the crowd. The two girls grabbed Tom's hands and led him to the port side where there were four other young girls. Ralph saw Tom crouch, and using their dolls as puppets, amused the little girls in a theatrical performance that despite the language barrier, just delighted the young children. At the conclusion, Johanna hugged Tom and skipped away.

Ralph took a final drag and flicked it overboard. He used heavy strides to reach his brother-in-law. "What the hell was that?"

Tom still had a large smile pasted to his face. "Playing with the kids."

"Aren't they a little young for a rascal like you?"

"What you have here with these young girls," Tom put his hands to his chest, "are simply my big brother instincts."

"You're getting too close to them, Tom."

"They're just little girls, Ralph. Lighten up."

AUGUST 15, 2016
CAPE LOOKOUT STATE PARK, OREGON

The ship was rigged for deep-sea fishing, except there were no fishing lines, rather, a submersible robot designed to inspect deep-sea oilrigs. The boat, the submersible robot and the skipper, Ron Scott, didn't come cheap. The submersible hugged the terrain deep below, its light probing into the inky darkness. The sea bottom was a flat, barren plain.

"They did a thorough job in cleaning up the wreck," Ron Scott noted. They had seen just bits of frayed metal. They patrolled back and forth in a grid-like pattern.

"This is the exact location of Buoy B, Professor," Scranton advised.

They looked hopefully at the video feed—nothing but the nearly featureless sea bottom could be seen.

"They have it," Roberts said.

They proceeded to the next location—Buoy A. The two were on the eastern side of the temporal ellipse. No sign of that buoy either. They trolled to the west towards the third buoy, triangulated between the other two on the western side of the zone. The camera revealed the barren surface, though a lot of interesting marine life swam about, flickering brightly in the lights.

Something glinted off the lights.

"Whoa!" Cosmo pointed at the video monitor. "That's a camera."

The ghost-like image sharpened as Ron manoeuvred the submersible closer, and with a joystick, hovered just before it. Careful not to stir up the bottom sediments with the downwash of the propellers, he crept within reach. "Nice, a Nikon," Scott said.

The arms of the robot stretched forward and with a claw, dextrously snatched the camera. Twenty minutes later, Ron Scott had secured the camera in a bucket filled with seawater.

"The camera needs to remain submerged until it's cleaned and dried. Electronics don't like seawater," Scott cautioned. "Less when they dry out after being in seawater."

"Any chance the memory card will have survived?" Cosmo asked.

"Hard to say, but I know someone who can salvage anything that hasn't rusted completely through." He glanced sharply at Fleming. "He's not cheap."

"Nor are you, Mr. Scott!"

MAY 5, 1848

Tom sat on the capstan, still in recovery after another day of classes. The disastrous third day of school wasn't much better than the first or second and had drained him to such an extent that his entire body trembled.

Anderson and Bodmar appeared on deck with black rods that looked like a cop's Billy stick with rings of chrome and white caps. The two worked together, waving the rods about like sorcerers conjuring up a dark spell. The passengers took some notice, but having seen Rood and Rodriguez appear daily for their navigational readings, they had become accustomed to their strange contraptions. Like a possessed Ouija Board planchette, their readings led them directly to Alvina-Kristina. She was taking a respite from the care of Edvard, enjoying the fresh air and took notice of them with a start.

"It's all right, dear." Bodmar attempted to ease her fright with reassurances, but despite the soothing voice, Alvina-Kristina cringed within her shawl. Anderson moved the wand up and down, from head to toe and tossed Bodmar a look of mild amazement.

"You're the one who spotted our ship?" Bodmar asked. Alvina-Kristina nodded. "Tell me, did you see any strange lights?"

Alvina-Kristina gazed about the deck, trying to find a saviour, then looked into Bodmar's soft face. "Yes." She swallowed hard. "Captain Liedberg said it was St. Elmo's fire."

"And some went on you?"

Alvina-Kristina seemed startled that they would know such a thing. But there was much more to it than that, and she refused to speak any further.

"It's not a bad thing, dear." Alvina-Kristina gave a very reluctant nod like she had been forced to confess to having an affair. "Thank you." Bodmar exchanged a stealthy smile with Anderson.

"What do your readings tell you?" Anderson asked.

"She experienced the exit flash as well as time dilatation," Bodmar said.

"She has absorbed enough to have experienced a complete time stoppage?" Anderson asked.

"Yes, for at least a couple of minutes."

"No wonder she's scared to talk about it."

"The poor thing must have been terrified."

Their actions peaked Tom's curiosity and he hopped down the stairs to the main deck. He felt the need to, in the very least, represent the interests of his class interpreter.

"Hey, what's going . . . on?"

Bodmar's gasp stopped Tom in his tracks. She glanced at her unit's screen. An instant of shocked, immobile silence stunned her. "We better get Trasler below."

Ralph and Tom sat in chairs similar to what movie directors sit in. Rood, Silver, Jackson, Rodriguez and Anderson watched as Bodmar waved the rod up and down both men. She stared something like in awe at Tom.

"Parker is below nominal, but Trasler," she quickly tossed Rood a look of naked disbelief, "is completely off scale."

"Off scale?" Rood's eyebrow soared.

"Off scale. I can't even tell you how much he's got, he's that much off scale."

"Just before the implosion event, when the TREP was at its maximum extent, were either of you in direct contact with any of the large TREP snakes?" Rood asked.

"I saw Tom get nailed by about twenty," Ralph replied.

"Jesus Christ bananas!"

"They were ignoring Ralph, but I was definitely their favourite meal," Tom said.

"You were supposed to avoid those," Silver said, showing increasing signs of agitation.

"You guys said the radiation was harmless and no one mentioned anything about avoiding them," Tom said. "Thanks for the heads up! So what's the concern?"

Bodmar spoke. "The Tachyon Residue Emission Phenomena is a by-product released during a temporal event which is absorbed into biological entities."

"Absorbed?" Tom asked. "Like we're all filled with this stuff?"

"Yes, and the equipment we had to extract it out of us didn't survive the Chinook's explosion."

"Which means?"

"We're stuck with it until it eventually dissipates. That could take years."

"Is it dangerous?"

"We're not exactly certain about long-term exposure," Rood replied, but Tom could tell he knew a lot more but wasn't willing to talk about it. "Had we not lost the extraction equipment, it would have been a moot point." He looked sharply at Ralph. "You may leave now."

Ralph left quickly, more like a jailbreak. Tom got up to follow, that is, until Rood's hand went on his shoulder, easing him back into the chair. Rodriguez turned the big hand latch, activating the twelve deadbolts, locking them in like they were trapped inside a bank vault.

"I need to run a simple test on you," Rood said. "It won't hurt much."

"Much? Like it's going to hurt, right?"

Rood looked at Rodriguez. "I'll need some restraints."

"Restraints? Sonuvabitch, guys, what are you going to do to me?" Somewhere deep inside Tom, a door opened, letting in a cold wind of pure dread.

* * * * *

Resembling a derelict Soviet moon probe, the spherical third buoy lay slightly on its side. At just 30 inches in diameter, it wasn't large but carried a lot of weight and took an effort to heave it from the water to inside the boat. They celebrated with smiles and handshakes. Ron Scott pulled on the rope trying to lift the buoy's anchor when something tugged back.

Ron Scott cursed. "The rope got tangled in my prop, dammit." He cut the engine, put on his scuba diving gear and flopped overboard. Jennifer went into a small rubber dinghy to hold the anchor rope clear of the engine. The water was calm, with just a light breeze and she enjoyed the lazy up and down motion over the light swells. It seemed so calming.

"Well, at least we got one," Cosmo said.

"May I point out that the military has two of them," Roberts said.

"Dude, they have no clue we even exist. They'll assume it was the Canadians who did it. You're always gloom and doom. Chill."

"I wonder if the data is intact," Scranton mused.

"It's the capacitor that was designed to trap the temporal static which is of interest to me," Fleming said. He got on his knees and with a Phillips screwdriver, unscrewed the cover. The inside sloshed with water.

"Unfortunate," Fleming sighed.

The crew picked up the unit and turned it upside-down, draining the water. Scranton pressed a reset button. Incredibly, they saw the unit's red pilot light begin to flash.

"It lives!" Cosmo laughed. "It lives!"

* * * * *

Tom felt like a condemned man strapped into an electric chair. He took off his shirt, revealing a well developed chest and arms. They bound him by the forearms, torso and ankles to the chair. After, they adhesived medical sensors to his forehead and two others to his chest.

Tom wrestled within the straps. Rood put a hand on Tom's shoulder. "Just relax, Barney."

"Relax! I'm about to be experimented on like a goddamn lab rat and you expect me to relax?"

Rood reached for an object on a desk. He tested it and sparks touched the two metal ends.

"That's a goddamn taser!"

"It will be just a pinprick." He smiled without humour and touched Tom's left shoulder.

Tom recoiled. "Sonuvabitch, Rood! That hurt like a . . . ahh . . . ahhhhhh . . . ooooh, oh boy."

A searing flash of silver-blue light exploded from Tom's body. He writhed and screamed in a cascade of sparks. Rood leapt two staggering steps backward. "Jesus Christ bananas!"

An expression of confusion ripped across Sharon Bodmar's face. "That shouldn't have happened."

* * * * *

Jennifer watched Ron Scott's air bubbles frothing to the surface while Fleming probed the inside of the buoy with a screwdriver, scraping away some muck that had accumulated inside. A brilliant flash burst off the metal. Temporal filaments streamed across the buoy in a plasma lightning ball effect. Fleming dropped the screwdriver and shook his hand that felt like it had been hit with a mallet.

"I must have shorted it out." A metallic-blue radiance consumed the probe, so brilliant they had to shield their eyes. "What have I done?" Fleming hushed, still shaking the pain from his hand.

Jennifer's heart took a high, frightened leap and she shrieked. Just a few feet from her, at the water's level, a glowing sphere of metallic blue shimmered with a glittering mist-like umbilical cord that stretched grotesquely, twisted, and linked itself to the buoy.

"Miss Burke, stay clear!" Fleming said.

"I'm staying clear!"

The professor looked in awe, wondering what dreadful power he had just unleashed.

* * * * *

"Chief!" Anderson's voice was hoarse with terror. "My God, look!"

An intense halo of light surrounded Tom. It appeared, for the moment, silver-white, with swirls and mists, all confined to just a half inch off his skin, like seeing the earth's atmosphere in orbit against the blackness of space.

"Is that green or blue?" Anderson asked.

"Can't tell yet." Bodmar waved a wand-like device before Tom. Larger than the one she and Anderson used on deck, it was tipped by what resembled an Egyptian ankh. "Let's hope it's green."

"It's blue," Jackson said.

"That's unfortunate," Bodmar said.

Tom spasmed within his restraints. He tightened his grip on the chair's armrest. His lips skinned back, revealing his teeth and a searing heat burned through his body. The pain wasn't on the skin—it burned inside him—deep, deep inside. His body pulsated within the metallic-blue glow.

"I think he's going to cross over," Bodmar said. Silver rushed to his laptop while the others stared at Tom with a corrosive mix of fascination and terror.

Tom screamed, but he couldn't perceive his own shrieks. The soldiers did not hear a scream, rather a dull, slow motion roar. Silver-blue vapours streamed out of the pours of his skin like a heavy mist.

"Oh God, oh God, he's crossing over," Anderson moaned.

"Don't touch him," Rood ordered.

Jackson was scared, and this wasn't watching a scary movie kind of fear, this was walking into an ambush kind of terror.

Bodmar looked at Rood. "What was the setting?"

"I gave him the minimum charge," Rood said like an apology. Still holding the taser, he verified the setting and showed her.

Tom's motion reduced to one-tenth speed, while the metallic-blue mists boiled off his body, glowing as bright as a welder's torch, forcing the soldiers to shield their eyes with their hands. Bodmar felt the surge of voltage pass through her and as she waved her ankh-like probe before Tom, her strawberry-blond hair levitated off her scalp like being weightless.

"He just crossed over," she confirmed.

"Don't touch him!" Anderson said.

"Triple-C event confirmed," Silver reported. "Do—not—touch—him!"

"Christ Almighty!" Rood muttered, "Sharon, don't touch him!"

"I don't have a hearing problem, gentlemen." Bodmar wanted to look away, but some unseen force stronger than any of her consolidated fears forced her to watch, twisting her head as if an unseen pair of hands were gripping her skull. She had a feeling that something bad, something horrible, was in the making, and there was nothing, absolutely nothing they could do but wait it out.

* * * * *

Roberts recorded the events with a video camera while Cosmo and Scranton activated their equipment. Jennifer paddled closer to the glowing sphere, careful not to touch the glittering stream of knotted rope connecting the sphere to Fleming's buoy. Through the brilliant metallic glow, a dark silhouette formed into something tangible, but not quite enough there to touch. For a moment, she was inside herself, almost detached from reality in her realization. She looked over at Fleming, holding inside her some kind of denial believing that her words were actually true.

"It's a person."

* * * * *

"People," Anderson said, "this isn't looking good."

"No," Bodmar agreed critically. "It's a disaster."

"We have a linear breach in progress," Silver reported.

Bodmar wondered how Silver's voice could be so sterile. She wanted to scream. The type of scream reserved for your death cries, trapped in an airplane spiralling out of the sky kind of scream. "Breach confirmed. Gentlemen, we have two coinciding timelines."

"Triple-C anomaly increasing," Silver reported. "Lost his bio readings."

"Dead?" Rood asked.

"Not sure." Silver's voice finally broke into terror and Bodmar was somehow immensely relieved he had done so. "If it continues like this, we'll all be screwed. The whole damn ship!"

"This is incredible," Bodmar said, trying to work outside of her fears. "We've got a stable singularity."

"Stable!" Rood shouted, astonished beyond belief. "Has this ever happened before?"

"No, it has not," Silver replied.

"A traversable wormhole?" Anderson asked.

"We'll find out shortly," Silver said.

"What I would do to have an extraction device," Bodmar muttered, more to herself than the others. "We could have stored all this temporal energy and played God at our whim." She had an impending feeling that something great, powerful and of monumental consequence was about to transpire.

Rood licked his dry lips. "We have a goddamn situation here."

* * * * *

A coolness crept around Tom's body and he felt a pressure form against his skin. Vague shapes began to appear. Blandness turned into contrast. He could see some motion. Waves like swimming in the ocean. At the very limits of perception, colour crept into the world. The cold, wet sensation of swimming in the water seeped through his awareness. He reached out, his arms—no longer constrained by the straps or the chair—moved through the water, but the resistance felt more like passing his hands in a strong breeze. He wasn't quite all there. He turned his head, and that's when he saw the young woman with the short brown hair. She floated in a yellow dinghy just a couple feet away. And she was staring right at him.

* * * * *

The man's head, glowing white-blue and translucent, rose from the water to his throat. Through the metallic mists, a hand stretched in slow motion towards Jennifer. The face of the man became sharper. She recognised it immediately.

"Oh my Lord! It's Tom Trasler!"

"Trasler?" Fleming asked. "Are you certain?"

She nodded—spoken words were not possible at the moment. Tom reached his hand out to her. He wanted her to grab it, to pull him through.

"Ask the dude when and where he's at," Cosmo said.

"Don't touch him," Fleming warned.

Too late. She grabbed his hand. It had the sensation of an electrified liquid, nothing solid but she could feel the tingles of electromagnetic energy. He tried to grasp hers as well, but neither could lock onto the other. Her hand passed right through his.

"Can you hear me?" she shouted.

"Yes!"

He spoke with a low, muted yes. Said in slow motion. The voice came from just a foot away, yet sounded if he called from a great distance.

"You're Tom Trasler, aren't you?"

"Yes!" in slow motion audio.

She forced her voice to full volume while trying to match his slow motion modulation. "My name is Jennifer and I'm a friend."

"Help me!"

"I'm here, Tom. What year are you in?"

"May, 1848. I'm on an emigrant ship." His voice had picked up speed, halfway to normal.

She reached for his hand again. It seemed a little more solid, but still unable to lock onto it. "How did you get on the emigrant ship?"

He struggled to stay afloat. "Arrived off the English Channel. They saw the smoke from our burning ship."

"What is the soldiers' mission?" she asked.

"They won't tell me. Help me get home!"

"I'm trying!" she said in a small, near-to-tears voice.

* * * * *

What Bodmar found moderately to seriously grotesque, was that Tom's body had lost its physical form and turned into a kind of silver-blue fog. She knew this was an illusion caused by the effect of him lingering within the corridor of the temporal wormhole, transitioning from one realm to the next. She said, "You know, during a disaster like this, one feels, that perhaps dormant TREP should be left dormant. Don't you have that feeling now?"

"Do you have any suggestions?" Anderson asked.

"Our only choice is to let it ride out," Bodmar said.

Jackson broke into a sweat—great big beads formed on his forehead and temples, running down his cheeks like clear oil. Rodriguez remained immobile, except for his eyes ticking from side to side. He reached into his pocket and got a stick of gum. The ship began to vibrate and it had nothing to do with the action of the sea, or the wind, or any other interaction from the natural elements.

"We've got trouble, people," Rood said. "I don't know what it is, but I know it's coming, big thunder."

The shaking of their surroundings continued to intensify. While screams exploded out of the steerage, equipment crashed off desks and shelves to the floor. They could feel the stress on the ship's frame through the grinding of wood, creaking and snapping lumber.

A pulse beating at her temples, Bodmar stared at Rood. She yelled to be heard over the background din of the steerage's panic. "I think Trasler's gone!"

* * * * *

Water gushed into Tom's mouth, salty and cold and he spat it out. He tried to arch forward to gain a foothold on the water but couldn't when the water's natural density remained half of what it should be.

"What happened to you to get this way?" Jennifer asked, trying to find that elusive grip. She could see miniature shockwaves in the water spread out from his temporal mists, creating tiny wavelets, but there was no vibrating coming from him.

"They gave me an electrical shock." Tom spoke at a near-normal speed and he seemed much closer. She could feel his skin coalesce around her hand, could feel the heat from his flesh and squeezed tighter as her hand strengthened around his. He had a great weight to him, as if tentacles from an unseen marine creature had grasped him by the legs, trying to drag him deep below.

She repositioned herself and pulled harder. A counter thrust heaved her off balance, dragging her to the edge of the dinghy. Their hands clutched in a death grip fighting a tug of war. Her free hand pushed deep into the rubber of the dinghy for the counter thrust—then slid off. Yanked forward on her stomach, her thighs pressed against the side of the dinghy, aware she had reached her last point of resistance.

"Let go!" Cosmo shouted. Others joined the chorus.

The weight overwhelmed her. She plunged headfirst into the water. Something dragged her towards a silver-blue light. She wasn't pulling him into her world—*he was pulling her into his.* Her fear extreme, she tried to pry her hand loose. His grip tightened. She continued to descend deeper towards the enveloping light that would take her to the one-way corridor to the ages.

Her free hand grabbed his wrist, squeezing with her full effort, regretting she chewed her fingernails. She bit his wrist, clamping down as hard as she could. He screamed with a burst of bubbles and lost his grip. She was free. She pushed away, kicked her feet and rose towards the surface. A flash, brilliant and blinding, detonated beneath her—then all became dark again. She broke the surface, gasping for air. She looked to the water below. Nothing. Just the darkness of the empty sea.

* * * * *

A flash sizzled from Tom's shapeless form and he became whole again. The ship lurched in a final spasm until a surreal calm smothered the mayhem. Kneeling upright, Tom was clear of his temporal cocoon. He stretched his hand towards the ceiling, as if he was reaching for something. The chair dropped next to him a foot off the floor, the arm restraints in place but empty. The medical sensors tumbled from the air as if an invisible hand had released them. Tom belched a spray of water from his mouth.

"Help me."

His last word became a snore and he collapsed into Bodmar's arms.

CHAPTER 11

Rood held the kind of disbelief that would make a man sit in a chair at four in the morning with his second glass of Scotch in a long night where there would be no sweet dreams. The world was insane and his mind an asylum.

"Sharon?" Rood said in a hushed voice. A don't-wake-the-baby voice. "He's soaking wet."

Bodmar's mind was a corrosive blend of fear and awe. "I see that."

The screaming in the steerage had subsided, but a lot of post panic trauma rumblings continued.

"If the taser had been a setting higher, we'd all be screwed," Silver said, his voice squealed in a high shrill like someone had a good grip on his scrotum.

"Define screwed." Rood's voice was also off nominal.

"Either absorbed into a temporal singularity—in other words, we'd cease to exist, or—we may have been extracted elsewhere. Different place, different time, perhaps different temporal branch."

"Jesus," Anderson hushed.

"How is he?" Rood asked Bodmar.

"Unconscious. He's choking on seawater. I think he almost drowned."

"Will he wake up?"

"Don't know. Don't ask me how he's still alive."

"I want answers on what just happened," Rood said.

"Here's the answer," Silver said, his voice still squeezed. "Trasler got rammed by dozens of TREP snakes and has absorbed no less than fifty times more TREP than the rest of us. He's a walking temporal Hiroshima."

"I used the minimum charge," Rood glanced at the taser. "All we should have seen was a little TREP sparkle."

"At normal levels, yes, but not when the subject is fifty times beyond normal," Bodmar explained.

"The next time could be worse," Silver warned.

"I'm aware of that." Rood looked over at Anderson. "Can we make an extraction device once we hit stateside with the materials of this time period?"

"Not a chance."

"What the hell are we going to do with him?" Rood asked, rubbing his jaw. "We can't let him go off on his own like this."

"If he has another episode anything like this," Silver said, his voice no longer high pitched, but reminded Rood of his ex-wife's nagging voice which was a recall as to why he had left her, "it could put in grave jeopardy everything that we hold dear."

"Then what do you suggest?"

"Weigh him down with a lead weight and toss him overboard."

"Silver, the man saved our hairy arses. Besides, all that temporal energy he's carrying could be used to our advantage."

"No! Just do as I say."

"We need a triple-C event to accomplish the mission," Rood said. "Without the extraction equipment, he's our primary TREP source with plenty to spare."

"We need a good source," Bodmar agreed. "Trasler could have very well saved the mission."

"You'll regret this decision!" Silver's voice retained its high falsetto. "I say it's best to destroy him right now!"

* * * * *

Jennifer lunged for the yellow dinghy and heaved herself up. She drew in a ragged breath and then coughed it out. Her eyes came into focus and turned to Fleming. His face—like the others—drained to a parchment white hue, his blue eyes blazed with crazy fire.

"Are you quite all right, Miss Burke?"

She stared at her feet, at her brand new shoes that were soaking wet and pretty much ruined.

"I'm good." She wasn't good. Something nearly dragged her to 1848, and the realization of how close she had come churned her mind into a liquid daze. She glanced at her right hand, at the empty spot on her middle finger where there should be a high school graduation ring, but it wasn't a big deal. Just high school with all its bad memories. She blamed herself for not pulling Tom to this side, to free him, to bring him back home. Had she been better positioned, she wouldn't have been dragged over the side. She could have pulled him to this side rather he pulling her.

Tom Trasler remained trapped in the ages when she he could have brought him home.

"I lost him." She stared into the dark waters. "I had his hand and lost him." She flopped on her back, leaning on the edge of the dinghy with her arms stretched out on the lip. Still breathing with heavy gasps, she stared at the endless horizon to the west but seeing nothing.

Ron Scott broke the surface. "Okay, the prop is clear. What a mess that was." He laughed, having no clue of what had just transpired, but he did notice Jennifer's tears, her soaking wet clothes and the forlorn looks on the others. "What was going on and what was that flash of light in the water?"

"The buoy shorted out," Cosmo said.

"It's completely ruined—Seawater," Roberts said.

Those in the boat were subdued and silent. They pulled Jennifer in. She sat in the back corner chair, huddling within her arms. Cosmo wrapped a towel around her shoulders, and she never acknowledged the gesture, just continued to stare into the abyss of her guilt. No one said a word heading to shore and Ron Scott, though knowing that it was a lot more than ruined equipment, let go of his curiosity. This was a cash job with no questions asked.

Jennifer never knew she could feel so much pain when there was nothing medically wrong with her.

* * * * *

Tom's eyes snapped open like a corpse waking up from the dead. He found himself in dry clothes on a cot.

"Just lie still for a few minutes," Bodmar said. She had a dry voice holding no bedside caring whatsoever.

"I feel lousy."

"I'm not surprised."

"What happened?"

"All that TREP you're carrying can be excited by an electrical charge. We expected that you might shoot off green sparks for a few seconds so that we could measure the amount and type you have. Instead, you went right into a triple-C."

"What exactly is a triple-C?"

"**C**ausality **C**rossover **C**ascade. You collapsed our space-time continuum. It appears that you somehow created your own temporal wormhole and nearly made it all the way through to the other side."

"It feels like a real weird dream. What did it look like?"

"Like cheesy Hollywood special effects. At one point, we could see right through your body."

"Right through my body?"

Bodmar nodded slowly. "It's actually an illusion. Your body remained intact—it was in transition from one realm to another. Would you mind explaining this?" She opened her palm.

"That's a ring."

"Yes. A grad ring. Based on the size of it, belonging to a woman."

"How do you want me to explain that?"

"It was clutched in your hand when you returned from your little excursion, to . . . I'd like to know where."

Tom paused for a moment. He felt no justification in telling her anything about the girl. "I don't remember."

"How about the teeth marks on your wrists?"

Tom looked down and he hadn't noticed the pain until now. She had taken a good chomp of him. "Maybe she was hungry?"

"No one else knows about this. It will be our little secret and I'll owe you."

"Like what kind of IOU?"

"Trust me when I say that over the next two months, that IOU may save your ass."

"Okay . . . I was underwater and surfacing. This young woman was in a boat of some kind. Might have been an inflatable raft, not sure. She offered her hand and I took it. Then I felt myself being pulled back. I remember she got dragged down with me and shook her hand free. I guess I pulled the ring off her finger. I wanted to go with her."

"You very nearly brought her back here."

"That would have been interesting to explain to the captain," Tom said with a grin that she didn't in the least bit like.

"So she touched you?"

"Obviously." He displayed the teeth marks on his wrist.

"That was a mistake."

"Why?"

"Because you were in a triple-C state. You were co-existing in two separate timelines, and she may have even branched time permanently. Second, because she touched you, she has absorbed your TREP. But not just normal TREP, but a TREP already in a triple-C state. Meaning, if she gets exposed to enough electricity—she could create a dangerous second timeline. Either temporary or permanent. Did you speak to her?"

Here is where Tom drew the line. "She tried. But her voice was super-fast. I couldn't understand a thing."

"What does she know about temporal mechanics?"

"How would I know?" *Another lie.* "Why did you bring me back?"

"We did nothing. The reaction wasn't quite strong enough to push you all the way through and you ran out of energy, like a battery going dead."

"Then give me a larger charge. I want to go home, dammit!"

"It's not just about sending you home, the time–space continuum is put at risk."

"I thought you said you couldn't change history?" She returned a blank look, saying nothing. "So you can—within a triple-C event?" Tom could see from her eyes that he was wading into very dangerous waters. An immediate change of topic was the most prudent course of action. He held out his hand. She put the ring in the middle of his palm and his hand snatched shut.

"What do you intend to do with the ring?"

He winked. "Give it back to her."

Her smile held a touch of humour even though she knew he hadn't been completely forthright, but then, she didn't blame him.

"I'm starving."

"That's a good sign."

Tom looked at his new clothes. They were contemporary, with a white striped shirt and gray-blue pants. "Who changed me?"

"I did."

"You saw me—"

"Grow up."

"It's just that . . . the water was cold."

She managed to break into a full smile. "That seawater must have been very, very cold."

"Oh, that's . . . just great!"

"Don't worry, Trasler, it will be our little secret—our very little secret!"

"You have a lousy sense of humour, Bodmar."

"Don't worry, Trasler, you're not my kind."

"I'm too young?"

She gave him a tidy little grin.

Rood, Anderson, Jackson and Rodriguez completed a full assessment of the crew and passengers. "That scared the bejappers out of the peasants and crew," Rood said with a chuckle rolling off his tongue. They stepped back into the office. "Liedberg thought we had run aground against an uncharted shoal."

Tom and Bodmar were still together. "You almost killed me!"

"Calm down, Barney. It was a miscalculation on our part."

"Miscalculation? I was see-through like goddamn Casper the Ghost and you expect me to calm down?"

"Trasler, if I give you an all-dressed pizza and a Coke, will you shut up with the goddamn whining?"

"Okay."

AUGUST 15, 2016
SALEM, OREGON

Jennifer sat down on the bed. A soft sighing noise escaped her. The motel, packed with tourists, had some drunken yahoos next door who were getting the better of her.

"He wanted to come home so badly."

"Trasler had you, Muffins, and he almost dragged you to his side,"

Cosmo said, trying to bring some kind of solace to her.

"You asked precisely the right questions, Miss Burke." Fleming caressed her arm. "The information will have enormous benefits to our research."

"We now know his exit location and the approximate date. This is huge," Roberts said. "We have two frame of references now, with Cosmo's little excursion to the past and this, we can likely infer the strength of the other events and exit paths as well. All thanks to you."

"They were rescued at sea by an emigrant ship," Cosmo mused. He lowered his National Enquirer and glanced at Roberts. "The yacht's on fire and the smoke happened to be spotted."

"Off the English Channel. Likely from Liverpool. That's where most of the emigrant ship's embarked," Fleming said.

"What caused the wormhole?" Scranton asked Fleming.

"A wormhole has two openings, Mr. Scranton. Trasler mentioned that he received an electrical shock. That set off his temporal static—a very powerful burst no doubt. Then I shorted out the capacitor, which had collected temporal static from the very same event. Through the realm of the singularity, the two events connected. Then, one of the doors closed, breaking the connection."

Cosmo took a table lamp and cut the power chord with a pair of scissors.

"What are you doing?" Jennifer asked, her voice still unsteady and frail.

Cosmo said nothing. He licked his forearm and touched the severed wire to his arm with a grazing glance. Green static flashed on his arm, joined a moment later by tiny temporal snakes.

"I hate it when you do that," Jennifer said.

The sparkling stopped after just a few seconds. "I absorbed some of the temporal static, Muffins. Whenever I come in contact with a shock, I glow like a Christmas light. The bigger the shock, the larger and longer the effect lasts. They must have nearly electrocuted him and the effect was so powerful, that it created a temporal wormhole. This means that I could become one door of a temporal wormhole, assuming you jolt me with enough electricity, and I connect with another door. Now, you were in direct contact with the singularity, Muffins. How about a shock and see what happens to you?"

"No, no, no . . ." Too late! Cosmo grazed her hand with the frayed wire. It lit up with metallic blue mists crawling on her hand and arm, right up to her armpit. She shrieked, amazingly loud those shrieks, and fluttered her arm trying to fling off the static. It finally vanished with a jolt, leaving her arm nearly numb. "You asshole!"

"Muffins, we needed to find out if you had the same stuff in you as I do, except yours is blue. At least we know that the two of us have to avoid getting electrical shocks."

"Cosmo's right," Scranton said. "And that's rare for him."

"Ha-ha."

"Miss Burke and Mr. Wynn must indeed avoid electrical shocks," Fleming agreed.

"I think we need to plant some biological specimens in the next event and see if we can duplicate the event," Cosmo suggested.

"Mr. Wynn, that is a superb plan. We need to do just that."

He grinned and put his full attention back to the Enquirer, devouring the scandals.

Jennifer slammed the door to her room, turned the lock and shot the bolt. She leaned against the door for a moment with her head back and her eyes shut. It was one thing staring into a temporal wormhole, linking her world to another time, but the feeling of holding Tom's hand and not pulling him to this side spiralled her into a depression she hadn't experienced since her father tore their family apart with his mistress and her bastard half-brother.

She tossed and turned in bed for hours. She had an uneasy sleep. Moaning in the darkness, she gave a cry loud enough to wake herself up and came out of the nightmare. She stared into the darkness, her eyes big and unhappy. She tried to rid herself of the awful guilt and sadness pressing on her like a big, heavy hand.

A man remained trapped back in time when he could have been back home, and she had his hand. All she had to do was to pull him into her realm. Because she failed, he was lost in the ages. She held the same severity of guilt as if she had just killed a man in a hunting accident.

Jennifer looked like death when she walked into the cafeteria. Cosmo brought her a coffee. At 7:00 AM, the others weren't too talkative—it had been a restless sleep for most.

Jennifer sat beside Fleming. "Promise me, that if I agree to take a semester off, we will do everything possible to bring Tom Trasler back home."

"Thank you, Miss Burke. Yes, you have my word. You have given our research a much needed end to pursue."

"I said it before, but I'm here to stay, Professor," Cosmo said.

"Thank you, Mr. Wynn and Miss Burke. I will be going to England shortly to secure financing."

"It doesn't look like you're that enthusiastic in going," Jennifer said.

The professor cracked a smile. "No, Miss Burke. It involves family."

"You look like me when I had to go to a family reunion," Cosmo said and chuckled. "That's always an unsettling event."

Jennifer grunted. "You haven't been to my family's delightful dinner table."

"Yes, family gatherings are often disagreeable," Fleming said, forcing a stiff upper lip and a prim British smile. "Mine? More anguish than you can possibly imagine."

MAY 7, 1848

Catching some fresh air on the poop deck, Tom saw a commotion break out below on the main deck. Johannes Wilhelm, a husky passenger in his late twenties, accused the carpenter, Magnus Högman, of theft while below in the steerage repairing a berth. Lars Göran Rödin ended the argument with a roundhouse punch. Rödin and Högman looked down at Wilhelm, twisted on the deck, more inanimate object than man. This wasn't the first time there had been an altercation with the crew. Rödin, though not usually starting the fights, typically ended them.

Captain Liedberg approached Tom. "Mr. Trasler, in my cabin!" Tom sauntered into the captain's cabin, anticipating a chewing out, though not certain why. "You are progressing well with the English classes?"

"Yes, sir."

"Capital. Keeping the tillers-of-dirt occupied will relieve us from the monotony of their confinement on board. Their boredom is a menace to myself and the crew."

"Is that all, sir?"

"No. I ask you this in complete confidence, Mr. Trasler."

"Sir?"

"What precisely occurred on the fifth of May? The crew and passengers felt the frame of this vessel vibrating with great fury which alarmed us to the highest degree."

"I believe it had something to do with Colonel Rood's plutonium generator, with some boil off issues inside the compressor. If there is an imbalance, it will shake. Once it starts shaking, the ship resonates with the vibrations. The same way a table will amplify a tuning fork."

"You are a cunning liar, Mr. Trasler."

"With respect, sir, that question should be directed at Colonel Rood, not myself."

"Then tell me this. The presence of the soldiers constitutes a permanent source of peril to the passengers and crew of this fine ship, until then so happy, and who might now expect still greater misfortunes. What is the importance of Colonel Rood's project that he has cast adrift eighteen unfortunate souls and has forced me under menace to bend to his intent?"

"I don't know, sir. Curiosity has a price, so I haven't pried."

"Colonel Rood mentioned to me that his mission is bigger than he or myself. What is that meaning?"

"I believe that the completion of the mission is more valuable than their lives. Just my opinion, Captain."

"Is Colonel Rood mad?"

"Determined, sir. Very determined to complete his mission, whatever it may be."

"Enough to put the vessel in danger?"

"He needs this vessel, sir."

"If he should be determined enough, Mr. Trasler, as to bring this vessel into any peril, I shall know precisely what to do."

"Do you have any idea of why Rood's crew deliberately time travelled into this time period?" Tom asked Ralph.

Ralph shook his head while sitting up in the berth. Tom handed him the bowl of gruel and Ralph gagged on the first bite. "No. Rood already mentioned that it would be a very bad idea to pry. You're prying. Bad idea."

"Apparently, Rood mentioned something to Liedberg about this mission as being a lot bigger than you or me. What could they be up to?"

"You can't change history, Tom. So I don't think they're going even to try to screw around with anyone's destiny."

Tom looked at Ralph critically. Obviously, Ralph wasn't aware of the power of the triple-C event. "Something big-time is up. Imperative, in fact, that they had to take all these risks to go back in time."

Ralph paused. "If it's something big, Tom, for Chrissakes, don't get involved and we'll be a lot safer if we're not in the know."

"Don't get involved? After what I went through? I am involved!"

"Yes, I've been told." Ralph stared down at his bowl of colourless slop. "And you got an all dressed pizza and Coke for your troubles which seems to me," he grimaced at his gruel, "that you got the better end of the bargain."

"MREs don't exactly come in extra large, Ralphy. It tasted like paste on cardboard. The Coke was just a concentrate powder in soda water. It was a bit of a rip off."

Ralph managed to swallow down some more of the gruel. "Tom, all we need to be concerned about is getting back home. Getting too nosy is a one-way ticket to permanent residency in this time period. Got it?"

Tom collected his daily water rations from the central station's distiller when Rood stepped in front of him and met his eyes head-on. "Don't get too curious as to why we're here."

"Curious?"

"You've speculated our mission with both the captain and Parker. Parker's right. Curiosity can be dangerous."

"My concern is to get back home. And when I do, whatever you guys are up to, will have happened over a hundred and sixty-eight years earlier. Not my concern."

"Textbook response. You may go now."

Tom prepared to leave when Silver scrambled behind him and tugged his shirt. "Trasler," he called with a half whisper. "Have you seen Selma-Olivia in her nightgown?" His lips formed a thin, deviant kind of grin that trickled ice water down Tom's spine.

"She's a girl, Silver, just a young girl who's barely developed."

"There's something that is so alluring about a young girl like her.

Pretty, unaware of her own sensuality—untouched by human hand."

"Christ, Silver, she probably hasn't even had her first period yet. Leave it!"

"Et tu, Bruté?"

It was stuffy in Ralph's tiny cabin from a recent cigarette. "What's your problem, Tom?"

"You stooled on me, that's what's up."

"Stooled on you? What are you talking about?"

"About me speaking to Liedberg and then you about Rood's mission. About what they are doing in this time period."

"I never said a word to Rood about it."

"Don't screw with me!" Tom thumped from the tiny cabin and slammed the door.

MAY 8, 1848

Attendance to Tom's English classes was mandatory by decree of the master of the ship. Participation, however, went unenforced and Tom got as much response as he would have from a room full of mannequins.

Alvina-Kristina, busy with her baby who had taken ill, left Tom without his translator. The kids were unruly and a couple of teenage girls were gossiping and giggling. Tom walked towards them, carrying a long, thin rod. He stood before the two girls, tapping the stick. They looked at him, giggled and continued to chat.

Tom swatted both. One on the left arm just below the shoulder, the other the right. "Silence!"

For a long moment, the only sounds heard were the slap of water against the hull and the wind whistling through the shrouds like a chorus of demons. Even two of the toddlers had shut up with their whining. With the full attention of the class, he continued with the alphabet, basic greetings and salutations. Tom broke the stick during the third class, right across the arm of a smart-assed fifteen year-old boy. Tom experienced no discipline issues for the fourth class of the day.

With Alvina-Kristina out of the loop, Anne-Sophie, who owned the tutorial, offered her assistance. She was a thin, ungainly woman with her ash-brown hair always clewed up and concealed under a scarf. Her second trimester pregnancy bulged from a homespun dress. She didn't have attractive features but she made up for it with a certain wit and a contagious love of life, and Tom enjoyed her presence immensely. The two sat on the forecastle steps planning the next class. She sat so close that Tom could feel her thigh pressing against his. She went over the book with childlike enthusiasm. She often stopped to giggle, staring at Tom with wide bashful eyes and Tom couldn't help but notice a secret sparkle reserved just for him.

"Anne-Sophie!"

She gasped and her eyes dimmed like a snuffed candle. She stood up and trudged down the steps. Her husband, with three kids in tow, slapped her arm and yelled out an overdrawn lecture. Tom had a pretty good idea that her husband, a miserable bastard with a shaggy beard, accused her of being inappropriate by sitting with him the way she did. Just before Anne-Sophie vanished below, she tossed Tom a sparkling glance, unabashed and beckoning an invitation for another rendezvous at some other time.

Another friendship Tom had inadvertently stumbled into was with Johannes Christoffersson, a bent old man with a long white beard from Småland. He often came to Tom to chat. Tom couldn't fathom why a man so old and frail would undertake such a difficult voyage and face the hardships of rebuilding his life in a strange land. He could never find out, since their Swedish conversations were completely one sided. Johannes Christoffersson would chat and chuckle with Tom for these half-hour monologues, then touch his cap in an adieu and contently walk off to entrap another to his conversation.

After his daily chat with Johannes, Tom paced back and forth along the decks trying to kill time. Desperately bored, he exercised on the deck—push-ups, sit-ups—but still had all this pent up frustration and he would like nothing more than a good fistfight to beat it out of his system. Rood had hundreds of hours of movies and TV shows, including a whole selection from the 1960's, and he knew they entertained themselves every night. Silver had a massive porn collection, as well as some action and horror films. Ralph got to watch the movies, but not him, because Rood was punishing him for his curiosity about their mission, which created a wedge between him and his stool-pigeon brother-in-law.

Forced into doing nothing, absolutely nothing, he stared at the watery wastes over the portside bulwarks—a miserable barren wasteland of marauding waves. The boredom was torturous.

The captain always kept his crew busy. Liedberg had a sailor swung over the prow with a hammer to chip off rust from the anchor. Anders Kallstrom, more boy than man, picked apart old ropes to collect the oakum, the loose fibres used for calking. The ship's carpenter, Magnus Högman, kept busy by belaying pins. A song accompanied every chore, and there were chanteys heard at any given point of the watch. They came from the shrouds, the three decks and deep within the forecastle.

Through the bustle of the crowded main deck, Tom noticed Silver ogling Selma-Olivia. She mingled along the decks, chatting to people. Silver never took his eyes off her. Silver moved discretely through the crowd, trying to manoeuvre closer. Catharina called Selma-Olivia and the two disappeared in the steerage. Silver caught Tom's look of disgust. He adjusted his wire-rimmed glasses and returned to the office.

MAY 9, 1848

Tom stared at Jennifer's graduation ring and she preoccupied his thoughts of late. He possessed a haunting image of the young woman. She was cute. Her name was Jennifer and she was a friend. He could only wonder what she was doing, such a young thing, poking around with temporal wormholes. But she gave him a semblance of hope. He had a friend on the other side and that was a great comfort.

Tyrone Jackson appeared on deck. Men tugged their women from his approach and the African American had long given up flashing his amicable smile. Tom saw one teenage girl stare and giggle at Jackson. That set him off. He turned and confronted the girl with a look of such fearsome scorn that it frightened her and she trotted off. Jackson leaned against the port bulwarks getting some fresh air when Tom joined him.

Tom found a pair of half-bloodshot eyes staring at him. "Remember what Gene Wilder said to Sheriff Bart in Blazing Saddles? What do you expect—*Kiss my kids good night? Please date my sister?*"

"How about—*good afternoon, Mr Jackson.* Is that too much to ask?"

"Jackson, they're freaking out on me because I'm not of the Swedish Lutheran faith and my hair is long. How many even knew that not all of humanity was anything but white? They detest me, too, so don't take it personally. Another minor detail, Jackson. You're one of the soldiers. You know, the bad guys. Even if you were white, they'd still hate you."

A child came to look at Jackson, staring the same way one would at a dog-faced boy at a Ripley's Believe it or Not road show. His mother yanked his arm and dragged him to the other side of the ship. Tom could see Jackson tense all up.

Rood joined the two. "Christ Almighty, Tyrone, what did you do to these poor people?"

Jackson's lips twisted as the bottled up words struggled to get out. He saved himself a lot of grief by not speaking his mind, and thumped back into the sanctuary of the office.

"He has issues," Tom mentioned.

Rood jutted his index finger before Tom. "This is exactly what I warned him of. The silly bastard still insisted on volunteering for the mission."

"He's going to lose it."

"Not Tyrone. He's an easy tease, but he'll eventually adjust."

Tom wasn't of the same opinion as Rood. Not at all. Tyrone Jackson was a ticking time bomb.

Tom found Alvina-Kristina by the portside ratlines cradling the baby. He zigzagged across the deck riding hard over rough waters. He wormed through the crowd and stood beside her.

"How's the baby?"

"Better."

The ship struck a wave with a thumping crash, tossing him off balance and he clutched the bulwark for support. Alvina-Kristina clung onto the lanyards with one hand, the other clutching the baby and spun off balance. For a skipped heartbeat, she nearly dropped the baby.

"I hate the sea!"

Tom rubbed his cheek, sandpapery with stubble. "I'm glad Edvard's better. I really need your help for these English classes." A hopeful smile flickered. "I'm useless without you."

Alvina-Kristina managed a faint smile. "Yes, you need much help." Her accent was still heavy, but she had improved immensely.

"We should start working on tomorrow's lesson."

"After I change Edvard." She caressed Edvard's cheeks, but the baby barely reacted. His mouth drooped half-open, his tongue sticking out slightly.

"What's the matter with him?"

"He has a weak heart."

"Maybe Sharon will have a look at him?"

"I don't normally make house calls," Bodmar said as she stepped inside the Gabrielssons' berth. She carried a small oil lantern and handed it to Tom. Alvina-Kristina, Sune and Catharina were present while they placed Edvard on the lower berth. With a stethoscope, Bodmar listened to the baby's heart. She examined the face, specifically the eyes, then the hands. Tom could read the sadness fill her eyes.

"You're right—the baby's heart is weak. There is nothing I can do. I'm sorry."

Alvina-Kristina, placid and calm, took the news better than Tom would have expected.

Tom crept through the office door and found Bodmar sitting before her laptop going over some colourful graphics. He recognised the implosion ellipse, an icon representing their ship, with three others—Carol, Alice and Charlie, in the water.

"Yes, Tom." Bodmar never took her eyes off the screen, her hand still on the mouse.

"What's this?" He held his index finger between her and the computer screen. She noticed on the tip of the finger a tiny little creature with a large abdomen.

She peered for a closer look. "It's a louse. Keep it away from me."

"They're in my hair!"

"In this cesspool, I'm not surprised."

"Don't you have any lice shampoo in your survival kits?"

"They'd only come back."

He squashed the louse with his thumbnail. "You must have something that will help."

"You'll have to cope. Wash your hair with vinegar and use a fine tooth comb."

"I thought lice transmitted typhus and other diseases?"

"Not head lice—body lice, different critter."

"Oh, they come in varieties?"

She rummaged through her field kit and gave Tom a tiny brass comb. "Brush several times a day. Once we've arrived in the States and out of this cesspool, I'll give you some lice killing agent we have."

Tom stared at the comb, then his eyes slowly rolled back to Bodmar who returned her attention back to her graphics. "What's up with Alvina-Kristina's son?"

She typed some notes. "He has a congenital heart defect."

"That's not good, is it?"

"No, it isn't." She continued to avoid Tom's eyes by focusing on the graphic. "He also has Down syndrome."

"You're kidding me?"

"I wish I was."

"Will the kid ever see his first birthday?"

She had no change of expression, just a slightly harder tapping of the keyboard.

"She's already lost a child!"

"And she's going to lose a second. Alvina-Kristina knows it, so don't worry."

"Don't worry? I'll be waking up some morning next to a dead baby and you're telling me not to worry?"

CHAPTER 12

AUGUST 17, 2016
LONDON, ENGLAND

The drawing room dwarfed Fleming's entire apartment. He despised his father's obsession with wealth, possessing more riches than they knew what to do with—other than gloat about it. The fireplace could fit his car, or burn it for that matter. The butler in a tux escorted him to the room. A pretty maid served him coffee. Their presence was another in-your-face boast of excess wealth.

Nothing was modest and that's what detested him the most about coming home. It had kept him away for all these years. Though there was more to it; much more. He sat on the sofa whiling the time by working on some equations with a pencil. He enjoyed longhand math. He erased a miscalculation. The door at the end of the corridor opened. The pencil between his fingers snapped.

The footsteps approaching on the Italian marble tile were in harmony with their ego, the aggression, the elevated feeling of self-importance, the upper class mentality that anyone lower than his standing was scum. His father entered the room with his sister in tow. Robert Fleming was a tall man, impeccably fit with a groomed beard. He parted his pure white hair with perfection and wore a custom tailored three-piece suit. He looked at Fleming as did the first ever tribal chief who proclaimed himself to be superior than those around him, who surrounded himself with yes-men so that they could feed off the toils of so many others. Nothing about this man conveyed happiness. Fleming never knew if his father had ever learned how to smile.

Lydia, his 47 year-old big sister, followed her father like a dog on a leash, dressed in a man's black suit with a striped blue tie and a Union Jack pinned to her lapel. The only feminine aspects of her attire were her bright red lipstick, manicured fingernails, and open toed stilettos. Her face was so pale, he wondered if she had ever seen the sun. Fleming could not help but notice the new breasts she acquired since their last and very much unpleasant reunion. His father stopped walking twenty feet away while Lydia ambled slowly towards Fleming, her five-inch porn star heels clicking on the tile that created an echo in the cavernous room.

"Hello, little brother."

"Good morning, Lydia." Fleming cracked a frail smile. She reached to kiss him on the cheek, but he leaned away from her. She grabbed his tie, jerking him closer to plant the kiss just above his beard.

"Still frightened of your big sister?"

"Hard habit to beat."

"So how long has it been?" his father asked with a deep, arresting voice.

"Three years."

"Three years, and now you just show up, begging for a handout?"

"We've made a discovery."

"A discovery?" Lydia taunted while flirting with Fleming's tie. It was all play until she made a mild adjustment to straighten it. "Another surprise about Jupiter's great magnetic field? Or the plasma torus around its volcanic moon?" She continued to fidget with the tie. "Yes, that was so exciting. It benefited all of mankind. Thank you for saving the world." She made one final touch-up then gave the tie a little jerk she knew her brother wouldn't like.

Robert maintained a strategic twenty-foot distance of pure loathing. "You make me puke! You haven't written, phoned or visited us in three years and you make some silly little discovery that no one, I mean no one, will give a rat's ass for and now you indignify me by begging for money?"

"Please, hear me out."

Robert Fleming owed his son at least the conversation where he told him to go to hell—but maybe not. "Why should I? Your quest for knowledge is for knowledge's sake. You have no ambition. You spent nine years to get a doctorate to study magnetic fields of planets. Other planets, for Chrissakes. Nine years of schooling to write a thesis on a plasma torus around Jupiter. Knowledge for the sake of knowledge is for losers. You're a disgrace and an embarrassment to the family name. You'll never amount to anything, just like your mother."

"Don't bring Mother into this."

Robert Fleming stuck his hands deep into his pants pockets. "Nothing would make me happier if I were to discover that you were the result of your mother having an affair."

Lydia flicked a hand through the heavy fall of her black hair. "So what is this great discovery, my little brother? Solar wind interactions with the Venusian ionosphere?"

"A little more significant this time around." He looked right into his father's tempered steel-blue eyes. "A closed timelike curve."

"In plain English."

"Time travel."

His father's facial features collapsed. For a moment, Robert Fleming stood motionless—then the breath shot out of him. Lydia took two stumbling steps backward as if he had just walked on water.

Fleming nonchalantly took his pipe from his shirt pocket and lit it. "Shall I go on?"

Robert Fleming looked at his son warily. "This better not be a joke," the God-voice said. His father walked towards him. More a stagger than a walk. Lydia's face became whiter than candle wax.

"It's no joke and it's not an untested theory. We experienced it firsthand."

"You've travelled through time?" his sister asked, her words a mere hush.

"One of my team has."

"You've invented a time machine?" she asked while Robert Fleming cocked his head, like a dog hearing an unfamiliar sound. She tried to mask the trembling in her voice, but failed.

"No. It's a natural phenomenon. We're still not certain how it works, but we've been able to predict these events and can measure their strength and polarity. Though we do not yet understand the mechanics, it is proven that these events create a closed timelike curve, or CTC, a loop that allows travel back in time, and, forward as well. Round trips to another time period are possible."

His father and sister sat in centuries-old white chairs spaced fifteen feet from Horatio's. They looked at each other across the distance, the implications heavier than a hostile corporate takeover.

"How did you discover this?" Robert asked.

"Last year, a colleague from John Hopkins University sent me some data. A European satellite had an instrument altered by a coronal mass injection—a solar storm. It changed the instrument's frequency and the data was garbled, except for some ultrahigh frequency energetic particles, impossible to pick up by standard instrumentation. The spacecraft's magnetometer, also altered and able to pick-up a higher frequency magnetism than standard equipment, showed an increase at these sites as well. It led me to a site in the Canadian Northwest Territories. The readings built up exponentially and then it took one of my young students to Utah nineteen months in the past. He showed up minutes later telling us of his adventures."

Robert Fleming sat ramrod straight in the old chair. "What did you tell your colleague who supplied you the location?"

"Nothing. I said there were no readings from the ground."

"Good call. Your students?"

"We're into our second summer of research and in the last year have observed additional events. After some experimentation, we were able to duplicate the radiation that altered the spacecraft's magnetometer and EPD, and apply it to our own equipment. With our modified gear, the data showed that there would be a very strong event five miles off the Oregon coast. I had three custom built floating buoys, with the ability to measure the fluxes of charged particles such as electrons and ions, high frequency magnetic fields and a capacitor to trap the temporal static we observed in earlier events. Unfortunately, the military showed up with a helicopter, along with a Canadian yacht. The temporal static, a form of magnetic radiation fallout, caused both to explode. The yacht rescued six soldiers from the helicopter before it was sent back into the 1840's."

Lydia's brow crinkled—her eyes grew serious. "The Canadian yacht that went to rescue the downed US helicopter?"

"Yes. The two Canadians went back in time to 1848."

"Which explains why they never found the bodies of the two Canadians. How delicious!" Lydia bubbled with excitement and his father's interest had peaked as he began to contemplate the possibilities and all its potential.

Robert Fleming leaned forward. "So the Europeans have all this data and have no clue what it is?"

"Precisely."

"Get more of it."

"I'll see what I can do."

Robert Fleming gripped the armrests of his chair. His knuckles were white. "You're not going to see what you can do. Just get it."

"I'll have to bring my contact in as part of the team."

"Then do it!" Robert Fleming jerked, making the old fabric of his chair strain and whisper.

"What is the motivation for your students to work with you?" Lydia asked.

"They understand the significance of the research, and have the passion to continue on with it," the professor replied. He wouldn't mention anything about rescuing Tom Trasler from the past.

Robert Fleming held up one finger like a college professor about to deliver a lecture. "Sooner or later they'll want a reward. Offer something to them."

"Such as?"

"A sightseeing roundtrip to the past or the future, little brother. A vacation of a lifetime, wouldn't you say?"

"I'll put them on the company payroll," Robert said, his voice significantly more conciliatory. "Get them to quit school and work exclusively for you. In case you've forgotten, we are the largest family owned defence contractor in the UK. I have a research department at your disposal. Any equipment you want, design it, give me the specs, I'll have it made. If you need logistical support—helicopters, boats, aircraft, weapons, security, muscle, name it—you got it."

"What's in it for you, Father?"

Robert Fleming let silence hang in the air for a moment, then straightened up. "I want a roundtrip to the future. Five to ten years. I'll come back with knowledge of the stock market, world events, my competition, enough to make some low, unassuming investments and we—you included—will be richer than your wildest dreams could ever imagine."

"You're not filthy rich enough?"

"You just don't get it, do you?"

"I suppose I don't."

"Can you make it happen?"

Horatio Fleming didn't react or respond. His stillness unnerved his father.

"I asked—can you send me to the future and back?"

"It's possible."

"Then we have an understanding. We own a small U.S. company. Lydia will make the arrangements to have your team put on the payroll, with full benefits, including medical. I want results in three months."

"Three months is too tight."

"Four months. Not a day more." He glanced at his son with a little bit of awe and walked out. The click-click-click of his heels could be heard long after he was out of sight.

"Congratulations, little brother. You've actually managed to impress Daddy."

He stood up. "I think I ought to get back to California."

"Come give your big sister a hug," Lydia said it in a taunting, seductive way that gave Fleming a chill colder than steel. "What's the matter, my dearest Horatio?"

He responded with a dead silence.

"You're making it into a much bigger deal than it really was."

He acted as though he hadn't heard a thing. His pipe blew off two rolls of smoke that were more explosions than puffs.

She leaned back in her chair and closed her eyes in thought, one finger twisting and untwisting a curl of hair by her temple. Her eyes rolled open. "You're completely tormented by it."

His stomach felt uneasy. "I'm over it."

"It's been almost thirty years and you are anything but over it."

He sat back down and tamped some fresh tobacco into his pipe. He needed to confront his demons, and with her, there were many. "I've moved on past my shame and guilt."

She tilted her head back, her eyes moving as though she was running through a mental checklist. "Things like that happen with families far more than you imagine. Every family has dark little secrets."

He said nothing while he topped up his pipe with a pinch of tobacco.

"Why do you smoke those archaic things, Horatio? Pipes are so passé."

Fleming would not justify anything with Lydia. He puffed contemplatively.

"Tell me," she crossed her legs, her shoe dangling from her foot while her toes twitched, making it wave back and forth. "When was the last time you got laid?" He refused to reply but she noticed a slight pause in his movements and suspected she touched a raw nerve. "Still lamenting over Maria?"

"I've been busy with my work."

"That's why you lost her. You had yourself the catch of a lifetime. Even father was most impressed, and that says something. What was going through your tiny little brain to lose her through neglect? You missed out on going to the Grammy Awards—with a winner. You're a fool. And look at you. You're a big pear. When was the last time you went to a gym? You've got bigger bosoms than I do."

"At least mine are real."

"Oooooo, touché!" She giggled and her teeth flashed brightly.

He continued to draw on the pipe creating big puffs of smoke, rising like Indian smoke signals. Lydia continued to sit upright and stiff in the chair, both hands on the armrest while the shoe waved about the tip of her foot.

"When was the last time you were with a woman?"

"You needn't be concerned."

"But I am. It is a basic need, dear brother."

"How long has it been since you got laid?" he countered.

She glanced at her gold wristwatch and perked up, a lewd grin twitching at the corners of her mouth. "Two hours, ten minutes."

MAY 10, 1848

Rood was restless. His crew continued to analyze the data from Trasler's incredible triple-C event, but he was a soldier, not a scientist, and he left the analytical work for his crew. He could only watch so many movies, TV shows and porn and found that time had gotten to be a hard thing to kill. Carlos, more than just being their security, was also a hell of an artist, and he occupied himself making sketches of life on board the ship. Rood had no such pastime to keep himself occupied.

He leaned against the bulwark and faced the mingling passengers. Carina Svensson made an appearance on deck wearing an elegant blue dress. A corset contracted her waist and uplifted her bosoms so high past the neckline they were nearly illegally exposed—and that was by 2016 standards of legality. The gentle wind blew her uncovered hair, white-blond in the subdued light filtering through the clouds. She flicked some hair from her face, her beguiling blue eyes set Rood's blood to a boil.

"Christ Almighty!"

Carina maintained a steady lock on Rood's eyes. She combed out the knots of her hair with her slender fingers, locked eyes with Rood once again and then swept across the deck, vanishing through the rear deck hatch into the steerage.

Rood was in immediate pursuit.

MAY 11, 1848

The ship allocated its food to the passengers every Thursday afternoon. Distributed by second-mate Polman, the flavour of the week was salted pork with a selection of dried peas, beans, barley grains and sea biscuits. Once in a while, Tom might get a nibble on a chocolate bar or energy snack from the soldiers, but other than the occasional treat, he ate as did the emigrants.

He, along with ninety others, swarmed the deck with the usual jostling in line. Three sailors rolled barrels and hauled tubs from the hold while Polman waited at the forward most part of the main deck with his wooden scale and measuring vessels.

Alvina-Kristina noticed Tom caught in the middle of the congestion. She gave Edvard to Selma-Olivia, using the excuse that she needed to bathe. She slipped into her family area and shut the canvas curtain tight. She opened the locker beneath the lower mattress. As she waited for her eyes to adjust to the shadows, she appraised Tom's possessions.

Ever since his arrival fourteen days earlier, he repeatedly warned them not to touch any of his belongings. Whenever he went through them, he always chased her and her family away. He was hiding something.

His secret.

The bright blue bag with the strange cloth was the largest of the pieces, but he went into it while they were present. There were three small bags with shoulder straps and two of them she never saw him open in their presence. The large suitcase sharpened her curiosity and she hauled it out, carefully placing it on the floor. Her fingers trembled as she examined the zipper. She had seen Tom use them and knew how they worked. Once unzipped, she pried open the lid.

Stuffed along within shirts, pants and the oddest underclothes she had ever seen, was a black and silver tube-like apparatus. It had silver ends that looked a bit like wheels, a black body and the silver middle part had a great many buttons on top of it. The black part had large circles that stuck out. She placed it on the floor. Every nerve tingled and her eyes were as wide with alarm as with fascination.

It looked evil.

Her heart pick up its stride. She hesitated twice before her fingers reached out to touch it. She felt a material completely unfamiliar to her. It wasn't made of metal or wood and it wasn't ceramic. Smooth and polished, it looked to be brittle should she strike it hard. The polished silver buttons on top were gently caressed and her fingers ran along a material looking like a glass window, but wasn't glass—it was smooth and a bit soft—an agreeable touch.

She made a vain attempt to convince herself that many well-to-do families from North America might have such devices. Alvina-Kristina, however, could not help but conclude the object was out of its natural element.

She primed her index finger and approached one of the buttons, stamped with the symbol "►" on it. She pressed it.

The world hung still.

The panel lit up. Lights flashed. A horrific noise exploded out of it. Huge, monstrous sounds. She shrieked louder than she ever knew she could shriek. She collapsed to the floor. The bizarre sounds screeched so loud her ears ached and she could feel it pounding all the way to the deepest depths of her body. The roar increased in pitch, louder, the sounds thumping into the very marrow of her bones.

Her terror complete, she crawled crab-like away from it. She reached the canvas curtain, clawing madly at her hair. She raised her scream to huge, inarticulate sounds of terror. Yet, if she were to scream twice as loud, the sounds blasting from this devil-box would still be many times louder.

The mounting noise peaked. Then all went quiet with just a piano chanting from the black ovals on each side, and . . . a voice came from the box! The intensity of the music dropped when a man sung, after, a hauntingly beautiful voice flowed like he was part of the orchestra. In a delirium of terror, she couldn't breathe. Death was closing in on her.

I read the news today oh—

A leg thrust through the curtain and a well-guided finger pressed the stop button. The instant silence deafened her senses. Tom's raging eyes stared down at her. Behind him stood half the ship's passengers and the crew, all horror drugged. The captain, frantic with fright, wiggled through, his eyes dark with fear. Colonel Rood, immediately behind the captain, touched his forehead with his fingers, shaking his head in dismay.

When Tom stared back at the crowd, they shuffled back, poised just below the point of panic. "What's the matter, Cro-Magnons? Never heard a music box before?"

The volume was on eight of ten. No wonder he heard it all the way up on deck. Right at the freaky part of *A Day in the Life*. He cursed himself for not removing the batteries.

Alvina-Kristina plowed her way through the crowd, fleeing as if all the devils of Hell were chasing her. Still unable to draw a breath, she zigzagged through the startled crowd on the main deck, leaping up the poopdeck stairs two at a time. She tripped while stumbling past the helmsman and collapsed on her knees. She pressed against the bulwark, gasping for air. She put a hand on her chest above the swell of her breasts, and with deep shaking breaths, sobbed in hysteria.

Some moments later, Tom stood before her, his hair streaming over his left shoulder. She clamped her knuckles between her teeth and whimpered low, in-the-throat sobs. She clasped her hands as a shudder twisted through her body. She would not be aware until moments later she had wet herself.

With her hair whipping across her face, Tom had trouble seeing through the tangle to find her eyes. "Congratulations, sweetheart. You just freaked out the entire ship and got me into some serious shit. I told you time and time again not to touch my things!"

Tom grasped her arm and yanked her up. She tried to twist her body away from his and to stop her, he grabbed both shoulders. He brought his face to within inches from hers. Her hair whipped at him in the strong wind, concealing the two within the golden dregs.

"Look what's happening. Everyone's freaking out. Don't you think I've got enough goddamn problems? Look! Look at them! They're all terrified of me!"

Alvina-Kristina shuffled back. Her hair tugged as it pulled past Tom's face. She unlocked her hands, grabbing her hair in her fists, then stared at the masses on the lower deck. Women were huddling behind their men while staring at them with a dull horror. Even the sailors had been scared out of their wits.

"It's just a music box. That's it."

Tom pounced back into the steerage and Rood greeted him, actually, not so much a greeting as a scolding. Silver and Rodriguez were there as well, positioned in the cluttered aisle right before the Gabrielsson berth.

Silver's thin lips trembled at the left corner. "Do you have any idea the impact your music has had on these ignorant peasants?" Silver said, attacking Tom like a prosecution attorney.

Tom shrugged. "Most people like the Beatles."

Rood's face wasn't a pleasant thing to see. "You scared the bejappers out of the entire ship's complement."

"They already know we are different," Silver said, his high-pitched voice had a natural whine that irritated Tom to no end. "You really did it this time."

"I didn't expect her to snoop."

Rood's features lost their humour. "I'm concerned on what Alvina-Kristina might suspect. We'll be keeping a closer eye on her."

"What happens if she discovers the truth?"

Silver spoke sharply. "She'll have a horrible accident and will be lost at sea."

MAY 12, 1848

Tom rubbed the pain from his arm. "You said it wouldn't hurt."

"Did it?"

"Yes!"

"That should be it for the shots."

"Thank God."

Those in the office were all occupied. Jackson and Anderson, hunched over a laptop, were discussing data involving exotic quantum particles and Tom's scientific illiteracy hindered any eavesdropping on their exchange. Silver, closer to him, had his face stuffed in front of his monitor. Rodriguez laid aside his sketchpad and seemed to be more in his natural element while cleaning his carbine.

"Trasler," Silver whispered, motioning with his hand to come to his computer. Tom timed his movements with the ship's climb over a towering wave and clung onto a ceiling beam while he leaned over Silver's shoulder. The seas were rough today, and the office was experiencing a significant up and down motion with plenty of down at the moment. "Check this out." Silver giggled like a pesky kid about to pull a prank on an unsuspecting sister.

Silver played a video of the inside of one of the berths, and despite the absence of direct light, the image quality was exceptional. It occurred to Tom that Silver planted a miniature camera to spy on a family! A young woman entered the camera's field of vision. He recognised her as one of the girls from his class—Henrietta Jacobson. She was twelve years-old.

She began undressing, working on the buttons of a pretty green dress. Silver's breath heightened—hollow, quick pants. Tom experienced an uneasy flutter in his gut that churned into a wrenching grip.

The dress slipped off.

Words of deep disgust were bubbling behind Tom's lips. "I'm outta here." He shifted to leave.

"Wait!" Silver grabbed Tom's arm. "Keep watching." He adjusted his wire-rimmed glasses.

"This is kiddie porn," Tom complained. "It's horrible."

"Pure as virgin snow."

Tom stood dumbfounded. Not at the scene, but the very fact that Silver was spying on the passengers in the worst possible way. Even more disturbing was that none of the other soldiers put a stop to it.

"Tell me," Silver said, his voice quivering. "Have you seen Selma-Olivia undressed?"

"Lay off with her."

The way Jack Silver nibbled on his bottom lip and continuously adjusted the wire-rimmed glasses gave Tom a chill so cold his skin ached.

"Silver, better come check this out," Jackson called. "Those three triangulated readings we saw in the implosion zone were definitely mechanical objects in the water."

"Don't touch a thing." Silver patted Tom on the shoulder and joined the others.

Tom found himself standing alone before the screen. He inched closer and saw other open windows. He flipped through them. There were other video transmissions. Many more. They tiled on the screen in thumbnails, all showing live images. There were twenty or so video feeds—including the inside of Liedberg and Ralph's cabin.

He glanced at Silver, along with Anderson and Jackson, were still discussing the data, and it was safe for him to snoop deeper into the computer. He opened other video streams. Some on the main deck, others in the steerage, even one right here in the office. Whenever there were conversations, the equipment automatically translated the Swedish conversations to English text. The transcripts were white against a black bar beneath the video. He recalled Anderson fiddling with one area of the galleyhouse, likely to change units to recharge them.

He maximized the window back to Henrietta, now in a light-blue dress with a white checkerboard pattern. Tom stood, swallowing back the bile. Rood came out of his private cabin holding hands with Carina Svensson. Rood was startled to see Tom standing unsupervised in front of Silver's computer.

"Enjoying Silver's kiddie porn?" Rood asked with a coarse chuckle.

Tom shrugged a no-comment and shot a not-too-kind look at Carina Svensson. "What the hell is she doing in here?"

Rood squeezed Carina's butt. "What do you think?" She jiggled her tiny purse to the sound of clinking coins.

"Sonuvabitch, Rood, you freak out over Alvina-Kristina going through the boombox and you bring a hooker right into the office?"

"She's a professional, Trasler. Client confidentiality. We used our translation devises to communicate the conditions of her employ quite explicitly. She's very well compensated, she doesn't understand a word of English and will be no threat."

Carina's hair flowed loosely over her shoulders and her perfume seemed everywhere. She slid her hand to caress Tom's neck and stood so close to him that he could feel the warmth of her breath whispering across his skin. To his disgust, he felt a hot flush creeping up his neck.

"Chief," Silver said. "We have a situation."

Rood studied the data while Silver provided the commentary. "Confirmed, there were three objects placed in the water that were responsible for some of the TREP readings. Perfectly triangulated. All were transmitting at a UHF frequency. Someone else was monitoring the event."

His eyes flared with shock and glanced sharply at Tom. "You are excused."

Tom knew that *the someone else monitoring the event* involved Jennifer, and he wasn't about to mention that minor detail to Rood. Stuffing his hands into his brown leather jacket, Tom tried to recall all of the camera angles, and as discretely as possible, to find their locations. He found the first located on the right side of the galleyhouse, facing forward, angled to the left getting most of the main deck. Very much like the tiny lens on his BlackBerry, a tiny black bead with a wire beside it for the audio. It had been installed in a casing and screwed into the wood just below the overhang. Unless you knew what you were looking for, it would be completely unnoticed.

Someone from his time period might see it and recognise it as a spy camera, but people from this century were blissfully ignorant of the ultimate violation. Rood could monitor just about every conversation and likely had a filtering program to red flag any security sensitive conversations. It explained how Rood knew he had spoken to first Liedberg then Ralph about the nature of his mission. *But to violate the sanctuary of the bedroom?* He went to his berth, checked out the entire area and found nothing.

AUGUST 19, 2016
PASADENA, CA

Fleming assembled his team for an important announcement. All were present except for Cosmo. Jennifer read the time on her smart phone while Fleming glanced at his watch every thirty seconds or so, each with dwindling patience. Cosmo finally lumbered in. He looked haggard and wore rundown jeans with a multi-coloured polo shirt ten years out of style. He hadn't shaved in two days.

Classical opera played on Fleming's stereo. Cosmo scratched the back of his head, his unruly black hair looking like a massive electrical shock. "That's Maria Simone," he said of the singer.

"Correct, Mr. Wynn." The professor had an odd smile, the type one has when containing a momentous secret.

Jennifer looked exasperated. "You don't look like much of an opera type of guy."

Cosmo walked up to her. "Sure. I like the classics, though my preference is metal."

"So why are you late?" she asked. "Are you on metric time?"

"We were playing Klingon Monopoly." He scratched his head again. "Ended really late."

"You're kidding me? Do you speak Klingonese as well?"

"Heghlu'meH QaQ jajvam!"

"Oh my God, what a geek!" He continued walking towards her. "What did you say?"

"Today is a good day to die."

"You're way too close to me, Cosmo. If you don't want to die, back off!"

"Geez."

"Seriously, I don't like being flirted on."

"I'm not flirting."

"Just keep out from my personal exclusion zone. That's a two-foot radius, to be precise."

"What's that in meters?"

"One of these days, I swear to God!"

"Pahtak!"

"What did you just call me?"

"Children, please," Fleming chided. Cosmo sat at the other side of the room from Jennifer. "I am pleased to announce that I have solicited the financial support of my father for our research. He is a very wealthy man. This will provide us with unlimited funding, and as his company is a defence contractor, he will also custom make any equipment we request. You will all be on a company payroll and very well compensated. I hope this will convince Mr. Scranton and Mr. Roberts to defer their studies for a year and stay on as full time employees. My father offered a bonus of three months back pay for any of you who sign on."

The looks on his team wasn't exactly what he expected. They shared a little worry and a lot of scepticism.

"What's in it for your father?" Jennifer asked.

"The same as yourself, Miss Burke." He cracked a smile. "It is my intent to ultimately take my team on a sightseeing tour to the past and back. A trip of a lifetime!"

"Just like Cosmo?" Jennifer asked, and her eyes lit up like twin novas.

"Significantly further back in time, I would hope. However, finding Mr. Trasler remains our top priority."

"It should be the only priority," Jennifer said.

A silence filled the room, and after a few stretched out moments, Cosmo looked at the professor. "So, how much are we going to get paid?"

Fleming scribbled an amount on a sheet of paper and handed all four of them a folded sheet. Cosmo gave a resounding *whoa!*, Jennifer burst into a smile mouthing *Oh my Lord!,* Scranton gave a long, high-pitched whistle; the same kind a sailor would give to a pretty woman. Roberts glanced at his copy and tried to mask the glow on his face.

"To hell with one semester, I'll take the whole year off!" Jennifer said.

MAY 13, 1848

Still unnerved by the boombox scare, Alvina-Kristina not only avoided Tom, she refused to help him with the English classes. Recovering after another day of tough classes and standing with Ralph on deck, Jackson's shoulder struck Tom as he passed by, spinning him off balance.

"What was that about?" Ralph asked.

"Sheriff Bart has issues with the town's folk right now."

"What the hell are you talking about?"

A woman restrained her daughter when Jackson walked by, and the African American's footsteps became a thumping tantrum until he returned to the steerage.

Tom smirked as a scheme came to him. "The passengers need to start interacting with Jackson in a more positive way."

"How are you going to arrange that?"

Two days later, Jackson took his typical morning stroll on the decks. There had been a change. People, mostly men, smiled and nodded greetings at him. They all had silly smiles and seemed nervous, like they were trying to be friendly to some kind of terrifying afterlife ghoul. Two of the men, both in their mid-twenties, approached Jackson. The first of the two shuffled in short Charlie Chaplin steps, wearing a stupid, awkward smile. He clutched his hat to his chest with high anxiety. Jackson paused and looked at the man with cool, appraising eyes.

The passenger cleared his throat. "Hey, broooh-ther, whaaaaas happenen'!" He stood there, a silly smile pasted to his face looking like one of those cheap fake lips you get out of a vending machine.

The other did a silly shuffle with his feet, spread his arms out and proclaimed, "I'm Kid a Dyyyynaaaamite!"

"Mr. Trahhh-sler!"

Tom knew he was in trouble. It took Liedberg a good four seconds to belt his name. These four pointers usually meant *big trouble.*

Liedberg's cabin door slammed shut and Tom stood, wavering with the corkscrew roll of the ship. Jackson stood there in a brown suit, stiff collar and a black cravat with his arms folded. His eyes, direct and challenging, were all theatrics. He gave Tom a covert, slightly soured smile.

"I have just received a complaint from this fine Negro. The passengers are greeting him in a manner as you instructed them to do so." A laugh nearly rifled out of Tom's mouth but he mustered it down, no easy feat. "As a result of this grievance, I have put my attention to your English classes. Yes, you have astounded me with the progress. Most of the passengers have mastered greetings and some can even form complete sentences on their own, but my God, Trasler, what are you teaching these poor wretches?"

"English, sir." Tom's face maintained a childlike innocence.

Jackson, very much over loudly, cleared his throat.

"English? There is a liberal usage of the word *man*, even if you are talking to a woman. Then you use the word *cool* to describe pleasure or satisfaction, even when it is not cold outside. Then there is this *far out, man* that these wretches seem to have embraced out of ignorance." The captain walked in a tight circle around Jackson without really acknowledging him. His attention momentarily distracted by his logbook on the table, he snapped it shut and focused his brooding eyes at Tom. "Mr. Trasler, I have twice circumnavigated the globe. I have gone through every possible and almost impossible adventure that a being with two feet and no wings could encounter, and yet, I have never heard the things you have been teaching them. Especially today concerning this unfortunate Negro."

"Such as?"

"Don't take me for the fool, Trasler! What about this gobbledygook concerning communicating to members of his race? In all my travels, I have never heard any man greet a Negro by saying—*hey, brother, whassss happennnnnin?"*

Tom smirked. "You've got the inflection just about right, sir."

"Enough! And what is this? When you believe a Negro is lying to you, you say . . . *Don't give me none of your honky jive talk."*

"It's possible that it might be a little bit out of date."

"And what is this?" The captain did a silly shuffle of his feet and his hands spread out in a gesture of self-adoring praise. *"Kid a Dyyyy-naaaamite!"*

"Captain, you've been practicing!"

"Trahhhhh-sler!" That was a five-second scream of his name. A five pointer was not a good thing at all.

"Okay, I admit, that's really out of date. But I beg of you, Captain, *hey brother, whaaaaas happenen'?* is something that has been used by the inner-city Negro. Ask Mr. Jackson."

"Is it so?"

Jackson cleared his throat. "Yes, sir, but—"

"Then why do you make this accusation against Trasler?"

"Sir, it is used by—" Jackson had to be careful with his words, "those of my people who are less refined. Gangsters, sir."

"You are teaching these poor wretches to speak as Negro gangsters?"

"Just a little slang."

"What about the other things, such as when you are excited, you say—*What a rush. That's hip. Groovy."*

"That's gangster talk as well, Captain," Jackson remarked, giving Tom a little elbow jab while a grin twitched his lips.

Tom barely contained his smirk. By the time they arrive in New York City, these Swedes will be the hippest speaking emigrants in the history of human migration.

"Trasler." The captain spiked his index finger under Tom's nose. "You know my unfavourable sentiments concerning these tillers-of-dirt, but you are to cease teaching them these Negro gangster phrases." Tom nodded his compliance. "I'm warning you, if I hear one more, *far out* and especially *Kid a Dyyyynaaaamite!*, either from you . . . or them, I will have you restrained in chains and your hair cut off!"

"You have my word, sir."

Liedberg paused, staring at Tom with his dark looks just for effect. "A man taking advantage of this simple Negro's good nature makes you a brute, Mr. Trasler. You have vexed him and he has rightly complained. The unfortunate Mr. Jackson does not have the same intellect as you or I. His fellow black-skinned creatures, when left in their indigenous abode, are savages, still living in the trees primitively and naked as do the untamed apes."

Jackson's eyes bugged.

"Savages? Living in trees as the untamed apes, Captain? Naked? Surely they cover their women!" Tom managed a perfectly straight face.

"With these very eyes, I have seen the savage women naked and their breasts shamefully exposed for all eyes, including children, Mr. Trasler. It is because of this lesser aptitude that the ignorant and unholy Negroes have allowed themselves to be inveigled so easily into slavery, and now, whom Province has entrusted under our charge."

A grin trembled on Tom's lips.

"This is not amusing, Trasler, remove that smile off your face!" Tom tried desperately to do just that, but the laughter building inside of him became an overheated pressure cooker about to explode. "Trasler, are you making a mockery of me?"

The laughter came out like a bomb. It rose from Tom's belly and exploded from between his teeth. A jolly go-to-hell, deep ruckus laugh. Seeing Liedberg's eyes flare into moons of outrage only throttled the laughter into all out hysteria. Despite knowing he'd be punished, he felt an enormous relief. He hadn't had a good laugh since his exile from his time period and rediscovered that wonderful sensation of a gut-heaving laugh.

Jackson tried to hold back his own laugh, but knew he was helpless to stop it. His chest heaved, the laugh at first squeaked through his lips like a whistle, then he cut loose like releasing a bombshell fart that you've been desperately trying to hold back in a crowded room full of socialites.

Tom glanced to his right, seeing Jackson trying to adjust to the iron cuffs. In the dim light of the deepest depths of the ship's hold, his eyes glowed like a predator hiding in the moonlight. "Trasler, honky went out with the Jeffersons."

"It did?"

"You are really out of date, you dumbass. And this *Kid Dynamite*, where the hell did that come from?"

"*Good Times,*" Tom said. "It was a seventies show. It was a huge sensation."

"Were you even born back then?"

"Retro TV, man. A black buddy and I watched these all the time."

"Somehow, I have trouble believing you even have a black friend."

"You're too stressed out about race, Jackson. Lighten up. Why did you sign up for this mission if you knew that racism would be such a factor?"

"I didn't expect it this bad. That dumb-ass captain."

"It's 1848, Jackson, it's the prevailing belief that whites had towards blacks. Ignorance doesn't make a man evil."

"I know that. It doesn't mean I have to like it."

"They're talking to you at least. You owe me that much," Tom said with another ball of laughter. Jackson's eyes stood motionless in the dark. Just staring unkindly.

"Don't expect me to thank you."

"When do you think Rood will get Liedberg to release us?"

"I don't know. He still hasn't stopped laughing, either."

CHAPTER 13

Tom learned one thing about Tyrone Jackson that night. He prays aloud for about thirty drawn out minutes before bedtime. Then there's this nonsense of him talking in his sleep. He has serious issues with an Aunt Clarice, who nagged him all night to eat his broccoli. Jackson denied he even had such an aunt, or any recollections of the dreams, but if Tom were to spend another night listening to his endless talk with God, or about goddamn Aunt Clarice's cruelty, he'd lose his mind. Worse, by sleeping vertically, Tom wrenched his back. The more he shuffled about, the more it stiffened and spasmed.

Following a stern lecture by Liedberg, their incarceration ended the following morning. Tom stepped out of the captain's cabin, standing with his posture warped by a knife-sharp back pain. It wasn't just the captain giving him a hard time, everyone was, and the voyage could take another month or even longer until they arrived in New York. Tom glared at the sea with contempt, then up to the crinkled sails fluttering in search of a stronger wind. With the lowest spirits since stepping on board nineteen days earlier, he went below decks to prepare his classes. Alvina-Kristina was waiting for him, sitting with the English tutorial.

"Captain Liedberg said I have to help with your classes, as you been teaching very bad." With eyes of liquefied ice impaling right into his mind, she asked, "What is your big secret?"

When Tom broke eye contact, he felt the release like a wave of vertigo sweeping out of his head. It took a moment of recovery for him to settle enough for a reply.

"It's a military secret, Alvina. Rood will kill me if I tell anyone and kill anyone who has learned of it. But I'm not bad. I'm sure those freaky eyes of yours can tell you that."

She put her back to him and folded her arms, holding herself as tight as she could. "You are not to speak of this to anyone."

"It's no big deal, Alvina. My wife's Aunt Clara has eyes just like yours. So what do those Aunt Clara eyes of yours say about me?"

She retained her back to him. "My Aunt Clara eyes tell me you have secret which is bad. Rood is the devil and he will bring much bad to ship. My Aunt Clara's do not deceive me."

"I won't let them hurt anyone, Alvina."

She spun around and grabbed his hands. Her hands were so cold they hurt his skin. "No! You cannot stop them! If you try, you shall die." The intensity in her features collapsed and softened into what looked more like embarrassment. "Do not speak of my gift with anyone."

"We'll just call them your Aunt Clara's, Alvina." He caressed her arm and his smile earned her some of his trust. "Now, let's start working on today's lessons."

The back pain hurt so fiercely, that immediately after supper, Tom went to bed, trying to get the full use of the berth until he had to share it with the others. The steerage, lit by the four evenly spaced lanterns running along its length, was always an active place at bedtime, and Tom wished to hell this one brat would stop her crying.

After an hour of sleepless rest, Alvina-Kristina crept in with Edvard, Selma-Olivia, Johanna and Stina-Sophia, getting ready for bed by first having a sponge bath.

Alvina-Kristina, standing on the first rung of the ladder, shook Tom out of his rest. "We are going to bathe."

Tom sighed. "All right, I'll get out." As he moved, something snapped and it felt like he had been shot. "Sonuvabitch!"

"What happened?"

"My back."

"Stay, but get on the other side of *The Walls of Jericho*. Don't look."

"The last thing I want to do is to spend another night in chains. Trust me, I'm not going to look." He rolled to his stomach and the pain shot like fire all the way down to his toes and right back up into his teeth.

Tom could hear Stina-Sophia and Johanna undressing and washing.

They were always giggling and playing and that brought a smile to his lips. The long voyage was especially difficult for the children—bored, eating rank and salty food, but these two paraded around the ship with total abandon, always happy and finding some game to play to pass time. After a good scrubbing, the girls skipped out in their nightshirts to play with some friends a few berths down.

Edvard fussed after his bath and Selma-Olivia took the baby so that Alvina-Kristina could wash. Tom could hear the washcloth ride all over her body. His mind's eye painted all kinds of visions of her—none of them that he ought to be imagining. After washing, he could hear her go into the bottom bunk for her nightshirt and shrugged it on.

"I'm finished."

He grunted while trying to roll to the edge of the bunk and struggled getting over the wooden edge of the bunk. Alvina-Kristina took his ankles and directed his feet to the rung of the ladder. As he made his way down, her hands slid along the lengths of his legs, riding him until they settled on his ribs, setting off a round of tingling and plenty of stupid thoughts.

The amber light of the four lanterns peeked over the clotheslined curtain, and in the shadows, Alvina-Kristina stood in a patched and repatched nightshirt. Barefoot and lovely but in tattered rags, Tom couldn't help but feel an outpouring of pity for the woman. One breast was nearly completely exposed and he tugged some material to cover it.

"You shouldn't sleep in that, Alvina, it's filthy and falling apart."

The comment hit a raw nerve with her. "I have another, but is for America."

"You can buy another in America."

"No money."

"You must have enough for a nightshirt?"

"Sune has only four hundred and sixty riksdaler."

Tom quickly calculated the conversion. "That's it? How are you going to manage a whole year on that?"

Her lips tightened into a frown. "By the word of the Catechism, a wife must be subject to her husband. Did God mean that she was obliged to follow him when he dragged her away from her home and out to sea? When we land in America, we will have nay a single nail for our walls, nay a board for our flooring, nay a shingle for our roof. We must live with the earth and build our house from the trees. And then build a farm from the forest. I was destined to be unlucky in life."

"Especially building a farm right out of the wilderness. I can't imagine the toil."

Those words didn't exactly belay her anguish. The look she gave him wasn't kind, not at all. "And you? What are you doing when we arrive?"

Tom winced, placed a hand on the bunk frame and hung his head. It took a couple of deep breaths before he could compose himself. Flicking the hair from his face, he looked at her. "Let's just say that it's going to be one hellova shock being dumped on shore."

"Are you poor like us?"

"I have money," he said—*assuming Rood kept his word.* He tossed her a quick smile and dug into his bright blue backpack. He fought through the back pain to stand straight. "But I also have an emergency source of financing." He handed her Carol's wedding ring.

Her mouth popped open at the lovely sight of the enormous diamond, flanked by a smaller pair on each side, mounted boldly on a golden band. She had never seen anything so beautiful in her life.

"It is very pretty!"

"That was Carol's."

She had no wedding ring of her own, Tom noted, while she slipped it on her right hand's ring finger. It fit perfectly and she stuck her hand out to admire the beautiful object, its five diamonds sparkling in the gloom, then hit Tom with a look close to being suggestive of the unthinkable.

"It look very good on me, you think?"

"I think not," Tom replied and motioned irritably for the ring's return. Alvina-Kristina admired it with one last fleeting glance and reluctantly twisted it off. Tom snatched it away from her.

Standing in the frail light within the rocking of the boat, her breasts swayed in and out of their hiding place and he could see one perfectly as it peek-a-booed through the torn fabric. She was beautiful, definitely sensual, but the ragged nightshirt gave her no justice.

"You're too beautiful a woman to be dressed in rags," Tom said as he left.

Her legs gave out and she dropped to the lower berth. She clasped her hands and a shudder twisted through her body. It wasn't the humiliation of Tom seeing her in rags—or her exposed breasts—it was the look of pity he gave her. Pity for a lowly peasant who must go to bed in rags not fit to wipe herself after using the chamber pot.

Selma-Olivia returned with Edvard and passed him to Alvina-Kristina for a feeding. Selma-Olivia slipped away and left Alvina-Kristina alone with Edvard. She slipped her breast from her nightshirt—her filthy rags—and as she fed the baby, the tears flowed down her cheeks.

It was the usual nonsense during the long nights in the steerage. Lights out, just a single, smouldering oil lantern providing illumination. The last of the arguments, people talking over loudly interrupting everyone else's sleep, the threats to be quiet, the indignations, snores, groans, talking in their sleep about their goddamn Aunt Clarices, someone imposing their personal prayers on the entire ship's compliment, babies crying. Always babies crying or whining. It never ended.

Tom lay on his back, arms folded and despite *The Walls of Jericho* offering some kind of sanctuary, he could nonetheless feel Sune's butt cheeks spread right around his thigh. It was downright disgusting. Sune never had difficulty falling asleep. It amazed Tom how he could lie down and in mere moments, hear the snoring. And this man could snore. Tom fidgeted and found a position that eased the back pain and he finally faded to sleep.

In the early morning hours on the 17th of May, a commotion disturbed the steerage. Above the background chatter, there were deep, heaving sobs. Jonas whispered something, then Alvina-Kristina banged on *The Walls of Jericho*. Tom slipped it open and she covered herself with blankets while Sune stirred from his sleep.

"Johannes Christoffersson is dead!"

"Dead!" Tom collapsed into the prickly hay of the mattress. Johannes Christoffersson was the old man from Småland who always chatted with him. At first light, while preparations for the funeral were taking place, Tom, his back having improved immensely, barged into the office. Everyone sat sipping on their first coffee of the morning and didn't look too chatty.

"Johannes Christoffersson is dead!" he said to Rood, who sat at the table, eating his MRE breakfast.

"We heard," Rood said. He had complete disinterest in his voice.

"A man died down here."

"These things happen," Bodmar replied, also at the table, sipping on a cup of their instant coffee. Tom was a coffee lover, but the rock hard pellets they used for their instant coffee were utterly vile.

"What do you mean, *these things happen?* A man is dead!"

"He was an old man," Bodmar said, "and with poor food, scurvy, and the deplorable water, these things happen!"

With the mainsail braced, the ship slowed to a crawl and the flag lowered to half-mast. The emigrants assembled on the decks wearing their Sunday best. Planks lay across two sawhorses and on those planks rested the body, wrapped tightly in canvas, with some pig iron at its feet to weigh it down. Standing on either side were Polman and Olsson, both men wearing long navy-blue coats with a double row of brass buttons. The men were hatless, women in scarves, many dabbing away tears. Liedberg, in his redingote, read from a prayer book. The emigrants, hands folded, bent their heads and listened to the Holy words.

There were solemn hymns and from the galley stove, the captain took some ash and sprinkled it on the body. *"Ashes to ashes, dust to dust."* The sea received the body with a dismal splash. They raised and lowered the ship's flag, repeated two times. Released to the wind, the wind took a grip on the mainsail, the mast creaked as the ship picked up speed. Women lined up for the galley, the men cleaned up the steerage and with one less soul aboard her, the *Margaretha* continued her voyage to the west.

Tom stared with wide, blank eyes at the sea, the back pain no longer a consequence but the shock of the death still numbing.

Liedberg stood next to him. "I can assure you, Mr. Trasler, that this ship will in due time arrive safely in New York. I can tell you with equal assurances, that the number of emigrants who will disembark will be less than the number who embarked."

"Do you always lose passengers?"

"People die on land, people die at sea. We are all destined to die, Mr. Trasler. It is inevitable that some will perish at sea."

"Ya," Tom nodded grimly. "These things happen."

AUGUST 20, 2016
SACRAMENTO, CA

Major General Charles Bishop leaned back into his chair. The morning sunlight spilled through a slit in the blinds, glinting off his two shoulder stars. The only sound in the room came from the rattling of an air conditioner grid. Colonel Cliff Nolan stood with his hands locked behind a back stiffer than wood.

Bishop took off his reading glasses, folded them and placed them on his desk. He rubbed the stress from his eyes, stood from his chair and peeked out his window, staring at the heat lines shimmering off the asphalt.

Nolan's face was oily from the heat of the office. "I don't believe for a moment that the Canadians were at the implosion zone by accident."

General Bishop's mask of military composure slipped and exchanged a glance with Nolan, one of those military burst communications that said far more than words could ever convey. "You're not alone in that sentiment, Colonel, but so far, everything checks out that they were."

"Canadian External Affairs was all over this within fifteen minutes of getting the phone call from Carol Parker. In less than one hour, the Canadian Prime Minster telephoned our Commander-in-Chief who ordered their quick release. Parker's father is aboard a charter flight—with a government official—in less than three hours to pick them up. Sir, government bureaucracy simply does not move that quickly, especially on a weekend. This was planned well in advance."

"You understand the close relationship that exists between the President and the Canadian Prime Minister? They have each other's cell phone number. Glenn Parker has the Canadian Prime Minister's personal cell phone number. It didn't take long."

"Yes, sir, but the facts are indisputable. The Canadian yacht showed up twenty minutes before the event and stopped at the implosion zone's northern boundary. That is not a coincidence."

"The official report has concluded the only reason they entered the zone at all was during their attempt to rescue our people."

"Sir, the authors of the official report did not have the clearance to know the true purpose of the Chinook's mission. Furthermore, the three in the water were temporally extracted, and then, twelve-point-six seconds after the event, appeared at swimming distance from shore. Sir, I personally experienced a temporal extraction. This is not what happens during an implosion. I smell a rat!"

"Colonel, we have salvaged the Chinook. Most of the equipment was destroyed in the blast and what is intact has been compromised by the exposure to seawater. We are attempting to salvage the data and we could be weeks away from having useful information."

"Are we keeping an eye on the Canadians, and can we pick them up at a moment's notice if need be?"

"They're off-grid right now but we're keeping a close eye on their friends and families."

"Off-grid! We were supposed to be watching them twenty-four-seven!"

"That was deliberate, Colonel. Let them put their guard down. I don't want any premature conclusions based on unsubstantiated suspicions."

"Not suspicions, General. Instinct. I may have gone through my basic training in the 1930s, but even today, they still teach a soldier to rely on his instincts. Instincts can mean life or death for a soldier in the field. My instincts tell me something isn't right."

"If they were deliberately there Colonel, they'd have some sort of credentials. With collaboration with the Canadian Security Intelligence Service and the Royal Canadian Mounted Police, and our own resources, we have analysed phone records, emails, internet searches and interviewed friends and colleagues. We are conducting an extensive background check of the five. We do know how to do our jobs, thank you." Bishop handed Nolan a large brown envelope with the flap unsealed. "This is what I have so far—real winners, here."

Nolan pulled out the paperwork and reviewed the files. The first picture was Tom Trasler—a police mug shot. Trasler's hair fell past the lower borders of the picture, his face concealed by a scruffy beard.

"God help the nineteenth century."

Next—a picture of Ralph Parker.

"Ralph Parker has a different father than his sister Carol. His biological father died when he was very young, and he never got along with his stepfather, Glenn Parker, who adopted him. Even though he was a millionaire's son and heir to the family fortune, he rebelled and joined the Canadian Army as a private when he was twenty-two. Unspectacular military career. He left the army two years ago. He performed two tours of Afghanistan in a non-combat role. He was a supply chain and logistics specialist and drove trucks for the army. He has been on several peace keeping missions as part as Canada's UN commitments. Once out of the army, he reconciled with his stepfather and joined the family business, in charge of the ground freight logistics department. He negotiates transport rates and books trucks. That's it."

Nolan shuffled the pictures and returned to Trasler's mugshot. "What a freak."

"Born and raised in Montreal, speaks French and English fluently and got an engineering degree at McGill University. Came dead last in his class and never got employed in that field. He has strong computer skills and had a brief career managing a company's IT until he fell off the wagon. He's been battling alcohol and drug addiction since high school. Plays guitar and has been in several rock bands, kicked out most of the time due to his drug issues. He has been charged four times: Twice for possession of drugs, once for assaulting his girlfriend's husband. One charge was for streaking stark naked in front of Her Royal Majesty while on a tour of Canada. Two of the charges resulted in convictions." Nolan became absorbed on the police mug shot. He was tight-lipped, intense. "A high-paid lawyer cleaned up his file and he got a pardon and pulled the right strings so he could travel to the United States. Got treated for his addictions a couple of years back through a twelve-step program and has been clean ever since."

"Alice Cousineau said she has known Trasler her entire life."

"Correct. They were next-door neighbours in Pointe Claire, a suburb on the West Island of Montreal. No evidence of a romantic relationship. They are, after all, fourteen years apart. She is a waitress in a sports bar. Word has it she is extremely sexually permissive. No military contact, no education past high school and certainly doesn't have the scientific know-how that would qualify her for the mission."

"A little bearcat, she is. Got a boob job. Saw it for myself."

"Yes, just a few weeks before their trip. We identified the clinic in Victoria. I assume it will raise the value of her tips."

"How long has Trasler known the Parkers?

"About a year. Once he was out of rehab, he cut his hair, shaved the beard and got into real estate and has done quite well. He was managing

Northstar Navigation's move from Montreal to Victoria, British Columbia, and that's how he met the Parkers. He and Carol were married for only six months."

"The bitch didn't take her husband's name."

"She's the millionaire, Colonel. She believes her family name is more valuable than his."

"It's downright disrespectful. Why did the company move from Montreal to Victoria?"

"Quebec politics and the desire to pursue the Pacific coast trade. Nothing suspicious. Carol Parker—"

"Christ Almighty, that dame has big bubs!"

"Colonel, please! Carol Parker is a pampered millionaire's daughter, and manages their overseas import and export department. She has taken numerous courses in export regulations and customs clearance and is certified. One note of interest—her family are gun enthusiasts and Carol Parker has been shooting competitively since she was thirteen. Nearly made the Canadian Olympic team for the London games in the pistol and rapid-fire competitions. Her father, Glenn Parker, has a better antique gun collection than most museums."

"What about Charlie Mason?"

"He's a computer nerd, likes techno music and is part of a Polaroid camera club. No steady girlfriends."

"If he's a computer nerd, why wouldn't he have a digital camera?"

"Everyone has their quirks, Colonel. Mason, as the IT specialist, was going to discuss computer issues with their client. That's it. They're all nobodies. They could not be agents and certainly not temporal experts."

"Perhaps that's the ruse, sir."

Bishop shuffled some paperwork on his desk. "Colonel, Henri and I have discussed this matter, and we need to conduct this investigation within the confines of our team to ensure security, and out of due diligence, I'm going to give your military instincts the benefit of the doubt."

"Thank you, sir."

"It is my intent to see that Parker and Trasler are posthumously decorated with the highest possible honour available to non-Americans for their sacrifice in attempting to save United States military personnel—the Congressional Gold Medal. Perhaps you should pay their families a courtesy call conveying our gracious intent. See if you can get anything off of them that might raise a red flag. Try to locate Carol, Alice and Charlie, their friends and family, and see what you can come up with. So pack up, Colonel, you're going to Canada."

MAY 18, 1848

Selma-Olivia walked towards the forward steerage hatch. Tom noticed Jack Silver standing near the hatch. He didn't move out of the way, forcing Selma-Olivia to pass just inches from him. A hand twitched and he was tempted to reach out for her. Tom glared a warning at Silver, who touched his wire-rimmed glasses and slipped below.

Rood and Carina Svensson stood side by side, both staring at the open sea. Their tryst became public knowledge, and if the passengers detested Carina Svensson before, their hatred for her was many magnitudes greater. With Rood distracted by Carina Svensson, Tom positioned himself where he knew the security cameras had a blind spot, and slipped out Charlie's Polaroid camera. He took three shots from various positions. He took a few of the steerage as well, documenting his journey. He wasn't certain what he could to do with the pictures. He thought about re-photographing the images with a contemporary camera once he got to shore, then bury them in a time capsule. It was just a ghost of an idea. When done, he reviewed the pictures he took, then those by Charlie before the temporal event. He found one of him and Carol. What disturbed Tom was the degree of disconnect from Carol. He didn't even miss her and yet his driving force to get back to his time was to be with her again. He tried to make sense of these feelings, but couldn't.

Tyrone Jackson appeared on deck. He hadn't shaved in a few days and his pencil thin moustache blended evenly with the stubble. Tom could see he was a man on the precipice. He passed a passenger by the name of Robert Sandburg. The emigrant yanked his wife, Maria Mansdotter, away from Jackson's approach with such urgency he yanked her off her feet. Jackson stopped, challenging Sandburg.

"You afraid of your wife touching a black man?" Jackson grabbed Sandburg's arm, tightening until he wrenched out a shriek. "Answer me, you white trash!"

"Jackson, stand down!" Rood shouted. On the other side of the deck with Carina Svensson, he shrugged her away and accelerated towards Jackson who blatantly ignored his command. Jackson's face twisted into a contorted mass of fury and struck Robert Sandburg down. He collapsed to the deck, stunned into silence. Tom ran over to help.

"Jesus Christ bananas!" Rood shouted, jerking his head as the word spat from his mouth and stared at Tom who joined him.

"He has issues," Tom said.

"He'll have more than issues when I'm finished with him!"

Maria Mansdotter—a pretty woman in her late twenties—shrieked when Jackson grabbed her, held her in a tight embrace, and forced his mouth onto hers. A shout of shock and outrage exploded on the deck.

Rood ripped Jackson away from the hysterical woman. "God rot your black ass!"

Maria Mansdotter's hands clawed as they came to her mouth, wiping and trying to scrub it clean. Then the wretched shrieking began. A mob instantly formed on the deck.

"We have a situation," Rood hissed.

"You think?" Tom said with a thick dosage of cynicism.

While Tom wrestled with Jackson, Rood took a walkie-talkie and barked into it. "Alert, alert, on deck!"

The crowd churned with outrage and the melee became louder, malignant. Robert Sandburg got up from the deck, and backed up by two tons of hellfire, grinned, showing several holes where teeth once lived and uttered death threats. Sandburg lunged for Jackson, his hands outstretched for the kill.

Tom released Jackson and charged to intercept, at first restraining Sandburg, but the enraged mob carried him back. The ship's crew joined in and the outrage swelled across the decks like a tsunami. They kept advancing, their faces wild with the intoxicated frenzy of mob insanity. Tom felt himself going down. He clung on to Sandburg's shirt, fearing they would trample him to death.

The imitation Remington Navy revolver flashed in Rood's hands. He fired four consecutive shots into the air and then pointed it right at Sandburg's face. Rodriguez hurled from the steerage with an unconcealed MP5 carbine. He fired over ten rounds into the air, scaring the bejappers out of the riot. The mob fell apart. First Sandburg and four others peeled off the edges, the rest fell back as the remaining soldiers poured on deck with carbines. Rood still had to contend with a horseshoe of extreme unpleasantness.

Liedberg wiggled through the crowd. "Your Negro Jackson has blasphemed the woman. She is forever polluted! I will have him flogged and chained!"

"You may chain Mr. Jackson until I say he is to be released. There will be no flogging."

"They will mutiny, Colonel, if they are not satisfied."

Rood marked Jackson with a look of disgust. Under any other circumstance his look would have frozen Jackson solid with terror, but this was not any other circumstance and it was Rood who felt the bolt of fear.

"I will permit five days in chains. After Jackson is released, I'll have him confined to quarters until our arrival in New York. He will have limited access on deck."

"Very well." He called Lars Göran Rödin to escort Jackson to the chains. It took about half an hour until the mood had placated to anything close to normal. Rodriguez collected the spent cartridges ejected from his carbine and tossed them overboard.

Rood put his hand on Tom's shoulder. "You did good, Barney."

"He completely lost it."

"Can't his people just stay away from our women? What is it with them? Being aboard a ship with so many blondes must heat his primeval African blood to a boil. Damn bastards, you never see white men pursue black women with such gusto as they do ours."

"I dated a couple of black women."

Rood's face looked like an obscene phone call. "I hope they were hot."

"One was sizzling," said Tom. "The other, not so much—just liked her."

"Your sister ever date a black man?"

"Not that I know of."

"What would have your big brother instincts have done had she come home with one?"

Tom didn't like the direction or where this discussion was heading. *Damn Americans and their damn race issues.* Rood may be a racist, but he was also Tom's only ride back home, *so keep the personal feelings out of the conversation.* "Based on some of the trash she was bringing home, a nice, clean-cut black guy would have been an upgrade. She had a habit of going for the bad boys."

"She's one of those girls?"

"Oh, ya. A few years back, I bought her a T-shirt for Christmas that read *I only date losers* and that didn't go over so well."

Rood grinned. "That's the problem, Trasler. Women have lost their way. They need to be protected."

"Or just kicked in the ass. I eventually beat the crap out of one loser boyfriend and told another to lose her phone number."

Rood looked at the decks, still concerned about the mood of the passengers.

"Damn that Tyrone. Look at everybody. They're totally traumatised. Do you blame them? One of their women getting kissed by a black man? We're not talking about women we know, Trasler, these are 1848 women. Getting kissed by a black man is the end of the world for them. She's considered permanently contaminated."

Tom looked at the woman, surrounded by other women, and the trauma was no less than if she had lost a child. "She's taking it bad, alright."

"Christ Almighty, if Jackson is this high strung about racism on an emigrant ship, just wait until we tour the great Confederacy."

"Confederacy?"

"Old South, Barney—The Confederate States of America."

"If my history is correct, we're thirteen years away from the Civil War. Why did you call it the Confederacy?"

"Your history is damn correct. I'm a Virginian, Trasler. The Civil War and the CSA have always been a fascination for me."

"You should speak to Ralph. He's a huge Civil War buff. He even goes on those battle re-enactments. He has an authentic Rebel uniform and a real black powder musket."

"Really?"

"Oh, ya."

"We'll have to have a chat!" Rood's face collapsed, and he looked drained, like half the life had just been sucked out of him. "You always hear it, Trasler, how the United States of America has never lost a war.

But, if you are a southern man, you have lost a war. I don't think many people understand to what degree that impacts Southerners."

"I didn't realize that. I guess our friend Jackson is interested in the Civil War: The war to free the slaves."

"That's crap. Five Union states were slave states."

"Hang on a second. Five states that were on the North's side were slave states?"

"You got it, Barney, and you can be sure that those five states weren't fighting to free the slaves. Another detail most don't get, is that when Lincoln freed the slaves with the Emancipation Proclamation in 1863, that only applied to the slaves in the breakaway states in rebellion, not the five Border States."

"I thought he freed all the slaves?"

"Nope, just those in the Confederacy. It was more a military tactic to have slaves flee to Union forces, and disrupt the economy, than heeding to the call of freedom."

"Really?"

"Really," Rood countered. "The balance of slaves were only freed with the Thirteenth Amendment late in 1865—after Lincoln was dead and buried. Lincoln is considered the greatest president of all time, but if he was alive today, he'd be labled a bigot for his views on blacks. Slavery had a lot less to do with the war than most people realize, at least the start of it. Even Lincoln said it was to preserve the Union, not to free the slaves. Robert E Lee and Thomas Jackson fought the Federal Army because they were men of honour who loved their native Virginia and viewed the Federal forces as invaders. General Longstreet is my idol. One of the most amazing personalities of the great Confederacy and the most brilliant general of the entire Civil War. He was dead-set against Picket's Charge at Gettysburg, which sealed the fate of the Southern cause. If he was in command and not Lee, we probably wouldn't have lost our Second War of Independence. It's a fascinating period in our history."

"Okay, I know this is classified and my lips are sealed. Can you at least give me a hint of why you deliberately travelled to the past?"

He slapped Tom on the side of his arm. "To save the women." Tom grinned a little uncertainly, not having a clue what *saving the women* meant. However, this was the first time Rood hinted anything of the nature of their mission. Despite his evasion, Tom's gut told him that it had everything to do with the Confederate States of America. Rood said something else that stood the hair up on his arms—*the great Confederacy,* and, *we wouldn't have lost our Second War of Independence.*

But what the hell was *to save the women* all about?

MAY 19, 1848

Another death from the steerage interrupted Tom's second English class of the day. The twelve year-old girl from Småland, who had been sick since he came aboard, withered away and died. For a while, it appeared the worst was over, but the poor thing was too weak to recover. Though Tom never got to know her, the dismal splash of such a young body set his mind off into a psychological rant about the unfairness of life.

These things happen.

The following day, Liedberg found himself staring with contempt at the limp canvas. The wind stirred the sails but could not bell them. The ocean was as still as a body of its size could be, so calm that two women sat on the top of the bulwark next to the main mast's lanyards, their bare feet dangling over the side of the ship. Despite it being a sunny day, the air was cool. Men were in vests, heavy shirts and wearing their caps or brimmed hats. Women dressed in thick sweaters or coats, most with kerchiefs patterned in red, blue and green, their hair tied back or braided while the more upscale women boasted fancy hats, dresses and footwear well beyond the means of the majority of the others.

Women mended clothing, some knit while others washed laundry in tiny vessels barely large enough to cook in. One combed her child's hair with a brass comb, then squished the lice on a clay tablet. A man with a walrus moustache entertained a crowd with a melodeon. Tom somehow recognised the melody, though couldn't put a name to it. The ship's sailmaker, Sten Lindblad, a wiry man in his thirties with a long pointed beard, sat on the deck, splicing rope, keeping time to the sing-song tune hummed by one of the other sailors.

The constant whine of children and babies crying was unrepentant. There were always babies crying—morning, noon and night. Up on the decks, below in the 'tweendecks, in the berths, babies crying and toddlers whining. It was torturous.

A chantey came from the shrouds as sailors swung high overhead through the rigging like Tarzans. Olsson stood by the bulwark smoking a pipe. He was in his late twenties, clean-shaven with a thick head of curly sandy hair like Larry of *The Three Stooges.* As with Polman, the passengers liked him, and he often joined them dancing on the deck. Rood's crew was rarely seen, but then, with a library of films, porn and computer games, as well as climate controlled fresh air, who needed to kill time on the decks?

Liedberg wiggled through the crowd to meet Tom at amidships. "The tillers-of-dirt crawl upon my deck like a plague of locusts!"

"I've never seen the decks so crowded, but the stench is getting really bad down there."

Liedberg shook his head, clearly agitated. "To think some vessels are designed from the keel to her decks specifically for this unpleasant, filthy living cargo. Many hundreds of the tillers-of-dirt who have never seen a body of water larger than a rain puddle. What captain would wish to command such an abomination? If these peasants had been as busy in tilling their soil as they had been toiling in their bedrooms, there would have been no need to emigrate!"

"Got the key?"

"Yes. Follow me."

Tom followed Liedberg to the forecastle into the cramped crew's quarters. At the far end, a hatch led directly into the hold, immediately forward from the bulkhead of Rood's office. Liedberg, holding an oil lantern, led the way down the long, steep ladder. They reached the lower hold, containing the ship's stores and passengers' belongings. After a brief search, Tom found his luggage.

Looking through both of Carol's suitcases, he found precisely what he sought—a light cotton nightie and some pyjamas. The balance of lingerie was definitely too daring for a modest woman of this time period. Astounded by how many pairs of underwear she packed for just a two-week trip, he grabbed a few then rummaged through the bras. They were a mélange of red, green, white, blue, purple and pink. He selected one white and another black. She had enough delicates to open an upscale lingerie shop. There were also three bikinis and he had no idea why when one would have sufficed. *Was this the wardrobe of a millionaire's daughter or what?*

On deck, Tom squirmed through the masses. He searched through the crowd and found Alvina-Kristina sitting on the galleyhouse's front bench, holding Edvard, snoozing quietly within his cocoon of blankets. She was mending Sune's pants.

"Do you have a minute below?" Tom patted his travelling bag. "I have a present for you."

Seeing the expectant look on Tom's face, her eyes lit up. She noticed his freshly shaven face and could smell his aftershave. A gleam entered her eyes. She handed Tom the baby. Edvard gazed up at Tom, big round eyes and broke into a wide, toothless grin. It broke Tom's heart knowing the poor kid was on such a brief tour of life. He smiled back and Edvard broke into a giggle.

"He never laugh like that." Tom impressed Alvina-Kristina with his charms. But then, the little girls often played with him. He was a man who adored children. Alvina-Kristina waved over Selma-Olivia, who squirmed through the bustling deck and took Edvard. She loved her nephew as if he was her own child and never refused Alvina-Kristina for his care.

It took a moment for their eyes to adjust from the naked sunlight to the gloom of the steerage—a longer adjustment to acclimatize to the raw stench. They stepped off the stairs into the midst of a vicious argument raging between two women that was degenerating into an all out catfight. Their exasperated husbands tried to break them up, though they separated the two, neither stopped the screaming and accusations.

"Lice," Alvina-Kristina said, then raised her voice a notch. "They are pigs from Småland. They cannot not bear to part with their precious vermin."

One, an Olive Oyl of a woman, blamed the other—a white version of Queen Latifah—for the lice. The white Queen Latifah countered by opening her shirt, intent on showing how lice-free she was—and displaying her rather imposing breasts by doing so—and it would have been a splendid striptease had her husband not intervened. The seven or eight men watching—Tom included—had a brief moment of high expectations, then silent disappointment.

"The only people who died or who are sick are from Småland." Although Alvina-Kristina said this in spite, she made an interesting observation. There were nine people who were critically ill and all were from Småland, a province south of Östergötland. Johannes Christoffersson, and the twelve year-old girl who died, were from the same tribe.

Once in their family area, Tom closed the curtains, but not completely. That would set off the alarms in a hurry. He smiled broadly. "Sit."

Alvina-Kristina sat on the lower berth, smiling expectantly. He tugged out Carol's ivory nightie. It had a decorated pattern of flowers along the collar and the short sleeves. Her face lit up like the sun emerging from a large, dark rain cloud.

"It opens at the front so you can still nurse the baby. It only goes down to here," he pointed to his thigh, "so you'll show a lot of leg. If there is a problem with that," he took out the pyjamas, "this has a top and a bottom and are really comfortable."

She took them, slowly as if they might shatter, and caressed her cheeks with them. He could see her eyes moisten with tears. The eyes dimmed and she shook her head, handing them back. "I cannot take these. Sune will be much mad."

Tom held up his hands, refusing to take them back. "Carol obviously has no further use for them." He plunged into the aquamarine of her eyes. "They're yours." She perked up, a mischievous grin twitched at the corners of her mouth and she put them aside. After a moment of further rummaging, Tom tossed her three pairs of underwear, then dangled a black laced bra before her.

"What is that?" she asked and giggled.

Tom showed on himself how it fit. "Put it on," he urged.

Alvina-Kristina blushed furiously. Tom smiled with perhaps too much affection, risqué as it could be construed as improper etiquette, especially by 1848 standards, but Alvina-Kristina's smile became a mirror of his own. He left the family area and closed the canvas curtain. The argument between the two women erupted again. *How was it humanly possible that the Olive Oyl woman, a tiny broomstick, could have rock concert decibels roaring from such miniscule vocal chords?* He heard Alvina-Kristina cry for help and he slipped back through. She astounded him by allowing him to see her back fully exposed.

"How do you do these up?"

"I'm not sure. I usually take them off."

She gave Tom a naughty kind of giggle while he connected the bra. She turned around. It was just her and the bra. Tom's eyes swept appreciably over the contours of her breasts, the perfectly positioned cleavage. The bra never looked this good on Carol.

"Is this okay?" Her voice was low and confidential. The sound of it affected him in a way that was both uncomfortable and excruciatingly pleasant. She gave him a slow, dark smile and he felt giddy like a teenage boy on his first date. Tom took a couple deep breaths to get his pulse back under control.

"It is," he stammered, "a perfect fit."

"I like it!" A large and guilty smile stretched her lips. For a moment he thought she was about to kiss him, and in that single shining moment of extremely reckless judgement, he would have permitted it.

Alvina-Kristina's face went blank. She clasped her hands together as a shudder twisted through her body. The content smile faltered on Tom's lips.

He knew by the woman's large, terrified doe eyes hovering before him, that whatever lurked behind was not a good thing.

Not a good thing at all.

The creaking oak planking betrayed Captain Liedberg's anger as he moved to within inches from Tom's face. "I spoke of this matter to Colonel Rood and he has given me full discretion in this outrage." Tom could feel the fear drip into the deep hollows of his body like acid on skin. "You have flagrantly disregarded my orders concerning any indiscretions with the women!"

"All I did was to give Alvina the undergarments that you and I spoke of, where you escorted me into the hold to fetch."

"Silence! Did I give you permission to speak?" Tom shut his mouth with a clunk of his molars. Liedberg backed off, put his back to Tom for a moment of contemplation, then spun around. "Your eyes have set-upon the nakedness of Alvina-Kristina Gabrielsson. She is forever ruined!"

Tom remained silent.

"Speak, Trasler."

"She was not naked. She showed me the undergarments to see if they fit as they should."

"Did they?"

"Yes, most definitely, yes. Superbly in fact. That's a hellova good looking woman." Tom cusped his hands before his chest, indicating large breasts. "She's really well built."

"Enough!"

"I saw far more of her breasts when she was wearing that disgusting nightshirt than with the new under garments. And it's not as if she's the first half-naked woman I've ever seen, sir. I've seen about five pair of bare-naked breasts since I came aboard. Mostly women nursing their kids and those undressing without their curtains completely closed. We're packed in the steerage like sardines, Captain, and every now and then, we catch each other undressing, washing or going for a crap or playing with ourselves. Inevitable and it's just part of the daily routine."

"What shall we do about this daily routine, Trasler?"

"If it will satisfy Sune Gabrielsson, then put me in chains." Tom didn't snort, but was pretty close to it.

Tom did not expect to find himself on the loft, with his wrists shackled in the heavy iron cuffs. He thought the captain pulled a joke on him when he ordered Polman to escort him to the loft. Polman blew out the lantern, taking his own with him. Tom could only watch the shadows stretch and recede until nothing but the darkness surrounded him. It wasn't so bad. He had his own spot and his back felt fine this time around. No Sune-butts pressing against his thigh. No point blank farts. The air stank but not close to the stench of the steerage.

A scurrying sound. The type produced by tiny feet. A skittering through the cargo and supplies not a yard from his feet. *Rats!* The scurrying returned, a little closer now, impossible to tell how near. A hop. He could feel it land on his loft. His breathing stopped. *It crawled over his ankle!* He could feel the naked skin of the feet, the tiny claws, the fur of its belly, the course stubble of its tail. Tom recoiled with a kick. The rat would have been launched into orbit had it not been for the ceiling above arresting its upward motion. The rodent ricocheted off, crashed onto something covered in canvas and scurried off.

Ten minutes of ghastly silence crawled by. Only the creaking of the timbers and the groaning wood of the keel filled the emptiness. Then it came back. The pitter-patter of tiny feet. More than one. It sounded like an entire rat nation as their nails scraped against wood and canvas as they climbed up over the clutter. Then came the gnawing sounds, some in front, to his right, to his left. The rapid grinding of rodents' teeth, surrounded him in the blackness. They went on for hours.

Tom sat bug-eyed in the dark, the hairs along the nape of his neck turning into hackles.

CHAPTER 14

MAY 21, 1848

After a sleepless night in the chains, Liedberg reinstated Tom back in the steerage just in time for the Sunday services. The critical tension between Tom and Sune was intense and Sune smouldered with ill temper. Tom thought it best to avoid him, and after Liedberg's dire warning, had been extra cautious with Alvina-Kristina as well. She wore her best dress for the services—with the bra. *Boy, did she look great.* Many other men thought she looked great and she attracted many silent accolades.

That afternoon, Tom delighted a crowd of children with another puppet show using their woollen dolls as the principle characters. Their giggles filled the decks, bringing smiles to the others. Rood and Ralph stood next to the front steerage hatch, they were not smiling, and in whispers, shared their concerns.

"He's getting far too close to the passengers, Parker," Rood warned. "This is going to create a hell of a problem if this isn't checked."

MAY 22, 1848

The water purled around the ship's hull like a gentle, slow running brook. The sails flapped back and forth against the masts. The canvas hadn't caught a wind in two days. Since the western route of the Atlantic crossing headed into the Gulf current, they could very well be moving backward towards Sweden. Catharina prepared salted herring for lunch, which Tom found so revolting he declined his portion and elected to cook his own swill. He stood behind Anne-Sophie and the two were chatting away in half understood conversations. She was unquestionably one of his best students and a great source of pride to Tom.

"Anne-Sophie!" Lars Göran Rödin's voice invaded the galleyhouse and he followed his voice inside. It was a tight fit for the three and the rank smell of liquor on his breath could kill a flock of starlings.

"Hey buddy, you're inside my personal space. Back off."

The mate stood for a moment, taunting Tom to continue his protest, then turned to Anne-Sophie with a T-Rex grin. He snatched her food basket and rummaged through it. She shrieked back while clutching the other half of her basket in a lopsided tug of war.

Lars Göran Rödin was a big man, and Anne-Sophie might be five-foot-three, pregnant, but she was no helpless damsel in distress. She flashed the cutting knife at Rödin. The mate chuckled fearlessly, daring her to attack. A knife attack would not be a good thing, so Tom shoved Rödin into the wall of the galleyhouse.

Rödin glared at Tom, stunned of his gall. Tom showed even more gall when he slapped Rödin across the face with a resounding smack. He backed out of the galleyhouse, grinning, his fingers motioning Rödin to follow. The mate released the basket and took two thundering steps forward. Anne-Sophie actually took a half-hearted swing with the knife, the other half-determined enough that she grazed his shirt.

The mate, drunk and slow, attacked with a right hook. Tom easily avoided it by ducking his head down and to the left. Rödin swung with such force that he couldn't help but follow his fist. Twirling and stumbling, Rödin caught his balance. Tom raised his fists, grinning. Excited passengers and crewmen stampeded over to watch the fight. As the cheering crowd circled them, Rödin paused to hock some phlegm over the bulwarks, grinned and stepped towards Tom. He swung again, grazing the side of Tom's head.

Tom stumbled back, shaking off the blow. "You're dead meat!" Tom drew his finger across his neck in a cutthroat gesture, raised his fists and closed in.

"Mr. Trasler!" Liedberg roared. A six pointer, that one.

"One moment, Captain, I'm about to beat the living daylights out of your asshole first mate."

"You will immediately arrest your actions!" He repeated his order in

Swedish. Rödin obeyed immediately and lowered his fists. Liedberg ordered the mate to stand behind him.

"He tried to steal food from Anne-Sophie," Tom said, his fists still raised and balled.

The volatile mob circled them. Anne-Sophie repeated the accusation, inflaming the rage. There were other accusations of bullying and theft by the crew.

Tom lowered his fists to his sides. His arms hung limply, but his hands remained balled. "The next time that asshole lays a hand on me or harasses any of the passengers, I'll give him the thrashing of his life."

"Lay a hand in anger against any of my crew and I'll throw you in chains."

"Then throw me in chains!"

"Best if you calm yourself, Trasler."

The mate's forearms were tensing as he locked his arms together, glaring at Tom with his dull blue eyes. Tom gave him the finger, licked it crudely and thrust it forward. Rödin lurched forward. Tom raised his fists, gesturing Rödin to go for it, and for a moment, it almost went down. Liedberg grabbed the material of Rödin's shirt and stopped him.

Tom spoke to the captain, still staring into the mate's eyes, the fighting lust still eager. "I'll calm down, but let me say one thing, with all due respects, sir, this is the last time he'll ever steal from the passengers or bully anyone. And, if it's a flogging and the chains that I'll get," his face grew defiant and determined and his voice growled, like he needed to clear his throat. "Then I'll make bloody well certain that by the time I get through with this maggot, it will be well worth the price."

Rödin broke eye contact and curled his hand into a fist, admiring the ridge of muscle in his thick forearms, then glanced over his fist and his eyes challenged Tom's, presenting a tableau of unregenerated hate. Tom gave him the finger with both hands now, grinning and smirking in contempt at Rödin's intimidations. No one had ever seen the finger used in that manner, but it looked funny and a ripple of laughter rumbled from the passengers. A teenage boy mimicked Tom and his mother slapped his hand. Tom wasn't scared of Rödin, and the mate was used to being feared. This wasn't sitting well with him and the laughter from the passengers enraged him.

Liedberg clamped his lips at Tom's boldness and contempt. Tom appreciated Liedberg's concerns. A passenger retaliating against the crew would set a dangerous precedent. The mate and cook were both despised and it wouldn't take much for other passengers to join in. Revenge could spread, control lost. This could degenerate into much more than just a personal dispute. Tom felt at peace with the consequences. *Completely.*

"Colonel Rood has given me full liberty with your discipline, Trasler. Lay a hand on my mate, or any of my crew, and I'll have you lashed with the cat-o-nine-tails delivered by the mate himself. Then it's the chains with bread and water for the remainder of the voyage."

Tom's shoulders slumped as he released the anger from his body and made a concerted effort to lower the sound of his voice. "Why do you allow your first mate to bully the passengers?"

"They, and even you, must be kept in line. When I first carried the tillers-of-dirt, I was lenient. They became unruly as time went by, aggravated by boredom and by foul food and rank water. One must deliver an iron hand early in the voyage and remind the tillers-of-dirt from time to time that mine is the sole authority on the water."

"How about theft?" Tom challenged, his voice returning to stridence.

"There will be no further theft," Liedberg said in a blessedly rational tone of voice and ordered the mate, along with the second-mate Polman, into his cabin.

It took about ten minutes for the excitement to settle down. People were soon about their business and Tom returned to the galleyhouse. Delighted by Tom's intervention, Anne-Sophie sang away. She cut up some salted pork on a ledge on the right side of the galley. This proved to be the most disgusting smelling meals offered by the ship's fare and the grease was this revolting yellow goop. She constantly glanced at Tom, smiling boldly. He smiled back, his mind still lingering on the terminated fight, frustrated by the captain's intervention.

She shocked him with a resounding smooch on the cheek.

The following day, another name was added to the passenger manifest. Karin and Carl August Nilsson gave birth to their fourth child. Two days later, the Captain led the baptism ceremony, bestowing the infant his name. Following seafaring tradition, the child was named after the ship's master—Olof Liedberg Nilsson.

The captain then outraged the assembly by announcing the child will cost Karin and Carl August Nilsson twenty-five riksdalers for passage. "You believed your child could have free passage aboard my vessel by smuggling him in your womb, but Providence has intervened in your dishonest schemes and the child is now a paying passenger aboard this vessel!"

Following the baptism, sailors swabbed the deck and sang their chanteys while one of the passengers entertained a good-sized crowd with his fiddle. Carina Svensson leaned against the windward bulwark, the wind whipped her hair and scoured her face. Tom too, enjoyed the weather. The sun's heat felt so good and refreshing.

The captain marched right for Tom, and he wondered what today's chewing out would be all about. "Come to my cabin." Carina Svensson, also curious, watched intently as Tom followed the captain like an apprehended thief into his cabin.

The brilliant sun peered through the aft windows and lit up the modest cabin. Ralph sat in a chair at the table, his arm still in a sling, and motioned for Tom to take a seat.

"So what's up?"

Liedberg's eyes glittered expectantly. He reached to the floor and grunted as he picked up a huge wooden bucket by its iron handle. He rolled up his white sleeve, reached into the water, paused and stared at Tom.

"It's time for a distraction from your personal woes." To Tom's delight, the captain held up a bottle of beer, the same ones he'd confiscated many weeks ago. He handed him one.

"Now that's a surprise!" Tom rotated the bottle, admiring it, seeing it as a long lost link to his banished existence.

"Captain Parker suggested I chill them in seawater."

"Good call, Ralph. What's the occasion?"

"I know you're supposed to be on the wagon, Tom, so we're limiting it to a single beer. We figured we needed time to chill."

"I'll drink to that." Tom opened the twist top bottles and he passed them out to first Liedberg, then Ralph. His nostrils dilated at the wonderful aroma fizzing out.

"I have never seen bottles such as these, Mr. Parker."

"They are ahead of their time," Ralph said with a ball of laughter tumbling out of his throat.

"Captain, it's been too long since I've tasted the nectar of the gods." Tom raised his bottle in a toast. "To your health."

"To the health of Captain Parker."

"How is that arm?" Tom asked.

"Useless as a limp dick."

"Nothing?"

He shook his head. "Barely any sensation."

The three bottles clinked together and Tom took a sip. It wasn't just his first beer since stepping aboard this century, it had been over two years since he had one. But one beer wouldn't harm him and Tom closed his eyes while the ale flowed down a throat burned and ravaged by poor nutrition. In all his thirty-three years, he never savoured a beer as much as he did right then. He leaned back and a contented sigh escaped from his lips. He held the moment, savouring it.

"Your brother-in-law has expressed concern over your affections of the passengers, specifically the children and the Gabrielsson woman."

Tom took a copious sip of the beer. "This conversation will cost you a second beer, Ralphy."

"Tom, listen to reason. Once off the ship, we're never going to see any of the passengers again. Don't make the goodbyes any harder than they need to be."

The captain finished his bottle, reached into the tub and opened another. "Your friendship towards the wife of Sune Gabrielsson is causing him much duress, and I am sympathetic to his angst."

"Alvina is hot, Tom, no arguments there, but she's a married woman!"

Tom took a couple of sips, closed his eyes to put his full attention to the flavour and the feeling of it flowing down his throat. *This has to be better than sex.* "We're just friends. And the kids? Come on, they're a delight."

"Rood expressed his concerns, Tom. You know the reason why."

"Ralphy, if Rood is so worried about me getting attached to the passengers, then he should have put me up in the office."

"No room. You'd have to share a berth."

"Ya, put me with Bodmar, that would be harmless enough."

"I do not understand," Liedberg said.

Tom finished his beer and motioned for another, and Liedberg passed him one, with Ralph eyeing his disapproval but not saying a word. "Sharon prefers to be romantic with other women, not men, so putting me in bed with her would be risk-free."

Liedberg chuckled. "These very eyes have seen women kiss and fondle each other. There is a gentleman's club in Rotterdam which has such a show . . . if you pay the right coin. A splendid sight!"

"To lesbians!" Tom raised his bottle. They shared a lewd exchange of chuckles and savoured more of the beer. "Will you please tell me when we'll arrive in New York?"

"It is tradition for the ship's master not to divulge the position of the ship! I am not one to break with tradition! I can tell you that progress has been cursedly slow. Tell me, Captain Parker, how many vessels does your enterprise possess?"

"Not my enterprise." Ralph chuckled a bittersweet laugh while he sipped on his beer.

"His family has been in the shipping business for years, but he's shown no interest in it," Tom explained.

"Yes, he has mentioned that to me."

"My mother's husband stole it from our family," Ralph said. "And I have virtually no experience in running a shipping line."

"Your step father?" Liedberg asked.

"I don't refer to that son-of-a-bitch as my father in any way, Captain." Tom never heard Ralph speak so poorly of Glenn, a man he admired a great deal. "My father died when I was a child and Glenn Parker just took over the company, even before he married my mother. He dismantled it, sold off the ships and now we just book space on other people's ships."

"You hold much bitterness, Captain."

"To put it mildly."

Tom felt quite uncomfortable, as he and Glenn forged a very close relationship. His own father passed away just before he and Carol got engaged and Glenn had been like a second father, very supportive and generous.

"If I got into the business," Tom began, manoeuvring away from Ralph's malice, "I wouldn't carry tillers-of-dirt, that's for damn sure."

Liedberg chuckled and toasted Tom with the bottle of beer. "How much does a new ship cost?"

Crow's feet creased about Liedberg's eyes as he wistfully smiled. "A new thousand ton packet will go for $40,000. A fifteen hundred ton beast will run $50,000. Not an insignificant amount of investment, yet, if run properly, an investment that would be paid off in just three to four years."

Tom finished his second beer, staring wantonly at the empty bottle. Those beers went fast.

"I have some brännvin, Trasler, should you desire another drink."

"Actually, that bottle of vodka you confiscated from us would really hit the spot."

"No!" Ralph stared hard at the captain. "Once he starts with the liquor, he won't stop for weeks."

"I regret, Trasler, I will heed to Captain Parker's caution."

Tom glared unkindly at Ralph, then looked at Liedberg. "Who owns this ship?" Tom asked.

"It is a family venture," Liedberg said. "Regrettably, I have two brothers of senior age. I may be the master of the ship, but I have little control over its business affairs, hence the tillers-of-dirt. I for one, have asked for a water tank and fresh water for the passengers, and have been rebuked."

Tom put the empty beer bottle down. He really wanted a third. "You really need to change the name of the ship. The *Margaretha* sucks. Where did that ugly name come from?"

The captain's nose flared. "My mother!"

AUGUST 21, 2016

PASADENA, CA

Cosmo ran a series of algorithms in an attempt to model the exit paths of the temporal events, and the lack of success frustrated him. The exit point was not a single spot like the entry—rather, it ran a long S-shaped route stretching potentially over 200 kilometers.

He glanced over at Jennifer and she seemed consumed by her computer. Just staring at it. He stood behind her, peeked down her loosely buttoned blouse admiring her frilly red bra, then back to her computer monitor. It was a Facebook page.

"Who's that?"

"Tom Trasler. Trying to learn as much as I can about him."

"You were doing that all day yesterday."

"And when I got home."

"What's your verdict?"

"His sister has done a nice job making him a Facebook memorial. He had a lot of friends. Had a rough time over the years—alcohol and drug addiction, but had been clean for the last two and was into industrial real estate."

Cosmo looked at a picture of Tom with long hair and a beard. "Whoa, is that him?"

"Ya," she replied with a troubled sigh. "Four years ago. His nickname at work was *Stoner.* Even his boss called him that."

"What was his job?"

"Loading trucks."

"Loading trucks and he had a degree in engineering?"

"Ya, and it says here he couldn't keep that job because of drugs." She looked at Cosmo. "You two would have gotten along great."

"I don't do drugs."

"Ya, right."

"I don't."

"There is no way you'll ever convince me you haven't done drugs. You speak Klingon and call people *Dude.* It's a known fact, that anyone who calls someone *Dude,* smokes weed!"

"I call people *Dude* because it's cool."

"It's anything but cool—it's drug-laden. You've never even tried?"

"No."

"BS, Cosmo, everyone tries weed."

"You've tried weed?"

"Ya, like in Grade 10."

"You've smoked weed?" Roberts asked. "Hey everyone, Jennifer's smoked marijuana!"

"On my Lord, I can't believe you just said that!"

All at once, everyone coalesced around her desk. "Miss Burke, this is distressful."

"None of you have ever tried weed?"

"It's against the law," Roberts said.

"Scranton's smoked weed," she said. "He's had to."

"Do I look that stupid?"

"That will explain all of Jennifer's errors," Roberts said. This wasn't a joke. He was dead serious.

"That will explain a lot more than just her errors," Scranton said. "Your poor brain cells!"

"I can't believe you're a pothead," Cosmo said.

"I'm not a pothead! I just tried it for a couple of years."

"Couple of years? That's not trying, that's an addiction!" Roberts said.

"Indeed," Fleming agreed. "We perhaps should consult a specialist on Miss Burke's behalf." Fleming was quite distressed.

"Oh my Lord, you people are crazy! It's just weed, and I haven't smoked-up since high school."

"It will explain so much." Scranton shook his head pitiably.

"We need to keep an eye on her," Roberts said to Scranton. "I can't believe we have a recovering drug addict in our group."

"I was not an addict!" She scrolled down the Facebook page. Tom, with the exception of a red cape and sneakers and a strategically placed pixelization, ran naked with a crowd of thousands looking on.

"Streaker!" Cosmo said. "Have you ever streaked, Jennifer?"

"No, I have not! You?"

"Just once."

"You streaked? Oh my Lord, that would have been too funny to watch!"

"It wasn't funny," Cosmo said. "I learned the hard way to never streak when you're cold."

"Uh-huh." She turned to the Facebook page. "Tom Trasler went streaking right in front of the Queen of England. Why would the queen be visiting Canada?"

"Maybe because she's their queen?" Cosmo said.

"Canada has a queen?"

"Your geography sucks!"

"I'm a physicist, not a geography teacher."

"You're really sure you still want to risk going back in time to rescue him? Like he's not the poster boy for clean-cut," Roberts said.

"More than ever. He's an interesting fellow. Besides," she glanced at her naked finger, "I want my ring back."

Roberts went to his desk, returned and dropped a brass coloured coin on her desk. She picked it up and noticed the queen on the back of it. "Canadians call their dollar coins loonies."

"Loonie?" She flipped the coin over and saw a bird on the water.

"That's a loon," Roberts explained. "Their two dollar coin is called a toonie."

"It has two loons, I suppose?"

"A polar bear."

She slapped her hand on her desk. "How do you get *toonie* from a polar bear?"

Roberts shrugged a big *I don't know.*

"Why don't they just use two loonies instead of making another coin? That's crazy."

"And Canada uses the metric system for everything," Roberts said with a tease.

"Thank the Lord I'm an American!"

MAY 24, 1848

After the final English class of the day, Tom grew restless. He sat on the aft steps to observe the masses swarming on the decks. Alvina-Kristina held Edvard tightly as she weaved in and out to join him.

"Have you seen Selma-Olivia?" she asked Tom.

Tom hooked his thumb over his shoulder. "She's on the poop deck." Selma-Olivia was down in the dumps and just stared at the sea, trying to cope with this horrendous voyage. Alvina-Kristina looked irritated. She stared at Sune, sitting with some other men. They usually congregated together when one of them brought out a jug of brännvin.

"What's the matter?" asked Tom.

"I need to bathe."

Tom suspected she was having her period. The women never discussed their periods, a topic so sensitive it could endanger national security. Perhaps they did so when together, in secret whispers.

"I'll take care of Edvard."

She looked at him as if he was a little deranged, hunched her shoulders and giggled. "Thank you."

Tom cradled the baby in his arms. Edvard's eyes lit up. Alvina-Kristina saw that Edvard was in good hands and left below. Tom smiled at the baby, walked his fingers along his tummy to the neck and tickled him. His mouth opened in a big smile.

Tom closed in and rubbed noses. "Ninga-ninga-ninga-ninga!"

The kid giggled. Tom continued to walk his fingers on the tummy, stopping every once and a while to flutter his fingertips. More giggling.

"You're ticklish, eh?"

He unwrapped the kid's blanket that looked something like a baptism robe. Holding Edvard by the underarms, he gave some raspberries on the tummy. The kid howled in laugher. Tom, smiling, buried his mouth into the kid's tummy and repeated the raspberry, sounding like one of those squishy farts. Edvard laughed uncontrollably.

Tom froze when the thought bubbled through his mind and popped. *Congenital heart defect.* "Oooooh-kay, little feller, settle down!"

Edvard wasn't settling down. The kid could die laughing. Not the worst way of going, mind you, but how do you explain handing a dead baby who laughed himself to death back to its mother? Edvard finally stopped and held his hand out and squeezed Tom's index finger. He cradled Edvard in his right arm, the fingers still walking on his tummy, still fluttering him into little giggles.

The two had a nice little chat and enjoyed each other's company immensely for about twenty minutes. Edvard, however, grew restless. Tom could tell he wanted more raspberries.

"All right," Tom lowered his voice to a whisper, "don't die on me, now."

He peeled up the tiny shirt and cut loose. Big wet raspberries. Edvard's all out laughing exploded out of him.

Alvina-Kristina arrived and smiled broadly. "You'd make good mother."

"Thanks. I like babies."

"Do you have any children?"

"Nope." He did another nose rub. "Ninga-ninga-ninga-ninga!"

Both Edvard and Alvina-Kristina were giggling now. "You are thirty-three and have no children?"

"Carol and I talked about starting a family."

"You don't have babies by talking," she said and giggled. *He couldn't believe she said that.*

"We've only been married for six months. I wanted the children more than she does. Unfortunately, Carol was more worried about what having kids would do to her complexion, stretch marks, weight gain, and she's been struggling with her weight since I've met her."

He tickled the baby before handing it to Alvina-Kristina. Edvard started to fuss. Alvina-Kristina tried to quieten him, then the crying began, not just crying, but a full-fledged screaming, foot kicking temper tantrum. Alvina-Kristina looked indignant as Tom turned to leave.

"He likes raspberries on the tummy."

"What is that?"

Tom showed her one on the back of his hand.

Alvina-Kristina had no success in calming Edvard's temper. Not even raspberries would work, or all the love only a mother could provide. Edvard wanted only one thing—and that was Tom.

Rood arrived on deck, breathed in the fresh air and stretched his arms out. He noticed Tom staring over the bulwark. He gave Tom a hearty slap on the shoulder.

"Afternoon, Trasler."

Tom returned the greeting with deadpan eyes. "Afternoon."

"You look worn out."

"Rough night sleeping."

"You're sleeping in the same bed as two women, you lucky dog."

"No, I'm sleeping, and I say sleeping in a figurative sense, next to a smelly hull and a smellier hulk of a man, Colonel."

"I'm certain that you'll eventually get an opportunity."

"Not on this voyage. Right now, I would rather have some Chinese takeout than a woman."

"Don't torment yourself, Barney."

"There was a little pizza place not far from where I grew up. Still there, actually. They made one helluva pizza."

"Stay away from those thoughts!"

"Tell that to my stomach."

Rood glanced over at Catharina, tending to Stina-Sofia and Johanna. "Catharina, she's a hell of a woman, isn't she?"

"An Amazon," Tom replied and smiled. "Unfortunately, she doesn't exactly like me."

"Even with the fresh water you're providing every day? We even upped the rations for you."

"Could you imagine how much she'd hate me without the rations?"

"So why does she hate you?"

"She doesn't trust me, especially you guys, and of course, I'm too close to Alvina—don't you start either! I'm getting it from everyone!"

As if on cue, Alvina-Kristina walked on deck and she immediately caught Rood's attention. "What's different about her? She looks amazing lately."

"Victoria's Secret," Tom said with a wink.

"No, seriously," Rood said.

"I am serious. I gave her some of Carol's bras."

Rood glared unkindly at Tom. "You shouldn't have done that. It's against the rules."

Tom smirked. "You look at her again and tell me that's not a justifiable exemption."

Rood gave a roaring laugh and slapped Tom on the back. "Goddamn, it's great to be a time traveller, isn't it?" They were quiet for a moment, both doing a little girl watching. All at once, his face turned sullen and he stared at Tom critically. "You and the children get along quite well."

"I just had this same conversation with Ralph and Liedberg."

"You're having another."

"What's the big deal? I like kids. Always wanted some of my own."

"When push comes to shove, Barney, you have to back us. There might be a tough call against the passengers. You're getting too attached to them and it might cloud your loyalties."

Tom smiled back, but Rood's eyes were difficult to read. "My loyalty is to myself to get back home to Carol, so you have nothing to worry about when push comes to shove."

Rood slapped Tom on the arm. It showed respect. "Going to be a great day." Rood rubbed his hands. "Started off with a great bowel movement. Nothing better than starting the day with an amazing BM, wouldn't you say?"

"Can't say I can boast of the same thing."

"A bowel movement is highly underrated. It allows you entire body to relax. Take your time, don't force it, it's a vacation from the rest of the world. Just you and your bowels. One of life's great, under-appreciated pleasures."

Tom gave a wry smile. "I'm fed up of squatting and the lack of toilet paper."

"Trasler, I squat. It's far healthier and half the planet uses squatting toilets."

"How can you relax while squatting, especially on a ship that's rocking all over the goddamn place?"

"Squatting allows the body to do its work better than sitting on the throne. And don't read, for Chrissakes. Focus 100% on your body, meditate on the plumbing. As for toilet paper that you and I know of, it's actually a late 19th century item."

"Whoa! Hang on here. Are you telling me, that in all of the 6000 years of civilized humanity wiping their bums, the same civilizations who built the pyramids and the other Seven Wonders of the World, the Great Wall of China, the Roman Empire that conquered all of Europe, the same genius who had plumbing to have mock sea battles in the Roman Coliseum, the renaissance of Florence, the Sistine Chapel, the brilliance of Leonardo de Vinci, all of that and no one—I mean no one—came up with a no-brainer like toilet paper?"

"That about sums it up."

"So there's no toilet paper waiting for us when we get to shore?"

"I'm afraid not."

Tom shook his head in complete dismay. "No toilet paper and the women have hairy armpits. God help us all."

CHAPTER 15

MAY 24, 1848

Silver shrugged into his brown suit jacket, paused in front of a mirror and adjusted his collar and cravat. He took a squirt of breath freshener, put on a bowler-like hat, slipped out of the office and made his way to the poop deck. Directly overhead, the mizzenmast creaked from side to side, frustrated while seeking a firmer wind. Below it, Selma-Olivia stood by the aft bulwark, staring past the ship to the big sky above it. Silver weaved his way through the crowd to make his way to the aft railing. He stood three feet to the right of Selma-Olivia.

She didn't glance at him fully, but what sideways glances she did have for him showed more revulsion than indifference. He was a tiny man with a big nose and had hands smaller than most teenage boys. She wondered how a man's body could stop growing while allowing its nose to grow big enough for a giant.

From his jacket pocket, Jack Silver pulled out a chocolate bar. With deliberate care, he peeled back the wrapper and caught the young girl's attention. She had never seen anything like it. It was dark brown—the same colour of animal droppings—and didn't look like it was something she would wish to put in her mouth. The bridge of her nose wrinkled with curiosity. He gave a reassuring smile, broke off a piece of the milk chocolate and slipped it into his mouth.

He closed his eyes. "Mmmmmmmmm."

She licked her lips and cleared some strands of hair from her face. He broke off another piece, was about to put it in his mouth and then faced her. He extended it towards her. At first, she refused, shaking her head. Urged by his smile, she took it. Cautiously, she put it into her mouth.

The most fantastic ecstasy imaginable exploded in her mouth! It was the most wonderful sensation she ever experienced! As she swallowed it, the delight spread, filling her entire body with great joy, and even after, her mouth still held the exquisite taste.

A grin twitched on Silver's thin lips, flickering in little spasms.

Selma-Olivia burst into a smile as Silver took a piece for himself and after offered her another. The expression of divine bliss never left her face. She thought what a happy fate it would be to have nothing but this food for her sustenance. After finishing each piece, she licked her fingers clean. Each time she did, her eyes slipped closed and an expression of delight flooded throughout her entire being.

When finished, Silver smiled and she giggled with exhilaration. She felt just wonderful, as if the black poison of this wretched trip had been drained from her body. Mr. Silver was not a monster the passengers spoke of. He was full of gentleness and delicacy. He offered her a little wave as he returned to the office, she giving him a much larger one in return.

Jonas tapped Catharina as he watched Silver vanish below. "That godless runt sniffs at Selma-Olivia whenever I turn my back. He often snoops about, stalking her like a wolf. Stalking God's pure lamb."

Catharina regarded the teenager. She was smiling, untying her braids and let the wind blow through her tresses. She spun around with an endless smile, her hair levitating in the gentle currents. Catharina's face became withdrawn and stern.

"I will speak to her."

Catharina sat on deck with her darning needle, mending Jonas' black jacket. She tried to teach Stina-Sophia how to sew, but Johanna, restless and bored, made teaching difficult, so she gave her a lump of sugar to keep the girl quiet. Catharina noticed Selma-Olivia appear on deck, heading for the aft bulwark. That was her spot when she waited for Silver and his candy. Catharina interrupted the sewing, walked to her and tugged sharply on the teenager's sleeve.

"Round about us crawl the brood of Satan. Do not accept any favours from the vipers. They have no grace to give us. Do not accept any of their devil's food."

"It is so wonderful to taste. And Mr. Silver is not what you perceive. What a jolly fellow he is."

"One sins mostly when one has the most joy from sin. Stay away from him!"

MAY 26, 1848

"Chief, we've come across some odd readings," Bodmar reported. Rood closed in on her monitor. She pointed at a graph on her screen. "Going through a temporal wormhole is like walking through a door. We know the event is highly decelerated from our timeline perspective and even after we passed through, the door, figuratively speaking, is still not entirely shut. It's like looking through a sliver of a door not quite closed."

"In other words," Silver said, "we still had a glance at the other side after the event."

Rood looked confused. "What are the strange readings?"

Bodmar continued. "Just over twelve seconds after the termination of the event, we registered three very powerful temporal spikes, on the other side, close to shore."

"Three?" Rood's mind drifted until the thought snapped into focus. "Carol, Alice and Charlie?"

"We think so," Bodmar said, "but can't confirm it."

"And they occurred outside the zone, close to shore," Silver said.

"How is that possible?" Rood asked.

"There is no explanation," Silver said. "None."

"First, the three metallic objects in the water within the zone and now this. What the hell is going on?"

"The three objects weren't put there by us, or by the yacht," Bodmar said. "There is an unknown faction observing these events. As for the mysterious temporal spikes, if that was Carol, Alice and Charlie, that opens a whole other can of worms."

Tom entered the office for his daily water rations. Bodmar was calibrating the navigator and curious, Tom closed in. "Can I look?"

"You can look." It looked like a bulky laptop the size of a briefcase. "This plots our position using the data from the sun and star readings, as well as the current location of the magnetic poles, which drifts over the years. On land, two readings ten meters apart using the telescopic pole will give it a 3D reading of the topography and matches the location. It uses a version of Google-like maps, but military grade and also shows the roads and railroads that existed in any given year. It works like your car's navigator. It will plot out the best route with all the options, travel time, the estimated costs, the works. All our temporal rides home are programmed as well."

She touched the screen and a menu highlighted the date of the implosion and date of the arrival, along with detailed maps. After his brief tour, she motioned him away, deciding he had seen enough.

Tom noticed Silver watching a movie on his laptop with earphones, the speakers muted. It was an action film and a helicopter exploded in mid air—destroyed by a handgun.

Tom tapped Silver's shoulder. "Did that helicopter get shot down by a guy with a pistol?"

He took an earphone out. "Yes—Steven Seagal. He's an excellent shot."

"That explains it," Tom smirked. "What movie is this?"

"*Exit Wounds*. Great film. I have a large collection of his films on my computer. Steven Seagal is my favourite actor."

"Actor? That's being awfully generous."

Tom watched a bit of the film, wishing Silver would turn on the audio. Tom went to see Rodriguez who showed him some of the sketches. The detail was so fine, so precise, the drawings looked like photographs. Tom argued with a suspender as Carina Svensson stepped out of Rood's enclosed berth. She had a dirty little smile on her lips and wore a pretty green dress, showing just a bit of bosom. He wondered how long it took for her to dress and undress in the layers of silk, petticoats, corset and God knows what else they wore under those things. Regardless of his less than unlimited sentiments concerning her, she was a stunning sight. She was no back alley whore.

"Christ Almighty, that was good." Rood stepped out, buttoning up his blue uniform. "I'll tell you something, Barney, sex is alive and well in the Victorian era." Tom remained silent. "Like Carlos' drawings?"

"I'm impressed."

"The man has a photographic memory and can reproduce it on paper like a goddamn camera. He does the same things for a face. All he needs is a second or two and he'll be able to reproduce it. A security bonus."

"I suppose." Tom went quiet and he carried a bit of a sulk in his posture.

"What's the matter, Trasler?"

Tom twitched with his suspenders and then glared at Carina. "What pisses me off is that you guys let her see all of this, go on deck with your navigation system without even trying to hide it from anyone, yet I have to wear these goddamn nineteenth-century clothes and goddamn long johns and these goddamn suspenders that never seem to fit."

"Tell you what, Barney." Tom wasn't used to seeing Rood so pleasant. "You can dress in your own clothes."

"Really?"

"Sure. Go ahead." Rood put his arm around Tom, who could smell the liquor on Rood's breath. He wasn't categorically drunk, but certainly not legal to drive. "Barney, I'll arrange for a private session with Carina, right here, right now, on the house."

"I'll pass."

Rood wasn't expecting such a resolute declination. "It will be better for you two to get acquainted."

"There's no way it's going to happen. Besides," Tom wore a smile that was a size too small, "I hope she's had her rabies shots."

"Bodmar cleaned her up, gave her all the shots and even one of those dissolvable contraceptives near the armpit. She's certified clean—no risk of STDs."

"How come she doesn't have any kids?"

"Had at least one, maybe more than one, according to Sharon."

"Really? What happened to it—or them?"

"Language barrier makes small talk impossible. That's why she's so much damn fun in the sack. Come on, Trasler, take the plunge!"

Tom smiled tolerantly as he flashed his wedding band, gestured trying to twist it off his finger. "It doesn't come off."

"You're supposed to be a grieving widower, remember? Besides, your wife won't exist for another hundred and sixty-eight years."

Tom glanced at Carina, who sat in a chair sipping on a drink. *Looked like brandy and God how he'd love to have that with a cigar.* She avoided Tom's line of sight, keeping her eyes well away from his. Obviously, she shared the same sentiments about him as he did for her.

"I hope to God she doesn't understand English."

"Sharon put her through tests to make sure she can't. Also, she's prohibited from your classes. Trust me, she's good as stone deaf."

"You don't think she's a security risk? She's seen computers and equipment, food and electrical lights. She's gotta know where we're from."

"This culture has no concept of time travel. There are only two fictional accounts of time travel written prior to 1848 and won't be popularized until works such as Mark Twain's *A Yankee in King Arthur's Court.*" He looked over to Sharon Bodmar sitting at her computer.

"Published in 1886."

"And of course, H. G. Well's *The Time Machine*."

"Published in 1905."

"Those works really got the concept rolling with the mainstream public, but until then, there's simply no concept about it. She sees all this equipment, and to her, we just have great stuff."

"How about Silver's films? That's a peek right into the future."

"You're right. Silver." He drew a cut sign across his throat. Silver wasn't pleased when he closed the lid to the laptop. Bodmar took Tom's canteen and filled it from the central station's reservoir.

"How are you going to keep her from talking about this?" Tom asked. "Will she have a terrible accident and become lost at sea?"

The words were like a bullet when they struck Rood. He gave no acknowledgement, but something just below the subsurface of the expression, the false smile of reassurance, seemed to confirm that's exactly what he intended all along. That's why Rood allowed her to see everything inside the office. There would be no consequences, they'd see to that. Tom felt the dread rise up inside his gut like a black column. He held no love for the woman, but she didn't deserve to be exterminated like a cockroach. This was no pseudo-intuitive nonsense, or a cognitive hallucination, he could read Rood like reading the bold print of a headline.

Carina finished her brandy and as she left, her hand went to Rood's shoulder, leaving it there as she passed him until it finally dragged off as she stepped through the door.

"Here's your canteen," Bodmar said, noticing Tom following Carina's departure. "Don't worry. I'll make sure they won't harm their toy."

Tom's mind flashed light years ago, more precisely, to when he was about ten. Tom recalled his dog Riley, a slightly less than purebred Springer Spaniel. Whenever his dad asked the dog if he wanted to go in the car, it leapt about wagging its amputated tail and barked up a storm. But if they were going to the vet, no matter how hard his dad tried to ask if it wanted to go in the car in the same tone as going to the corner store, the dog somehow knew it was going to the vet, and cowered under the coffee table until it was dragged out. Bodmar was trying to hold the tone of going to the corner store when she knew goddamn well that they were going to the vet.

MAY 27, 1848

Silver loitered about the decks. Women tugged their children away from him, their eyes filled with loathing and mistrust. He went to the aft bulwark and took the chocolate bar from his jacket pocket. Within moments, Selma-Olivia stood beside him. He smiled into her twinkling eyes as she took a piece and slipped the milk chocolate into her mouth.

He smiled at hearing the blissful *mmmmm* whisper from her lips. This time, he let her have nearly the entire chocolate bar. After finishing each piece, she licked her fingers. Each time she did, her eyes slipped shut, her head tipped back and an expression of ecstasy filled her features, radiating out through the smile. When she finished, he left, then turned to her and indicated for her to follow him. She didn't hesitate. With a wide, expectant smile and a skip to her step, she followed him below.

Jonas sat near the forward deck hatch with Carl-Johan and some other men, chatting away. A young woman's scream shrieked from the 'tween-decks. Its desperation pierced the background din of the steerage and rose to the decks. A slap followed and then a suspended silence. Another scream. Deeply throated, delivered with terrible fear. It was Selma-Olivia!

Jonas ran to the steerage. Just as he landed off the stairs, more screams, swallowed, broken, then a man's shriek of savage agony. Selma-Olivia burst through the closed partition of her berth, her dress ripped past her waist, her undershirt ripped open, one breast exposed as she collapsed onto the steerage floor. Silver stumbled through the curtain, one hand clutching his right eye. Blood gushed from the socket and he screamed in wretched pain.

"He violated me!" Selma-Olivia shrieked, straining her vocal cords with the force of her cry and still her voice was so small. A terrible rage rose in Jonas, blending his emotions into a volatile mix of brutal violence.

Silver stumbled towards the sanctuary of the office. People rushed from their berths and Jonas charged towards him, cutting off Silver. Clutching his right eye with blood pouring between his fingers, Silver looked this way and that with the left eye, seeing nothing but a encroaching circle of rage. Two of the men grabbed and held him.

Rood heard the triple beep from the security system sounding a warning. Glancing at the monitor, he saw the mayhem with Silver in the middle of it, and it wasn't difficult to understand what had happened.

"Christ Almighty!" Rood grabbed his holster and hurled out of the office with Rodriguez.

"What did he do to you?" Jonas asked.

Selma-Olivia's mouth opened, in shock, breathless, then finally formed the words. "He kissed me against my consent, then ripped open my dress and laid his vile hands upon my naked bosoms!"

Two passengers restrained Silver from the back as Jonas charged towards him. Wearing a horrible grin that wreathed his lips back from his teeth, Jonas let out a low, ripping scream. "You have blasphemed God's innocent lamb!"

Silver's good eye bugged back at him in total terror.

Jonas' fists were a flurry when they smashed into Silver's teeth, his nose, gut, neck and head. A front tooth spat from his mouth. Now it was Silver who screamed in agony and fear and panic.

Rood's shot drilled into the main mast, roaring through the steerage. The flash of the gun lit the gloom and the silence was instant. Rood's lips stretched into grim anger. His eyes were clots of acid as they burned right through Jonas—burning all the way to the center of the earth and straight into hell.

Tom burst down the aft steps. The rational part of his mind had been harbouring the hope that he imagined the whole thing, but that hope died when he saw Selma-Olivia's ripped dress, Silver's bleeding eye, his bloodied teeth showing a black spot and Rood's gun thrust under Jonas' jaw. He turned around, his hands clutching the side of his head.

With their backs against the front of the galleyhouse and facing the main deck, Tom stood with Ralph, armed with a short-barrelled imitation musket loaded with twelve 9mm rounds. Tom wanted to beat that little pedophile senseless, especially considering Selma-Olivia was part of his Swedish family, but he knew the consequences would be terrible. Rood was worried about his loyalties. He capitulated and decided he'd prove his loyalties just to appease the sonuvabitch. Anything less than his full support would be catastrophic. He felt sick. Silver was a monster, and other than Rood threatening to delete all his porn, and like Jackson, confined to the office, there would be no discipline. Jonas had been fully justified in beating Silver, but Rood explained that no matter what Silver had done, as heinous as it was, a passenger hit one of their own. For that, they had no choice but to set an example to prevent it from happening again.

Next to Tom stood Ralph, his right arm in a sling, holding a Colt revolver with his left hand. On the forecastle deck, Rodriguez watched for trouble, and hidden beneath his long beige coat, an MP5 carbine with a high volume magazine, just in case things got out of control. On the poop deck, Anderson and Bodmar stood alert with their imitation muskets. Jackson, forbidden to go on deck, kept guard with a carbine and watched the proceedings on the security monitor, switching from one camera to another like a director of some sick reality show. He could communicate instantly with Rood, who wore a wireless earbud.

Silver had a white eye patch covering what was lucky to still be an eye along with a scattering of lurid facial scars courtesy of Selma-Olivia's fingernails. Before them, Jonas Gabrielsson was shirtless, his wrists bound and tied to the main mast. Liedberg stood with Lars Göran

Rödin, clutching his cat-o-nine-tails, the strands fluttering menacingly in the breeze.

Every passenger, with the exception of four who were critically ill, were ordered on deck. For a moment, a death-like silence passed through the masses like a black wind. Only the creaking of wood, the rustle of canvas, the splash of water against the ship and the whistle of the rigging hushed though the eerie quiet. Liedberg held the written statement given by Rood. The paper trembled in his hands while he translated the English into Swedish and read the first part.

"For the punishment of assaulting a member of the United States military, Jonas Gabrielsson has been condemned to receive twelve lashes." He lowered the paper and nodded at the mate to execute the sentence.

Rödin jiggled the cat-o-nine-tails, untangling the knotted strands, then raised his arm and brought the whip down to Jonas' back. It was a multiple shriek of leather striking skin. Jonas recoiled and a terrible grunt wrenched from his body. Catharina covered her eyes and turned away. Stina-Sophia and Johanna screamed and cried with Alvina-Kristina trying to cover Johanna's eyes, but the little girl squirmed away, intent to look. Carl-Johan, blubbering away, squinted his eyes shut.

Tom stared ahead, blankly facing the crowd. Carina stood before him. When his eyes coupled with hers, they exchanged the exact same look—the awful guilt of association with Rood and his criminals. Rödin swung again. The screams shook out of Jonas, sobs wrenched from the women and children while the men stood silently.

Silver trotted to Rödin in short little shuffles. His voice climbed to the high, clear octaves of fury. "Harder!"

Not understanding, the mate looked over to Liedberg. "A little more effort, Mr. Rödin."

Rödin was a man of good physical courage, but he felt something turn over in his stomach. He jiggled the chords again, executing the third lashing and then the horrible screaming began. They were big, lusty, filled with red agony.

"Harder! Harder!" Silver shrieked with a horrible smile, the missing tooth-spot the focal point of the maleficent grin, wreathing his perch-like lips.

Rödin submitted the fourth lashing.

Silver went right to Rödin's face, inches away, his uncovered eye sparkling with warm and lunatic joy. "Harder!"

Rödin gave it everything he had and the knotted chords whipped up a spray of blood. Silver stared up at Jonas mercilessly, his fists shaking with violent lust.

"Harder!"

Another explosion of blood sprayed from Jonas' back. The strength was gone from his legs now. He just hung from his wrists. Rödin continued with the lashing, when he completed the twelfth, he stared at the deck with the bloodied chords staining the deck with crimson like tiny paintbrushes. For a big man, he was on the verge of tears.

"That's it?" Silver complained. "More! More!"

"The punishment has been executed in full, Mr. Silver." Liedberg's hands had locked behind his back, squeezed so tightly he had no feeling left in them.

Silver shuffled to Rood, his feet moving in tiny, agitated steps. "That's not enough!"

"You know goddamn well that should have been you up there, Silver. Stand down!"

Liedberg read the second part from the paper. "If anyone so much as bumps any of the soldiers—including Mr. Trasler and Captain Parker—they won't get off as fortunate as Mr. Gabrielsson."

The crew released Jonas from the mast. He collapsed into a writhing pile and the crew doused the fire from his back with several buckets of seawater. Catharina, Alvina-Kristina and Selma-Olivia rushed over to care for him.

Jonas lay perfectly still, just trying to negotiate with the pain. Catharina looked at Alvina-Kristina, her eyes blazing with wrath. "Imagine my anguish when I heard the first lash fall upon poor Jonas. I had never thought that I should be compelled to hear such fearful sounds, and nothing can efface from memory the disgust and horror of that moment. I had heard of such things, but had not realized men could be beaten like dogs, much less that other men not only could sentence such barbarism, but could actually stand by and see their own manhood degraded in such disgraceful manner."

Ralph tapped Tom's arm. "Look at his back."

"The Lord Christ our Saviour took thirty-nine lashings, Mr. Parker, to redeem us of our transgressions," Liedberg said.

"Thirty-nine would kill a man."

"Indeed it should have. The precious Christ paid dearly for the exonerations of our sins."

"I'm going below to barf," said Tom.

Tom passed a long, lonely night. He got the cold treatment from everyone, including Alvina-Kristina. It was bad enough participating with the soldiers, but things only got worse when Liedberg declared to all that he and Ralph were put under Rood's protective umbrella. Tom would have preferred to take his chances with no association with the soldiers. Jonas suffered in terrible pain and several times during the night, he woke up grunting in agony, trying his best to stifle the screams. Tom spent the next day—the one month anniversary since he came aboard—pretty much ostracized. Being a Sunday, there were no classes to keep him occupied. The day crawled by slower than the ship's lethargic ride.

On Monday, the passengers led an organized boycott of Tom's classes to protest his involvement in the lashing. Liedberg intervened and personally saw to it that everyone made it to the second class. It was already a tense class when a woman keeled over in a dead faint. One of the well-to-do wives of a merchant had her corset drawn so tightly it caused her to faint. It gave Tom the scare of his life and couldn't understand why she insisted to wear that horrid thing, especially on this wretched little ship. Carina Svensson, okay, he understood, but a merchant's wife?

During the third class, Tom felt some itching under his shirt. He wore his jeans and a plaid shirt, his Prada leather jacket and his beloved Montreal Expos baseball cap, and couldn't understand why the clothes were causing so much discomfort. Just before lunch, the itching was driving him insane. Immediately after he dismissed the third class, Tom scurried below and removed his shirt. Red spots covered his chest and armpits. Then he saw it in his shirt. The shriek could be heard from the crow's nest.

Bodmar backed away from Tom when he made the revelation. "That's not head lice—it's body lice. Go away."

"Head lice, body lice, what's the difference?"

"Not much—just habitat."

"They're not, like, you know . . . crabs?"

"You've been humping someone?"

"No."

"Then they're not crabs."

"How do you get rid of these little bastards?"

"They're quite sensitive to temperature change. Just wash your clothes in hot water and keep clean as possible."

"Keep clean as possible? In this cesspool?"

MAY 31, 1848

The louse infestation exploded throughout the steerage. Alvina-Kristina's shoulders, stomach and chest were dotted with louse bites. Baby Edvard had been spared, but Sune seemed to have it worse than anyone. Alvina-Kristina took quicksilver salve and rubbed it over their bodies. Tom was in his berth, getting ready to boil his clothes when he heard Bodmar calling him with a whisper.

"I'm in here."

She slipped into the enclosure and handed Tom a tiny vial holding an ounce of a yellow fluid.

Tom knew immediately what it was. "Oh, God bless you."

"I owed you one. Consider us even. Do you have any shampoo in your luggage?" Tom took out an eight and a half ounce bottle shaped more like a perfume bottle than a shampoo. "Good God," Bodmar said. "Do you know how much that stuff costs?"

"It's Carol's."

"That's over $100.00 a bottle!"

"Carol is a millionaire's daughter, remember?"

"How could I forget?" She opened the lid and sniffed. "It smells like a hundred dollar bottle of shampoo." She put about a quarter of the goop into the shampoo, and slowly rocked it back and forth.

"That's it?"

"This is highly concentrated." She went through Carol's toiletries. "Nice conditioner, another hundred at least." She took out some body wash and put a similar amount in there as well. "This will kill what you have and keep them at bay for a few days. Give yourself a body wash every couple of days but most importantly, wash your clothes in hot water every day. Unlike head lice, they lay their eggs in the clothing and aren't that hard to kill. And Trasler, I never gave this to you." She put the half-full container inside Carol's bag. She slipped out and continued to the deck, hoping her actions wouldn't cause an alert to the security network.

Tom's hair, still wet from the shampooing and sponge bath with the lice killing shampoo and body wash, felt lush and vibrant as any shampoo from a $100 bottle of shampoo ought to. He had other shampoo bottles in his, Alice and Charlie's luggage, but he felt no guilt in spoiling himself with Carol's. He changed into fresh clothes he had hadn't worn since coming aboard and he knew they had to be lice free. He put some deodorant on, brushed his teeth and felt human for once. He sorted his laundry for the delousing wash when Alvina-Kristina entered the cubical of canvas enclosing their living space.

"Hi, Alvina."

It was not quite a full smile she gave him, but the closest since Jonas' lashing. She stared curiously at his light blue polo shirt and jeans. She had never seen him wear them before and they were indeed strange looking clothes.

"My mother said to me, when I was little girl, that only unholy people and whores breed vermin on their bodies."

"It's disgusting, yes, but it's not our fault. Don't get upset."

On deck, the two worked merrily side-by-side, scrubbing, rinsing and scrubbing again while Catharina tended to the baby. Other women washing their clothes crowded the deck, making it difficult to find a spot. Women sat around, picked lice from their clothes, squashing them one at a time on a wooden plate. In the galley, they boiled all their underwear in a strong lye soap.

Tom and Alvina-Kristina passed the time chatting away, both enjoying the warmth of the pleasant spring afternoon. They put the rinsed clothes in another basket for Selma-Olivia to take into the steerage to be hung on the clothesline set-up for washing days. The captain strictly prohibited hanging the clothes on the decks to dry.

Alvina-Kristina ran the zipper back and forth on a pair of Tom's jeans, fascinated by it.

"That's a zipper."

"Zeeeper?"

She saw zippers many times from Tom's belongings, but never on the pants and she giggled while running the zipper up and down the jeans. "It's more fun to do it," Tom said while motioning the zipping back and forth, "when someone else is in them."

Alvina-Kristina's eyes bugged with shock and sharp disapproval, yet betrayed a promiscuous kind of appreciation for his boldness. Tom smiled back, his eyes of molten chocolate boldly making love to hers.

She zipped it back and forth again, giggled and said, "Groovy, man."

"Shhhh! Don't let the captain hear you say that or I'll be put in chains!"

"Groovy!" she shouted and bent into laughter by the terror in Tom's eyes. Tom's hand covered her mouth and she continued the forbidden words muffling out of the side of his hand. It was unabashed flirtation and he loved it as much as she did.

"Why are you being so nice to me today?" Tom asked.

"You gave me the very good night clothes. And . . ." she giggled and closed in for the whisper. "I love the bras."

His eyes slipped to her breasts and his lips curled into a grin. "You look great in them." She didn't mind his glance at her breasts, not at all, and the look she returned certainly encouraged his praise.

After they finished the wash, Alvina-Kristina prepared to wash her hair. "Stop, woman!" Tom gently slapped her hand, continuing to do so until she dropped the homemade soap. "Look what it's doing to your hair." She showed her the last two frayed inches of her waist-long hair. He put his hands in front of her. "Stay there. Don't move."

Tom returned with a case of Carol's toiletries and a clean towel. He led Alvina-Kristina to the forward deck hatch's latticed cover. With a surplus of distilled water from the central station, and before a growing crowd of curious onlookers, he rinsed her hair and took out Carol's $100 bottle of shampoo.

Alvina-Kristina looked on curiously when the shampoo oozed like thick molasses into his palm. Its aroma enchanted her. She hunched her shoulders and giggled softly in anticipation. His hands caressed the top of her skull. Alvina-Kristina felt herself slipping, slumping, as his fingers massaged the shampoo into her scalp. He began at the crest of her skull, then outward in concentric circles to the nape of her neck, scratching behind her ears and to the outer fringes of her hairline.

Alvina-Kristina's eyes took on a dreamy quality and her lips stretched into the fullest of smiles. She felt herself lapse away into another world—a utopia, far, far away from this miserable ship, her husband, child, sister and their resettlement to America. All that mattered was the magic emanating from his fingertips. She leaned harder into the thrilling thrust of his fingers. It had been a long, long time since she completely lost herself with such a simple pleasure.

A slow, soft moan escaped her lips.

Tom took his time, seeing the bliss settle on her full lips and noticed how her entire body softened. He allowed her hair and scalp to absorb the shampoo's lice killing agent—not to mention its high priced ingredients. He rinsed her hair, and to her delight, took out a bottle of white conditioner, which cost about as much as her passage on this ship, and massaged it into her hair for ten minutes of ecstasy. He gave her a final rinse using the remainder of his distilled water to ensure her hair would be as clean as possible. He'd be going to bed thirsty tonight but he didn't care.

She moaned in delight when Tom brought out a comb. It wasn't a discrete moan, either, and more than one woman on board covered their mouths in shock at Alvina-Kristina's public indiscretion. Her eyes slipped shut while the enchanted comb ran through the full length of her hair. Tom placed her head down as he combed her hair back from her forehead, then parted it to the sides. He raised her chin and continued to comb, patiently untangling the knots. He combed first from the outside, then from underneath the hair. Often he would lean down, cheek to cheek to whisper private little compliments into her ear. She responded with mischievous giggles. Alvina-Kristina felt a few strands being tugged, then her eyes snapped wide open when she heard the first snip.

"Thomas!"

"Don't worry, kiddo, I've been cutting chicks' hair for years." He cut off more as he worked his way down. "Everyone thought I was the type of guy who wasn't into women when I took the hairdressing course. *Au contraire,* it was to pick-up chicks that I did. It worked. Boy, did it work.

I mean, it really worked." After he finished with a layer, he pinned it across to the opposite side of her head with hair clips.

Two dozen spectators assembled tightly around them as Tom completed the haircut. He used a brush unlike any Alvina-Kristina ever saw, with bristles circling the entire shaft. Reaching underneath her hair, he twirled the brush while he worked his way down. When finished, he center parted her hair, showering freely over her shoulders and tapered inward. He raised Carol's big vanity mirror before her.

A sharp gasp betrayed her surprise. Her hair, once waist long, fell just half way down her back. Instead of falling evenly, it was layered and tapered, shorter in front and longer in the back. Her hesitation turned into approval and she decided she liked the way her hair complimented her facial features, enhancing them even.

"Admit it, that woman in the mirror is the most beautiful woman you have ever seen."

She giggled, thoroughly intoxicated by his charms. Glued to the mirror, her smile glowed like a sunrise. "Thank you. You are very kind."

The assembly had mixed looks. Most giggled at the foolishness of this new style, a select few, less rigid in convention, clearly liked what they saw. Some looked on with envy.

"Now for the final touch." Tom sprinkled a touch of perfume behind her ears and neck. He placed his hands on her shoulders, leaned in and sampled the aroma from one side of her neck then the other. He gazed contently, proud of his handiwork while he plunged into the aquamarine sea of her enamouring eyes.

She inhaled deeply and absorbed the fragrance. She felt like a queen!

"Admit it, she looks amazing," Tom said to Ralph. He contained a proud boast to his voice.

"She does, Tom." Ralph was less than enthralled. His eyes dimmed. "Her husband made a complaint to Liedberg."

"For crying out loud! About what?"

"Fool, you two were flirting like lovers. This is the nineteenth century, moron, with very strict protocols concerning the sexes—which you completely overstepped."

"It was just a haircut."

Liedberg approached the two. "Will you gentlemen be so kind as to follow me." Ralph shook his head at Tom, who still held a childlike innocence in his eyes. The two followed Liedberg to his cabin. Once inside, Liedberg closed his door. The two stood, shifting side to side to compensate from the ship's corkscrew roll. Liedberg stood behind his table. He lanced Tom with his brooding looks.

"You and the Gabrielsson woman seem to be getting along quite capitally."

"Yes. We've become good friends."

"Can you tell me, on your oath as a gentleman, that beyond the commonest civilities, that nothing improper has transgressed?"

"Absolutely nothing."

Liedberg lurched towards Tom, nose to nose, the captain looking like the quintessential drill sergeant. "Are you trying to make me a fool?"

"No, sir. Never."

Liedberg eased back, though just slightly. Tom could still feel his breath puffing against his face. "Your intimacy with the wife of Sune Gabrielsson was much advanced by the cleansing, the grooming and the cutting of her hair. The entire family has been mortally affronted by your shameless improprieties."

"It was a shampoo and haircut."

"Lord forgive you, Mr. Trasler, and for what you have confessed this very moment, may you never be truly sorry."

Tom said nothing.

"When your impudence and passion begins to cool, how wicked you shall begin to feel." The captain waved Tom and Ralph to leave his cabin. Tom stepped out and turned to Ralph.

"What the hell did he just say?"

"I'm not sure," Ralph said with a ball of laughter rolling off his tongue. "But I think he wants you to keep your paws off the bitch."

Tom had a blank face for a moment. "Could you imagine if we had gone further back in time to when people spoke like goddamn William Shakespeare?"

"We would have needed an interpreter!"

Alvina-Kristina leaned against the bulwark on the windward side of the ship, taking refuge within her private little utopia. She had been there since supper and contently stared into the pleasant breeze, admiring the gold painted clouds. The sun hovered low over the sea, its rays reflected across the waves like burning flames and shone brilliantly on her hair, uncovered and fine as golden silk threads, fluttering erotically. Only very young girls have hair this fine, this delicate, but no child possessed hair this thick, luxurious, soft or perfumed like hers.

Tom had given her the underclothes, the bra, the nightie and pyjamas, and transformed her hair like a miracle. Never in her life did she feel this beautiful. Never did a man make her feel so complete as a woman as she felt now. There would be a dear price to pay for it. In a way, she had sold her soul to the devil and there would be hell to pay. She knew it, accepted it, and right now, she didn't care.

She heard the thunder of the devil's footsteps approach. Approaching to collect.

Here it comes.

PART III

THE PAST IS BUT A BEGINNING OF A BEGINNING, AND ALL THAT IS AND HAS BEEN IS BUT THE TWILIGHT OF THE DAWN.

H.G. WELLS (1901)

CHAPTER 16

AUGUST 22, 2016
PASADENA, CA

Cosmo and Jennifer spent much of the day reviewing the video of the temporal event that hurled Cosmo to his nineteen-month long journey into the world of reruns. They were on the second floor of a lower scale apartment they just leased for their research. The soothing scent of Folgers brewed from the kitchen. The office furniture was new, and despite the windfall of cash, bought at discount store prices and wasn't comfortable for these long sessions.

Jennifer sat on a black vinyl chair supported on five wheels, one always seemed to lock in the wrong direction. Her legs were crossed and the short red skirt rode up high. Cosmo stood behind her, leaning slightly on her chair. Cosmo thought her scent was like lilies, sweet and subtle just after a gentle rain. He hovered above her left shoulder.

"Proximity alert! Proximity alert!" Jennifer said.

"What are you talking about?"

"You're inside my personal space, Cosmo. Avast!"

He edged back slightly. "Play it back one more time, Muffins."

"I'm going to kill you, Cosmo, I swear to God." Her hands flew as the next words exploded out of her. "Why are you calling me that, anyways?"

"It just seems to fit."

"Fit? What do you mean, fit?" He shrugged out of the interrogation and she breathed heavily in an overkill of bad theatrics. "So what's with you buying those trash magazines?" Jennifer asked, her voice carrying a significant amount of disdain. There were two copies of the scandal magazines next to Cosmo's keyboard.

"Got to keep up with the celebrities, Muffins."

"Like, who cares who cheats on who?"

"Like, who doesn't?"

She gave her eyes a little roll in their sockets and played the video in reverse motion. Cosmo liked the smell of her perfume and he appreciated her short, thick hair even more, yes he did. He hovered just above her left shoulder. Her fingers wrapped around the mouse were long and delicate. She had beautiful hands—a shame she chewed her fingernails as if they were breadsticks. The imploding shockwave recorded from the video camera rushed by in reverse at high speed.

"Now, here's the birds," Jennifer said. She got no comment from Cosmo. She glanced over her shoulder and his eyes weren't exactly on the video monitor.

"You're looking down my blouse again!" She recoiled and punched his shoulder.

"I was not," he protested, standing upright, rubbing his shoulder. She had a good clout.

She buttoned up her light green blouse. "What colour is my bra?"

"Robin egg blue."

"You little—"

"Okay, I got caught. Fine, I'm a guy. You wear your shirts way too low cut and when we take the bait, we're condemned. We don't take the bait, girls wonder what's wrong with us, or them, but either way, we lose. Lose-lose, that's exactly what you women want. You're all evil."

He hit a nerve with her. She stared at the monitor and then hit the pause on the video. She turned and faced him. "Do you know how Fleming handpicked us?"

"Because the initial event was in the summer and everyone had gone home for the summer break?"

"No. He put a lot of thought into selecting the team. It's because we're all top of our class for our respective disciplines. We should be honoured. But, there's more to it. I caught Fleming one day with his guard down. After, he asked me not to talk about it." She stared ahead, not feeling too good about herself. Or anyone else in the team. "He handpicked us because all of us are geeks and none of us have a life."

"What do you mean?"

"All of us are single and none of us have a close circle of friends. Meaning, we won't spill the beans to anyone."

"We have no social life because we're top of the class. We spend our uninteresting lives with our studies and research."

"Exactly," she said, but it wasn't a happy acknowledgement. "I haven't dated seriously since grade nine when Danny-boy messed me up so bad I've never recovered. My so-called best-friends-for-life are pregnant, divorced and pregnant, single and pregnant, still behaving like they were fifteen year-olds, or need to be put into rehab. You spend the odd night playing board games with some other geeks, or paintball, or Warcraft, but you're single and have no best friend." Her words were running so fast she needed to pause for a breath. "Did you ever have a serious girlfriend?"

"A few . . . nothing serious. Just one. Thought I was going out with her." Cosmo fell into a deep pit of anguish. He worked his mouth a little then swallowed, then tried to look like he didn't care, but did a poor job of it. "I guess her definition of going out was different than mine. Nope, nothing serious. Ever."

"Our buddy Scranton," Jennifer continued. "No social life. Goes home and is on the computer all night long, writing software or hacking into websites. Every now and then he finds a one night stand on line and gets laid—the only one of the team that's getting it—but that's it."

"He's getting laid?"

"Ya, did you know he's Jewish?"

"Scranton isn't a Jewish name!"

"His father married a Jew and converted. He sneaks off to synagogue every now and then, too."

"What are religion are you?"

"Non-practicing Methodist."

Cosmo shrugged. "What about Roberts?"

"Divorced."

"Roberts is divorced? At his age?"

"Don't talk to him about it. He knew the girl since, and I'm not kidding, pre-school. They got married when both were nineteen. Three months later, she dumped him—for whatever reason, she moved to

Canada. Roberts goes to see her about three times a year trying to convince her to come back. That's why he had Canadian coins to show us. He's a big mess inside but never shows it. But Roberts wasn't even Fleming's first choice."

"He wasn't?"

"No, it was Gail Tucker."

"I know her."

"Real hottie. That's the problem. Guys are always after her, she has the smarts but she also has a social life. Didn't make the cut because of that."

"Wow. And the professor?"

"Doesn't talk about himself much. Single, but it looks like he had a girlfriend, quite a catch, apparently, and lost her because of his research. His research is his life—like the rest of us. All of us spend just about every minute of our spare time here. During the last school year, when I wasn't studying, I was here. I went out of my way not to be social so I could come here. All of us do the same. We have no life, no friends, no hobbies, just this damn work."

"It's interesting work."

"It's an addiction."

"A good addiction."

"Is it?"

The professor entered the apartment with a short, stout man in his mid-forties with brown hair in a crew cut style. He wore gray slacks, a white shirt and wingtip shoes that must have hurt his feet, but they sure were classy. An awkward little man, he looked like he belonged in the late 1950's.

"This is Patrick McKenzie, from Johns Hopkins University Applied Physics Laboratory. He has been the source of providing the locations of our magnetic anomalies. I have recruited his services and he is now part of the team. He has been fully briefed."

"Welcome aboard. I'm Russ Wynn." The man shook Cosmo's hand, nice and tight. "We were hoping you'd be joining us."

Jennifer remained casually slouched in her chair and offered her hand. "Jennifer Burke." He gave her a tidy little bow and for a bemused instant, Jennifer thought he would kiss her hand. His hands were small and smooth and she guessed he never did yard work, or ever owned a

Lawnboy, for that matter.

Fleming arrived with a trimmed beard and his auburn hair clipped above the ears. "Dr. McKenzie is an expert in solar, interplanetary and magnetospheric plasma physics and planetary magnetic fields. He has been involved in numerous unmanned space missions, the most recent was the Messenger spacecraft that orbited Mercury."

"Sounds impressive," Jennifer smiled stiffly. "Is the spacecraft still orbiting Mercury?"

"No. It impacted the surface last year when all its fuel was exhausted."

"Miss Burke is our Ultrahigh Frequency Overhauser Magnetometer expert, much of the design modifications were her own, while Mr. Wynn's fancy is the Elementary Charged Particles Detector, as well as the Ultrahigh Frequency Fluxgate Vector Magnetometer, both modified by Mr. Wynn to detect the temporal phenomena, previously undetectable, among many other talents."

"Ya," Jennifer said, "especially looking down lady's blouses."

"Hope he doesn't look down mine," McKenzie said with a tolerant smile.

"I wouldn't put it past him." Her face twisted in a grimace. "And he speaks Klingon."

Cosmo looked Jennifer squarely in the eyes, his own by no means pleasant. *"DenIb Qatlh!"*

"Impressive!" McKenzie gave a roaring laugh and slapped Cosmo's shoulder affectionately. "Dr. Fleming speaks very highly of his students. You are missing two others of your team?"

"Bob Scranton and Stuart Roberts—they're field testing some new equipment that just arrived from England," Fleming said.

"I see, then if I may impose," McKenzie said, "is that fresh coffee I smell?"

"It is," Cosmo said, getting up and returned with coffee for the professor and McKenzie, then making a second trip for his and Jennifer's caffeine fix.

"Cosmo makes good coffee," Jennifer said. "One of his few uses."

"Ha-ha."

"All of my team have modified their equipment to hone in on our mysterious anomalies," Fleming said with a boast in his tone.

"The high frequency magnetism, I understand, is only the by-product of the event but not the actual process?"

"Correct," Cosmo said. He glared briefly at Jennifer, his eyes brooding, then faced McKenzie with an entirely transformed face. "It's like monitoring a sonic boom but not able to locate the aircraft breaking the sound barrier. The charged particles are the direct result. That's what we're focusing on."

"We see the magnetic and charged particle fluctuations, but still don't have a clue what's creating the effect," Jennifer said and followed up with a sweet smile.

"Hopefully, we can solve this puzzle." McKenzie glanced at Cosmo, who hadn't shaved in about three days. "Russell Wynn—an actual time traveller. It's an honour."

Cosmo grinned with a little uncertainty. "It's not as if I did anything special, it just happened."

"How did you survive for nineteen months?"

"Here's the interesting thing. Two years ago, my bank account got cleaned out. Credit cards maxed out overnight. The only way someone could have pulled it off was to have duplicates of my bank and credit cards, my on line passwords and PIN numbers. Even the cops were dumbfounded. When I found myself in Utah and figured out that I went back in time, I realized that I was the thief, having to wipe out my accounts to live off. Then I made some heavy-duty coin on sports betting, kinda like Biff in *Back to the Future II.* I made a fortune off the Super Bowl, along with the world series, NBA, NHL and other events."

Jennifer looked a little puzzled. "You never mentioned that."

"No one ever asked me what I went through, Muffins—just the science part of it. I had a really rough time, but no one cares about that, or the hippy commune I stayed at, or that freaky chick with the hairy legs and Arnold Schwarzenegger physique who wanted me to give her a love child. No, you don't care."

"You're right, I don't care." She wasn't taken in by his Basset Hound eyes. "How much did you make with the sports gambling?"

"Seventy grand."

"Seventy grand!" Jennifer shrieked. Fleming's eyebrow soared while McKenzie tabulated the possibilities. "You just go back in time, cheat and break the rules and . . ."

"Cheat?" Cosmo looked quite indignant.

"You broke the time travel rules. That's a no-no!"

"I never changed history, Muffins. My bank account was robbed by me before I went back in time. I made no attempt to alter the outcome. I just placed a few bets. And the burden of student loans? I needed this cash."

"With all that cash, don't you think you could invest in some decent clothes and a razor blade?"

Cosmo masked the hurt, but the hurt went dagger deep.

"What was it like, living in a world where you knew future events?" McKenzie asked. "Since my ex cleaned me out, going back in time like you did is a temptation. Maybe even to stay there!"

Cosmo was still lost by Jennifer's comment. "Kind of like watching a movie the second time, but there are parts of the movie you missed. I knew the big events, but the day to day events in your own little world were still unknown."

"Incredible experience. I hope to do the same shortly!"

"You mentioned you have an ex?" Jennifer asked.

"Yes," McKenzie said.

"We're all single with our own sob stories, so feel at home."

McKenzie really didn't know what to say. An awkward transition passed until the conversation resumed.

"I think we're onto something, professor," Cosmo said. They eased closer to the video monitor. "Here's the Northwest Territory-Fort McPherson temporal event. Note the birds fleeing from the trees as the shockwave closes in."

"Mr. Wynn, we have seen this video dozens of times."

"Yes, Professor, but what did the birds sense that we did not?"

"We have been unable to ascertain that."

"Birds see colour as we do." Jennifer's arms were still tightly crossed, leery of Cosmo's straying eyes even though she had done up her blouse to the top button. "But," she held up four fingers, "their eyes have a fourth colour receptor that is sensitive to ultraviolet light."

"Also, many birds are also thought to have magnetoception, which is a sense that allows them to detect a magnetic field to perceive direction, altitude or location," Cosmo added.

"With the magnetic fields going amok during the events and possibly the event visible in ultraviolet wavelengths, the birds will see and feel it while we stood there in ignorant bliss," Jennifer added.

"Interesting." Fleming nodded to his new companion.

"Now check this out," Cosmo said. "The shockwave that terrified the birds played in reverse, at high speed, mimicked a shockwave one would see from a powerful explosion." They played the altered video, which clearly showed an expanding shockwave. "This proves it was a massive energy burst. The event we saw, relative to us, is happening in reverse time at drastically reduced speeds."

"We ran the data in reverse and highly accelerated, and it all starts to make sense," Jennifer added.

"The other issue was that we never found a localized source to explain the energetic partials, or the magnetic anomaly," Cosmo said. "We can only conclude the event was caused from an outside source."

"This is why Stuart Roberts couldn't find anything in the ground," Jennifer explained.

"If we were to look at the temporal event in reverse time," Cosmo said, "we will see a massive explosion, then residual temporal radiation and high frequency magnetisms declining predictably at a half-life decay. Slow it down by a factor of thousands, at reverse time the way we see it, the magnetic and energetic partials readings we picked up before the event, are actually the temporal fallout increasing until time zero. After the temporal event, there is a dull magnetic imprint at normal time-space speed."

Fleming closed in on the monitor, quite impressed. "This is why we can detect these zones before the temporal event occurs."

"Bingo!" Jennifer said. "We actually see it in reverse time."

"The professor speaks highly of his young team," McKenzie said smiling. "Backward time travel requires matter with negative energy density. I believe you have discovered it."

"Right there," Cosmo said, pointing to the screen. "The event is likely caused by a quantum phase of exotic matter randomly impacting Earth. We can detect them because of the relative reverse space-time causality from our perspective, we can predict them before the actual impact."

"That's amazing." McKenzie grinned.

"Dr. McKenzie has an important finding to share with us which I believe will tie into Mr. Wynn's hypothesis," Fleming announced.

"Mr. Wynn or Cosmo? Which should I call you?" McKenzie asked.

"Russ," said Cosmo.

"Cosmo is perfect," Jennifer said. "It's not just because he's a complete geek and speaks Klingon, once you get to know him, you'll understand what makes him Cosmo." Jennifer again rolled her eyes, this time highly exaggerated. Her overblown theatrics continued to be substandard if not downright pathetic. Cosmo was damned fed up with it, but Jennifer's personal morale was pretty much rock bottom today and decided to cut her some slack.

McKenzie took a sip of the coffee. "Strong."

"As it should be," Jennifer said.

"And your important finding?" Cosmo asked.

McKenzie took another sip. "As you know, the Europeans have an earth orbiting satellite—OARS—**O**cean and **A**tmospheric **R**esearch **S**atellite. Launched in 1996, it is in a highly elliptical orbit that takes it through and then past the Van Allen radiation belts. One of the experiments on board, the Energetic Particles Detector, was altered last year after an intense solar storm while it was near its orbital aphelion well outside the Earth's protective magnetosphere. It was transmitting data no one could make sense of. The principle investigator solicited my assistance and couriered me the disks, as well as the software to encrypt the raw data. Combined with the readings from the spacecraft's magnetometer, I discovered that the anomalous readings showed a unique form of charged particles attracted to a similarly unique magnetic field. One of the areas with the highest readings was last summer's Fort McPherson magnetic anomaly. And after three passes, it showed the strength of these charged articles was increasing exponentially. That's when I contacted Dr. Fleming."

"Dr. McKenzie has mapped about twenty percent of the planet with the so called defective EPD experiment and has found dozens of these hot spots," Fleming said. "Most cluster about the Earth's magnetic poles." Fleming held his unlit pipe his right hand as he continued. "The north magnetic pole is in Canada, the southern magnetic pole just off shore from Antarctica. There are very few hot spots in Antarctica, which can only be explained that ice cover does not retain the temporal signature." He put the pipe back in his mouth.

"Who else knows about this?" Cosmo asked.

“I consulted with Professor Fleming first,” McKenzie said. “He then said we should talk. And we did. I advised the Europeans it was a defective instrument and sent them a software patch to filter out the readings. In other words, restoring the instrument to its normal operating mode, albeit degraded, while masking our temporal readings through a four level encryption process and keeping the raw data concealed for our later retrieval.”

“No one other than us in this room knows the altered EPD is locating temporal activity centers,” Fleming mentioned.

“Do we have access to new data for the rest of the planet?” Cosmo asked.

“Yes,” McKenzie replied. “But as stated, the data is masked by four layers of encryption. It requires a tedious four-pass process and is extremely time consuming. Once encrypted, however, it will eventually give us 100% coverage of the planet. We will be able to map both the impacts, as well as the exit paths.”

“This might explain why the rest of the world doesn’t know of these events,” Jennifer speculated. “They are in remote areas near the poles, far away from cities, or civilization to be seen.”

“Precisely,” Fleming said. “Only a handful—the strongest—make it to lower latitudes and the impact area is relatively small. This will explain why the temporal events remain virtually unknown.”

“Except for Uncle Sam,” Cosmo said. It was a stark reminder that chilled the room.

JUNE 1, 1848

A sharp, penetrating cold blew in from the northeast as the sun hovered above the eastern horizon, peeking through the thunderheads while struggling to kiss its warmth onto the new day. To the north, lightning flickered against a slate black sky. The weather changed dramatically from last night’s placid sunset to the stormfront closing in on them like a freight train.

On the pitching deck, men turned up their collars and the women huddled tightly within their shawls. Catharina and Alvina-Kristina appeared on the windswept deck carrying food baskets and cooking pots and joined the line-up for the galley. Alvina-Kristina wore a thick shawl, concealing her new hairdo that irritated Tom to no end—then he saw the fresh welt on her cheekbone.

His temper flared, and when he spotted Sune, pounced towards him. "You sonuvabitch!" Spitting into his hands and rubbing them together, his feet slapped the planking as he thundered towards him. Sune turned to face Tom with defiance, which changed to alarm once he saw the violence of Tom's temper.

Olsson intercepted Tom. "Easy, now," Olsson urged in Swedish.

Tom continued to claw forward with no loss of momentum. The second mate, Polman, rushed to the aid of Olsson and together they contained Tom's charge.

"You'll be put in chains if you fight," Polman warned in Swedish.

The spurts of his breath were coming out fast. Tom stopped his charge and freed an arm, pointing at Sune. "You beat your beautiful wife, you miserable sonuvabitch!"

"Settle down, Trasler," Olsson said. They both held their arms around Tom, feeling his strength ripple through his shoulders.

"He hit her," he responded despondently in English. "He beat up his poor wife just because I cut her hair!" He loosened his body, the shoulders, legs and back softened. Tom took a deep cleansing breath as Olsson escorted him to a quiet spot to calm down.

Carina joined Polman. "Sune acted as a man should," she said. "Thomas needs to mind his own affairs."

"I agree. It is not Trasler's concern if Sune Gabrielsson asserts his God-given authority over his wife," the second-mate said to Carina. "She disgraced him yesterday."

"I fear his feelings for her are strong," she said.

"Too strong," agreed Olsson.

By noon, the wind swept over the sea, driving its surface into gnarled ridges that pounded against the ship, hurling torrents of water across the bow. Tom was about to retreat below when Liedberg plunked his hand on his shoulder, guiding him into his cabin. He closed the door.

"Have a seat." It was an order, not a request.

Tom sat, clasping his hands on his lap. He expected another chewing out because of his loss of temper. It created much chatter among the passengers and crew. Tom was still not completely calmed down.

"The Sabbath past, I was observing your participation in the Holy service. I see that you are not a praying man."

"That I am not."

"I also note you sit on the woman's side of the congregation and not with the men."

"I'm not in favour of segregating men and women, sir."

"I see. You attend the services, but you do not believe. Even the whore Carina Svensson bows her head in prayer."

"Good for her."

Liedberg's face went dark and troubled. "You will soon be a praying man."

"What could possibly turn me into prayer, sir?"

"A tempest, Mr. Trasler. One that will soon be upon us."

He had Tom's full attention. "A bad storm?"

"Regrettably, they are frequent during the seasons of the equinox and are above all terrible over this immense ocean, which opposes no obstacle to their fury. I assure you, Trasler, you will soon be a praying man."

"I don't believe there is anything to pray to, sir."

"Lord forgive you, Mr. Trasler, that this great tempest is not for your benefit, so that you will be put in such extremity of peril, that you become a believer and beg for deliverance."

Stepping out of Liedberg's cabin, the wind hit Tom with a blast that caused him a couple of missed steps. His hair whipped straight ahead, obscuring his vision and his pants flattened against the back of his legs. The change of weather in just the past few minutes was dramatic. The sea turned into an expanse of marauding gray mountains. The waves felt hard as concrete, crashing into the ship and jolting people right off their feet.

Stumbling past the galleyhouse, Tom heard a woman's yelping shriek through the open door. Liedberg peered into the galleyhouse to see. Burned by scaling water, she screamed furiously at the captain, as if he was negligent for not calming the waters.

"Must I hold your pot as you cook, you old sow? Get below. Be gone!"

The ship rammed into a mountain of a wave, sending a deluge from the weather bow right to the main deck. Liedberg's voice rifled back and forth along the decks. The crew climbed aloft and crawled out on the swaying yards while they struggled to reef the big sails. The first mate gazed at the mass of clouds churning towards them. He was a tough man who feared no other, rarely feared the wrath of God, but he was a man who feared the sea.

When Tom arrived at the Gabrielssons' berth, the critical tension was extreme. The purple-black welt staining Alvina's temple and cheekbone extended well below the eye. This wasn't just one punch—it was an all out beating. It must have happened last night, and Tom, having gone to bed early, slept behind *The Walls of Jericho*, and this morning he didn't see her, only noticing a change of mood, and assumed it was just the tension from the haircut. Now it was much more—this had become *the Cuban Missile Crisis*—with Sune and Tom on the precipice of all out war. Tom faced Sune, sitting on the bottom berth with Jonas. He stared back at Tom with a bold defiance. Alvina-Kristina was quiet and submissive. Selma-Olivia and Catharina looked on with frightened faces, fearing the fight they could see coming. Tom looked over at Alvina-Kristina.

"No man has the right to beat or even hit a woman, no matter what she's done."

The beating had its effect on her and she turned away from Tom, fearing further punishment. Tom pointed his finger at Sune. "All right, you miserable wife beater, I'm going to give you what you gave to Alvina." He raised his fists. Sune rose off the berth, raising his own. Jonas stood beside Jonas, his fists also raised. Tom's fists trembled with raw fury. He began to recoil his arm. Sune flexed, eager to put Trasler in his place. Johanna wailed and clutched Tom's legs, blubbering away. Tom caressed her skull and eased her back. He flipped the bird with both hands.

"Asshole."

He wheeled around and stepped into the aisle, not certain what he'd do next. Carina, who like the rest of the passengers, had watched the drama, nodded with a *c'est la vie* kind of shrug, inviting him. Despite there was no love lost between them, Tom considered the alternative—and accepted the invite. She looked relieved when he arrived, obviously not wanting to be alone during the storm. Her crate was too large to lower into the hold where most of the emigrants stored their belongings and became her bed. There were layers of canvas folded on top providing a rudimentary mattress. Secured with one end bound to the mast, it ran along the direction of the aisle to where the other end was roped to a ceiling beam.

Carina wore a dark green dress, one of her three cotton dresses she used when washing or cooking so not to spoil her more lavish wardrobe. With Tom present, her clotheslined curtain remained open to prevent unfounded rumours concerning the two. Still, many took careful notice of the two sitting together, but none so as much as Alvina-Kristina.

The ship rode up and down the monstrous waves like a deranged stunt pilot joyriding an airplane. Desperate mothers cradled their infants, grasping for supports to prevent toppling off their bunks. The storm intensified, predicating a sharp increase in retching. Vomit flowed on the floor and the stench was ripe.

The ship struck a wave with a tremendous, jouncing crash. Rood flew upward, hitting the ceiling beam with a shower of stars sparkling in his field of vision. It was a shock and also pain as he rubbed the top of his head. "This is going to be a bad one, big thunder!"

Jack Silver, nauseous when the ship rode a calm sea, crawled on his hands and knees to a plastic pail. His body convulsed up a barf, but nothing came out other than a deep belch. The floor beneath him fell away and he slid downhill. He crawled uphill. The deck rose and he fell downhill. He clutched the central station with both hands and there he clung, waiting for the ship to get back onto an even keel. She did, except only to roll over on the opposite side. Downhill became uphill, then uphill downhill. Over and over again. And again.

Still wearing the white eye patch, Silver tumbled like a little kid rolling down a hill. The walls tightened around him. He needed to get out of this awful place. Now. Right now.

He burst through the office door into the steerage. He climbed the stairs to the main deck, crawling up on all fours like a crippled dog. He pulled and pushed at the lattice hatch. It wouldn't move. He had the same extremity of panic as would a burial victim waking up inside a coffin. With the terror-induced strength, he jerked an opening. He squeezed through. The decks were completely awash and the rain beat down so hard it stung the skin. But at least he breathed fresh air and the cold helped to dampen the nausea. The deck beneath him fell away and rolled to his left, and then rose and leaned to his right. Grunting and moaning, Silver leaned over, his gut heaved and he puked until nothing but empty air belched from his body.

Heavy footfalls clumped overhead, then an ominous silence fell upon the steerage when the crew shut the two sliding deck hatches, battening them down. The passengers found themselves locked shut from the outside—trapped below—the only source of fresh air cut off.

"They just locked us in," Anderson reported.

"Silver?" Rood asked.

Anderson's face paled.

Rood glanced at the security monitor and toggled through the cameras until he found Silver. *He was still on deck!* He was leaning over the bulwark, puking. The animation died out of Rood's face. Lightning flashed, multiple detonations like an air raid and inside the office, every monitor went blank.

"Your computer's out," Anderson said.

"You have an amazing power of observation!"

"They were programmed to shut down during an electrical storm," Anderson explained.

Rood charged into the steerage. People around him groaned, swore, puked, prayed, moaned and cried. He went up the staircase. The hatch was locked tight. He ran through the aisle, thumped up the stairs, and grabbed the aft hatch, heaving with his full weight, but it too was locked. He shook it for anger's sake and swore profanely. Rood banged on the hatch, yelling at the crew to open up. No response. Rodriguez joined him, both trying to force open the hatch.

"Can't open it, Chief."

"Jesus Christ bananas! Silver's up there!" Rood swept back into the office. "I need the video feed!"

"The system is surge protected," Anderson explained.

"Reboot it!"

"Can't. It won't permit a reboot during lightning events. I can't exactly go to a shop to replace the motherboard."

"Override it!"

"That will take a minute."

"We don't have a minute!" Rood's screaming didn't make any difference. The computers couldn't care less if he screamed at them. All this screaming only slowed Anderson down.

Silver stumbled drunk-like for the hatch. He tried to release the locking latch. The deck rolled, pitched, every direction at once it seemed, and Silver couldn't find a proper footing to unlock it. Sten Lindblad, the sailmaker, appeared directly before him.

"Open the hatch, you stupid galoot."

A wave crashed over the side of the ship, flushing Silver to the starboard side. Lindblad clung to the rim of the hatch, staying put while Silver gulped and spat water. The sailmaker shot Silver a sideward look of cunning he could not see.

Silver crawled on his hands and knees. "Open it, you idiot! That's an order!" Silver felt himself heaved up by his belt. Lindblad held him with a single arm. Silver folded like a limp rag. "Let me down!"

Silver saw the bulwark shift position from his left to his right. Then all at once, below him—the churning sea. Silver felt himself freefall. He was below the waves before understanding what just transpired, and worse, what it all meant. He kicked to the surface. He could see the ship move past him! It moved further away. He reached for the hull. It was beyond his reach! Silver screamed and his terror was extreme. No words, just a high-pitched shriek. A wave pulled him under. It was lights out for Jack Silver before he even realized he was dying.

The security monitor flickered back to life. Rood could see the tempest beating down on the ship with visibility reduced to just a few feet. He switched from one camera to another. No sign of Jack Silver. Rood's face paled into a lost gaze. Bodmar did a security search for Silver. The system would recognize and isolate him with the best available video feed. *No person matches your search.*

Rood swore and kicked Silver's empty puke-bucket. "Secure the equipment."

The snapping sounds from the ship's fabric revealed the horrific stress it fought against. A convulsion shook down the entire length of her keel that felt like it was about to shatter. Debris, garbage and human sewage flowed along the steerage floor. Locked below, the physical misery of the storm accentuated the complete indignation of not being able to tend to personal hygiene with any privacy.

Inside the office, the soldiers retreated to their berths. Jackson sat beside Rood. "We're screwed without Silver. Did he get flushed over the side or was he tossed?"

"Silver was too much of a coward to get flushed. Let's face it, Tyrone; he was the most hated man aboard ship. He was tossed, all right." Rood lay flat on his back on his mattress. He was in a state of shock. "Christ Almighty, whoever is responsible better get their speech ready for God, because by the time I get through with them, they'll be giving it in person."

Payback is a bitch.

Their world was a wild ride of ups, downs, lefts, rights, and often a perverse combination of all of them. All feared that at any moment, the ship would shatter into pieces. The water would flood in, filling their lungs. They would disappear below the waves never to be heard from again. There would be no marker, no gravestone, no message to the living world—their fate forever a mystery.

Despite all the suffering below deck, Tom could not help but wonder about the poor bastards above, fighting the elements with every shred of wit, courage and strength they possessed to keep the tiny ship afloat.

In the feeble light, Carina pulled out two Bibles—one in Swedish, a smaller one in English. She flipped to the Gospel of Mark. It was on Chapter 4, verse 37, and she handed him the English Bible, her finger on the verse. Tom just stared at her with a little bit of awe, dumbfounded the prostitute knew the Bible well enough to find a particular verse. She found the same verse in her Swedish Bible read aloud. Tom had no clue what possessed him to follow in English.

> *And there arose a great storm of wind and the waves beat into the ship, so that it was now full. And He was in the hinder part of the ship, asleep on a pillow: and they awake Him and say unto Him, Master, carest thou not that we perish? And He arose and rebuked the wind and said unto the sea, Peace, be still. And the wind ceased*

> *and there was a great calm. And He said unto them, Why are ye so fearful? how is it that ye have no faith?*

"There's one certainty, Sister Carina, there's no Christ on this ship to calm the sea."

She smiled and patted him on the lap. She prayed for both of them.

The hours crawled by, minute after infernal minute.

The only indication morning had dawned came from slivers of light curling around the fore and aft deck hatches. Little fresh air could seep in, yet when the waves came crashing onto the deck above, water rained down, soaking everyone and every mattress. The air Tom breathed had been breathed a hundred times before by ninety filthy mouths. Only a half-breath of fresh air entered the steerage, and there was more water than air pouring through those openings.

Another full day of insanity passed until the lines of light around the deck hatches vanished as they entered into another dismal night. Matters worsened when they extinguished two of the four ceiling lamps to keep the others fuelled. A short time after, they poured the oil from the third into the last. The air was exhausted and Tom had visions of the crew opening the deck hatches and finding ninety suffocated corpses.

Throughout the tempest, Carina clutched Tom's arm, sometimes holding hands or embracing him completely. Tom clenched his eyes shut, desperately wishing for the seas to be calm, to be able to breathe fresh air, to wash and to have a hot meal.

To sleep.

Sometime around midnight, the ship leaned into a long list to port. The ship passed a point it had never before breached. A dreadful hush crept through the steerage as a clatter of loose items slid across the steerage floor. The ship maintained its roll to port. Bodies tumbled out of their berths and crashed onto the floor like a mass suicide. The list continued.

They were capsizing!

Death screams ripped from ninety throats. Tom could feel Carina's fingers gouge into him like claws, cutting into his skin while she nearly split his eardrums with a searing scream.

Tom thought of himself as accepting death, but he didn't want to go like this, not in a reeking hold, dying within the mortal cries of ninety others. Carina clutched him, her lips seeking his and she gave him a crushing death kiss until the shifting gravity tore their mouths apart.

Tom clung to the mast, feeling the throbbing vibrations snapping from it. He could feel Carina's arms wrap around his waist, holding on only by sheer desperation. The ship wallowed for an eternity of the worst kind of terror. Shrieking souls rolled across the deck along with a shrapnel of chamber pots, tables, benches, chairs, crates and cooking utensils. The collision of debris and bodies shrieked throughout the steerage. Even while fighting the elements above, the crew would have surely heard the wailing from below.

Tom lost his grip on the mast. Carina clung onto him while they tumbled across the planking that was more wall than floor. Tom saw the terrified family he was about to smash into, seeing a young girl's face, screaming in fear. Someone struck up against Tom.

The skin he pushed away was cold and waxy—a dead person! A shriek burst from his throat.

A dead person was next to him!

Who? Who was it?

They hurled through a canvas partition, striking the frame of a berth. The corpse followed Tom until it plowed into him a second time. He turned to look at the body.

It was Anne-Sophie.

His throat tightened with shock and disbelief. A shriek ripped from his mouth. Carina Svensson's screams joined Tom's. Anne-Sophie's mouth and eyes were opened in a twisted, silent scream while her limbs flayed unnaturally as all three crumpled against the berth.

The ship clung at the tipping point, as if waiting for a final push that would ultimately set her over. Then—a sudden heave. The ship rolled amok to starboard. Bodies and debris fell towards the opposite side. People in the portside berths toppled out by the dozens, sounding like a load of pumpkins being dumped out by a truck.

Tom, Carina and Anne-Sofie's body tangled and tumbled towards the starboard berths. Carina smashed her ribs into the corner of her tied down crate, grunting as she bounced off and clung onto Tom's ankle. They took out a canvas partition and crashed into a berth, snapping the bottom planks. Tom found himself sprawled on top of the deceased woman while Carina followed, crumpling into him along with some loose boxes and buckets striking both in the back and ribs. Tom could only sense his own screaming, both in pain and panic. Carina wailed in a depraved scream.

The ship recovered in what seemed to be a nonchalant manoeuvre.

The din subsided and for a suspended heartbeat of an instant, it was dead quiet. Tom could see a passenger raising his hands to Heaven.

"Oh, almighty God, mercifully hast Thou preserved us!"

Then the excited chatter rumbled, the children's screams and crying rented the air as others praised their God while they gathered their wits and crawled back to their berths. Carina, on her hands and knees, two-handed jerked Tom off his dead student. Anne-Sofie's grieving father-in-law and husband grabbed the body by the left ankle and dragged it back to their quarters while the remaining limbs flayed this way and that without any dignity whatsoever.

Tom and Carina crawled back to her crate. They clung to the mainmast and clutched the other. Both were in pain, hungry and thirst burned their throats. They were soaked in human sewage and vomit and the stench was sour. In the half-light, their emotions taxed, Tom and Carina kissed fiercely, weeping into each other's arms, sharing their lips for any comfort they could find.

It was fear, desperation, madness—all of it.

Four hours passed since the ship nearly succumbed to the tempest. Alvina-Kristina lay on her upper berth with Edvard, Sune and Selma-Olivia. Sune somehow slept. She kept checking on the baby, each time expecting to find a tiny corpse, but Edvard seemed to weather the storm quite well—just like his father. She took him to her breast and he fed quite greedily.

"I have faith that the Almighty will do everything He can do to help us cross this dangerous sea," Catharina said, her voice vibrating into a tremble. Selma-Olivia chewed on a biscuit, hard as rock, breaking it into smaller pieces.

"Why would He so anger the sea?" Selma-Olivia asked in a tiny, frail voice.

"God has let loose this tempest to test our faith."

"I don't understand why His faithful servants must be punished for the sake of a trial." Her tiny voice was jagged with confusion.

"The devil is always near, trying to tempt a sinner, making him doubt that God could help in trouble and tribulation. Jesus calmed the storm and walked upon the sea. He can save the faithful from any peril He chooses."

"Anne-Sophie and her unborn child are dead!"

"It was her time. Preordained before her birth. She is now with the blessed Saviour in all His glory."

"I wish God would choose this peril to go away as Christ calmed the sea."

"We must trust to the mercy of Him who rules the elements. Already the sea is less tumultuous and the agitation of the waves diminished. Pray with me, child." Catharina took a prayer book, flipping to the Ninety-third Psalm.

After Alvina-Kristina finished nursing, she handed Edvard to Selma-Olivia and stood to stretch some stiffness from her back. With just a single lantern remaining, the steerage was as dark as twilight. She looked back to Anne-Sophie's family. She could see the body covered in a blanket, only a foot sticking out. It was white and waxy, the toes curling in slightly. She heaved out a half sob and forced it back. She stared at Anne-Sophie's husband. He glanced up, resenting her intrusion. She never liked the man, but her heart filled with great sorrow for him.

She peered deeper into the gloom over to Tom and Carina Svensson. They were on the floor beside her crate, wrapped in what she first believed was a terminal embrace. Their cheeks were pressed together, their eyes closed, their faces and clothes smeared with filth. They looked like the two deadest people she had ever seen. Fearing the worse, she stumbled towards them, getting close enough she could see the minute twitch of their faces, the eyelids squinting.

That filthy whore had her man, and then realized what she just thought. It wasn't *her man*. Her man was in the berth contently snoring. She could not understand her feelings, but they were embracing like lovers—and they kissed madly—and it irked her, not just a little but a great deal. She touched the left side of her face. She could feel the welts rise above her skin with her fingertips, their touch causing her face to burn with fire. Feeling sadder than sad, more alone than lonely, she took another look at Thomas and Carina Svensson, and then turned towards her berth, weeping all the way back.

When the final lantern exhausted its fuel, the passengers saw their world go black. They waited out the tempest in total darkness.

It was well into the fiftieth hour of this perfect storm when the deck hatches opened with synchronized precision. The diffused light of the overcast afternoon flooded the compartment revealing their un-dead tomb. There was no cheering, no praise to their God—just the overwhelming silence of nearly ninety living cadavers.

CHAPTER 17

Like ragged spirits, a bone-tired lot crawled onto the main deck. Many held their hands to the skies, collecting rainwater to splash their faces clean. It was as if they had been released from the lowest depths of Purgatory, exonerated from their sins and baptized clean by rains bequeathed from Heaven.

Tom crawled up the forecastle steps and stumbled to the windward side of the ship's bow. He clung to the bulwark while the ship pitched down. The torrent of water breaking off the deck washed him to the capstan. Despite floundering, he welcomed the frigid water that revitalized his strength and cleansed him of the reeking filth. Feeling almost human again, he crawled back to the bulwark and clung on more completely now, relishing the wash of the spray as it scoured the stench from his body.

Shredded topsails, braided into dangling ropes, were being replaced by an exhausted crew who climbed high aloft. The main lower topsail swung out on its booms. The wind grasped the canvas and shook away the clinging moisture, creating another thunderclap and brief downpour, hauling the ship into its march through the water. The captain pulled in next to Tom, forcing a cadaverous grin to crack his chiselled face.

"That was a bit of an adventure, wasn't it?" Tom said.

Liedberg shook his head, his hair pasted to his forehead and temples. "We lost the helm for a moment, got trapped in a trough and I perceived it certain my command was to be lost. I'm even more astonished I didn't lose a man."

"For your information, I never did pray."

"You ought to right now and give praise. It was Providence alone whom delivered us from a watery tomb."

"Oh? I thought it was your cunning skill as a captain backed up by a great crew."

"You are correct in your accolade, Mr. Trasler. Thanks to their valour and vigour of their muscles, this crew is one who would get out of a scrape to which most others would yield."

Both men braced themselves as a wall of water heaved across the pitching deck, drenching both. Tom shook the water from his face and hair. "How do you keep control of a ship in such weather?"

"Employ only the topsails and a jib. The sails must be low enough for reefing, but high enough to keep a hold on the wind when the ship is low in a trough. With minimum canvas, the masts and rigging won't get over taxed and we can still hold her course."

"We must have made good mileage with that kind of wind at our backs."

"We reaped excellent mileage—in the wrong direction!" The captain paused and the pitch of his voice lowered to a mere hush. "I understand there is a fatality?"

Tom nodded grimly. "Anne-Sofie."

"She! How?"

"I don't know," Tom sighed. "Maybe her pregnancy had something to do with it. I didn't even hear her dying or any commotion and she wasn't that far from me. I was very fond of her. She was a sweet girl."

"That she was. I am deeply saddened."

Tom took a deep, shaking breath. He looked below to the main deck. The passengers' nerves were ragged. No one had slept or eaten in two days, and they looked disoriented as they mingled about. "How are we going to dry up the steerage? It's a sewer down there and it really stinks."

"We have to form some work teams."

"What about the straw mattresses?"

"Regrettably, they are a curse to dry out—perhaps impossible." Liedberg looked up at the three masts, the crew working hard without complaint. "Before undertaking new fatigues, my crew must first of all recruit their remaining strength to repair the sails and rigging. My cook has to re-light the stove and my crew takes precedence for a hot meal.

They still have much to do, as do I. I beg for your leave."

Tom knocked on Ralph's door. It eased opened and Ralph's face was gray. The seas still rough, Tom clutched onto the door while forcing a false smile on his lips. "You don't look so good, Ralphy."

"I don't smell so good, either."

Rood appeared on deck with Rodriguez. Rood looked bewildered. The unsteady way he walked solidified Tom's impression the man was in shock. He knew two nights trapped in a tempest would do it to a man. It did it to everyone, but this was a different kind of shock. And he knew it was big trouble.

Rood walked to Ralph and Tom. "Silver's lost," he said with chilling simplicity.

"Lost! How?" Ralph asked.

"Panicked and went on deck. Never made it back in," Rodriguez said. "Someone must have thrown him overboard."

"In the office, both of you," Rood said. "There's about to be some payback, big thunder!"

Tom and Ralph arrived at the office, greeted by four soldiers dressed in black fatigues, battle armour and combat helmets. They carried carbines and were packing nine millimetre Colts.

"Your uniforms are over there." Rood pointed to the floor.

Tom looked at the soldiers in black and swallowed. "Are you kidding me? We're going on deck in 21st century battle armour?"

"This is all about payback, Barney, and to scare the ever loving bejabbers out of the rest of the crew and passengers so that the rest of us will be left unharmed until we ditch this rat infested tub."

It had never been discussed, but no one, not a single soul in the office, carried any doubt Silver wasn't swept away without some direct involvement from the crew. This wasn't an accident—it was a homicide. An unspoken unanimity prevailed that action must be taken. Any one of them could be next if an example wasn't set.

Tom knew he would be a witness to terrible violence. When Anderson pulled out a makeshift torch, a wooden swab handle wrapped with linen and stinking wet of lamp oil, his stomach twisted and his heart raced.

Payback is a bitch.

Anderson assisted both into their battle armour and handed Tom a carbine. It was a thing of handsome, barbarous beauty. Anderson gave him a quick tour of the weapon as Rodriguez distributed the ammo. They were long banana clips holding 9mm rounds.

Ralph, with his right arm in a fresh sling, was limited to a nine-millimetre Colt. Rood slapped the clip into the gun, jerked back the slide and handed it to Ralph.

"Careful, Parker, safety's off."

"I've handled a nine before," Ralph said, feeling a little insulted.

"You haven't fired a shot since basic training," Rood said. "Today may be your big chance to finally become a real soldier."

Ralph's face soured, but it was true, really. He served in combat missions but never on the front lines or never discharged his weapon against the enemy. Still, he resented Rood humiliating him this way.

"How do I look, Ralph?" Tom's helmet hung low over his brows, the large chinstrap pulling in his features while his shoulder length hair spilled well past the helmet.

"You need a haircut to look like a convincing soldier."

"You with us, Barney?"

"Yes, sir!"

Rood smiled and smacked Tom on the shoulder with a loud slap, but it carried respect. "Sharon and Terry, take the poop deck, Tyrone and Ralph, the forecastle. I want only you people on the elevated decks, so the helmsman has to be taken care of. If he resists, just shoot the bastard. Carlos, Barney and I will remain together on the main deck." Even Bodmar was in agreement with Rood on this one. They all nodded. "Move it!"

Rodriguez and Anderson were, militarily speaking, the best of Rood's crew. Rodriguez went first, Anderson last, and after locking the office with the full twelve security latches, they moved swiftly. Anderson and Bodmar marched through the entire length of the steerage to reach the aft steps. Bodmar, for the first time since Tom met her, wore bright red lipstick—a form of warpaint, he surmised. She led the way with gasps from the startled passengers, having never seen a woman dressed that way, with the helmet strapped tight, her pursed crimson lips, black pants and men's boots. Bodmar's strides were imperative—like a man's. They yanked their children out of the way. Others cringed into their berths, poking their heads out cautiously after the soldiers passed. One woman, seeing the weapons and knowing there was about to be terrible violence, clasped her hands into desperate prayer.

Tom marched behind Rood and in front of Rodriguez. He kept the carbine close to his chest. Safety off, finger against the trigger guard—just like Anderson showed him. Moving fast, they ascended the steep staircase. When they arrived on deck, the rain continued to fall, but the wind settled into a calm and the waves had diminished to long, slow swells. The deck was crowded and passengers hurried aside, clutching their children and each other. Tom found his stride, matching Rood's with long, heavy thumps splashing on the rain soaked deck. Bulldozing through the crowd, he felt a perverse kind of thrill he was somehow terribly ashamed of.

Rood fired a short burst into the air. The passengers were exhausted, on edge and it didn't take much to create a collective panic that swept across the decks. One woman cut loose with an endless shriek so exaggerated it sounded like a bad actress in a low budget horror movie.

Liedberg and the sailmaker, mending one of the ripped sails, saw the approach of the armed soldiers. The captain stood, his voice climbed to the high, clear octaves of fury. "What is the meaning of this?"

"I'm missing a man—Jack Silver."

"Silver is missing?"

"Continue to yank my crank, Captain, and I will put a bullet in you. You know damn well that one of your crew threw Silver overboard."

"This is the first I have heard of this matter!"

"All your crew on the main deck," Rood ordered. "Passengers, too. All of them, even the sick. Now!"

Liedberg replied in a vehement whisper, "We have a funeral in just minutes."

"There will be a second funeral, I assure you, once we find out who murdered my man."

Liedberg motioned for his two mates. "Mister Rödin, have the crew assemble on deck. Mr. Polman, all passengers on deck, even the infirm."

A hundred souls jammed the deck. Dead tired and hungry, most were so exhausted they had little room left for fear. Liedberg explained it was a certainty someone threw Jack Silver overboard.

"I implore the guilty one to reveal himself," he pleaded. "For the sake of all others on board, I make this appeal."

No one moved. Rood was not a patient man. He levelled his eyes on the youngest member of the seventeen member crew—Anders Kallstrom, more boy than man. Rood grabbed him from the line of crew standing before him.

"I assure you he is not responsible or capable of any wicked act," Liedberg begged.

"I don't doubt that, Captain." Rood smiled as he held his hand out and Rodriguez handed him a water bottle containing the lamp oil. He spilled the contents over the boy's hair, shirt, pants and back. The odour spiralled into the rainy air. Rood took out a lighter and lit the torch. His grin turned his expression into a skull's face.

Tom saw the exact moment when Liedberg realized Rood wasn't sane, that he was dealing with a lunatic. They realized it together. A gasp murmured through the crowd while Rood's face held a serene placidity that even Rodriguez found disturbing. The boy leaned away from Rood's torch.

"Whoever killed Jack Silver has ten seconds to come forward, or else this charming young lad will become a human inferno." A smile emerged on Rood's lips, managing to unite cordiality and cruelty at the same time.

Liedberg relayed the ultimatum. The crew remained firm. The passengers tensed up, and it was the most horrible sense of quiet Tom had ever endured. He felt the dread rise up inside as the rain hissed against the torch, making quiet little whispers in the breeze. Bits of the torch fell from the shaft, falling like shooting stars on the deck, igniting bubbled drops of lamp oil splattering the wet deck, burning above the film of water with a blue corona.

Anders Kallstrom called out a plea, his young voice filled with tears and terror. Women in the crowd whimpered to stop this madness, hushed quiet by others who feared reprisal from the soldiers.

"Six . . . five . . . four," Rood paused as he brought the torch closer to the boy.

The boy repeated the plea, his voice hoarse with huge, innocent eyes of blue ice. Tears filled those amazingly blue eyes and spilled from them.

"Three, two . . . one—"

"It was I!" Sten Lindblad, the sailmaker, stepped forward.

"You!" Liedberg roared in fury.

"I threw the pig into the tempest."

"Do you have any mind of what your evil has brought to this ship?" Liedberg roared, his voice a blend of outrage and tears. Lindblad knew this was an execution. He tightened his face, his body stiffened, standing there, waiting for oblivion.

"Captain, I'll take care of the punishment," Rood said. His face was docile, completely at peace when he handed Rodriguez his carbine and drew the nine from his holster, shoving it in Sten Lindblad's mouth like a grotesque cigar.

Liedberg looked at Rood with pleading eyes. "He is indispensable!"

"I intend to see the colour of his brains."

"We have sustained massive damage to our canvas. Only he has the skill to mend the sails. If you wish to arrive in New York, Colonel Rood, we need a sailmaker!"

"Very well." Rood withdrew the pistol and holstered it. He gave Lindblad a one armed shove back into the line of sailors. Within the same motion, Rood put the torch to the boy.

Tom stood directly before Anders Kallstrom with a miserable half-sanity. It wasn't the sight of the flames engulfing the boy as Rood slid the torch down his body. Or the arms flaying, the legs giving way or the splat of the body on the deck, or the rolling, the legs kicking madly, arms thrashing from side to side, or the face melting away that curdled Tom's blood. It was the boy's screaming. Screaming the way only a human being on fire can scream.

A collective outrage instantly exploded and the crowd turned into a tempestuous mob. Rood expected them to cringe in submissive fear. It was very much the opposite. Rood tossed the torch overboard as Rodriguez handed him his carbine. Tom slipped his finger from over the trigger guard to the trigger itself. The gun pointed at the passengers and crew, menacing them by swinging it back and forth. For the briefest of moments, Tom found himself pointing the gun directly at Alvina-Kristina. She clutched her baby tighter against her body. Tom felt a shock like a transformer blew inside him. A deep apology filled his eyes while rainwater vibrated off the barrel of his MP5.

Gunilla Jonsdotter, a short middle-aged buxom woman, burst from the crowd. She took off her shawl to beat out the flames and stomped towards the boy, yelling fearlessly at Rood. She looked right at him, cursing him all the way to the devil.

"Smile for the camera," Rood said. He squeezed the carbine's trigger. The top of the woman's head tore off. What remained of her face toppled on top of the burning boy. Her hair flashed in flame like those old disposable flashbulbs. The mob's screaming rose, all anger. Not fear, but abhorrence and fury.

The depraved yell came from the right. The cry of a man no longer with his senses. Carl Gustaf's hands outstretched in the strangle position, homed in on Rood. Others flexed to join the charge. Rodriguez took a quick step and slashed his dagger across his neck. Carl Gustaf's throat peeled open like a second mouth. Blood mist sprayed out of the throat from a scream venting from two holes. His hands motioned to his neck, but halfway there, they went limp and he collapsed next to the dead woman.

A sick and horrible chill ran down Tom's back. The mob exchanged an unspoken unanimity to attack. There would be casualties, yes, but militarily speaking, acceptable losses. You could see it in the faces, the abhorrence seething in their eyes, the hate contorting their bodies. They had been pushed too far and no matter what the consequence, the soldiers were going to die. *Each and every one of them.* Tom knew he could fire for a few seconds, but eventually they would get to him. The four covering the higher ground might hold them off, but Tom knew with cold certainty that he, Rood and Carlos Rodriguez, would be torn to shreds by the mob's bare hands.

Liedberg lunged forward, intent to stop this insanity.

Rodriguez, with blood dripping off his blade, flashed a cunning grin at the captain, brandishing his knife with mute savagery. Tom didn't hesitate. Pointing the carbine up with his right hand, he lunged forward. His left hand grasped Liedberg's face and shoved him down. The captain landed hard on his back. Tom stood over him, one foot on his chest, the carbine clutched in both hands, his face screwed up in an expression of desperate intent.

"Do not move, Captain! I repeat, do not move!"

Liedberg uttered a deep groan, a sound of utter, hollow despair.

"They're going to charge," Bodmar warned.

"If they attack, we're finished!" Ralph cried out.

Rood wasn't concerned. His crew was scared, terrified in fact, but nobody fights as ferociously as a terrified soldier.

"Come on, bring it on!" Rood taunted the crowd.

"They're about to charge!" Ralph's full scream was decibels below the roar of the outrage.

Tom felt a debilitating fear grip him. The captain continued to resist beneath his boot. Speech all at once seemed hard.

"Stay down, Captain. Do not move!" Liedberg continued to squirm under his foot. Tom pressed harder. Rodriguez lurched to intervene. Tom locked eyes with him.

"Stand down, soldier!"

Rodriguez stopped his approach, but he was too wired with killing lust to stand down. Tom also looked deadly, he looked determined, but he was also dreadfully tired.

"Do something, Chief!" Bodmar shrieked.

"We're losing control!" Jackson shouted.

Tom flashed a look at Rood. He could tell the colonel finally accepted they were in a goddamn situation. Rood's mind went blank, uncertain of what to do next.

His entire body still ablaze, Anders Kallstrom screamed wildly, inciting the madness infecting the mob. It wasn't just the screaming, it was the smell, that burnt human flesh-stench no other odour equalled. It acted like an opiate, intoxicating everyone, amplifying the outrage past the point of deterrence and reason. The crowd acted as one. They lurched forward, tightening the circle of rage around the soldiers. Everyone in the crowd looked at each other, nodding, ready for the final thrust against the soldiers. There was no fear in the crowd, just fierce resolve.

Tom took his foot off Liedberg, rode the ship's descent into a wave and pivoted to face the burning kid. Tom never realized how a body could be so horribly burnt and yet still have so much life. He thumbed the carbine's selector switch to full auto, firing a burst into Anders Kallstrom's chest.

Blood and charcoaled flesh exploded off the body with a fine mist and a fresher stench rose up, driving into Tom's nose like an upper cut. The boy's tortured screams, instantly stilled, created a sudden silence. The end of Anders Kallstrom's screaming, thrashing and pain placated the mob. The sea breeze carried the gunsmoke, its cordite aroma, fresh and ripe and hot, away from the deck.

Rood's face went from a ferocious intent to outrage. Tom could see the livid lines in his neck. He slapped Tom's shoulder and spun in front of him. His carbine pointed at Tom's forehead. Rood's wild eyes bored right into his. Tom knew he crossed the line. *Rood's line.* He didn't like Rood staring at him with those wild, crazed eyes. No, he did not. Though the gun hovered just inches from his face, he drilled his own crazy fire deep into Rood's eyes.

"They get the point, sir!"

Rood lowered his carbine and put away the lunatic like removing a Freddy Kruger mask at the end of a Halloween party. Tom briefly looked at the faces in the crowd; they accepted this as an out to the attack, and pulled back. He turned and faced Liedberg, still flat on his back and offered his hand. The captain knew Tom saved his life and accepted his hand. Tom clasped it and tugged Liedberg to his feet.

"Tell the passengers to go below and remain in their berths," Tom said.

Liedberg knew what he was going to ask. These wretches had been locked in the steerage for over 50 hours and they were going to be forced below again, but witnessing three savage executions takes a lot of the go-to-hell out of an angry mob. They were quite willing to comply with the order. Liedberg told his men to lock the hatches, and ordered all, including himself, to their quarters.

Just as the rain stopped, the decks lay empty, just the soldiers in black and the three bodies, the kid still smouldering. Tom felt Rood's eyes back on him, still not certain if the carbine would appear back in front of his face, the flash from the barrel, then instant oblivion. Instead, a serene smile curled Rood's lips.

"You did good, Barney. For a half-faggot real estate agent, you did better than some of my crew. You proved where your loyalty lies, and I admit, I wasn't so certain at first. You should consider a career in the military. You'd make a first-rate soldier."

"I just killed a goddamn boy," Tom muttered, his voice trembling. "I don't feel so first-rate."

Bodmar took a bucket of water and doused the kid's body, curled in a position of terrible pain. They stood there, none of them speaking, each in their own world, a million thoughts, images, sounds and smells invading their minds, their thoughts plunged into corrosive pools of acidic emotions.

The soldiers entombed the bodies in canvas and laid them down on the planks supported on the sawhorses. The crew retrieved Anne-Sophie's body and prepared for it burial. Only after they scrubbed all traces of the carnage, were the passengers allowed back on deck. The emigrants were subdued when they assembled around the four bodies, lined-up beside each other. Rood, Rodriguez and Liedberg faced the assembly.

"The United States military are not to be interfered with again!" Liedberg shouted. "They have put explosive devises in the hold of the ship and wish to demonstrate their dominion over any ill-conceived insurrection."

Rodriguez showed an empty salted pork barrel and tossed it overboard. When it was a hundred yards past the ship, he held up a device in his hand with a red button. Showing it for all to see like an auctioneer, he depressed the button. The air rent from the explosion. The passengers, already past the snapping point, recoiled and gasped. Shrapnel from the barrel hit the side of the ship, the sails and pieces fell to the decks sending passengers ducking.

"That is their power!" Liedberg roared. "It will manifest itself below the waterline if they perceive they are defeated. Do not menace the soldiers. Do not menace Mr. Parker or Mr. Trasler." The assembly stared at the captain, wide-eyed and trembling. *They got the point.* He turned and faced Rood. "I have discharged your instructions."

"You may proceed with the funerals."

The soldiers returned to the office and Ralph retreated to his cabin. Tom remained on the forecastle deck. Still in his helmet and black battle armour with the MP5 cradled in his arms, he sat on the capstan. He bowed his head and wept.

A little at a time, the colour returned to the world. There remained a terrible dread in Tom's eyes, something so dark it would always dim the light from the world even during the best of times. Alvina-Kristina stood before him, cradling Edvard. Tom's battle armour and his carbine did not unnerve her, rather, it seemed to have kindled an odd stirring in her. Her bruises from Sune's beating were a stain on the left side of her face, from the forehead to her jaw. Just a few days ago, she showcased beautiful, golden hair, now it was a filthy tangle of soiled black strands. Her stained red dress reeked with grime.

Tom touched the bruises with the tips of his fingers. "You okay?" She nodded, retreating beyond the range of Tom's touch, fearing Sune might be watching. "How's the baby?"

"His heart may be weak, but he is also very brave."

"I pointed the gun right at you. I'm so sorry."

She gave him a twitch of a grin. "You wouldn't have harmed me, Thomas."

"No, I couldn't."

The passengers congregated for the funeral at amidships, but Tom and Alvina-Kristina remained on the forecastle deck, participating in the service from there. Tom learned one thing about Alvina-Kristina during the funeral hymn—she had a horrible singing voice. Carina Svensson sat on the rim of the aft hatch, her head bowed into her hand, heaving the sobs from her body.

When Liedberg sprinkled ash on the canvas covering Anders Kallstrom, Tom shook his head. "That poor kid. Probably never kissed a girl."

"What a lonely way for your earthly body to rest. Alone in the ocean. I don't want to die like that."

"It's not as if you're still in your body, Alvina."

"I want to be laid with my family, with a marker. I don't want my body to be alone."

Tom smiled at her, somehow feeling the same way. Rood appeared on deck back in his blue uniform, still heavily armed, with Rodriguez close to his side. They took their navigation reading.

Alvina-Kristina's eyes filled with a loathing that frightened Tom. "Rood is the devil. I know you are not. Everyone is talking about you. You saved the captain. You took the boy from his pain. You saved many others."

"If there is a devil, there must be a God," Tom said, frowning. "I don't feel God's presence anywhere on this ship."

"God is somewhere. We must find Him and throw ourselves upon His blessed bosom. He will give us strength and His divinity will allow us to defeat those who desecrate his flock."

He could see the anger and resolve in her eyes, plenty of resolve. Too much and it frightened him. She touched his shoulder pad and put her attention back to the funeral service. Following the mournful hymns, the four bodies were offered to the deep. A gleaming ray of sunlight burst through the clouds like fingers from Heaven guiding home the souls of the dead. The sun's angle against the waves made it appear they were glowing by an inferno lit deep below. Alvina-Kristina looked automatically for the rainbow and found it, far out over the water, a misty and mystic crescent. The passengers dispersed, sailors took away the burial planks and the mainsail shook out its wrinkles. The breeze freshened and the masts gave to the pressure of the sail.

Sten Lindblad moped about in a lost daze. The horrendous guilt of Anders' death would be something he would have to carry with him for all his remaining days. The crew had little to do with him. He worked alone, assisted by others only by the obligation of duty.

Tom and Alvina-Kristina drew closer together. "I really liked Anne-Sofie," Tom said, giving a long, sad sigh.

"Our time in this world is very short." She also sighed, blinking away the tears.

"Need a hug?"

She looked down at Sune, who was watching them with a deep mistrust. She shook her head. Her tears splashed onto Edvard's tiny face. It was plainly evident she wanted the hug.

God knows he needed one.

CHAPTER 18

Rood and Ralph stood near the aft quarters, staring at Tom sitting on the capstan on the forecastle deck. He had a good scrubbing, a shampoo and changed into his civvies, wearing his Expos hat. He sat there, staring at nothing, absolutely nothing.

"He's just sitting there."

"Leave him be, Parker. There's only once in a lifetime when you take your first human life."

"You have a soft spot for him."

"Trasler may be a recovering cocaine and alcohol addict, and a real estate salesman, which in my opinion, is as low as an existence as a man can lower himself to, but he knows how to handle himself in a tight spot. He took the initiative, even though knowing I just may put a round in his head for defying my command. He showed where his loyalties lie and he saved our hairy arses, Parker. I have a lot of respect for him."

Rood nodded at Carina Svensson, sitting next to the deck hatch. Her entire body convulsed and they could hear the sobbing all the way across the deck. "Well, so much for tonight's entertainment. Hey," he tapped Ralph's good arm. "I've got seasons two and three of *Seinfeld* on my PC. Interested?"

"How about Silver's porn?"

"Ahhhhgh," Rood grunted. "Just people humping. I've got tons of great shows from the 60's as well. How about *The Beverly Hillbillies?"*

"Nothing wrong with watching people hump."

"Truth of the matter, is that silly bastard changed his password and it doesn't match any he was authorized to use, so we're locked out."

"We're locked out of Silver's computer?"

"Locked out tight. I threatened to wipe out his entire porn collection after he accosted the young girl and he put in a new password. Our security protocol is that three wrong passwords in a row, the computer shuts down for 24 hours. So we get three tries per day until we can break the code."

"There's a lot of great porn at stake here."

"Bodmar is working on it. *Gomer Pile?"*

"Hogan's Heroes?" Ralph countered.

"You're on soldier!"

Carol had a selection of other insanely priced specialty shampoos in tiny travel-size containers, as well as body washes from the same brand. Tom filled one shampoo and a body wash with the lice-killing agent. He took them to Alvina-Kristina along with some distilled water. "Wash yourself with this," he handed her the body wash, "and your hair with this. Just use a small amount like I did when I shampooed your hair. Okay?"

She opened the cap. "I like the smell."

"And you'll smell real nice after!"

Polman delivered swabs and mops to the passengers as the steerage cleanup began. It was a damp, reeking latrine. Everything was wet, specifically the mattresses, which would be impossible to dry out which meant they were going to rot. Many of the passengers suffered losses in food and clothing, and those fortunate enough to have spare clothing and supplies stored in the hold, waited for their turn to go below. Three hatches, all kept locked, accessed the hold. The large square floor hatch at the back of the steerage, one located in the soldiers' office, the other through the forecastle in the crew's quarters.

The steerage's aft hatch was the only one accessible to the passengers, required an escort as the ship's stores were vulnerable to theft. The captain took personal charge to assess the conditions in the steerage. Inside the cramped, dark hold were ship's stores, water, spare parts, large crates of personal belongings, farming implements, spinning wheels and even an enormous plow someone insisted in taking to America. Under the flickering glow of the lantern, Tom found some oversized yet fresh clothing from Charlie's suitcase, as well as some ground sheets from the camping supplies taken for a planned trip to Yosemite National Park. While Tom and four other passengers were leaving the hold, Liedberg grasped Tom's shoulder.

"Follow me, lad." The captain led Tom through the narrow, cluttered passageway and pointed to a loft located above some kegs of pig iron. A spot Tom knew intimately well. "I wish to speak to you here in private. About this loft of which you are so familiar."

"About today's events?"

"It did not seem possible that the essence of such a fine young man could have ended in such a vulgar fashion." Liedberg grasped Tom's shoulder with great affection. "You saved my life, Mr. Trasler, and the lives of many others. You were prepared to face death today to save the poor boy from further pain. I thank you. I will spare you from further incarceration on this loft. It is my debt I have contracted to you."

"Like a *Get out of Jail Free* card?"

Liedberg smiled, obviously not fully understanding Tom's humour but grasping just enough. "Yes." Liedberg slapped a large key into Tom's hand. "I entrust to you this key to the hatch, Trasler."

"What for?"

"You shall be its custodian and escort passengers here to fetch their belongings when needed."

Tom stared at the brass key. "That sounds just fine. I only wish I could sleep away from the Gabrielssons. Aside from the soaking wet mattress, Sune and I aren't exactly on speaking terms over that harmless haircut."

Liedberg eyed Tom sharply, signifying it was anything but a harmless haircut. "There shall be no change, Trasler. Behave your passions with the Gabrielsson woman, and there shall be no further cause for Sune Gabrielsson to be agitated by your presence. Your *Get Out Of Jail Free* card, as you refer it to, is not exempt from transgressions against the women!"

"Oh, so beating up the first mate is also out of the question?" The burning look in the captain's eyes quite conveyed the response to that question. "Captain, by any chance, could I sample some of that vodka?"

"Mr. Parker forewarned that once you start drinking, you cannot stop!"

"I can take liquor in small quantities, Captain. I drink brandy when I smoke cigars, or spiced rum with a couple of ice cubes. It's when I get past the halfway point of the bottle that my booze switch gets thrown."

"I will heed to Mr. Parker's caution."

"Captain, even though this is against every recovering alcoholic's advice, my wife finds it helpful for me to have a drink from time to time, as it releases some of the desire."

"Your desire at this moment is too severe, Mr. Trasler. That is a danger which you must not dispute."

Tom knew the captain was right, but he felt Liedberg had affronted his dignity by merely having to ask to have a drink. He prevented a massacre, saved the captain's life, and a little grog should have been an automatic offering.

The moment Tom arrived at the berth, Sune hurled his handbag at him right for his face. Tom reacted just fast enough with a stellar two-handed catch. He wanted to hurl it right back. Sune yelled something at him—it didn't sound too much like a welcome back home—and pointed to Carina's enclosure.

"That was just a temporary arrangement, asshole. Trust me when I say I'd be a lot happier than you to stay there."

Sune didn't understand Tom's English and called Carina Svensson. "Trasler was your guest during the storm, and a happy guest when you two gave into your unholy passions and touched each other with your mouths."

"It is called a kiss," she replied, dipping her words in ice. She turned from Sune and went on deck. He pursued her and she refused to heed to his calls. When he arrived on deck, the congestion of other passengers had stalled her, allowing him to catch up.

"He stayed in your berth during the storm, you keep the pestilence!"

She spun and faced him with a challenge. "He had no choice. He was no longer welcome in your berth. That was made quite evident."

"You two were embracing each other like lovers. He is your problem now, not ours!"

Carina pointed at Sune, her finger jabbing in the air. "Do you deny Captain Liedberg's decree that Thomas must stay with your family?"

"Are you telling us what to do?" Catharina hissed, her arms flying.

"You, the whore of all Östergötland and Marseilles, have the impudence to tell us what to do?"

"You snivelling sow!"

"You . . . you who have disgraced womanhood by bedding hundreds of men, dare to call me a sow?" Catharina roared. "I can only wonder how many bastards have passed through your womb. You ought to ask forgiveness of all those women whom you insulted when you gave yourself to their husbands!"

"I did not give myself to any husband. Not a single time!" Carina's face went placid and she wore a smile revealing her complete contempt for them all. "It is they who came eagerly to me with coin or brännvin." She pointed at the obese woman who had punched her into the steerage the day Tom had been brought aboard. "That fat old sow, Margot Hankinsson, her husband Ivar came running to my bed. And more than once, I assure you." Her husband, standing next to his wife, cringed with mortification. Carina smiled wryly. "Tell me, Ivar, each time that you came to me with your tiny pecker in one hand, a riksdaler in the other, that it was not the best coin you have ever spent?"

"You should weep tears of blood!" Margot screamed.

"A leper can be hated no more than Carina Svensson when she spreads her evil among our men!" Catharina shrieked, straining her vocal cords with the force of her cry.

Carina remained calm, delighted she could finally speak words dammed in her mouth for many, many years. "I have never spread evil. It is your men who walk about the decks and lust over me. They can't get their seed ground here on the ship by their homely sows, so they must walk about and squeeze and suffer and lust after me instead. Is that my doing, or your unholy neglect of your men?"

"You turn your wicked eyes onto our men, tempting them with beautiful dresses and exposed bosom while you seethe with lust," Catharina shouted.

"It is they who seethe with lust by preferring to have my beautiful body in their thoughts and not their unsightly wives." Alvina-Kristina and Catharina both screamed their fury at Carina, both held back by their husbands. Carina smiled back with an impish little grin. "In any case, Thomas must bed with the Gabrielssons, by the decree of the captain."

"That son of a whore is no longer welcome with my family!" Sune declared, turned sharply and walked off with childlike stomps, paused and shouted over his left shoulder, "Never!"

Carina brushed against Jonas as she passed to leave. It flustered him. It took little effort to do so. Moments later, Liedberg arrived with Sune.

"I am aware of your hostile feelings towards Mr. Trasler," Liedberg said to the entire family, "but that is not my concern. I command him to remain with you as per my previous decree and I order all of you to comply." Sune's temper heated to a full boil, provoking Liedberg to wave his finger just below his nose. "I am fatigued by your misgivings of my decree. Fatigue me further, you, like your brother, will become well acquainted with Mr. Rödin's cat-o-nine tails!"

Assisted by the second-mate Polman, Tom refurbished the upper berth to his personal specifications. Alvina-Kristina arrived at bedtime, finding their re-instated guest administering the final touches to the berth. Their mattress lay in a crumpled heap of rotting hay. Polman dragged it out to throw overboard. Many other passengers were doing the same.

"What do you think you doing?" Fatigue made her accent thick.

"I'm not sleeping on that damp, critter infested mattress. I covered the planks with some canvas I mooched off Polman. Then I got three groundsheets from my luggage. So the top bunk will finally be comfortable. No smell, no critters, nice and dry. Unless you prefer the company of your vermin?"

"No . . ."

She took a close look at the three groundsheets, placed perpendicular on the bed, that were just about a perfect fit on the berth. They were about half an inch thick, bright blue with a texture she never before touched. It gave her the same unsettling perception as the so-called *music box*. Just another one of his possessions that was out of its natural element.

"I have to change," she said.

Tom slipped into the aisle, lit by the four evenly spaced lamps running along its length. He stepped out of the way from Polman and another sailor who dragged out soiled mattresses to throw overboard. Alvina-Kristina called and he passed through the curtains.

She stood before him in the shadows, with only a trace of reflected amber lantern glow touching her. Wearing Carol's nightie, she appeared like something out of a fantasy novel—a beautiful and enticing siren of the woods. It was the first time he saw her naked legs. They were long and slender and endless, soft hued as delicate china. The beige fringes of the nightie fluttering her thighs concealed the rest of her legs like an unhappy dead end. He raised his eyes to her breasts, full, tantalizing, and swaying deliciously with the ship's lethargic roll over the waves. Her hair, cascading over her shoulders like a golden waterfall, framed a round and soft face with eyes glittering like turquoise gems as she relished the worship of his eyes.

What heavenly beauty! Tom's soul cried out.

She touched his forearm with her fingertips and he felt a tingle like a low-grade electrical shock and she closed in for a whisper. "You asked me on deck for a hug, and I said no, as Sune was watching. My heart is still oppressed, so hug me now, before Sune's eyes are upon us."

"Okay."

She put her arms around his neck and she pulled him to her body. He could feel the imprint of each breast flattening sweetly against his chest.

"Why did you kiss Carina Svensson?" she asked with a whisper. Immersed in the warmth of the beautiful landscape of Alvina-Kristina's body, it took a moment for him to clear his mind enough to respond.

"We were scared, Alvina. It wasn't romantic kissing, it was just seeking comfort."

"Do not kiss the vile woman again."

He traced the jaw line on her face with his finger, enjoying the slight flush it brought to her cheeks, one horribly stained from Sune's beating.

"I wish it was you who I was kissing." He projected his voice low and inviting, drinking in the twinkle in her cerulean eyes. He underestimated how much those words pleased her. He ran his fingers through the sheen of her blond hair. He could tell by her scent, fresh and flower-like, she used the body wash. Her hair held the brilliance and freshly shampooed softness. "Your hair and that nightie brings out the best in you, kiddo. You look really pretty."

A large and guilty smile stretched her lips and she gave him a blush that climbed out of her nightie and flushed her skin. She bit gently on her lower lip, her eyes, deep blue, round and large and soft in the frail light, floated into his.

"Thank you."

He could hear the smile broaden in her voice. Alvina-Kristina stood there, nibbling on her lower lip. While he continued to hold her eyes, the moment grew long, magnified by the silence between them. Then, somewhere deep inside his mind, the stupid switch went off. He leaned towards her lips. Her eyes slipped shut, her mouth pouting ever so slightly. He paused, just to be certain she wasn't going to resist, before bringing his mouth to meet hers.

Johanna and Stina-Sophia burst through the curtains!

Tom leapt back from the shock. They ran to Alvina-Kristina telling her about another girl, something to do with her baby teeth, then turned to Tom, smiling and giggling and jumping up and down. They were so excited he couldn't understand a word they said. They ran back into the aisle, shrieking and giggling.

Tom's heart beat with so much force it pounded his entire upper body. Somehow, he managed to take control of his impulses. Clearly annoyed by the interruption, it took Alvina-Kristina longer for her head to clear.

"I better get into bed before anyone catches me seeing you in that."

"Yes." She breathed in shallow pants. At first, the girls' sudden entrance infuriated her, but the scare of the close call dampened her passions. She nodded and giggled, acknowledging with swimming eyes it was a near thing. "Sune will have a big fuss if he sees us like this."

"As will the captain and the mate's cat-o-nine tails!"

Tom flopped flat on the bunk and snapped shut *The Walls of Jericho.* He appreciated of just how close they were from getting caught, and the consequences would have been terrible. He had been forewarned by Liedberg his *Get Out Of Jail Free* card wouldn't be enough to keep him out of the chains—and perhaps a lashing—for what would have been the ultimate violation. His thoughts were in disarray of how quickly his passions had been ignited. Even more shocked how she permitted a hug just wearing the thin nightie, having his chest flatten her breasts and waiting quite willingly for a kiss just millimetres away from being sealed.

This was no puppy love. She was a twenty-three year-old woman raised with 19th century values and a strict orthodox religious upbringing.

He supposed that Sune's beating fuelled some serious rebellion against a man who treated her like a punching bag. The same man who dragged her away from her home and family to the assured misery of cutting a house from the trees, living in a log cabin with a dirt floor, while expected to be equal in the chores yet bearing child after child. Tom couldn't help but wonder if she perceived him as an available widower—and how easy would it be to step off a gangplank and disappear with him deep into the North American continent. Whether or not those represented her true feelings for him, any involvement with Alvina emotionally would be a disaster, destroying any chance of him returning home, back to Carol; his wife. *Yes, his wife in that forgotten, other life.*

Sune arrived with Catharina, Jonas and Selma-Olivia, who had Edvard. Sune inspected the mattress and looked at Alvina-Kristina, as if she were to blame.

"We will be arriving in America with ruined backs."

"We will be dry, at least."

He touched it again. Curious, but no longer objecting. "Where is that son of a whore?"

Alvina-Kristina pointed to the canvas sheet on their upper berth. "He won't see me nursing the baby." Sune surprised her without issuing a warning.

Lying in the gloom behind *The Walls of Jericho*, Tom fiddled with his wedding ring. The lack of guilt or shame of nearly kissing Alvina alarmed him. He had no wife, not in this existence, and for a while now, felt a growing awareness that he may never get back home. Whether he liked to admit it or not, his feelings for Alvina, his inappropriate actions with her, and unfulfilled desires, was being unfaithful to Carol. Deep down inside he knew it, but it just didn't feel like cheating; not in this new life where he had been portraying himself as a widower. The harsh truth was that she was another man's woman, and any pursuit of the passions he had for her would be no less self-destructive as falling off the wagon. He had to distance himself from Alvina-Kristina, *goddamn had to.*

The women were settling in bed when Tom realized something was amiss.

"Uhhhhh . . . Alvina, aren't the men supposed to get in first?"

"No. Sune said he doesn't want to sleep next to you."

"So . . . who's sleeping next to me?"

"Me." His heart took a fantastical leap right into his throat.

Alvina-Kristina crawled up along with Selma-Olivia, while Catharina, Johanna and Stina-Sophia took the lower bunk. Sune, Jonas, Carl-Johan, and the little girls entered and changed.

"Why did Sune agree to this sleeping arrangement?"

"The Walls of Jericho separates us."

"Ya, right. Tell me something. When you two are alone, does he ever hold your hand, put his arm around you and cuddle?"

"No," she said, thinking nothing more of the question.

"I didn't think so." Tom could feel Alvina-Kristina's thigh flat against his as she also lay on her back. "Good night, Stina-Sophia, Johanna," Tom said sweetly, trying to distract his instincts.

"Good night," replied Johanna.

"I want a good night kiss," Stina-Sophia demanded in English. Tom kissed loudly into the air. Both girls giggled delightfully.

"Good night, Sune." No response. "Night, Jonas, Carl-Johan." Silence. "Good night, Selma-Olivia."

"Good night." *That was actually borderline cheerful.*

Softly, he completed his row call. "Good night, Catharina."

"Goot night, Thomas." *Well, that was a first.*

"What about me?" Alvina-Kristina demanded.

"Sleep tight, kiddo."

He felt Alvina-Kristina's body nudging next to his, and as the ship corkscrewed over the waves, his body pressed into hers, then hers into his. Over and over. The rhythm was maddening erotic.

Alvina-Kristina felt quite well of herself. Having two men on either side of her created quite the thrill. She could never admit to such a thing, naturally. Her mother died before she reached womanhood and she never had the benefit of a mother's wisdom about the affairs of the bedroom. Her grandmother said to her on the eve of her wedding a woman having sexual desires was shameful. A woman must never admit or reveal any such shame to her husband. When a woman gives into her husband's will, she must do so only for the sake of his satisfaction. A woman can never succumb to her own cravings or reach rapture lest her husband's satisfaction becomes subservient to her own.

She always doubted the wisdom of her grandmother. She knew lying squeezed between two men created great shame. And she felt quite delighted to feel shameful.

Alvina-Kristina touched the bruise on her cheek. It still hurt. Her foot slipped through *The Walls of Jericho* and crossed over Tom's legs. He caressed the soft, warm skin of her leg, gave it a little love tap and when the ship rolled to sharply starboard, could feel her press tighter against him.

Sometime after the midnight watch, her hand slipped under *The Walls of Jericho* and grasped Tom's.

He squeezed back and didn't let go.

CHAPTER 19

JUNE 5, 1848

Tom stood at the entrance to the office. "Another death!" Rood and Jackson glanced over at him, resenting the interruption.

"We heard," Rood said, hunched over a computer with Jackson and Bodmar sitting next to him, trying to come to terms with some data.

"It's from the same tribe from Småland who have been sick ever since we've been aboard," Tom pointed out.

"It's called scurvy, add malnutrition, rank water, that dreadful storm and some people simply not fit enough to survive the crossing," Bodmar said. She never took her eyes off the monitor.

"These things happen, my ass. Something really nasty is going on with that gang from Småland!"

"You may leave now," Rood said.

Tom slammed the door. He glanced over to the family area of the Smålanders. He knew one thing, that was a spot best avoided and if he had his way, the entire section would be under quarantine.

AUGUST 22, 2016
VICTORIA, BC

Glenn Parker cleared the files from his desk and fidgeted with a pen. He stood up from his mahogany desk and opened the white vertical blinds to expose the gray weather outside.

A blend of footfalls approached from the reception area. The short shuffle of Charlene, his administrative assistant—and the heavy thuds of a big man. He came into view and Glenn noticed Cliff Nolan's eyes getting sidetracked on Charlene. Her previous employer—now in prison for murdering a 15 year-old girl—invested many thousands of dollars in aftermarket upgrades on her body, and, although modestly dressed, her figure wreaked havoc with Nolan's yearns.

They shook hands only as a civil formality. "Have a seat, Colonel."

"Thank you." Nolan smiled amicably. The smile was pure theatrics.

"I'm having a difficult day, Colonel, so we'll have to keep this short."

"Of course. I'm here to personally convey my condolences on the loss of your stepson, Ralph, and son-in-law, Tom Trasler."

Glenn smiled with forced graciousness. "Thank you. It has been a difficult adjustment."

Nolan's voice was smooth as silk when he continued. "The United States Army does not take their sacrifice lightly. They gave their lives in an attempt to save men and women who were under my direct command. Do not underestimate our appreciation for their sacrifice."

"Thank you."

"We intend to see they are posthumously awarded the Congressional Gold Medal. It is the least we can do to give recognition to their valour."

"You're very kind." Glenn was impatient with the bullshit. "Why are you really here?"

Nolan gave a long, slow smile. "What was the purpose of their voyage to Long Beach?"

"Ralph was working on a contract to manage a Long Beach based shipping company's cross border traffic into Canada. He planned to entertain them aboard the yacht. Carol is our custom's expert, Charlie Mason the IT specialist. Alice and Tom went along for the ride, but Tom also has IT skills, and he was going to back Mason up. After, they planned a weeklong camping trip at Yosemite National Park. What importance is this to you?"

"There are some irregularities regarding the investigation."

"Cut to the chase, Colonel."

"The yacht just happened to arrive at the precise moment and exact location when we entered into the operational phase of a highly classified test flight. Outside of the crew, the number of people who knew of this test was less than ten. I cannot help but be curious as to how *The Salty*

Dog arrived with such precise timing."

"Tom and Ralph happened to be in the wrong place at the wrong time. There is nothing more to it than that."

"How was it you were able to solicit the Prime Minister's assistance on such short notice? And on a Saturday, no less?"

"I've known the prime minister for many years, well before he was even leader of the party. We've gone fishing together on several occasions. I consider him my friend and happen to have his personal cell phone number. Furthermore, I am not ashamed that I used my political contacts to come to the aid of my daughter."

"Just exactly how were you able to find, charter and take off in an aircraft in just three hours—with a government official?"

"Have you no shame in respecting our grief? This meeting is over!"

Nolan's face became an immobile marble bust. The looks just as cold. He stood up and smoothed a wrinkle in his uniform. "Do you have any knowledge of Charles Mason's whereabouts?"

"I do not. He tendered his resignation. His whereabouts is none of my concern, nor is it of yours."

"You daughter is in hiding as well?"

"Not in hiding. On leave of absence. She has just lost a brother and a husband. I will not tell you where she is."

Glenn held his arm towards the door. The theatrical smile Nolan forced at the beginning of the interview was gone, and after giving Charlene a final look-over, the colonel left without saying another word.

Though with Nolan for just a few moments, Glenn could read that beyond the polish and the drapings of a uniform, he was a creature of no conscience capable of great harm. He lifted the receiver to make a phone call when Charlene came in with a folder.

"I found Ralph's Thacker Shipping file." A peculiar tight expression of concern lingered on her face.

The tension mounted in Glenn's shoulders. "What did you find?"

She struggled with the words. "Well, all of Ralph's emails may have been deleted, but there was a hard copy in the filing cabinet."

"And?"

"There was no meeting ever scheduled in Long Beach. Thacker Shipping told Ralph at the end of May that they weren't interested in our services."

Glenn's jaw slid forward. He took the folder, browsed through it, and after all the staff left for the night, shredded the file.

JUNE 7, 1848

After finishing his last English class of the day, Tom stood next to the bowsprit trying to relax when Alvina-Kristina tapped him on the arm.

"When you are mad at somebody, you called them ass-hool. An ass is a beast of burden. It was the blessed beast that Jesus rode on. It has a cross on its back, because it rode Jesus. But, I don't understand the *hool.*"

Tom's eyes twinkled. "There's two meanings for ass. One is for the donkey, the other is for . . ." Ensuring no one could see, he gave her a firm tap on her butt. "So if someone says you have a great ass, they're not talking about your donkey."

Blushing furiously, she wheeled away from Tom and rushed down the stairs. Halfway across the main deck, the laughter exploded out of her. She doubled over, gasping and snorting, water running from her eyes. The cook ambled by. She faced him at point-blank range and shouted, "Ass-hool!"

Still in the throes of laughing hysteria, she vanished into the 'tween-decks. From there, Tom heard another resounding *ass-hool!* and he could only wonder who the recipient may have been.

JUNE 12, 1848

There had been a change in the women. They possessed an odd confidence about them. Some challenged their husbands' authority, others shamefully playful in the berths at night. Sune and Jonas were on deck with a group of men, passing around a jug of brännvin, discussing the matter.

"Their minds are being poisoned by that disciple of Satan." Jonas pointed at Tom. Rather than teaching, he stood behind the capstan like the Antichrist on a pulpit, preaching blasphemy to his misguided disciples. There were just women in this particular class as Alvina-Kristina stood next to Tom, translating his evil, her hands flying for emphasis.

"Your wife is much excited," Wilhelm noted.

Sune took a quick shot from the jug. "She is like soft wax in his hands."

"She is innocent of fault," Jonas said. "I cannot wonder at his devotion to ruin our women."

Stefan Johnson scratched his head like something—a louse, perhaps—had bitten him there. "His pollution of our honest women must be checked."

"He is a deceitful, bad-hearted wretch." Mans Samuelsson spoke with a low growl. "There is no good in him."

"Come, let's hear what is being taught," Sune said. The men crept to the forecastle steps and eavesdropped on the class.

Liedberg was not pleased. The ship hadn't taken hold of a good wind in days. This made him irritable. He kept the crew busy with chores but they were getting edgy as well. Even Polman was uncharacteristic in his curses when he hauled up a wooden bucket filled with grease boiled out of salted beef and pork. Liedberg ordered him to take it to the main topmast and rub it down to prevent it from drying out. An equal lack of joy came from the decks, and though the crew sang their chanteys while swabbing the deck, there was little enthusiasm in their voices. Liedberg detested the grumbling, and if they didn't cheer up soon, he'd reduce their rations of grog.

A commotion erupted from the galleyhouse. A growing crowd of spectators gathered there and were extremely agitated. They watched a half dozen females clapping, laughing and jumping up and down. The captain ambled to the poop deck rail and looked down.

The ship's cook wasn't sprawled dead on the deck and he couldn't possibly fathom anything else that would bring such joy to the women. One young maiden raised her fist in some sort of a menacing-looking gesture while stomping out of the galleyhouse. She came face to face with Trasler and they greeted each other with the resounding *high-five* he had been teaching them as of late.

Stefan Johnson pounced up the stairs, followed by at least another dozen of the tillers-of-dirt. "He has gone too far this time. Do something, Captain, or you will leave us no recourse but to act upon our own."

"Act upon your own and you shall bring upon yourselves the terrible wrath of the soldiers. Trasler is protected."

"But the soldiers have given you dominion over his punishment. You can act."

"That is so."

"You must have Trasler flogged and chained," cried out another and an angry roar of agreement shouted from the growing mob.

"What has Trasler done this time?"

Stefan continued to be the spokesman for the group, now composed of over twenty enraged protesters, most of them men. "He is encouraging the women to burn their corsets!"

Liedberg's left eyebrow soared. "Good gracious! What on earth for?"

Stefan's face—beat red—looked as it were on the verge of detonating into miniscule fragments. "To liberate themselves!"

"Liberate themselves . . . from what?"

"Trasler, the devil incarnate, told them to shed their corsets because they are not healthy. He said it forces the bosom upwards in an unnatural posture for the sole purpose of pleasing men."

"All this just because he saw one woman faint from a tight corset," one of the other men added.

"Other than the whore Carina Svensson, few other women wear a full corset," Liedberg countered.

"But, that is only part of his atrocities," Stefan continued. "He is teaching them heresy which opposes the sacred word of God!"

Anders Danielson, a Smålander, raised a Bible in the air, waving it so hard it nearly shook apart. "*Neither was the man created for the woman—but the woman for the man,*" and, "*For the husband is the head of the wife!* The Holy words."

"What is Anders Danielson getting at?" Liedberg asked.

"Trasler is teaching the women much more than just English," Stefan continued. "His third class of the day, all women, he teaches them heresy about . . . women's rights."

"Woman's rights? What in God's hallowed name are woman's rights?"

"Unholy sacrilege!" Anders Danielson said.

Stefan continued. "After the class, these misguided women then speak these despicable words to the other women. Now they are all speaking of this nonsense."

The Smålander again roared, fisting his Bible. "*Wives, submit yourselves unto your own husbands, as it is fit in the Lord!* The devil Trasler is rebuking these holy words!"

"Mr. Danielson, I am well versed in the Holy Word, thank you." Liedberg's eyes roamed across the agitated crowd. "Is it truly so?" They all nodded, confirming the incredible accusations.

"Another thing," Stefan added, wagging his finger as if it were afire. "He is telling our beloved women they are not to be subservient any longer to their husbands!"

"Surely not," Liedberg gasped. "Sune Gabrielsson, is this so?"

Sune's eyes were dark and brooding. "Even the virgin Selma-Olivia is declaring that she is a liberated woman!"

"Tell the captain about the other wretched things he's been poisoning their minds with," Stefan snarled to Sune.

"Yes . . ." Sune rubbed a jaw coated by a three day supply of blond stubble. "He says they should be equal to their husbands in the bedroom."

"Surely you jest, Mr. Gabrielsson. No man, not even Trasler, would be so audacious as to discuss bedroom matters to a woman."

Sune flapped his hands in the air in complete frustration while a cacophony of anger exploded from the crowd. "He is telling our women, even the unmarried ones," Sune screamed at the top of his lungs to be heard over the near riot, "that they can have complete sexual relations with a man on certain days without becoming with child!"

"Which days? Tuesdays? Thursdays? I've never heard of such rubbish!"

Stefan offered the explanation. "Certain days . . . before, during and after . . . well, when a woman is . . . unclean."

"God the almighty! He actually speaks of such vulgar matters?"

"Flog him! Flog him!" someone in the middle cried out.

"Those are dangerous words, Captain," Stefan added. "Such talk could bring anarchy and many of our women actually agree with him."

"My wife agrees with him wholeheartedly," Sune grunted. "Then, he told them that someday women will not just claim the right to cast votes, but be elected into government!"

A roar of laughter mocked the audacious words.

"This must stop." Liedberg rubbed his bearded jaw. "It will stop!"

"Hang him from the yards," demanded Stefan. "It is your duty!"

"Nobody here," Liedberg raised both his voice and his finger, "has a right to teach me my duty."

Within moments, the entire mob demanded the same.

"Yes, Captain, you were looking for me?" Tom nonchalantly poked his head through Liedberg's thick oak door. He knew exactly what this chewing out would be all about.

"Come in and close the door."

Tom did and stood indifferently.

"You have been onboard this ship now for how many days?"

"I've lost track, sir."

Liedberg verified his log, flipped through the pages and nodded stiffly. "It has been forty-six days." He slapped it shut. "There is much disease below. There is poor food, rank water, an infestation of rats and vermin, and then, Mr. Trasler, there is you."

"You seemed to have catalogued me along with the pestilence, sir."

"Pestilence? Trasler, you are in a category all of your own. There is not a single passenger on board who is not as restless as a caged beast. This is the first time in these wretches' lives they have not tilled the soil and missed the spring seeding. They have never known such an extent of idle time. It creates restlessness, leading to domestic squabbles and even fisticuffs. But most of the passengers restrain their urges to create a state of total anarchy aboard the ship. Until that glorious day when you and your gang of hooligans disembark in New York City, I expect you to restrain your impulses to create anarchy!"

"Anarchy?"

Liedberg's eyebrows lowered from his brows like sharpened sickles. "You have been teaching the women things other than the English tongue."

"The advanced class, which coincidently just happens to be all women, has been taught some history of the Roman Empire, and now we're into . . . social studies."

"Social studies! What in God's hallowed name are social studies?"

"Women's place in society. Making them feel better about themselves."

"Women voting? Women in government?"

"Okay, in retrospect, giving the women the vote might be a really bad idea."

"Effective immediately, you are to cease social studies. You are to cease all talk with the ladies concerning their place in society, specifically their so-called liberation. Not during your English classes, not afterwards. This is not a request."

"That's fine. There's no further need. The seed has been planted."

"You are an anarchist, Mister Trasler."

"Women aren't a man's possession, sir—they're a man's life's partner. They are the mother who brought his children into the world and a best friend he has the privilege of growing old with. A woman's place is at the man's side, not under his feet."

"A woman's place is between the sheets."

Tom glared at the captain with sharp reproof.

"What of the burning of the corsets?"

"Dramatic symbolism but those things are really a danger. They crush themselves to the point they have trouble breathing. They're uncomfortable, in many ways dangerous, and it's us men who are to blame, sir. Imposing our warped standards of what a woman's shape must conform to."

"And what shape do you think they should conform to, Mr. Trasler?"

"Au natural, sir. Nothing better than watching the bounce and jiggle of a breast." Liedberg bowed his head while Tom continued without shame. "Some of the men on this ship treat their women no better than they do their hogs and cattle. The men expect to be served like they are a king and the woman a chambermaid. You often see them slap their wives about and—"

Liedberg slapped his desk. "It's not your concern! Stay away from the women with such talk. Stay away from all of the women, or I'll have you flogged and chained!"

"I thought I had a *Get out of Jail Free* card?"

"It has just been used!" Liedberg's finger pointed at Tom like a loaded weapon. "Also, another improvement I would enjoy to see, Mr. Trasler, is your hair cut to the respectable length of a gentleman."

Tom reached for his shoulder length hair that had grown nicely over the last six weeks. "The chicks really dig the long hair."

"Any further indiscretions will commence with me personally

attending to the grooming of your delinquent hair." Tom's smirk evaporated like spit on a barbeque. Liedberg dug into the deepest reservoirs of courage to muster up the words. "What is this vile talk, regarding . . . well, a woman being . . . unclean?"

"You're talking of their periods?"

"Enough! Enough! Enough! Whatever you wish to call it, I cannot comprehend how you can so casually discuss such repugnant matters!"

"A period is a natural bodily function and is—"

"Stop it!" Liedberg held up his hands to dam the flow of blasphemy. "I will be paying special attention to your activities, Mr. Trasler. The mate will have nothing more to want in life should he have the pleasure with the cat-o-nine-tails on your back!"

JUNE 13, 1848

The entire ship's complement, and specifically the bulldog woman, Beritt Larsson, scrutinized Tom's lessons to ensure English, and only English, was taught. They chaperoned him day and night, even when he wasn't teaching, and the classes degenerated into a chore rather than something meaningful for him. In the middle of his fourth class, Maja Bergström, the Olive Oyl of a woman with rock concert vocals, lost all expression. She keeled over dead to the world.

Class cancelled.

Tom, badly shaken up, recalled that Maja Bergström came from Småland. She broke out in a high fever yet shivered with the chills and complained of terrible headaches. Her eyes held a dreamy quality and she was unaware of her surroundings.

Liedberg made a rare appearance in the steerage and brought with him his medicines in a wicker basket. A sizable crowd horse-shoed around him as he made his examination. He looked at some of the others from Småland who were also infirm. They all had signs of advanced scurvy and he realized the scurvy was a disguise for the true ailment. Liedberg's face turned pale as death.

Tom stumbled back, stunned by the dread he saw in Liedberg's eyes. "What is it? What's the matter with her?"

Liedberg couldn't manage direct eye contact with the Tom. "Typhus!"

"Sonuvabitch! That's contagious and it kills people!"

"Yes. Among the healthy, perhaps one in five who contracts it will perish. Among the unhealthy . . ." He turned about and gazed at the passengers—beaten by the elements, malnourished, worn down from the rigors of transatlantic travel. "Last year was horrendous. Over twenty thousand perished at sea from the plague."

"Twenty thousand! In a single year?"

"I met a mate from the *Virginus* last year who told me that out of four hundred and seventy-five souls, they lost one hundred and seven at sea—and Lord knows how many after. And the captain," a cold shudder ran through Liedberg, "perished the day after they arrived in port."

Rood and Bodmar stood in Liedberg's cabin, clutching onto his upright wardrobe for support as the ship swooned along the wave crests.

"You are certain of this?" Rood asked.

"Yes, Colonel," Liedberg replied. He sat deep into his chair, hands clutching the armrest. "Four cases confirmed, possibly more."

"How come we're only finding out about this now?" Rood asked. "We've been on board for almost seven weeks."

"This couldn't have just happened," Bodmar said. "The disease had to have been aboard since departure."

"It has," Liedberg admitted. "Those with the infliction are all from Småland. A twelve year-old girl was ill when she came aboard and eventually succumbed. The old man perished and another after him. God be praised, others who had contracted it recovered and there was little spread of the infliction."

"Tom did mention that something bad was going on with the passengers from Småland," Bodmar said, furious at herself for dismissing him. "We assumed it was just scurvy."

"We're going to have to isolate anyone inflicted and clean up the filth down there," Rood said.

Liedberg nodded. "I will make the arrangements."

"Sharon is going to give you and your crew a typhus vaccine," Rood explained as Liedberg's head moved in little ticks to face him. "It will prevent you and your crew from getting the infliction."

"What of the passengers?"

"The crew will all but exhaust our medical supply." Rood's voice held no emotion or remorse. "The passengers will be on their own."

"It is imperative the crew avoid any physical contact with the passengers for at least a week," Bodmar said. "It takes that long for the vaccine to take effect. Are any of your crew infested with lice?"

Liedberg shook his head. "No, I see to it they are kept free of the vermin. What does this have to do with the Typhus?"

Bodmar did not answer the question. "Lice is a sign of filth. The filth impacts the survival rate of those inflicted. We must clean up the steerage and get rid of the lice. It's disgusting."

"This must be strictly enforced," Rood added.

The captain nodded stiffly, his lips pressed into a thin line. "Very well. When do you want to see the crew?"

"Immediately," Bodmar replied. "I'll get my things."

Seeing the parade of crewmen go in and out of the captain's cabin, some clutching their arm, it didn't take Tom long to realize they were getting vaccinated. He waited until Bodmar left Liedberg's cabin.

"Typhus vaccine for the crew?" She continued without responding. Tom remained in pursuit. "What about the passengers?"

Bodmar stopped walking. She stared straight ahead. Her eyes did not meet Tom's. "Not enough to go around."

"Not even for the kids?"

"No." Her response was a mere hush.

"The children are the most vulnerable."

"I can't help them."

"Not even the family I'm billeted with?"

"The passengers aren't our problem."

"What about the lice? We gotta tell them they're the carrier."

She turned and faced him—her eyes were bleak. "We're decades away before the connection between lice and typhus is identified. We can't tell them that it is. All we did was to encourage Liedberg to have them clean the filth below."

"Prime Directive?"

"Remember that typhus would have been on board this ship with or without us. You've already been vaccinated, Tom, be thankful for that." She stopped halfway down the steerage steps and looked back at Tom. "It's already cast in stone who will live and who will die. That's what a benign violation of causality is all about. No one ever said fate or destiny was just, fair or pleasant."

Tom watched Bodmar continue down the steps like a demon descending into Hades. He glanced at the passengers surrounding him, at the men, women, boys, girls, children.

All those children.

The mainsail braced up and the ship hugged the wind as it rode hard. The decks remained angled sharply towards port, making it a challenge to walk. Tom heard a shuffle of steps from behind. Bodmar tapped him on his shoulder and he turned around to face her. She slipped a small metallic tube into his hand.

"The autoinjector comes with a single dose. You can inject into the thigh or the ass. It will go through clothing if they're shy. There is no guarantee. If they've already been infected and are in the incubation period, this will be too late for them. I need the applicator back in twenty minutes."

Tom's hair whipped across his face from a sharp wind. "I understand."

"Don't waste it on Carina Svensson, she's had her shots."

Tom glanced over and saw the prostitute standing by the bulwark. Despite their intimacy during the storm, there remained a mutual feeling of impartiality and had not interacted much since. Alvina-Kristina had seen to that.

One dosage, one lousy dosage.

He stepped into the steerage. The stench drilled into his nose and mouth and he could taste the air. Alvina-Kristina sat with Edvard on her lap. Her bruise had just about faded away and his eyes drank in her beauty, savouring it like a sunset. He took the applicator from its case.

"Do you trust me?" he whispered.

At first she glanced at the applicator with suspicion, but when she met his eyes, it reassured her. "Yes. Of course."

"I need you to hug me."

Without hesitation, she placed Edvard on the lower bunk, wrapped her arms around him and squeezed. Tom took the applicator, pulled up her dress—she was wearing Carol's panties he had given her—and stabbed her in the butt. She stiffened but she remained in his embrace.

"Shhhh. I just gave you some medicine. It will keep you healthy."

She relaxed immediately, although her butt still squeezed tightly. "What medicine?"

Tom showed her the empty applicator. "It's a vaccine to prevent you from getting the typhus."

She rubbed her stinging butt. "Why in my . . . ass?"

He smiled crookedly. "Doctor's orders. Bodmar gave me just one dose."

Her voice became desperate. "But what of the children?"

"I only had one dose."

"Why me?"

"You're my special friend."

She offered him a frail smile, pleased with his sentiments. "And you?"

"I had mine when we first got on board. That shampoo and soap we've been using kills lice, Alvina. I'll give you some more and make sure everyone in our family washes both their hair and body with it." He didn't elaborate about the lice-typhus connection, but keeping her free of the lice may have already saved her life.

"That is why I have been free of the vermin since you cut my hair?" She seemed to understand the connection between the lice and typhus, but he wouldn't confirm it.

"Yes."

She smiled gratefully. "Well, we shall both be healthy and able to tend to those who are not."

He caressed her arm, put the spent applicator in its case, returned to the main deck, and discretely slipped it back into Bodmar's hands.

"You gave Alvina-Kristina the shot?"

"How did you know it was her?"

"She's the one you care about the most. She's also the one who will eventually set you against us."

JUNE 21, 1848

Wrapped in a blanket, the six-month-old looked asleep. The young mother shook her child, as if trying to wake it. Its head skewed to one side, then flopped to the other. She wailed as she brought the dead child to her bosom. Her husband drew in his two other children who were only beginning to grasp the enormity of their loss. The child was an adorable cherub a week ago. Now it was a limp corpse.

Raised by appalling images on television and the internet, Tom saw sights of African children starving to death, monstrous images of the Holocaust, victims of earthquakes, tsunamis and terrorism. He'd seen mangled body parts and bloody carnage just about every night on the evening news. He willingly paid good money to watch gore projected within the movie theatres.

Nothing could have prepared him to live it.

The grieving woman held the baby towards Tom, as if he possessed a power to awaken it from its final slumber. It set him off shrieking. He scrambled for the main deck and clutched onto the ratlines while gasping for breath, grasping for sanity.

Polman brought the baby's body to the deck. It was a tiny little bundle and the congregation assembled for yet another funeral. Tom never saw Liedberg's eyes look so empty when he conducted the service.

Tom waited by the galley to cook lunch with Catharina and Alvina-Kristina, but they were long overdue. Going into the steerage, Tom could see the somber crowd gathered by the Gabrielsson berth and he knew something horrible must have happened. His first thought was Edvard. He moved in slow motion, terrified of what he might find. Alvina-Kristina turned to Tom. Her eyes were wide and blue, sparkling with tears.

"Sune has been stricken!"

A chill turned Tom's skin into something tighter than leather. She rushed forward and collapsed into his arms, squeezing so hard he had trouble drawing a breath. Catharina wiped Sune's face with a wet cloth and he could barely respond. Alvina-Kristina didn't want to cry—it might take the hope away from Sune—but she could feel the tears brimming and cast Tom away before the levee would break.

Later, on deck, a commotion confronted Tom. A crowd of passengers, mostly women, circled a spot on the deck. Waved over by a group of women, Catharina hurled out of the hatch. She knelt on the planking and the sobs heaved out of her. Tom nudged his way through the crowd. A hollow pain knotted his stomach. His fists clenched until they were bone white—trembling.

Little Johanna was sprawled unresponsive on the deck. Tom stood silently now, closing his eyes to shut out the abusive world that refused them peace.

CHAPTER 20

LATE JUNE 1848

The amber rays from the four steerage lanterns peeked above the clothes-lined canvas divider, and what light not absorbed by the ceiling shone onto the tiny form, now more corpse than girl. Johanna's fever hovered over one hundred and four, yet she often complained about being cold.

The child continuously cried for Tom's presence and he steadfastly obliged her request, rarely leaving her side. The sick, now over ten cases, were isolated at amidships, the most stable location on the ship offering the most possible comfort. Next to Johanna lay Sune and another inflicted woman.

The stench was so ripe that Polman dipped a red-hot iron into a bucket of tar to deaden the smell, only to replace it with a new, pungent odour. As bad as the stench was, it was the moans of the sick that was the hardest to take.

Jonas respected the adoring care Tom tended to his daughter. He kept her clean, comfortable, fed her and constantly encouraged her. By God's mercy, Carl-Johan and Stina-Sophia were healthy and kept well isolated from those who were not.

On June 22nd, a red rash began to spread over Johanna's body. The colour faded from her cheeks and a leaden look crept in. Tom patted her arm. It felt so frail beneath his palm, as fragile as the bone of a canary's wing. Johanna looked at him and tried to smile. Tom reached over and kissed her on the forehead.

Next to Johanna, Sune opened his eyes and seemed grateful by Tom's presence. "You're doing okay, Sune," Tom smiled, knowing damn well he wasn't doing okay. Tom knew it and so did Alvina-Kristina. He was burning up and a thick, red rash covered his torso. Sune Gabrielsson was 20,000 leagues away from doing okay.

Liedberg stood next to the helmsman. This was the worst epidemic he ever witnessed on his watch, and though his was the ship's sole authority on the sea, he humbly sought the mercy of Providence. He noticed Tom stepping onto the deck, walking to the aft steps and sat. He looked rung out, like an old rag. Liedberg sat beside him.

"I have never before sailed in such absolute destitution."

"It's hard enough seeing them, but it's the moaning that goes right into your brain."

"I was tending care to Margot Hankinson this morning."

"I noticed. How's she doing?"

Liedberg's eyes were grim, unblinking. "She remains in a continuous state of drowsiness and symptoms of delirium have begun to manifest upon her. As I left, she fell into a prostration so profound that sight and hearing failed her."

Liedberg turned his eyes away from Tom to the main deck. There were no men congregating about the steerage hatch sharing a jug of brännvin, no women in their homespun dresses and tight scarves mending shirts or trying to entertain a young child. No one played the fiddle, no one danced to the tune of the melodeon. No children rolled downhill on the pitching decks, no child's laughter. The sailors executed their chores, yes, but long gone were the chanteys.

"What misery, grief and despair has manifested upon my blessed ship!"

AUGUST 24, 2016
SACRAMENTO, CA

Colonel Nolan's phone rang and he could sense the urgency before he picked up the receiver. The message was short and to the point. *Do not pass go. Go directly to Lucy Lewis' laboratory.* They found Lucy Lewis next to a gray and blue contraption with about thirty spools of thread-like copper wire jumbled in seemingly no pattern set on a tripod, hooked into a gray box. A standard USB cable linked it to her computer.

Dressed in civvies—a high skirt and a peach blouse—Lucy Lewis held that kind of glaze to her eyes one would have just before telling your dad you just took out the front end of the car.

She took a quick, sharp breath and adjusted her black glasses. "Our friends in D-Block were calibrating this wonderful brand new high frequency magnetometer which is specifically designed to measure TREP wavelengths at extreme distances. Looking back at two weeks' worth of data, they noticed some odd readings."

"Odd readings?" Henry asked.

"A massive triple-C event."

"Jesus, Joseph and Mary!" Nolan said. "When?"

"August 15th. Now, D Block doesn't have clearance to know what a triple-C event is, but just a cursory look at the data, this was a monster."

"Where did it happen?" Nolan asked.

"North," Lucy replied.

"There's a 99% probability it would be north," Henry said.

"Let me be blunt." Lucy sat down and keyed in a command. The monitor showed a green bell curve. "This was an impressive six minute event."

"Good God," Henry hushed. "That's never happened before!"

"Not that long," she said. "The only way you can get a Triple-C event—that we are aware of—is for a biological entity, filled with enough TREP, receiving an external electrical stimulus. The only way a biological entity can absorb enough TREP to go Triple-C is to pass through a significant temporal event. Therefore, there are only two possibilities of what caused this. Either one of Rood's crew has managed to find his or her way back and nearly got electrocuted, or, someone else outside our organization has passed through a significant temporal event and nearly got electrocuted."

"Someone else?" Nolan exploded.

"Don't shoot the messenger."

"There's no way we can determine a location?" Henry asked.

"Not with just one unit," she said. "We need three of these deployed about five miles apart, triangulated and programmed to alert us immediately so that if this happens again, we'll be able to pinpoint the location down to a closet in a house in Cleveland. It's not just someone else being involved, they pose a very real danger to the timeline."

"Whatever it takes, do it. If this happens again, we'll dispatch the black team and take them in," Henry said.

"Just take them out!" Nolan said.

"Cliff, I'd rather consolidate the knowledge than take them out," Henry said tolerantly.

"How is this possible? Who else could have done this?" Nolan asked, and it looked like a hidden tourniquet tightened the skin around his face.

"Our three little pigs off the yacht were drained of their TREP. Not them." She managed to grin through her stress, which caused her front teeth stick to out, and she was cute as a chipmunk. "Get that dumb cow-look off your face, Colonel, and accept the facts. We have competition."

"Get back to Canada, Colonel," Henry said. "Find out everything about those Canadians. There has to be a link between them and the triple-C event!"

JUNE 26, 1848

Tom carried Johanna through the aisle to the office. Her tiny limbs were limp as a rag doll. Bodmar saw his approach on the security monitor and waited for him, with Rood standing directly behind her.

"What is it, Trasler?" Bodmar was cold and Rood just glared at Tom from behind Bodmar's shoulder, resenting the theatrics.

"She's dying."

Bodmar met his eyes head on. "I can't help you."

"You have the antibiotics that can save her, that can save Sune!"

"Out of the question." Rood had no inflection in his voice whatsoever and Tom wondered how any human being could be so inhuman.

"If we help just one kid, Trasler," Bodmar explained, her voice rising with anger, "we'll have a rush on this office that we wouldn't be able to control."

Rood stabbed his index finger in the air, just under Tom's nose, so close Tom could have snapped it with his teeth. "Desperate people become a mob, Barney, and that's the last goddamn thing we need right now."

"One secret little shot. Please, she's just a little girl."

"We can't interfere."

"This isn't about breaking the Prime Directive, God damn you, it's about saving a six year-old girl."

"Fate has already decided who will live and who will die." Rood crossed his arms, his uniform stretching around his chest. "Don't anger the gods."

"Please!" Tom begged. Rood saw a tear blurt from Tom's right eye and he flicked it off his cheek.

"That's exactly why we've been telling you, time and time again, not to get too close to these goddamn lowlifes!" Rood slammed the door.

Tom stood there, pounding his fist against it. Sobbing. "God damn you all. She's only six!" He looked down at the girl. Her eyes opened momentarily. "I'm sorry, sweetie. I'm so, so sorry." He kissed her on the forehead and trudged back to the berth. A slow shuffle of dragging feet.

JUNE 28, 1848

The sails were depressed and wrinkled. The sun burned high overhead, beating down on the tiny ship. Rood came on deck with Rodriguez and did their usual noon measurement with the navigator. Liedberg joined them.

"If you know a way out of these doldrums, Colonel Rood, I will be much in your debt."

"You're within 250 yards of the course I gave you. Considering the bearskins and stone knives you navigate with, my compliments. You're doing a first rate job."

"An ox travels faster than we."

"A couple more days, I think, we'll be fine. The weather is finally changing."

"I subscribe to your opinion. These mares-tails are cirrus clouds, scattered in the zenith. Their presence often announces a change in the weather."

"We're still two weeks at best from port."

"That is my opinion."

Rood searched the decks for a moment, then turned back to the captain. "Haven't seen Trasler in two days."

"He is below, tending to the young Gabrielsson girl."

"Have you heard anything about her condition?"

"I fear the worst."

"And yet he won't give up?"

"He is a gentleman who can undertake and persevere even without hope of success. It is the true measure of the human spirit, Colonel Rood. He knows he is losing her and this morning, I went below and I found him lying next to the berth of Johanna Gabrielsson, overcome by fatigue, he managed to forget his sorrows in a brief interlude of sleep until he awoke again. He is a man of a good sort."

Tom was tired almost to death—that's what it felt like—but Sune looked far past even that. Alvina-Kristina knelt next to Tom, brushing Sune's thick hair with her long fingers. His eyes slid open, smiled, then closed his eyes, as if mustering all his strength for the words. "I'll be well soon, Alvina-Kristina."

To Tom, Sune didn't sound in the same solar system with getting well soon.

While Alvina-Kristina tended to Sune, Tom turned his attention back to Johanna. He tried to get some honey and water into her. She reached for him with one woefully skinny arm. The sight of her adorable face—thin and frail, but still trying to smile—made Tom feel like screaming. He knew life could be cruel, but goddamn it, this went too far beyond cruel. It was utterly barbarous.

THE EARLY MORNING HOURS OF JULY 1, 1848

At about 2:00 AM, a desperate, whimpering sound woke Tom up. He eased open *The Walls of Jericho*. Tears streamed from Alvina-Kristina eyes.

"What's the matter, kiddo?" She gave no reply. He glanced at Edvard, terrified he'd find a tiny corpse, but he was breathing in a sound sleep, as was Selma-Olivia. Tom placed a hand on Alvina-Kristina's sternum, the edge of his hand grazed her breasts and he felt the crashing thump of her heart. She was soaked in sweat and trembled—but wasn't feverish. His hand felt damp and sticky from her skin. "Kiddo, speak to me."

She appeared oblivious to his touch or his words. Alvina-Kristina scrambled over Edvard and Selma-Olivia, and in a single motion, leapt off the berth. Her frantic footsteps receded down the aisle towards the forward hatch. Wearing nothing but a pair of navy blue boxers, Tom charged after her. Alvina-Kristina shot through the fore hatch onto the main deck wearing Carol's thin nightie that showed all those legs. *What would those wretches on duty do to her when she appeared up on deck?*

Tom emerged out of the hatch into a warm summer squall. A low roar enveloped the ship, accompanied by the rattle of rain he found refreshing. The opaque veil of precipitation obscured the ship's lanterns, rendering more shadows than light. The ship rode over smooth, low waves and the wind, steady from the stern, breathed a sigh just sufficient to take hold of the light night canvas.

Standing behind the bowsprit railing, two sailors had already taken keen notice of Alvina-Kristina. Tom's feet splashed their way towards her. Her hair fell in dregs against her back, and her nightie, wet and translucent, clung to her like a second skin. Her butt shown through the wet material so clearly she might as well have been naked. Her endless legs stretched past the nightie's hem. She coiled her arms around her while balancing to the lethargic rise and fall of the ship's prow. Pulling in behind Alvina-Krisitna, Tom touched her shoulders. He felt the anguish vibrating right out of her.

She spun around and clutched Tom's forearms. "You must save Sune and Johanna. I cannot!"

"They'll be fine," Tom replied, his voice soft and gave her a reassuring smile. "Little Erin Nilsson broke fever yesterday and she had it just as bad, if not worse than Johanna. Sune is tough. He'll pull through."

"Last winter, we lost our son, Johannes. Edvard has a weak heart and will die young. I can't lose Sune, too. What will become of me? And of Selma-Olivia? I'm scared, Thomas, so scared."

Two more sailors came into view to watch. "Alvina, let's get back inside. That nightie is soaking wet and you can see right through it. It's a really, really bad idea to let the crew see you like this."

Alvina-Kristina glanced down. If she was appalled at her exposure, the intensity of her eyes, wide and wild, masked it. She shook her hands loose from Tom's forearms.

"When Sune told me about going to America, I submitted to his will. Is that not what a wife must do? I should have never given in! Aunt Clara warned me this would go very bad. I knew before I stepped aboard this horrible ship that all Sune promised about our new life would never come to pass. I knew this ship would be our tomb!"

A long throated wail wrenched from her mouth. She stepped into Tom's caress, pressing herself against his body and clutched him with her arms. Alvina-Kristina sobbed with long hissing cries. He kissed her tenderly on the cheek, tasting her tears. She responded by squeezing him tighter, almost rough.

The rain throttled into a deluge with a rumble, whipping off the deck and sprayed off their heads and shoulders, creating a halo-mist about them. Alvina-Kristina released Tom, grabbed the snagged dregs of hair, giving him a hard, searching look. The kiss on the lips took him by complete surprise. It was a light, polite kiss, like a New Year's smooch to your best friend's wife.

Tom heard one of the sailors chuckle and knew this would be the hottest gossip to hit the ship since it departed Sweden. He was so terrified of the consequences he couldn't possibly enjoy the moment.

"We better get below."

She threw herself against him and hooked her arms around his neck. Within the shadows, Tom could feel the firm and individual touch of each breast press against his chest and the heat of her breath caressing his neck. The erotic roar of the rain enhanced the intimacy, thundering his pulse throughout his body. He put his arms around her, still feeling the quivering after-effects of the crying —but—there was no further crying. Just the after-effects.

"Alvina, we're going to get into some serious shit for this!"

Her body remained against his like soft fire, setting his own ablaze. After what seemed an eternity during which neither of them were willing to move, she spoke in a mere whisper.

"I need this, Thomas. My heart is so much oppressed with anxiety."

He started to make a reply but her lips closed over his, muffling the response, and this was no polite New Year's kiss. Her hand reached up to cradle his skull, drawing him closer while the other slipped behind his back, containing him. He tasted her lips and felt her chest heave with fast and frightened breaths. She was completely overcome, as if she had never been kissed before.

The sailors were hooting and howling.

The sensation of her tongue slipping between his lips stunned him. So startled, he was slow to receive her and she coaxed him into an exquisite dance. Tom broke free from the kiss with a loud sucking sound. The sailors were whistling and applauding. Tom heard nothing. Nothing but the satisfied sigh escaping from Alvina-Kristina's lips.

"I'm going to get a lashing for this!"

Without any further hesitation, his mouth descended to hers. She seemed utterly unwilling to let go of him while her kiss plundered his mouth. Everything else in the world vanished except the overwhelming sensation of the shared embrace, sharply in-drawn breaths, sealed lips and caressing tongues. This was something he wanted to do for many weeks, something always in the corridors of forbidden thoughts, but never imagined possible. He held her tightly and they continued to kiss, slower and more thoroughly this time. They knew, both knew, of the terrible consequences awaiting them, yet both longed for a release from the heartbreak and suffering, comfort theirs just for a few illicit moments.

The thumping of footfalls splashing the deck came from the first mate and this meant trouble. Tom grasped Alvina-Kristina's hand, evading Rödin by running down the starboard steps. Nearly yanking Alvina-Kristina's arm from her body, he hauled her off balance and scurried along the port side. They slipped and stumbled past the galleyhouse to the rear hatch.

The crew roared in laughter, content to have a good look at the running girl, wet and beautiful and an awful lot of bouncing beneath the transparent nightie. Scurrying below deck, with Alvina-Kristina still in an off balanced tow, Tom went to the berth, grabbed his hand luggage he kept slung over the bunk support and doubled-backed to the aft end of the steerage. Unlocking the cargo hatch, he plunked her into the hold and crawled in right after. Tom took a disposable flashlight from his handbag he kept available. He turned it on. Alvina-Kristina gasped in shock, as Tom knew she might.

"Don't tell anyone about this light. It cost a lot of money and I don't want it stolen."

"I won't. Who is Garrity?" she asked.

"Garrity?"

She pointed to the name of the flashlight. "That's the name of the company who made it. I knew a Garrity once." Tom rolled his eyes.

“And you think I’m weird? Let’s get into some dry clothing before we both catch our death.”

They followed the slender cone of light and Tom came to his pile of luggage. Tom gave Alvina-Kristina the red flashlight to hold and she studied every molecule of it. He took out a green lighter and held it up.

Rather than hide it, he said, “Watch this.” He flicked it and lit the lantern hanging from a beam hook. The amber flame filled the hold with its flickering glow.

Tom took the flashlight, put it away in the traveling bag and searched Alvina-Kristina’s expression for some reaction. He found none, as if seeing a disposable lighter was an everyday occurrence, but then, she saw Rood use one to light the torch before setting the boy on fire. After seeing him in the battle armour and carbine, nothing could be a shock anymore. He took Carol’s suitcase and unzipped it. He found a towel and rummaged for something for her to wear.

“Well, there’s not much here you can wear, kiddo. Just this.” He pulled out a bright red sweater with a blue stripe about the middle part, a strange looking “C” in the front, an “H” engraved inside the C, with the number 4 painted white on the sleeves and a huge one on the back.

She looked at it unfavourably. “I will feel silly in this.”

“No one feels silly wearing a Montreal Canadiens sweater.”

“What is that?”

“It’s a sports team. Carol was very fond of that sweater. Just put it on.”

She looked at him, her eyes telling him she had no idea what a sports team was. She would still feel silly wearing it.

He went through Charlie’s luggage, found some boxer shorts with green dancing froggies, and went to a shadowed corner to dry off and change. Charlie was a big boy and it wouldn’t take much for the boxers to slip right off. Alvina-Kristina giggled at the ridiculous sight Tom and the extra-large sized boxers presented, but she still hadn’t changed.

“Why are you still in that wet thing?”

“I need some help to take it off.” Tom’s eyes were wide and alarmed. “I will tell no one.” She hunched her shoulders and giggled sweetly.

Tom knelt on one knee, and from behind and very much aware this was a serious lack of good judgement, slowly rolled up the nightie. He admired a taut, flawless butt, provoking a brief hiatus and a significantly higher pulse rate, then quickly finished disrobing her. He handed her the towel and turned his back. He wiggled a coat hanger free from Ralph's suitcase, using it to hang the dripping nightie on a deck beam.

He turned around. She stood stark naked before him. She looked—with the exception of the faint underarm hair—like a centerfold girl, the warm tones of the lamplight soft and complimentary. She held the sweater and towel in each hand and shuffled towards him in a slow, suggestive way.

"Help me put this on?"

He snatched the towel from her and dried her back, butt and legs. She turned around and raised her arms. He paused, admiring her beauty while she relished in the accolades gleaming from his eyes. She put the sweater on a crate, took his hands and brought them to her breasts. They were large and firm, and he gave himself a note of caution that these were lactating breasts. She leaned in for another kiss. It was a hard kiss. For the briefest of moments, he almost took her, all of her, right then and there and he knew damn well she wanted him to.

He continued to kiss her and jerked to a stop. She was well past the point of no return and he knew that if he didn't stop now, *right now,* he wouldn't, he couldn't. It wasn't as if she was on the pill. In this day and age, sex was very efficient at making babies.

He took the towel and patted her dry. A commotion from above began as a few murmurs became a rumble. That sobered both out of their sexual intoxications, and she shimmied into the sports sweater. It barely concealed her, leaving nothing but those lissom legs he wished he could run his lips all over. She sweetly twirled about, revealing her lowest extremities for Tom's grateful yet frightened eyes. He opened Carol's suitcase and after some rummaging, pulled out some red silk pyjama bottoms.

"Put these on." She did so, but every motion was slow and deliberate and she jiggled beneath the sweater something awful. "Let's go."

She looked at him, her eyes soft in the flickering light of the lantern. "Thank you, Thomas. You are a very good friend. I needed this . . . I am very scared."

"I'm scared of what they're going to do to us!"

"Yes, we will get in much trouble . . . but . . . I needed this. Thank you, Thomas. You are my best friend."

"We'll get through this, kiddo. Together." He gave her a firm love tap. She stared at him, her eyes glossed as a fresh layer of tears welled in her eyes. She pushed her lips into his. This was not the ravenous kissing she gave him on deck. She kissed him softer, deeper, with much more affection. *How could something that was wrong, so terribly wrong, feel as if it was meant to go on forever?* The commotion going on above continued to intensify and he turned his head to one side to break the kiss.

"Come on, kiddo. Let's go face our Waterloo."

He snuffed out the lantern, opened the hatch, crawled out and crouched with his hand stretched below for her to grab—then he noticed the assembly. Passengers in their nightclothes lined the aisle, seventy of them, old and young, all eyes lined up on him. Catharina and Jonas stood in the center of aisle, side by side, as terrifying as those ghost girls standing in the hallway in *The Shining.* He pulled Alvina-Kristina out, and she saw what he saw. She wanted to keep holding his hand, but that would be fatal, and she released it. He locked the hatch and they moved forward, side by side, walking slowly.

He realized he was just wearing boxers, and this was only going to make the scandal worse. As they walked slowly through the aisle, it was like passing through a gauntlet. They squeezed past Carina's enclosure. He would have expected a lewd, lustful grin, but instead, her hand covered her mouth in claws of distress. Alvina-Kristina noticed the blank looks, seeking reproach but finding none. She wished for reproach rather than the long, drawn out faces.

Jonas stood there, empty of face. Catharina's eyes were wide, glistening with tears in the lamplight. Selma-Olivia couldn't be seen—just heard—crying with deep, shuddering sobs that chopped into Tom's head like a dull axe.

Catharina burst forward and grabbed Alvina-Kristina's hands, clutching them together and kissed them. Her voice was wet and jagged with pain.

"Be brave, Alvina-Kristina. Sune is dead!" Alvina-Kristina stared at Catharina nakedly. She knew Catharina had more to say. She spoke the dreadful words with a hush. "And baby, too."

"And baby, too?"

CHAPTER 21

The morning dawned with a feeble light crawling from the east to awaken a gently creased sea. It was a cool, colourless day, with featureless clouds hanging just beyond reach of the masts. The ship sat all but motionless in tranquil waters while the canvas stirred restlessly. Catharina, Selma-Olivia and Jonas surrounded Alvina-Kristina like a praetorian guard. It was deemed best if Tom did not participate in the funerals.

Tom couldn't imagine how Alvina-Kristina would cope. She lost her husband and a child and faced an uncertain future. Kneeling at Johanna's bedside, he picked up her hand. It was limp. He dropped it and picked it up again. "Johanna?"

She opened her eyes and smiled. "I love you, Thomas."

"I love you, too. You gave me a fright, you!"

Tom wiped her face with a washcloth. He knew the hand of death was closing its grip on her. He kissed her forehead and it was hot to the touch. A shadow crossed over Johanna and turning to look, found Rood and Ralph standing behind him. Their looks were of concern, even a little compassion.

"Rough night," Rood said.

Tom forced a grin. "It started off well enough."

"How's Alvina-Kristina coping?"

"She's lost," Tom said. "She'll be under the care of her brother-in-law. Same with her kid sister." Tom looked off into an empty space. "I can't imagine what it's like, first losing her firstborn last year, and now, her new baby and husband. These people really rely on their faith."

Ralph put his hand on Tom's shoulder. "How are they treating you after the big scandal?"

Tom tossed him a forlorn glance. "The passengers are blaming Alvina for the deaths of Sune and Edvard, that her indiscretion invoked the wrath of God. She's having a real tough time, especially from that bulldog woman, Beritt Larsson. She may have no teeth, but, goddamn, she'll give you a mouthful. As for me?" He smiled without humour. "I'm pretty much Satan in their eyes, but Alvina went to the captain this morning and asked him not to punish me, saying she's the one who started it. Liedberg has so much compassion and pity for her, he spoke to me and I'm off the hook."

"So how far did you get with her last night?" Ralph asked. "By all accounts, you two were really going at it in the pouring rain. She was wearing a thin nightie in the pouring rain. She must have been the grand prize winner of the wet T-shirt contest."

Tom was in no mood for lurid details. He took a few wayward strands of hair from Johanna's face and didn't face Ralph. "We didn't go the distance."

"You two went into the hold. So how far did you get?" Ralph pushed.

"That's a private matter, Ralphy."

"She's suddenly single and available," Rood pointed out.

"And no baby, either. Makes it convenient," Ralph said.

"She has a kid sister. Still a package deal, Ralphy."

"Do you two have a future?" Rood asked.

Tom glanced at his wedding ring. "Just because she doesn't exist right now, I haven't exactly been faithful to Carol, but you know that Alvina and I don't have a future. Hopefully, Carol and I still do."

"Good response."

"Trick question?"

Rood grinned. "Just checking."

"I'm going to miss her, though." He took a damp cloth and wiped Johanna's face.

Ralph said, "It's just like saying goodbye to a summer friend, Tom."

Tom looked sharply at Ralph. "We've been through life and death, Ralphy. She's more like a war buddy. You can relate to that."

Rood grinned. "I know exactly what you mean. How is she?" Rood asked of Johanna.

Tom caressed Johanna's face with the back of his fingers. She had no reaction to his touch. He glanced at Rood, his eyes resigned.

"She's dying."

AUGUST 26, 2016
POINTE CLAIRE, QUEBEC

Nolan was quite thrilled to be squealing around corners in the black Corvette convertible with the top down. He enjoyed his hair flying in the breeze and wearing his cool sunglasses. He was looking for a house just a hop from the tavern where he ate lunch. As much as he detested all things Canadian, their beer had a better edge to it and the tavern served one hell of a steak. He found the house sitting in the shadow of the large municipal water tower bearing the town's coat of arms. The house was an older wooden dwelling on a large lot.

He eased into the driveway and parked behind a faded red Honda Civic, suffering from severe rust erosion. A red Corolla parked just down the street came to life and it did an abrupt U-turn. He couldn't see the occupants, but all at once, he felt watched. He stared at the empty spot for moment, then turned his attention back to the house. The car and the house told him this wasn't an affluent household. The lawn was recently cut but infested with weeds and scorched with dead spots.

He rang the doorbell and heard the aggressive yapping of a small dog close in on the door. The front door opened and from behind the screen door's dusty window, Nolan found himself staring into the prettiest brown eyes he had ever seen. The young woman was in her late twenties, strawberry blond hair with a side part coursing about her naked shoulders, just long enough to touch the top of a red tube top wrapped around a nice but not too large bust. This girl's eyes, the palest of brown, ensnared him. He admired her round unblemished face, pert nose and full sensual lips. She wasn't wearing makeup and didn't need any. But underlying the pretty face, he could see the sadness of a sister who was still mourning the tragic passing of a sibling.

The woman took in Nolan's stunning stature, who looked dashing in a military uniform. He took off his cap and tucked it under an arm. The white poodle yapped and snarled at him.

"Snoopy, stop it." She bent down to pick up the dog and held it in one arm and the wretched beast continued to bare its fangs at him. She cautiously opened the aluminium screen door open, just enough to expose her face. She knew by Nolan's uniform what the visit concerned.

"Jane Trasler?"

"Yes?"

"Ma'am, I'm Colonel Cliff Nolan, the commanding officer of the crew who lost their lives in the helicopter crash. I wish to offer my condolences on the death of your brother, but I did not come here just to offer condolences, but to offer a thanks. Your brother knowingly risked his life to save six lives of those under my command, and I do not take this supreme sacrifice lightly."

Jane's breath got trapped just for a moment. Something about Nolan was quite arresting. His eyes were pale hazel and the tailored uniformed wrapped around an incredibly lithe body. The poodle kept snarling and Jane clutched her fingers around its snout to keep it quiet, to the point of it whining in pain.

"I had no idea there were survivors."

Nolan's heart leapt. He couldn't believe he had been so reckless and said there were survivors when all the reports said there were none! *Christ Almighty, a hot broad in a tube top and all at once national security is compromised.*

"You must understand that a classified operation requires disinformation. However, I thought you should know that your brother's sacrifice was not in vain. Do not speak of this to anyone."

"My lips are sealed." She gave a gesture of zipping her mouth shut. "I'm so thrilled Tom helped save some lives."

"He's a hero, ma'am. There's no other word for it. Hero." Nolan smiled inwardly. *Great recovery, old boy.*

"We lost my dad just ten months ago and now . . ." Jane choked up and tears welled in her piercing brown eyes. "Would you like to come in?"

"I would. It's very hot."

Jane Trasler wiped her eyes delicately with her free hand as she dumped the dog down the basement stairs and the slammed the door on it. The dog yapped away. Non-stop.

"Would you like something to drink?" Jane asked.

"That would be appreciated, ma'am."

"Ma'am is so cowboy. Call me Jane, please."

"All right, Jane."

"I have Molson, Coke or tap water."

"A Molson would hit the spot nicely."

She went into the kitchen with the slapping sounds of her flip-flops following her. She wore a tight pair of shorts and Nolan had a good look at Jane's legs. They were nice but milky white, oddly untanned, despite this being the height of summer.

Nolan stopped just beyond the porch and glanced at the living room. There were a few pictures on the pale green wall, mostly store bought paintings, but one section had some of the family. One picture of Tom had hair halfway down his back and a full beard similar to the police mug shot. There were bouquets of flowers scattered on various tables, most wilted and well past their time. There were dozens of sympathy cards standing open on the tables. A couple of guitars were in their stands, decorated with wilted flowers and cards. This was a house still in mourning.

With no air conditioning, the house possessed a stuffy, hot smell. Nolan was melting inside his uniform. Jane banged the door to try to quieten the dog, but it only throttled the yapping into something even worse. She brought a glass and a Molson for the colonel but drank hers directly from the bottle. She wriggled her feet out of the flip-flops and sat in a green upholstered chair, with one leg folded on the chair and he took notice of her feet. The toenails were painted in crimson with little white flower decals on them. *Very cute.*

Nolan was taken off guard by his lost self-control around this young lady. She was nothing spectacular. He had seen prettier women, much prettier, but something about her was incredibly alluring. Each part of her taken on their own merit was overall plain, but put all together, the fit was perfect.

A moment of drawn out silence heightened the sexual tension building between them, just the incessant barking of the poodle. *Why the Christ would anyone own a breed that is so goddamn annoying?*

Nolan continued with a low, soothing voice. "I can assure you that Tom didn't suffer. We expect that death must have been instantaneous."

Jane remained composed. "That's what we were already told. It's kind of unfair he went like that."

"Unfair?"

"If it's that fast, Tom never knew he was going to die. I'd like to know, to prepare myself, even if it was only a few seconds."

"You can tell your mother that her son died a hero. She can, at least, be proud of that. Your mother is not at this address?"

The tears flowed like someone opened a tap. "Mom . . . she took this real bad and Tuesday, she completely lost it. Now she's in the nuthouse."

"Nuthouse?"

Jane looked embarrassed. "In the psychiatric wing of the local hospital. She's in total denial and believes that Tom is still alive."

"Unfortunately, we had to give up the search for the body."

"A body would have really helped." She wiped her tears and took a couple of big gulps from the bottle, then chuckled without humour. "She believes he is living in the past, of all things."

Nolan's mind reeled. He had to control himself. Even if the mother was a complete crackpot, there had to be some hard evidence to lend credence to this. He paused, making certain the words wouldn't stumble out of his mouth. "How did she come up with that?"

She chuckled the nervous tick from her throat and took another good swig from the bottle. "At first, she seemed so calm and surreal, then just like that, she became obsessed. Said he was still alive in the past."

"How far back in the past?" Nolan tried to keep his voice level.

Her mouth skewed a little over to the left side, like she just had a mini stroke. "Cowboy and Indians, like—the Old West."

"That's a rather incredible thing to believe."

"No kidding." She took another sip of her beer and stared contemplatively at the bottle. "Like, it's really embarrassing. Tom used to be into cowboys and Indians even when all the other kids were playing Star Wars. I think she somehow turned that into where she believes Tom is living."

"I'm so sorry, Jane. This must just add to all your heartache and grief."

"I'm not far from the loony-bin myself," she said and gave a waterlogged chuckle.

Nolan took a quick sip of his beer to conceal his total shock. Jane looked humiliated and an awkward giggle just eked out. She chugalugged half the bottle as tears flowed, leaving lines of silver streaks on her face. She hiccupped a sob, snapped some Kleenex out of a box, and wiped her face. "Sorry."

"I have to deal with the families of those who perished. It's the most difficult part of being in command. But the military has a superb support system for families."

"Thank you for coming. It's . . . it's a great comfort knowing Tom didn't die in vain."

Nolan glanced at the two guitars. One was a classic red Fender Stratocaster, the other a Gibson twelve string acoustic. "Your brother was a musician?"

She smiled. "Everyone wants to be a rock star, right? Tom tried, got to give him that much. The most he ever did were the local pubs."

"I'm here for more than just offering my gratitude." Nolan found himself melting into her glittering, sad eyes. "The United States Army wants to begin the process of ensuring both Tom and Ralph receive public recognition of their heroism and sacrifice through the Congressional Gold Medal."

"Thank you." She had a little cry and blew her nose, soaking the Kleenex. Nolan pulled a few additional tissues from the box and handed them to her. She tilted the beer and drank the bottle dry. His lingered at two thirds full. "How about lunch?" she asked.

"Lunch would be wonderful." Nolan just ate a steak, but for her, he'd find the space for another meal.

"Nice Greek restaurant just below the hill."

"Air conditioned?" Nolan's sweat trickled from the side of his face into his collar.

She broke into a broad, wide smile and grabbed Nolan's hands. "You bet. By the way," she leaned into him, "I just love riding in Corvettes, pedal-to-the-meddle, with the top down!"

Nolan smiled and melted into the chocolate of her eyes. He confessed to himself that he just might be falling in love.

JULY 3, 1848

Carina Svensson took a moment of rest on deck, leaning against the bulwark at her customary spot amidships. She wore her lavender dress, stained and torn after two months at sea, and her hair was like a mop.

She noticed Carlos Rodriguez on deck with a pad of paper and a pencil, doing some sketches of the unfolding tragedy. How a man would want to record all this sorrow was beyond her comprehension. She was at least doing something about it, not just drawing pictures.

Liedberg joined her. "You are much admired for your care of the sick. Many of the passengers have accepted you."

"It is the least I can do. God be praised, I still have my health."

"Death at last took possession of the Hankinson woman."

"Yes. I have learned as much. The ravages of the disease are terrible."

"I am aware of your attempt to offer your care."

"She refused."

Liedberg led Hankinson's service. Carina stood there, suffering from a wrenching emptiness. It was Margot's husband she transgressed and regretted she boasted about it before all the others.

Tom stuffed his hands in his pants pockets and ambled about, still absorbing the deaths of Sune and Edvard. He and Alvina-Kristina exchanged a few words from time to time, but they now slept in separate bunks, with Tom on the bottom with Jonas and young Carl-Johan. The big scandal spoke on everyone's lips, and as much as he tried to avoid it, it was always there—on the decks, in the galleyhouse, in the steerage. There was no escaping it.

Alvina-Kristina didn't only grieve the loss of her husband and child, but Jonas took her under his care, raising a lot of uncertainty about her future. Her only way out was marriage. That was the harsh reality of her situation and *she'll be damned if she marries another farmer.* She felt lonelier than she ever thought a person could feel alone. She remained withdrawn and she wasn't just avoiding Tom, she avoided everyone.

Beritt Larsson came up to Tom, cursed him to the devil and swatted him with an ear ringing wallop. He took off his Expos cap and bowed to the old lady. "I love you, too."

She hit him again, her toothless mouth cackling away and thumped across the deck, still muttering her disgust at him. She was in her late sixties and strong as an ox. Both Tom, and the old bat herself, knew she was somehow immune to the plague. She'd live to be an ancient old hag and pity on her kin.

"Thomas! Come quickly!" Alvina-Kristina's voice held a tremendous urgency to it. She rushed back down into the steerage. Just as Tom arrived at the steerage hatch, the second-mate and another sailor, both wearing grim looks, started down the steerage stairs—with a sheet of canvas.

They only used a sheet of canvas like that for the dead.

"Out of my way!" Tom shoved the two sailors aside and rushed to Johanna's berth. The entire family circled the bunk as Tom drew near.

Alvina-Kristina turned to Tom. Her face glowed like a sunrise. "The fever has broken!" Jonas moved aside to let Tom look. When Tom touched his lips to Johanna's forehead, her temperature was drastically reduced, almost normal.

Jonas, weeping, hugged Tom, as did Catharina, Selma-Olivia, Stina-Sophia, even Carl-Johan. Tom leaned back against the coarse wood frame of the bunk with a sigh of naked relief. In that one glittering moment, he found himself giving thanks. He checked himself after he said it in his mind—but he just thanked God. He hadn't prayed since a child doing his bedtime prayers. Still not certain how it happened, or how long this moment of being a believer would last, he caressed Johanna's face, feeling relief tears brimming in his eyes.

Thank you, God. Thank you!

"You alone saved her and we will be forever in your debt," Alvina-Kristina said. Johanna's survival would be at least some form of atonement from the awful loss of Alvina-Kristina's husband and child. Because of the scandal, Alvina-Kristina did not hurl her arms around Tom, although she should have. Tom had saved her niece's life with love and care she thought only a mother could provide.

Catharina placed her hands on Tom's shoulders. "When he was first put here, we rejected him. Now, he whom Providence has made our brethren, is greatly loved. If he has committed any transgression with Alvina-Kristina, which has shamed our family in the eyes of others, he has most certainly expiated it, and in our eyes, he is absolved."

Catharina leaned down, kissed him on his stubbled cheek, and held the kiss there for a long moment, the moist heat from her lips sent tingles long after she broke the kiss. For the first time since forcibly billeted with the family, Tom was accepted as a cherished member of the household.

There were sudden cries of anguish. Polman and Olsson paused as they looked about. Someone pointed and they continued past the berth to another young family. With help from friends, they took away the body of someone's dad.

JULY 5, 1848

Tom found Alvina-Kristina sitting on the bottom berth. Johanna was still weak and she gave her honey and water. He sat beside the young widow. "How are you coping?"

"My breasts are full. When I hear a baby cry in hunger, I can feel them nearly burst."

He repositioned Johanna and with the three of them together, slipped an arm around Alvina-Kristina's shoulder. She initially resisted, but then softened. She needed this and her head leaned against his.

"It's a nice day. Let's go on deck," Tom suggested. "The sunshine will do you both good."

"No. I hate the sea. The very sight of it makes me ill."

He kissed her on the cheek. "You know, I had gotten attached to Edvard. I really liked that little fellow."

"He liked you, too."

She stroked Johanna's head and the girl drifted off into sleep. Alvina-Kristina's face looked perplexed. "Do you suppose that Edvard in Heaven can ever forgive his parents for bringing him into the world with such great defects?"

"I'm certain, Alvina, that God brought him into the world like that, so Sune would not have to travel to the afterlife alone, but holding the hand of his son."

"That is very beautiful Thomas, a pity you are an unbeliever and do not believe even your own words." He took her hand and kissed it. "You know, Thomas, you are different from any man I have met. You can sit and talk with a woman, almost like another woman. Even matters of the toilet without shame. I like talking to you. I trust you. So, please, tell me. In America, what will you do?"

He caressed her face, took a deep breath and decided she deserved at least some semblance of the truth. "Ralph and I aren't invited to stay with Rood and his crew, so together, we have to go to California, which is on the western coast of America, a great distance to cross. We'll set up a date to meet Rood in San Francisco, then finally we'll get to go home."

He expected a long, sad face, or possibly, a request he take her with him. What he got caught him off guard. It was pity. He wasn't certain if her Aunt Clara's were speaking, but the look in her eyes told him one thing—*he wasn't going to make it home.*

"Why do you need Colonel Rood to go home?"

"It's complicated." He kissed her cheek with a firm, lingering kiss and cuddled her tightly. "We cannot have a future together, Alvina. It's not possible." Snug and warm in her arms, he could feel the jolt of heartbreak and lost hope. "I'm going to miss you when we get ashore."

"I think I will cry big tears when you say goodbye." The tears pooling in the blue of her eyes were like drowning in the depths of the sea. They both hesitated, but they finally found a way to kiss on the lips. They shared a gentle, brief moment. Somehow, it felt more wrong than when Sune was still alive.

They remained there for hours, cuddling and kissing occasionally. During this time, Tom thought about his feelings, both toward Alvina-Kristina and to Carol, a deep, penetrating, honest and sincere audit of his two loves.

Even though they did not have the bond of lovers, he never felt so complete in another woman's arms. Carol seemed to be a distant ship, just a vague outline, drifting off into the fog, slipping away until consumed by the mists. He rocked Alvina-Kristina gently, kissed her on the cheek, just as he did with Carol on a sleepy Saturday morning, back when she'd been his wife, back in that distant, near-forgotten other life. He looked down at the golden hair feathering around the angelic face. It wasn't Carol. It was another woman. In a different life. In this life. *In the only life that mattered right now.*

He looked at her face, knowing if he did ever make it back home, she would have been dead for many, many years. He wondered what it might be like, returning to 2016, knowing that she, Johanna, everyone on this ship had turned old, ancient and withered, and died. He looked at Alvina-Kristina's beauty, at Johanna's cuteness, and couldn't imagine them as dead of old age. But that's exactly what they would be—rotting skeletons in the ground—and this contemplation was driving him a little bit mad. He shook the thought from his head.

How was he ever going to be able to say goodbye to her?

They remained in the comfort of each other's arms in a half sleep, both feeling deliciously at peace.

JULY 7, 1848

By the time the last of the typhus patients either broke fever or succumbed to it, a total of nine were dead with three survivors weakened to mere invalids. With no new cases in a week, Bodmar was cautiously optimistic the epidemic had run its course. Liedberg inspected the steerage twice daily, to ensure it had been scrubbed and tidied. He would not permit water rations until the steerage passed a rigorous inspection. The lice population plummeted and morale improved significantly, bolstered by rumours of their imminent arrival in America.

Whenever the weather was fair, they brought the sick up on deck and this helped speed their recovery. After many weeks at sea, even the healthy children were less active and many had lost their appetites. The food was so salty, many were refusing to eat sufficiently.

Tom resumed the suspended classes and his students were far more enthusiastic, anticipating they would soon be speaking their new language, not to one another, but to Americans. Tom continued taking Polaroid pictures. This was a remarkable document of these times and he had to find a way of releasing them without the world knowing the truth of how they were made.

Alvina-Kristina, free of the care of Edvard, helped the recovering patients in the other berths. The aftermath of their indiscretions lingered ever present, and they rarely met together in public view and continued to sleep in different berths.

JULY 8, 1848

Tom huddled in the gloom of the hold while rummaging through Charlie's clothes, looking for some fresh socks and underwear. He noticed Charlie's passport and he still had his, Carol's and Alice's. Not that would do much good right now, but he'd have his handy should he ever make it home.

He browsed through the top flap of Charlie's suitcase where he found a tourist guide of California. It was a lost world. It seemed so far away, as if it never existed at all or was a half-lost dream he had once, long ago. But there it was, displayed in living colour—California and its fantastic attractions. He settled his emotions and read, almost to convince himself he actually used to live in that 21st century world. It had been over two excruciatingly long months since he came aboard, and yet, wondered what happened to the time. Flipping through the pages, he paused and grinned at the irony of it all—*Explore California's Past.*

He chuckled aloud. *Most of the history hasn't even taken place yet!* It stirred an excitement in him, as he'd be going there shortly. He read an article on the California Gold Rush, detailing some of the most lucrative gold sites. He immediately recognized this was an extraordinary finding. The timing couldn't be more perfect and it directed him to a huge placer on the Feather River—*Rich Bar.* He could get in and out before its actual discovery in 1850 and never even change history. *Whatever he left behind, would be what the original discoverers would find!* He had to go to California regardless and decided he'd take this little side trip. He would secure his finances—just in case he could not get home—and if he did get back home, take back as much bullion with him as possible—or leave it buried for later retrieval. His head spun at the mere thought of it. There were four additional gold sites, all fit perfectly to his timeline to get there prior to the original discovery.

He felt some eye strain and decided to resume his tour through the pages later on in better lighting. He put it in his handbag, and with the last of the fresh socks and underwear, made his way back to the Gabrielssons' berth.

The canvas belled with a warm summer breeze at her back, the *Margaretha* tore through the water like a warship on the attack. From time to time, a sheet of spray hurled over the bulwarks. The decks were crowded that fine day. Alvina-Kristina stood behind the helmsman, with his shirtless back bronzed by the scorching sun. She listened to the wake with contempt as it boiled with a deep hiss, almost a roar. She just wanted to get off this death-ship with all its horrible memories. Just behind her, Carlos Rodriguez drew pictures again. She wasn't certain if it was just a ruse to spy on the passengers. She resented his presence.

Alvina-Kristina had deep concerns for Selma-Olivia. Her sister was very fond of Sune and really didn't know Jonas and Catharina until the meetings began to plan this ill-conceived emigration. Now both she and her sister would be under Jonas' care. She was worried he'd take all of Sune's money, leaving her and Selma-Olivia with nothing but obligations, forcing them into free labour to build his farm. Captain Liedberg said slaves were only those of the Negro race and confined to the South, but she suspected he might be wrong. Sune had such high expectations, hopes and dreams for their new life in America. What was hardest for her to accept was that Sune never got to see America.

She looked about for Tom but he wasn't on deck. She had difficulty understanding her feelings for him. She loved him, deeply, but it was a confusing kind of love. She always wanted to feel his arms wrapped tightly around her. She could stand perfectly naked before him and enjoy his touch on her body, and yet, the thought of her bearing his children was completely removed. More than just a friend, much more, perhaps a lover, but not a spouse. *Did that make any sense?* All she knew was she cherished his friendship more than life itself and the thought of losing him once they arrived in America created an unbearable torment.

The hard facts smashed into her mind like a psychic fist. Only Thomas could free her from the slavery and misery awaiting her and Selma-Olivia to build a farm from the trees. Regardless of the consequences, she had to find away to keep him from walking out of her life—even if it compromised her faith. She had less fear of God's wrath than digging a farm out of the wilderness for another woman's man.

Rodriguez stood up and walked off. Knowing he always maintained a military alert, she decided to annoy him by tailgating him about three feet behind. He went to the forward hatch, down the steps and she continued to tail him until he turned for the office. Since her family was on deck, she knew when she saw the closed curtains at her berth it was Thomas. It must have been that Aunt Clara thing, but it alerted her to pause. With stealth, she drew the curtain open just enough to peek inside. She could see him reading a book she had never seen before. The cover had strange artefacts on it. She wasn't certain what saw on the front and back covers of his book, but her Aunt Clara's knew exactly what it was.

His big secret.

Tom looked for Alvina-Kristina. She wasn't on the decks. He slipped into the steerage and noticed the closed canvas curtains. "Alvina?"

"Gooooh away!"

He had startled her. He knew at once she wasn't undressing, bathing or using the chamber pot. It wasn't that kind of do-not-disturb. It was an *I'm-up-to-no-good* kind of evasion. He thrust the curtain aside. A gasp choked out of her.

Alvina-Kristina sat on the bottom bunk—the tourist guide in her clutches! Her eyes met Tom's with such an impact he could feel them impale into his mind like spears. He could sense the bewilderment and fear converging in them. Alvina-Kristina's darkest fears burned into his mind like clots of acid. He managed to free his eyes and then all at once, the only contorted emotions remaining in his mind were his own.

"Give me the book." He shouted in spite of himself, furious at her again for snooping through his things.

She responded with a chilling silence that drifted into a standoff setting both into stone. She glanced down at the booklet, still keeping a watchful eye on Tom as she flipped from page to page, absorbing the photographs, mesmerized by the strange sights. There were monstrous flying machines, bizarre carriages, thousands of them on huge black roads. There were titanic ships, gleaming white with no sails and a horrid rat-like creature with big black round ears, a silly smile and a man's body. It stood beside an equally horrid creature resembling a yellow dog. She was in the grip of panic, fascination, wonder, terror; all of it combining into a single, depraved emotion.

He lunged for her.

She leapt up and shoved Tom aside with such unexpected speed and force that he careened head first into the berth while she hurled out of the steerage.

"Sonuvabitch!"

Alvina-Kristina dashed to the decks. Squinting from the brilliant daylight, she scurried around the mingling passengers towards the bow. Tom shot out of the steerage as if he had been blasted out of it, winced in the sunlight, then located Alvina-Kristina in the shadow of the foresail. Hunched over the book, she flipped through its pages. She paused on occasion, trying to decipher the caption. Terrified she'd be picked up by the security cameras, he pounced up the forecastle stairs. Alvina-Kristina didn't evade him, rather, she waited, demanding an explanation. He arrived beside her under the foremast ratlines.

Her lips trembled as the words struggled to be released. "Where are you from?"

He grabbed her bicep and led her to an area he knew was a blind spot for the surveillance cameras. His eyes locked with hers. Each confronted the other like two prizefighters just before the opening bell.

"If Rood finds out that you know, he'll put a bullet in your head. Don't you get it?"

Her features softened. "We are best friends, Thomas. I love you." She hugged him and only then could he feel the fear tremble from her body.

He kissed her on the forehead. "I know, I love you, too, and I'm trying to keep you safe."

"Where are you from? Please." Her voice was soft, her cerulean eyes softer. They were as deep blue as the sky above and Tom wished he could fly through them like a dove.

He took a long, deep breath. "It's not so much as where I'm from as it is . . ." he again kissed her on the forehead, "when I'm from."

"When . . . when?"

"This year is 1848. My world, where I come from, Alvina-Kristina Gabrielsson, will only exist in the year 2016."

Alvina-Kristina's face remained remarkably composed by the revelation—she had already come to that conclusion, she just couldn't make any sense of it. But hearing it from his lips, and all at once everything made perfect sense. Right from the moment when she saw the explosion of emerald static that slithered on her fingertips, and when time briefly came to a standstill. His hair, clothes, the soldiers and their weapons and armoured uniforms, the so-called music box, the bright blue material they slept on and his liberated views of women. It seemed too obvious now.

"I knew . . . something like that. I knew all along."

He nodded. "I'm from a hundred and sixty-eight years in your future."

The bulldog woman stared at their embrace in sharp disapproval. Beritt Larson's toothless mouth moved and twisted as she muttered her disgust.

"Mind your business, you old sow. Be gone!" Tom shouted. He spoke Swedish quite well now. He picked that line up from the captain along with other words from his maritime vocabulary, which are absolutely unfit for the company of women. The old lady's face looked as if she had been pinched in the ass. She moved off, chatting away to herself.

Tom leaned against the bulwark and stared past the deck and ratlines towards the distant rim of the horizon. The ship rode hard over the choppy waves. Alvina-Kristina shuffled next to him. In the strong breeze, strands of her hair brushed against Tom's face.

"Why are you here?"

He couldn't help himself. He gave her a firm smooch on the lips. "I'm not here because I want to be, trust me on that," he said, finishing with a tense kind of laugh.

"You were trying to help the soldiers' boat, is that how you got here?"

Tom's voice faltered as he recalled that horrible day. "It's difficult to explain. The United States Army had this flying machine." He attempted to describe the Chinook, and then with vivid detail, told her of its crash, the grizzly search for survivors, finally, Rood commandeering the ship. "Rood and his people are here on some kind of mission. We don't know what. They promised Ralph and me that if we cooperate with them, that in two years, we will go through another time warp to go home. Carol, Alice and Charlie are not dead—they never made it into this time period."

Tom could see the heartbreak darken her eyes. "Then, you are still married?"

"I am." He kissed her forehead again, then held her in his arms.

"I thought you were a man with no wife . . . why didn't you tell me?"

"I didn't expect us to have feelings for each other, Alvina. I never intended to hurt you. I'm so sorry." He could hear her anguish through a sigh, that had she not held back, would have been a full-blown cry. "Carol doesn't exist right now, but I will be going home to be with her once again. That's why I never took off my wedding ring."

She wasn't certain if she had anger against him for the deception, or heartbreak, but she wasn't happy right now. "But, you permit yourself to kiss me?"

He kissed her, a soft, lingering kiss. "It's wrong, I know, even though it feels so right."

"When you get home, I will be dead, for many, many years."

"I've been thinking about that, too. It's difficult for me to grasp, but really, you'll always be alive, simply living in the past." He gave her a deep hug and her arms sailed around his. She leaked out the little sob she was holding back. The answer to the question she pondered for the last two months was finally revealed, the answer numbing as the question itself.

A man from the future. A man she could never have. A man who could not help her avoid the fate of clearing the wilderness for a home that wasn't even her own. Her destiny and her sister's were sealed, and all at once, her fate became a miserable existence of servitude without hope.

Within the foresail's shadow, Alvina-Kristina drew closer to him, staring ahead at the empty waters, the strands of her hair wrapping around his neck like golden tentacles. Tom kissed her on the cheek. He thought the trembling was coming from her, until he realized it was pounding out of his own body.

AUGUST 27, 2016
PASADENA, CA

Fleming bent closer to Jennifer's monitor. A smile lit up his face. "Confirmed, Miss Burke. That is indeed a spectacular temporal event! In just ten days' time!"

"Where?" Cosmo asked.

"Victoria Island—that's in the Canadian Arctic," Jennifer said.

"Can we get prepared with so little time?" Cosmo asked.

"I will notify my father. Time is tight, but we can do it, I'm certain."

Scranton burst into the office with an expectant grin. "We got the pictures from the camera found on the ocean floor. Photographer was Carol Parker and we managed to salvage 109 frames off the memory card!" They went to the kitchen table where the rest of the crew waited. Scranton grinned as he slipped the memory stick into the USB slot.

"Carol Parker was a hell of a photographer. Wait till you see this." Scranton loaded up a sequence of shots of the Chinook exploding and impacting onto the water. "She must have just held the shutter. This is almost a movie sequence."

The crowd sitting around the monitor were muted by the violence of the crash. There were additional shots of the rescue, of the severed fuselage floating upside-down. Some shots were only partially complete, with large, black blocks where the data could not be salvaged. The temporal static seemed to glow so bright and surreal it looked like a really bad Photoshop job. The final frames showed the military crew getting rescued and emerging on deck.

"This confirms six soldiers survived the crash," Fleming noted.

"Uncle Sam would be, how should I say? Somewhat irate that we have these pictures," Cosmo stated.

"Indeed, Mr. Wynn." Fleming gave Scranton a sharp look. "How much does the lab that salvaged the images know?"

"I was there during the entire process, and the guy who salvaged the SanDisk drive was just looking at ones and zeroes. He saw maybe three frames and I made sure he didn't save any. He was a long-haired hippy-type of guy. I don't think there would be an issue even if he had seen the shots."

"That is fortunate," Fleming said.

"If we could ID just one of these guys," Scranton said, "we'd be able to find out where they're based out of."

"They never released the name of the casualties," Roberts mentioned.

"Nor will they," Fleming said.

"They have nametags on their uniforms," McKenzie observed.

"It would be best if we did not pry," Fleming cautioned. "We need to maintain a great distance from our colleagues."

"Let's see what the five Canadians were up to before the encounter with the helicopter," Cosmo suggested. "You know, check out their backstory."

Scranton grimaced they were wasting their time, but relented. The thumbnails tiled on the screen and he clicked the first frame. It was a shot taken in Victoria a couple of days before they departed. Carol wore a tight red blouse and Cosmo could be heard muttering his approval under his breath. Another shot was of Alice standing with Tom, with Victoria's Empress Hotel providing the picturesque backdrop. She was in a tight little beige dress—she was all legs, but not much else.

"I thought you said she had a nice rack," Scranton observed. He pointed at the screen.

"She does," Cosmo countered.

"Oh my Lord, stop it!" Jennifer complained.

Scranton shook his head. "Sorry, man, but those sweet rolls are a carpenter's delight."

Cosmo stared hard. He blinked and had a long, searching look. "You're right, dude. The babe has no paw-patties. Nothing. Training bra material!"

"Will you two pigs stop it!" Jennifer shrieked.

"Mr. Wynn!" Fleming snapped, low on patience while McKenzie caught on that this involved much more than just men being men.

"Don't you get it?" Cosmo said. "Alice Cousineau has absolutely no muffins!"

"Muffins!" Jennifer gasped. "What do you mean by she has no *muffins*? Is that why you call me Muffins?"

"Oooooops," Cosmo gasped as she squeezed her fingernails into his forearm.

"You are so dead!"

"Please," Fleming chided both. "Enough of this pettiness!"

"This is not petty!" Jennifer tightened her grip around his arm and knew he had to be in severe pain right about then. Cosmo angled his head away from her like a dog caught chewing on his master's slippers, and gave a prayer of thanks she had a habit of chewing her fingernails.

"Miss Burke." Fleming lost all patience with their constant squabbling. "You and Mr. Wynn may discuss your infantile issues once we're through here, but not until. Is that understood?"

She clenched her jaw so tight her molars were endangered of shattering. "Uhhhhh!" she grunted. "Yes, but I swear to God, Cosmo is sooooo dead!" Jennifer tossed away her grip.

"Get pictures on the yacht again," Cosmo asked, his voice was tentative and a little frail. His arm hurt but wasn't going to give her the satisfaction by admitting it. Jennifer crossed her arms. She had a low-cut blouse and she concealed her *muffins* as best as she could.

Scranton sped through the shots to the sequence on the yacht just prior to the encounter with the Chinook. Alice was in her yellow tube top. "Flat as a board," Cosmo said.

"Like I really care about Alice Cousineau's lack of muffins."

"Because, Jennifer, when I saw her coming out of the water, she had very nice twangers."

"What are you saying? Temporal events makes your boobs grow?"

"Touché."

"Professor, I've had it with him!"

Fleming glanced at Cosmo. A fire raged in his eyes and he realized Cosmo was definitely onto something. Cosmo took his laptop and placed it beside Scranton's. He loaded up the pictures of Carol, Alice and Charlie being helped out of the water. He found a solo, frontal view of Alice. She wore the same yellow tube top and cut-off shorts. But there it was—a full handful and even a little more to spare.

"Oh my Lord!" Jennifer gasped. "She has boobs!"

"Bosoms, indeed," Fleming acknowledged.

"Hold the presses!" Jennifer's breath heightened as she looked at one screen then the other, back and forth. Her tone became elevated while the profound implications were beginning to fall into place. "The clothes are different! Similar tube top and jeans, but not the quite the same."

"Same with Carol and Charles," McKenzie noted. "Similar clothes, but not the same. Just trying to look the same."

Jennifer's heart was racing. "Oh my Lord, I've got pictures of them, too!"

"How's that possible?" Cosmo asked. "You guys bugged-out before they got to shore."

"I took some tourist shots when we first arrived. I only glanced at them once but I just recalled seeing that yellow tube top." She placed her laptop on the table. There were several shots of the scenery, then one of the park's entrance. There were perhaps twenty people in the shot and in the far background, she could clearly see the bright yellow tube top. She zoomed in. Though heavily pixelated at that magnification, it was them—Alice, Carol and Charlie—heading for the beach with backpacks.

"When was this picture taken, Miss Burke?" Fleming asked.

"Two hours before the event!"

"How can they be on the yacht and on shore at the same time?" Roberts asked.

Fleming's voice trembled. "There is only one possibility, Mr. Roberts."

"Look at Alice's height," Jennifer shrieked. Alice's head was past Carol's shoulder on Cosmo's screen, on the shots from the memory stick, well below. "She . . . grew, she must have grown two inches and . . . grew boobs!"

"They weren't hurled from the zone. They swam out there," Cosmo said.

"Correct," Fleming agreed, and his voice rose sharply. "They were not hurled from the zone as we were deceived to believe, Mr. Wynn. They passed through the temporal singularity, went into the past, then somehow, they found the means to return prior to the original temporal event. They released a temporal charge, deceiving the military—and us—that they were hurled from the zone, when in fact, they had not."

"What did I tell you?" Jennifer said, her voice carried the full exoneration she imposed on the others. "All along, I've been saying that this makes no sense. No, you all thought I was a nut, wrong, stupid, smoking dope, having my period—well I was right! You guys were wrong!"

"And, your point?" Scranton asked.

"I—was—right!"

Roberts got up and wrote on the calendar's current date—*Jennifer was right*. "There we go. Of course, if I was to write all the times *Jennifer was wrong*, you wouldn't be able to read any of the dates."

Jennifer's hands tensed and flew up, as if she were about to play the piano during the final climax of an epic musical score. "You were wrong, I was right. You owe me!"

Fleming shook his head in depleted patience and tapped the picture on Cosmo's laptop, of the three after their rescue. "They all appear older. Look at Charles Mason. He was chubby before the event, now quite fit. Twenty, thirty pounds lighter. Carol Parker has gained weight and look at the lines on her face."

"She's got a nasty scar on her forehead, above the right eyebrow," Jennifer pointed out. "She doesn't have it on the before shots. Sometime during her temporal trip, she got whacked in the face."

"Looks like Alice had a boob job," Scranton noted.

"Fake—yes," Cosmo agreed.

"Oh, you're that much of an expert you can tell?" Jennifer chided.

"Yes," Cosmo replied pointedly. "That's definitely an aftermarket upgrade." He looked at Jennifer's breasts for a good half-dozen seconds. "Yours are way too small to be fake."

"Oh—my—Lord, I hate you!"

"Her bust size may have increased during their two year foray into the past and got an enhancement as part of a cover-up," Roberts speculated.

"You don't leave on a trip and come back without taking precautions. She needed the enhancement to have it on record there was a boob-job. How else do explain growing breasts naturally in just a few hours?"

"I suspect two, three years passed," Fleming concluded. "Then they returned to the present before they left, and were attempting to deceive the military that they had never departed at all."

"A round trip," McKenzie said with a disbelieving kind of awe.

"A round trip, indeed," Fleming acknowledged. "A two or three year foray into the past and somehow, somehow, they had found the means—more specifically, the assistance—to return!"

"Unless it was planned all along," said Cosmo.

The silence in the room was deafening.

AUGUST 29, 2016
SACRAMENTO, CA

Nolan lurched forward as Henry dropped the enlargements onto his desk. The images so incredible, so impossible, he blinked, still unable to believe his eyes. He stared at General Bishop, Henry Mitchell and Lucy Lewis in stunned disbelief.

"Ralph Parker and Colonel Rood—together in Kandahar City?"

"Confirmed," Bishop said. "The Canadian Army has given Parker's movements during both his tours of Afghanistan. Rood and Parker were in the same region for no less than six months on his second tour. They're drinking buddies."

"An officer drinking with a private? What's this world coming to?" Nolan said in disgust. The pictures showed the two together, arms around the other's shoulders. "I had utmost confidence in Rood."

"This establishes that, without a doubt, Ralph Parker was at the implosion zone with a private arrangement between himself and Rood. Colonel Rood is compromised!"

"For what purpose?" Nolan asked. "And what was in it for Parker?"

"Or the other four," Lucy Lewis added.

"What are they up to?" Bishop's voice trembled at the very thought of Rood tampering with the mission.

"Trasler's mother said he's living in the past, she obviously knows," Lucy said. "They had planned this all along. He must have said goodbye to his mother and told her."

"We have to dig deeper, Colonel," Henry said. "I'm not talking about scratching the surface—I want a complete excavation into their activities for the last five years. Anything outside the military. You're going back to Montreal."

"I just got back."

"And you're going right back!"

JULY 9, 1848

The *Margaretha* leaned into a hard starboard tack. Under her topsails and top-gallant-sails, Tom stood alone by the bulwark. He heard rumours they were less than a week away from America and kept a watchful eye on the horizon. There were no telltale signs they were close, such as birds or even other ships to be seen. It didn't look like they were any closer than a month ago.

He had mixed feelings about landfall. It would spell the end of this maritime voyage and the beginning of a new adventure as he headed out towards California. Though the ship was a nineteenth century environment, he had a regulated daily routine. He knew where he was to sleep, to whom he would see and speak, when and what he was going to eat. He had no need of money. On shore, he would be thrust into the full nineteenth century environment. In a way, the ship was a halfway house from his world into theirs.

He looked about the decks. He knew everyone by name. In one week, or less, all this would be gone. Carol had been on the back burner of his thoughts for much of the trip. She would surface from time to time, but with her out of his life for the next two years, he focused on the here and now. Right now, Carol wasn't on the back burner. She wasn't even on the stovetop.

He glanced about, looking for Alvina-Kristina. She was on his mind constantly. She was not coping well since the loss of her husband and child. Every time a baby cried in hunger, she touched a breast. That special intimacy between a mother and her infant was taken from her in the most horrible way. He was battling images, too. The carnage in the Chinook, Anne-Sophie's corpse hitting him during the storm, the typhus victims and of course, that poor kid burning to death, and then, pulling the trigger on the lad. The rank smell from the bullets exploding into his charred body would always remain with him.

He never saw or even heard Carina Svensson's approach. It was her perfume that alerted him. He ignored her as he continued to search for the elusive landfall. He heard that the first one who spotted land got a bottle of rum and three hearty cheers. He'd pass up on the hearty cheers. The bottle of rum would do just fine. Or the bottle of vodka Liedberg embezzled when he first came aboard would do much better.

Wearing a lavish green silk dress buttoned to the neck, Carina stood right next to him and leaned her arms on the bulwark. An awkward silence drifted by, then the incredible words were spoken—words spoken in flawless British English that nearly made his knees buckle.

"I know who you are and when you are from. As soon as we are in sight of America, Rood intends to escape in his inflatable boats and blow-up this ship and destroy all her living souls."

CHAPTER 22

Tom's breath locked in his throat and his head nearly spun off his shoulders. He continued to stare ahead at the horizon, then glanced briefly at Carina. He understood the risk she made in speaking to him about this, unaware how he'd react. Cautious about the security cameras, he broke his silence with a low, quivering voice. "Rood has no security cameras in the hold."

"Perhaps, if we were punished and put in chains."

"Punished?"

She yanked his arm so violently he spun around. Face to face with her, she stood so close he thought she was going to kiss him.

"Bastard!" she screamed in Swedish, and whipped a hand across his face as loud as a gunshot.

"Bitch!" He slapped her right back. Harder. Her punch appeared out of thin air, striking him below the eye with a wallop and a shower of sparks blew into his vision. He collapsed and she spat on him while he lay on the deck, trying to shake reality back into his world. Trying to figure out where that fist came from.

He grabbed her ankle, gave it a good yank and brought her down. He crawled to his knees, whipping his fists at her. She fought back and a flurry of punches were exchanged. The noise around them exploded—cheering, hooting, laughter—and just moments later, they were separated. Both fought against the restraining arms of the others, both still intent to attack.

"A tiff with the whore?" Liedberg said, chuckling.

"Mind your goddamn business!" Tom yelled back.

"You fat old pig!" Carina shrieked at Liedberg in Swedish.

For a moment, the captain's face was idiotic with surprise. Then it filled in with black rage. Tom gave him a wink and held his hands before the captain, in a gesture to have them cuffed.

"Just chain me and get it over with." By reading Liedberg's features, Tom knew he succeeded in making Liedberg understand this was some kind of deception and of the importance for the two to be alone. "You can let us calm down and speak to us in about . . . say an hour?" He gave Liedberg another wink.

Liedberg winked right back. "Agreed, one hour, Trasler." He slapped his hands. "Mr. Polman, install these two vagabonds to the chains!"

Alvina-Kristina came on deck just as Polman escorted the two down, both still swearing at the other. She sensed this was much more than an altercation with the filthy wench. Whatever it was, she didn't like it. Not at all.

Tom's hands were at head's level, constrained by the rough iron cuffs. In the slanting light of the swaying lantern, he glanced to his left at the prostitute chained three feet away. She stirred uncomfortably within the cuffs. Her beautiful dress took a good measure of abuse, heaped in folds about her thighs while her pale legs were nearly fully exposed. Her legs were nothing less than spectacular.

"Did you have to punch me so goddamn hard?"

She gave a satisfied little smile. "I had to make it look convincing." Her smile withered into tightly pursed lips and she levelled him a chilling look. "You were quiet convincing yourself." A stain grew on her cheekbone.

"Your English is pretty damn good for someone who went to Marseilles for five years?"

"I have no idea where that rumour came from—I was in London."

"I always wondered why you had an English Bible."

"Yes, I was careless when I gave it to you."

"I suspected when we first met you couldn't understand French. So you deliberately infiltrated Rood?"

"I am going to America to start anew, Thomas, like everyone else. However, I mistrusted Rood immediately when you people were rescued. Something about his equipment, his guns, you, nothing fit. Especially you."

"Me?"

She rolled her eyes. "Let's not even go there. I let Rood pursue me and then I observed."

"I was kind of hoping you were a time cop from the 21st century who had infiltrated Rood."

"Sorry, I'm just a 19th century whore."

"What's the purpose of their mission?"

She shook her head. "I do not know. They would never discuss that while I was present."

"What about him destroying the ship?" Tom asked, his voice stammering—it took a lot of courage to ask.

"As soon as they are in range of Sandy Hook, and after it's dark, Rood will lower his rubber boats into the water and Rodriguez will set off the bombs. The passengers have seen too much of the future and of their atrocities. I know I certainly have seen too much."

"What are Rood's plans for Ralph and me?"

"You are full of temporal energy. They need you."

"For their mission?"

"Yes. That much I know."

"Then they intend on changing history?"

"I don't know any more than that."

"When are we going to be off Sandy Hook?"

"Tomorrow night."

"Tomorrow!"

"Yes. I trust you, but if you betray me, I will only be shortening my life by a single day."

"That doesn't give us much time."

"If we are to be saved, then you will have to oppose Rood. Once he discovers you are against him, he will try to kill you. If you do not get killed, it is a certainty you will never see home again."

"I got to think about this." *How could he possibly stop Rood without getting himself killed?* His mind swirled with hundreds of images. The images were not of home, of his culture, his friends and family. It wasn't of Carol, his sister Jane or Mom. The only images were of his family here on the boat—Johanna, Carl-Johan, Stina-Sophia and Selma-Olivia, of the children laughing and playing on the deck. Even Liedberg, for

Chrissakes. He had this odd, strong affection for the captain. Alvina-Kristina's image was the strongest and she had been tormenting his affections for the last month.

It was an easy decision to make. "I'll do whatever it takes to save my Swedish family."

"Are you in love with Alvina-Kristina?"

He wouldn't answer the question. The question terrified him—the answer even more. "She knows who I am."

"She knows?"

Tom cracked a smile. "She just recently found out. She didn't take it all that well."

"We cannot defeat Rood by might," she cautioned. "Even if we have the entire crew attack, Rood will destroy the ship with the bombs."

"We need to put him in a position where he can't destroy the ship," Tom mused, looking about the hold. "He can't destroy the ship if he's stuck on it! We need to deny him use of his rubber dinghies, either by destroying them, or . . . taking them ourselves."

"Escaping in the rubber boats . . . Yes."

"Then he needs to stay on the ship to arrive on shore."

"We have to do this tonight."

"And get a good head start before Rood discovers that we're gone."

"He has cameras everywhere."

"We will have to disable the security system."

"How?"

"I'll have to try to get into the office, somehow get alone and try to figure a way to disable it."

"Silver's computer is right here in the hold, with the soldiers' other belongings."

"Ya, but Silver changed his password just before he was killed so that no one would be able to delete his dirty movies and they can't log on. They tried for weeks and finally gave up."

"His new password is *Longdong Silver*."

Tom looked sharply at her. "How did you get his password?"

"I have all of them."

"All of them!"

She nodded her head. "I just watched them as they touched the letters, knew they were important to start their computers, so I wrote them down in my Bible. Just in case."

"Aren't you a cunning . . ."

"Whore, just say it. I won't be offended."

"We'll need Liedberg to feign a malfunction in order to stop the ship. While the attention is on the repairs, we'll sneak out on the rafts."

"If I can get their navigation equipment, you can use it to get home."

"That's a big risk."

"I wish to live in your time." She paused, the intensity in her eyes were like liquid fire. "If you agree to take me with you, I will assume the risk."

"Deal. How do you plan on getting it?"

"There is a hatch leading to the hold in their office. Get the key from Captain Liedberg. I will slip it through directly into the hold."

"Then all we need to do is to figure out how to pull this off without getting ourselves killed."

They went through something like fifteen scenarios, looked at what needed to go right, and what might go wrong, and nothing seemed to be anything less than suicidal. A little less than an hour later, Liedberg stepped down the ladder and joined them.

"What is the purpose of your self-inflicted incarceration?" His burning eyes seared into Tom's.

"We are close to Sandy Hook?"

"It is tradition for the captain not to divulge the location of the vessel to the—"

"As soon as Sandy Hook has been sighted, Rood intends to destroy the ship with all hands on board."

"Blackguards! Pirates! Bashi-bazouks! Brigands! Sons of John Bull!"

"Easy, Captain Haddock!" Tom pleaded. "Shhhh!"

"I speak perfect English, Captain Liedberg, and have heard all of their wicked intents."

"I see," Liedberg's lips twitched into sly smile. "That is quite the deception."

"The information she has gathered will save our lives, Captain."

His eyes darkened in the lamp light. "Colonel Rood is a miserable creature who dares claim to be called a man."

"He is noxious vermin and must be treated as such," Carina said.

"It might justly be asked if there were a soul dwelling in his body, or if the brutishness alone survives in him."

"We can debate Rood's insanity all day, it will do little to save our lives," Tom cut in.

"Forgive me, Mr. Trasler. I have been obliged to share my beloved vessel with another master. For two months, I have been under Colonel Rood's dominion and I am very much anxious to exterminate Rood and his pirates like I would scurvy dogs. We must take counsel how to prevent the devastations with which the soldiers threaten this ship and all her precious souls."

"Can you please unchain us?" Tom shook his bindings. Liedberg did and with Tom and Carina still using the loft as a seat, the captain vented his anger by pacing back and forth in the cramped aisle.

"It may be necessary to fight, to destroy every one of these scoundrels, so unworthy of pity and against whom any means would be just. I assure you, Trasler, they will soon die an ignominious death!"

"The general idea is to avoid a shooting match."

"This good ship and her crew and passengers are now menaced with terrible peril. The best thing to be done now is to openly give chase to these wretches."

"They out gun you. You've seen their weapons."

"I believe we're not fellows to be afraid of a bullet. We can have satisfaction of these pirates."

"I'm terrified of bullets! Please Captain, we can't afford any more bloodshed so close to America. They have bombs placed in this very hold ready to destroy the ship should they know defeat is imminent."

"Then we shall dispose of the bombs," Liedberg said.

"We cannot remove the bombs unless we have the remote detonator," Tom said. "They will explode if tampered with."

"I too have also heard this from Rodriguez," Carina added.

"I apologize for my reckless words. Under the influence of violent excitement, I am prey to a thousand embezzled thoughts."

"Stealth and deception, Captain, not vengeance, is what will save this ship and her souls." Tom rubbed his chafed wrists. "I need to sneak off this ship with his rubber boats. For that, I'll need some kind of breakdown to occur. While your crew is working on it, others will help us take Rood's rubber boats and he'll be forced to stay aboard and keep the ship and its crew alive until you are safely in port."

"I expect landfall this afternoon and depending on the winds and tide, be in New York harbour by sunset the following day, or first light the day after."

"How close can you get us to land? We have to do this tonight."

"Immediately after Colonel Rood performs his midnight navigation reading, I will alter coarse to bring you as close to shore as possible. Sandy Hook is to the south in New Jersey. I will steer sharply to get the boat closer to Long Island. I will then see to it that the rudder will require emergency repairs."

"Can you tell Rood you're having trouble with the rudder? That will take us a bit off course so he won't get excited if we deviate a bit. I'm planning to do this while they're asleep, but if they do wake up, and notice the ship isn't moving, faking the repairs will be necessary."

"Agreed. This will close the distance to fifteen miles. After I will bring the ship to full stop, we will lower you over the side amidships while my crew creates the deception of repairs on the poop deck. How do you intend to make your way to shore in the rubber rafts?"

Tom didn't even try to hide the facts. "The military has developed a small, fuel powered engine that drives the rafts at high speed. Fifteen miles will be perfect. Now, as soon as Rood discovers we're gone, you have to tell him that I also changed all his computer passwords. If he wants them back, no one gets hurt. You also have to promise him you won't try to attack him. This has to be peaceful."

"What is a computer password?"

"It's like a changing the keys for a lock, and his mission cannot be accomplished without them. Where can I agree to leave them?"

"The front desk of the City Hotel. It is one of the better establishments."

"All right. Carina and I still have work down here. Come back in an hour. And Captain, Rood has eyes and ears everywhere, including your cabin. The safest place to talk to your crew is just behind the bowsprit." Liedberg looked at Tom curiously. "Remember, only behind the bowsprit and in whispers."

"The passengers, in common with the crew, are still in entire ignorance of the extremity of peril to which we are exposed and it must remain thus to avoid panic."

"Agreed. We only tell others on a need-to-know basis."

"A few hours soon separates us from an eventful moment. One clasp of the hand, my friends."

Tom placed Silver's computer on the loft, opened the lid and it automatically booted up.

"Hopefully, its battery still has a good charge to it. It's wireless, so as long as the battery holds out, it should connect to the network."

He entered the password.

L-O-N-G-D-O-N-G-S-I-L-V-E-R.

"What is Longdong Silver?"

"Wishful thinking. Sonuvabitch, we're in! This is a lot easier than I expected." He went into the network configuration.

"You are good on these." She put her arm around Tom's shoulder.

"Charlie was the computer guy for Carol's company and he doesn't know half of what I know. He buggered up the security settings and I was the one who fixed the damn thing. Charlie was almost out of a job. When I wasn't in a drunken stupor, I did a lot of cool shit on the computer."

He could see through the network that Bodmar was active on her computer, but Rood, Jackson and Anderson's, though logged on, were dormant. The security computer was logged on with the cameras transmitting, along with the audio converted into transcripts, translated and screened for key words that might set off the alarm.

He manoeuvred into Rood's computer. It prompted the password.

"Rood's is *Stonewall.*" Carina said.

"As in Stonewall Jackson. All right."

"What are you looking for?"

"I want to change his password."

She giggled sharply. "He will have a fit."

"Won't he?"

CHANGE PASSWORD?

YES

ENTER NEW PASSWORD.

S-N-O-O-P-Y

CONFIRM PASSWORD

S-N-O-O-P-Y

"Child's play. Next time he or I log off, he's screwed. They never expected to be hacked in this time period."

"What is Snoopy?"

"Name of my sister's dog. It's a horrible tiny white poodle that yaps and yaps and yaps."

"Yes, I've seen them. A popular toy of the rich. They are wretched beasts."

"You have absolutely no idea how much I detest that damn animal—almost as much as that damn animal detests me. Okay, I was in a drunken stupor when I kicked him and it never forgave me."

"Did it deserve to be kicked?"

"It deserved to die. As far as I'm concerned, it got off easy. All right, tonight we'll make sure all the computers are logged off so that their alarms are silenced—sonuvabitch, I hate that dog—Do you know the other passwords?"

"The security is *Big Brother*. I don't remember the others, each has more than one, but they are all written in my Bible."

"I'll need them and then wait for Bodmar to get off hers to get into her settings."

Tom went into the security laptop and after a bit of fumbling, found the security cameras. Nine transmissions tiled across the screen, a lot fewer than before. Most of the cameras required recharging, but perhaps this late in the voyage, they couldn't be bothered. He went into the settings and tried to understand the security system preferences. He wanted to alter the sensitivity so that unusual activity wouldn't set off the alarm. After ten minutes, he gave up. With too little time to figure out the parameters, limited battery life and frayed nerves, he decided he'd have to shut down the entire grid. Tom glanced at the battery. It crept towards low. He turned off the computer and concealed it beneath the loft.

Once she returned to the deck, Carina Svensson stretched a kink out of her back. Tom appeared shortly after, she gestured crudely at him and Tom shot back with the finger. He searched for Alvina-Kristina and found her in the steerage on the top berth. She was lying down, curled fetaly. Seeing Tom, her eyes flashed to life and a strained smile formed on her lips. Tom crawled up the ladder, joining her.

"Stay away from that vile woman."

He grabbed her free hand and kissed it, then kissed her lips. "We have to talk. Quietly, in whispers." He snuggled next to her, kissed her again and leaned into her ear. "Carina understands English perfectly. She has been spying on Rood and has just learned that he intends to blow up the ship with all aboard."

She gasped sharply.

"Carina, the captain and I are working on a plan that would make it impossible for Rood to destroy the ship. We intend to sneak off the ship tonight in Rood's boats. Then we'll meet later at a boarding house Liedberg knows of. We have to be very careful when we talk or meet. Rood has tiny cameras all over the ship and is spying on everyone, day and night. That's why Carina and I pretended to fight so we could be alone and talk."

He saw her eyes flash in the light of the flickering lanterns. They were filled with the prospect of adventure. "I will help you."

"I was counting on you."

She had an excitement that was brightly displayed on her face. Tom realized with a peculiar sort of warped humour she was absolutely thrilled by the danger and the challenge facing them.

He had just made her day.

"Colonel Rood, a moment if you please."

Rood seemed to be quite jovial and smiled broadly at the captain. "Yes, Captain."

"We shall be in sight of Sandy Hook tomorrow."

"I concur."

"Once we do we will have a pilot come aboard."

"Yes, I am aware of that."

"I do not wish to alarm you, Colonel. However, I must report to you that my helmsman is struggling with the rudder. I see nothing that will impede our arrival, but we may be delayed or slightly off course. We must be cautious as we enter crowded ship lanes, and if there is much loss of control, we shall be ordered by the pilot to lay anchor until the repairs are affected."

The colonel's jovial look darkened like a tempest. "I want no delays."

"Nor do I, Colonel. Nor do the passengers, I give you my utmost assurances."

"As long as we are on the same page, Captain." Rood walked away, his thumps betraying his anger like a spoiled child.

Just before sunset, land was spotted and it wasn't Tom who received the bottle of rum and three hearty cheers. Three other boats could be seen in the distance and the excitement among the passengers was very great. They remained on deck long after sunset just to see lights from shore before Polman herded them into the steerage.

Rood and Rodriguez completed their midnight readings with the navigator, and once they were below, the captain ordered the helmsman to gradually alter the ship's course to the north-west for Long Island. The clouds cloaked the sky so the rotation of the stars would not betray them.

Tom could hear Carina entertaining Rood from his spot directly beneath the office. He would log off all the computers with the new passwords once everyone was asleep. Then he'd shut down the security grid. Hopefully, they'd only notice the lockout in the morning, long after he made his escape.

Carina gave the one final scream of her fake orgasm, a predetermined signal loud enough to let Tom know she finished. They agreed on twenty minutes for her to freshen up and then she'd drop the navigation equipment through the office cargo hatch. Tom checked Bodmar's computer, still logged on but with no activity for twenty minutes.

Dressed in jeans and a plaid blue shirt, his Nikes and baseball cap, Tom navigated into the network, keeping a close watch on the dwindling battery power. He flipped through Carina's Bible and found where she wrote down the passwords. First, he altered Anderson's password, then Rodriguez and Jackson's. Just Bodmar's left. He heard the *Mission Impossible* theme song play inside his head while he went into Bodmar's settings to change her password.

INCORRECT

His heart leapt. Bodmar had been using four. Two more chances left.

He went to the second one in Carina's Bible.

INCORRECT

Bodmar had long gotten used to Rood's antics with the whore-toy, but my God, this was overkill. She finished her snack and returned to her computer. She got an alert. Two failed attempts at altering her password.

"What do we have here?" She tucked her chair in closer to the desk.

She went into the network settings and noticed another active computer—*Silver's computer!* Someone was using Silver's computer yet she could account for everyone in the office. *Parker, perhaps, who she didn't trust? Trasler? No, neither could have ever gotten past Silver's password. If she couldn't, they certainly couldn't.* For a fleeting moment, she thought Silver might somehow still be alive, but he couldn't have remained concealed all this time. The hacker just got out of her settings. She slipped her holster around her beige dress and stepped out of the office. She looked through the aisle and it was as peaceful as the aisle could ever get for this time of night.

Tom tracked Bodmar through the security cameras and noticed her sidearm. She had been alerted! She passed each berth slowly, then realized she held an electronic device in her hand. It occurred to him she was going to detect his computer!

"Gotchya!" Bodmar said.

Tom powered off. *But it was too late!*

Bodmar's device pointed down and she knew the signal originated from the steerage. She went up onto the decks heading directly for Ralph's cabin. She opened the door without knocking, just wide enough to peer through. Ralph was in a deep sleep and never even knew she peeked at him. She closed the door and stared at the captain's cabin, seeing the glow of the lanterns wrap around the doorframe. She knocked on the door.

Liedberg thought it might be Tom and Bodmar's presence startled him. "What is it?"

She peered past him, seeing no one else in his cabin.

"I have some equipment I need in the hold. It's urgent."

Carina glanced in a wall mirror and touched up her hair. Rood stepped out in a crimson robe and noticed Bodmar absent from her station. He knew she'd be up a while yet as this was the final day she'd be able to work for quite some time.

"Sharon?"

No reply. Rood was a creature of habit, never trusted change or the breaking of routine. He looked at Carina with a look colder than a serrated blade.

"You know your way out."

Something was already amiss with the plan. Rood wasn't going to bed like he always did, instead, the bastard was getting dressed. Carina glanced at the navigation equipment. There were two pieces to it. The navigator, which looked similar to a laptop though a lot bulkier, and the telescopic pole with the black dome. Knowing she'd have just seconds to act, she went on her hands and knees, took off an earring, and placed it under the dinner table, which was against the forward bulkhead. She unlocked the hatch with the key Liedberg gave her.

Tom stashed Silver's laptop under some luggage and waited directly below the office's cargo hatch. He could hear Carina unlock the padlock. Then, behind him, he heard the rear cargo hatch open. A lantern's light slanted through the hatch, half eclipsed by a clutter of cargo, projecting long, warped shadows into the hold.

"What are you exactly seeking, Miss Bodmar?"

Liedberg had a naturally loud voice, but raised, Tom understood the warning. There was no place to hide. *He was going to be discovered!*

"I told you—a piece of equipment," Bodmar replied, irritated by Liedberg's resistance.

Carina opened the hatch, and poked the long pole of the navigator through it. Tom grabbed it and pushed it right back to her. He poked his head through the hatch, seeing no one else, heaved himself into the office. He quietly closed the hatch while Carina put the navigator back.

"Carina, you still there?" Rood asked, hearing movement.

She responded in Swedish that she didn't understand him.

"Get the hell out!"

Carina and Tom slipped out the office door. She looked furtively at the navigator and closed the office door. Tom couldn't speak to her without revealing they understood one another, so he motioned for her to go to her living area and he ducked into his berth, joining Alvina-Kristina, waiting there for the next phase of their operation.

"You disturb me at this unholy hour, search the hold and comeback empty handed?" Liedberg grumbled.

"It's a woman's prerogative."

After crawling out of the hatch, Bodmar paused at the back of the steerage. Whoever was using the computer in the hold left, or, some kind of electronic deception perpetrated by the person on Silver's laptop rechannelled the computer's signal. Liedberg returned to the main deck and Polman urgently trotted over.

"I fear the plan has gone astray," he hushed.

"It must be acknowledged that as yet, the stealth of the project has not been attained. We may have to execute our plan in a way we had hope not to, Mr. Polman."

Bodmar went to the Gabrielssons' berth. "Trasler?"

Tom grunted. "Sharon?" He tried to sound groggy and confused. It worked.

"Never mind." She continued through the aisle and slipped into the office. She met Rood just as he stepped out of his enclosure. He had dressed into his uniform. "Planning another hot date?" she asked.

"I was about to ask you the same." Rood tugged his uniform down and slipped on his holster. "What were you doing?"

There was open suspicion of the other. Bodmar couldn't help but suspect that Rood somehow activated Silver's computer and tried to change the passwords. It wouldn't explain the signal originating from the hold, but Rood, being a crafty son-of-a-bitch, may have done just that to throw off any search.

"I have a headache and was getting some fresh air."

Rood felt the boat lose her stride. "You feel that?"

"Yes. We're stopping."

"Goddammit! It's the rudder. Come on."

"Sonuvabitch!" Tom whispered to Alvina. "They we're supposed to fake the broken rudder after Rood's crew were all in bed!"

"Now what do we do?"

"Improvise. Dammit, I had this all planned out and now we're screwed!"

Bodmar and Rood mounted the staircase for the decks. Carina slipped through her curtain and trotted to the office. Rood hadn't locked the door and she crept through. Rodriguez, Jackson and Anderson were asleep just beyond their canvas partitions and she had to be quiet. She opened the hatch and carefully slipped the navigator's probe through, then the navigator and closed the hatch. She got the key to lock it—someone yanked her hair hard from behind. It was Anderson.

"What are you doing here, sweetheart?"

She concealed the key and pointed to the empty pierced ear hole, hoping he wouldn't notice the missing navigator.

"I don't think so." He wouldn't let go and she grasped at his hand, gouging her fingernails into his wrists. "Rodriguez!"

The Hispanic got out of bed in a flash, wearing nothing but army issue boxers. "What's she doing here?"

"Looks like she was snooping. Keep her on ice."

Jackson joined them. He wore a pair of blue cotton pyjamas, tops and bottoms, and in bare feet. He was still half asleep. "What's going on?"

"Ship isn't moving and we caught the bitch snooping around."

Alvina-Kristina and Tom crept out of their berth. Jonas grabbed Alvina-Kristina's wrist. She briefed him on part, but not all, of their plan.

"I saw Carina go into the office and she has not returned."

Tom understood the Swedish response, and stared at the office. There wasn't much he could do at the moment. He and Alvina-Kristina moved swiftly through the aisle to the back of the steerage, then through the hatch and into the hold. He turned on the flashlight. The light beam went to the hatch at the other end, the one directly under Rood's office. He saw the navigation equipment.

"Okay, she accomplished her mission. Let's find out what's happening in the office."

He dug out Silver's laptop and booted it. He went to the security cameras and looking at the office camera, Anderson, Rodriguez and Jackson surrounded Carina. She sat in a chair, the same way she would if they were interrogating her.

"This is not good," Alvina-Kristina said with a hush.

"It's a disaster."

Carina spoke in Swedish and with a written transcript translated live, she explained she was looking for her earring that fell off when she was with Rood. They weren't interested in her excuses.

Tom scratched an itch while watching the monitor. "If we leave without her, they'll kill her." He switched to the outside cameras and saw Bodmar and Rood still on deck. He asked Alvina-Kristina to hold the flashlight as he flipped to the last page of Carina's Bible. He had two more passwords but only one more chance. *Which to choose from?*

"I need your Aunt Clara's. Which is the right password for Bodmar's computer?"

She stared at the passwords. It wasn't a crimp of concentration, rather, she let go, allowing her mind to tune into a frequency where Tom could never follow. Her eyes blinked, bringing her back. She tapped the fourth.

He typed it in. "Oh, you're good."

"Mother said only wicked people and witches do such things. She had the gift, too. She said never to use it on purpose."

"You're saving lives, kiddo. Nothing wicked about that."

Having successfully changed the password, Tom ordered Bodmar's computer to shut down and switched back to the outside camera. Bodmar and Rood were making their way towards the poopdeck. Seven sailors and Liedberg peered below at the rudder while they lowered a sailor by a rope to the top of the rudder. Liedberg spoke harshly, belting instructions. Tom read the translation printed on the screen. The rudder was not responding. At least that part of the plan was going right.

"What exactly is the problem with the rudder?" Rood asked.

"A more perfect survey has to be made to determine the fault, Colonel. In the dark it is next to impossible." The skies were clearing, but the moon was in a fierce struggle to break free of the clouds.

"Can't you just jury-rig the goddamn thing? We're so close."

"Colonel Rood, I am as anxious as you to get to New York and put an end at last to this sorry voyage." Liedberg put his revised plan into play, hoping Rood would take the bait. "Without the ship's boat, which you had dispatched along with eighteen souls to the mercy of Providence, we have to use ropes, which has greatly inconvenienced the investigation. It will take time!"

"Would it help, Captain," Rood's voice was frustrated, "if I provided you with one of my dinghies?"

He took the bait!

"Indeed! I shall have one dispatched immediately."

"Sharon, I want the three stooges out here, pronto."

"That's just great," Tom said. "Now they're all out of bed. Someone's going to discover they're locked out of their computers and if we're still on board, Rood will be merciless to get the passwords out of me."

"What will he do?"

"Either torture me, or more likely, threaten to start killing you guys. Likely, you first."

That didn't go over too well with Alvina-Kristina.

Bodmar returned to the office. Rodriguez was still in his boxers, but Anderson and Jackson had since dressed. Anderson in his soldier blues, Jackson in contemporary civvies. Bodmar found Carina sitting on the chair, staring at Rodriguez's pistol. Carina had this odd, bored expression on her face.

"What's this?" she asked.

"Caught her snooping."

"I'll watch her. The chief wants you three on deck. He's going to inflate one of the dinghies to assist in the repairs."

"Repairs?"

"Rudder's out."

They changed and left and Sharon noticed her computer was powered off. She knew immediately this was not a good thing. She pressed the power button and waited. She entered her password.

INCORRECT

That little bastard.

She said nothing. She was furious at herself for not putting a new password after the first alert. She stomped her foot in frustration for allowing this to happen. She went on the security computer. Powered up, but locked on a dead camera. It wouldn't permit her to toggle to an active camera. The mystery hacker could use the security grid, but denied them use of it. She stared at the screen for a time and was about to power it off to deny them its use, then reconsidered. She stared up to the security camera peering down at her and gave a tidy little wave.

CHAPTER 23

"She's onto us." Tom tugged his baseball cap tighter. He rerouted the security feed through Silver's computer to ensure they wouldn't lose the camera grid. "We have to get Carina."

"But how will you manage to achieve her deliverance and also escape ourselves?"

Tom knew their plan was in shambles. He only had a ghost of an idea—nothing resembling a plan.

"I locked them out of their computers. They're screwed without them. If they ever want to get back in, they'll need the navigator and the new password." Tom tapped is head. "And it's in here."

"But he'll torture you—or kill me."

"I'll have to try to reason with Rood."

"How will you get home without the navigator?"

"I'll get the information I need before I give it back."

"What if Rood does not wish to reason with you?"

"Let's hope it doesn't come to that. I'm not so good dealing with torture."

Bodmar closed in on Carina. "What were you doing?" She feigned she didn't understand, just pointing to her missing earring. Bodmar bent down, looking on the floor, and then found it. She pinched it and still on her knees, held it to before Carina.

"Is this what you've been looking for?"

Carina nodded.

"No. I think you planted it there, just in case you were caught."

Bodmar crossed her arms. "What's going on?"

"Rood's intent is to destroy the ship along with all her passengers."

Bodmar was shocked into a laugh and she didn't care for the sound of it in the slightest—high and slightly hysterical. "Oh my God!" Bodmar's face twisted into a blend of horror and hearing the funniest joke of her life. "If Rood finds out you speak English, he'll shoot you in the head without a second thought."

"You are the one who assured him I was dumb to the language. He may shoot you, also."

"Good point, it will be our secret for the time being at least. What is exactly going on, here?"

"You plan to leave the ship tomorrow night once the ship is off Sandy Hook. You, Anderson and Tyrone were not in the room when Rood discussed with Carlos to blow up the ship once you are at a safe distance."

"You heard this?"

"I hear everything. You'd only find out watching us all die. Myself, the crew, the passengers, all those children."

Bodmar always questioned Rood's state of mind, especially when he torched the boy. Willing to kill over a hundred souls so cold bloodedly is proof positive of his madness. "Who changed the computer passwords?"

"If you want your passwords, I need safe passage off this ship, tonight, along with Thomas and Alvina-Kristina."

"So it was Tom." Bodmar shook her head, smiling. "I always knew it would come to this." Their arrogance put them in this predicament. Their network security was lax. Of course it was lax, on a nineteenth century sailing ship. *Who would have the skill to hack the system and shut them out?* Bodmar stared at the ceiling mounted camera and put her hands on her hips. "You win, Trasler. We need to talk. No guns, I promise."

Tom had Alvina-Kristina gather their luggage while he opened the cargo hatch to the office. Either Bodmar was going to force the passwords at gunpoint, or worse, threaten to kill his Swedish family—or she was going to keep her word. It was a hell of a gamble, but he already made up his mind not to bend. Even if they started to kill those closest to him—Alvina, Johanna, Selma-Olivia, if he gave up the passwords, they'd all be dead. Everyone on board. He would have to ride the torture all the way to hell. As their faces met, she was wearing the holster—but at least she wasn't holding the gun.

"Where's the navigator?" Bodmar asked.

"You'll get it back in New York City—only after I have confirmation that everyone is safe. My guess is that you're dead in the water without it."

"Quite dead in the water. How are we going to get our passwords and the navigator back?"

"Liedberg suggested the front desk at the City Hotel. Apparently, you won't have any difficulty finding it—it's the best hotel in town. I'll deliver them only when I have confirmation the ship and all passengers are safe and sound. If Rood retaliates even against one passenger—no passwords, no navigator."

"Agreed. I'll hold off Rood so you can complete your escape."

"What will Rood do to you?"

"He'll be fine once he calms down."

"And until he calm down?"

"That could be a problem."

"What exactly is your mission?"

Tom never actually expected her to say anything about it, but she flowed right into the conversation. "Ever watch *The Terminator?"*

"What, you're knocking off Sarah Connor?"

"Exactly. Except our Sarah Connor is a slave from Austin, Texas, by the name of Nat Brady."

"He's your Sarah Connor? A black slave?"

"He's certainly not a white slave."

"Why are you going to alter history?" Tom asked with heightened suspicion.

"Tom, our history *is the altered history."*

". . . What!"

She glanced at the activity on the monitor. Liedberg's men were getting the dinghies. "We have enough time for me to lay it out for you. Two years ago, we detected a massive exit node in the middle of nowhere in Western Australia. An exit node is like a knot in a rope, the rope being the long S-shaped exit path. That indicates that someone, or something, will exit a temporal wormhole. We identified the temporal origin as being February 1972 in the south-eastern region of the Yukon.

Hours before the predicted exit time, we were joined by our Russian colleagues, who had also detected the event. To say the least, there was a tense standoff until we agreed to investigate this jointly. What happened was completely unexpected. There were nine soldiers inside a snow covered barracks, six from the Soviet Red Army, three from the Confederate States of America."

"Soviets and Confederate soldiers coming from the Canadian Yukon? In 1972?"

"It that reality, the Soviet Yukon. When we learned of the alternate reality, things got ugly between which side would get which men. Some of the Soviets wanted to defect, one CSA soldier refused to be taken in by the Americans, since the USA and CSA were engaged in a severe cold war, hence the Confederacy aligning itself with the Soviets. One of the Confederate soldiers from 1972 that we retained was Brent Arbing, one of our colleagues killed in the Chinook crash."

"Arbing . . ." Tom paused and then the name flashed into his mind. "I saw him dead in the Chinook. I remember him more than I'd like to."

"Our friend Arbing came from a world where the Confederacy had successfully ceded from the United States."

"Rood mentioned the Confederacy to me, so I thought it might have to do with your mission."

"Yes, everything. In both Brent Arbing's world and ours, the Confederacy sent two diplomats, James Mason and John Slidell, who tried to get diplomatic recognition by England and France early on in the war, but their diplomatic efforts were a failure. According to Arbing, in his timeline, Confederate Vice President Alexander Stephen commissioned a secret diplomatic mission from Texas, through Mexico aboard a French vessel to bypass the Union blockade. Nat Brady, a slave owned by Joseph Walker of Austin, Texas, would be the new emissary. Having an educated, pro-Confederate slave pushing for European recognition would be far more effective than sending two slave owners.

"Knowing the tide of war was going against them, the CSA had no recourse but to offer a Slaves' Bill of Rights, championed by Nat Brady and his master Joseph Walker, which would eliminate the cruelty and guarantee them medical care and a retirement pension. Nat Brady also convinced the Europeans that freed slaves would be worse off as they didn't have the intellectual faculties to thrive on their own. The Slaves'

Bill of Rights would make slavery more palatable to the Europeans and ease the recognition of the Confederacy. Slavery would eventually transition to indentured servitude, where they work for a set number of years then go free—and shipped off to Liberia.

"On January 14th, 1863, Napoleon III met the Confederate delegation, which promised recognition of France's intervention in Mexico that already began in early 1862, and promised cooperative military operations through Texas. The major European powers were concerned by the rise of America and it was in their interests to see it cut apart and weakened. France was the first European nation to formally recognise the Confederacy. The Netherlands were next, Britain and Spain followed shortly after and then Brazil. Under the threat of global conflict with the CSA's new allies, Lincoln capitulated on May 9th, 1863. With the break-up of the Union, the Alaska Purchase never occurred. Remaining in Russian hands, it flourished with the gold rush—with only Russians citizens permitted. The Alaskan territory spread during that time, which now included the Yukon and part of the Northwest Territories and northern British Columbia.

"With the Soviets under Stalin and a weakened United States, there was a Soviet stronghold in North America. During the Second World War, the CSA was neutral and with a military impotent USA, Hitler and Stalin, under an unholy alliance, conquered and divided Europe, the Middle East and northern Africa. There was a nuclear conflict in the late 1950's that killed over ten million North Americans and equal number of Soviets, but ultimately, the Soviets came out on top. Imagine a much darker world that never knew the Beatles or the moonshot. All because the actions of one Confederate slave."

"How did our timeline get altered?"

"Obviously, Nat Brady never went on his mission. Someone must have gone back in time, met Nat Brady and managed to initiate a triple-C event, and during that event, killed him."

"So why do we need to intervene a second time?"

"Since the Russians had the same intel on the altered timeline as ourselves, we learned of a Russian plot to ensure the survival of the alternate timeline to ensure a Confederate victory and a non-sale of Russian Alaska to restore the glory of the Soviet Union. Arbing was to be our guide on this mission to identify Nat Brady, but unfortunately, was killed when we lost the Chinook."

"If Nat Brady has already been stopped, why try to stop him again?"

"The other side will seek to protect Brady earlier in the timeline than when he was killed, so we have to terminate him even earlier. If we succeed and kill him over a decade before his mission, and create an earlier temporal branch than the previous, we know he's out of the way."

"The Confederacy will just pick another slave."

"Nat Brady was highly educated. He's the one who proposed the Slave's Bill of Rights to appease the Europeans. His legacy was his persona and negotiating skills and convincing each of the Confederate States to accept his new deal for slavery, which was no easy task, but he prevailed. His dedication to the Confederacy convinced Europe that blacks were not so bad off as slaves. His selling point was that blacks needed the care of the white populous. Slavery offered his people shelter, food and clothing; something they'd struggle to have as a free people. As outlandish as it sounds, that was the prevailing consensus of the African-American for the time. Lincoln opposed blacks having the right to vote, to be on juries, certainly not to hold office or marry whites, and wanted to ship freed slaves out of the United States. Lincoln wasn't for black equality, despite how history remembers him.

"Nat Brady's view is like a Jew defending the Nazi cause."

"He looked at what the free black man would face. He firmly believed blacks were better off as slaves under the new deal than those struggling under the burden of prejudice and struggling to put a roof over their heads or putting food on the table."

"That's crazy."

"To you, a 21st century man, yes. You have to put everything into its historical context. You have to put your mind into that of a 19th century man. If Abe Lincoln were alive today, he'd be destroyed politically and branded as an ignorant, racist bigot. People weren't evil because their values seem to be archaic by our standards. Never judge any man or woman based on your 21st century, politically correct, pompous rational—judge by the values of this time. It's a whole new world out there for you, Tom, and if you are to survive, don't even think of putting your 21st century morals into the context of the mid-nineteenth century. This was a lot of our training, and we trained for a long-term mission, to work and live in these times. We were trained on the trades of this period so we could get work since we were faced with the prospect of perhaps waiting years to find Nat Brady."

"How does the triple-C event work to alter history?"

"It branches time temporarily, and if you are going into a crossover state, as you were, you can create a temporary second timeline branch and alter history through a violation of causality. The problem we are facing, without Brent Arbing to identify him, is that in our history, we have no idea who Nat Brady is. There are no records of this insignificant slave in our timeline. Therefore, we have to go to Austin and seek him out—assuming he's there. He may not even be in Austin yet. He may not be there for ten years."

"How are you certain that our history isn't the right one and Nat Brady's history the altered?"

"The position of Arbing's temporal branch precludes that we are in the altered timeline."

Tom's mind reeled. "Rood is a Confederate sympathiser!"

A black emptiness paused the conversation for a long moment. "I beg your pardon?"

"He and I were talking about the Confederacy. He's quite affectionate about it. He was talking like he regretted that the South had lost the Civil War."

"He's a Virginia man." Bodmar froze for a moment, the revelation making the hair prickle on her scalp. "What else did he say?"

"That every southerner feels a sense of defeat as their side lost the war, their *Second War of Independence,* he said, and then, something about *saving the women."*

"Saving the women? Good God, from what?"

"I have no idea."

"This changes everything. It's now up to you."

"Wha—whaah whoa! What does this have to do with me escaping?"

"It has everything to do with you escaping, and unless you want to own a large part of the responsibility for the end of everything you've ever known—I advise you to shut up and listen."

A slow pause. "I'm listening."

"You have to become Nat Brady's terminator."

"I just want to go home!"

"The home you might end up going to, may not be the same home you left."

"What's preventing you from saving the day?"

"You're filled with a wealth of TREP, Trasler. That is your weapon. You have to shock yourself. I'll give you a taser for that purpose. Once you're glowing, you'll need come in direct contact with Nat Brady and have someone to pull the trigger on him. Hopefully, you and I will meet up and work on this together. If not, you're on your own."

"You expect me to hunt down and kill an innocent man?"

"Saving the world isn't always pleasant. Not only that, you have to take out his master, Joseph Walker, as well."

"Why?"

"He created the new working deal with slaves. What started off as a wager, his plantation practiced a new deal with slaves. He insisted they were properly clothed, had appropriate footwear, permitted marriages and didn't split up families, limited the hours they worked each week, gave them vacation time and never whipped insubordinate slaves. Then, most outlandish, a sort of profit sharing plan if productivity rose to a certain level that allowed them to eventually pay for their freedom. He was probably the only ethical slave owner of the Old South, and we can't allow his model to survive and be adopted by the Confederacy. The North will lose its moral authority to free the slaves if it means they'll be no better off free."

"And you're telling me I have to kill these poor bastards?"

"Let's review." Bodmar was all business. "The name of the slave to be terminated?"

"Nat Brady."

"His Master?"

"Joseph Walker."

"Where?"

"Austin, Texas." Time was short, too short. He had no time to contemplate of what she asked of him. "Tell me again what I'm going to do?" Tom asked.

"Save the world."

"If I don't, then—no Beatles?"

"No Beatles. No moonshot.

Carina had been invisible during this entire time, just as she had always been—a fly on the wall. She touched Tom's hand. "I like the

Beatles, too."

Tom went to the security monitor, keyed in his password, then toggled the cameras. Anderson was on deck with the dinghy after dragging it out of the hold—it was safe for him to return down there. Bodmar gave Tom a piece of equipment about the size if a small laptop.

"It's a solar powered charger for the navigator and laptops, and here," she handed him the same taser Rood used on him. "Get below and pack up. I'll keep Carina here for the time being so that things look normal. Go!"

"I could do with some weapons."

"Cash as well?"

"Sonuvabitch, I completely forgot about money!"

"I'll take care of that, too, but only enough for the short term. You'll have to find a way to make a living. Sorry."

"I have a tourist guide that has a map to the largest placer during the California Gold Rush, called Rich Bar. I can get in and out before it gets discovered in the spring of 1850."

"Do it!"

"But it will delay me from finding Nat Brady."

"There's no rush, Tom. You have years to get this done. Rood will head right for Austin. That's a given and you'll be safer if you go to California. Get financed, then you can save the world."

"Okay." He logged out of the security laptop, ensuring they were locked out of it.

"Go!"

"Oh, one last thing."

"We're running out of time."

"I gotta know! Why does Rood call me Barney?"

"Ever watch Barney and Friends?"

Tom's lips puckered up. "When he said it *Barney style*, was he saying it because he thought I was stupid?"

"You've caught on."

"That sonuvabitch! He named me after a goddamn purple dinosaur?"

"Go, Tom!"

Alerted by the activity on deck, Ralph awoke, dressed, stepped out of his cabin and walked over to Rood's crew as they prepped the dinghy.

Polman dropped the rope ladder and lowered the dinghy by a rope into the water. Anderson climbed down the ladder, clinging to it with one hand like a monkey in a tree, the other deploying the raft. A compressed air container blew into the dinghy, inflating it in just seconds.

"I was getting worried you guys were leaving without me," Ralph said to Rood with a forced chuckle, nervous they were going to abandon him.

"We're not leaving, Parker. The rudder's out."

Ralph sensed something wasn't right. He wasn't certain if it was Rood, or Liedberg, or something freaky from the shared bloodline with kooky Aunt Clara, but a deception was in play, clearly, that's what he sensed. He returned to his cabin and pocketed his 9mm Colt. He went across the deck to the forecastle where Polman stood before the cargo hatch.

"What's going on?" Polman didn't understand, but something in his expression alerted Ralph. He was concealing something beyond the hatch. "Open it." Ralph gestured with his good arm to swing it open. Polman stood firm. Ralph lunged forward and bent to grab the handle.

Lars Göran Rödin attacked from the shadows to his left. He flattened Ralph against the wall, keeping his hand against Ralph's mouth, lowering his captive into the hold.

Alvina-Kristina was gathering the luggage while Tom put his entire focus on the security system, watching Bodmar and Carina, and hadn't seen Ralph's capture. He heard the noise behind him, startled by it, and felt naked without a gun.

"Jesus Christ, Tom!" Ralph, still in Rödin's grip, stared at Tom sitting before Silver's computer. Rödin looked on curiously while Alvina-Kristina greeted Ralph with dark suspicion.

"Got a situation here, don't we Ralphy?" Tom said.

He looked at Tom, then at Alvina-Kristina with luggage in her hands, adding them to a pile. "What's this about?"

"Rood intends to leave the ship tomorrow in the dinghies and once at a safe distance—poof! A ship full of innocent families baked into crispy critters."

"Are you serious?"

"Oh, ya. We're taking off as soon as Rood goes to bed. I changed all the computer passwords and I have the navigation equipment. If he wants them, this ship, and every single passenger, has to arrive safely in New York."

"If you're making a get-a-way, I'm in."

"Don't trust him," Alvina-Kristina said.

"Alvina, he's my wife's brother, for Chrissakes!"

"Thomas, no. He's one of them!"

"How could I possibly be with them? If I stay behind after you leave, they'll kill me, Tom. Rood is totally wacko!"

"My Aunt Clara's are not deceiving me. Do not trust him, Thomas!"

"What does she know about Aunt Clara?" Ralph asked.

"Enough not to trust you, Ralphy. Sorry."

"You're going to have to face Carol and tell her you let me die, Tom. Her brother. How are you going to explain that to your wife? Think about what you're doing!"

He thrust a finger at Ralph. "All right, but I'll be watching you."

"And I'll be watching out for you." The relief on Ralph's features was enormous.

"No! No, Thomas!"

"He's family, Alvina. Besides, even if he is on Rood's side, he knows what we're up to! We can't let him go."

"He can be held by the sailors!"

"He's coming with us."

Alvina-Kristina flapped her arms in disgust. She couldn't believe was happening. Tom asked one of the sailors to keep an eye on him, and Ralph sat under guard in the shadows.

Jackson watched the sailors climbing down the rope ladder to the dinghy when he tapped Rood on the arm. "Can we go back to bed?"

Rood waved a hand at Jackson and Rodriguez, dismissing them. He followed the progress of the crew examining the rudder. To Tom's dismay, Rood wasn't going back to bed. *That sonuvabitch will stay on deck until the repairs are made, except there are no repairs to be made.* Sneaking off on the dinghies would be impossible—unless Rood was taken out.

Jackson and Rodriguez made their way to the office and found Bodmar at her desk and Carina Svensson still tied to the chair.

"I found her earring." Bodmar got up and pinched it into the palm of Rodriguez's hand.

"She was telling the truth?" Rodriguez asked.

"Apparently."

Jackson closed in to look at it. Bodmar stepped behind the men. They spasmed and both looked at the source of the pain, seeing the syringes stuck in their shoulders waving like bamboo sticks in the wind. Jackson folded and dropped, but Rodriguez jolted towards Bodmar. She forced him away, trying to push him down. Rodriguez shuffled towards her in slow motion. Against the wall, he trapped her, grabbing her throat. Bodmar gasped, pulling his wrists, countering the choke. Carina, strapped into the chair, shrieked as Rodriguez continued his attack. He shook Bodmar, and then, like a battery powered toy running out of juice, he slowed, ceased all motion, and crumpled to the ground motionless—the syringe swaying from side to side like a miniature spear.

The floor hatch opened. "Hurry," Tom called, "Anderson's just about done."

"I need two more minutes." Bodmar dragged both unconscious men into their berths and packed the cash and weapons for Tom.

"Stop!" Tom hissed from the hatch, dropping into the hold, shutting the hatch as fast as he opened it.

Anderson came in. Bodmar knelt before Carina, feigning she was verifying the bindings.

"The chief wants the navigator."

"That's unfortunate." Bodmar turned around just as Anderson saw it was missing.

"Where's the navigator? Where is it, Sharon? Where are Jackson and Rodriguez?" He looked into their berth saw the two unconscious men. "You traitor!" He reached for his pistol.

"Terrance, let me speak!"

He wasn't going to let her speak.

Her holster flap was already unbuttoned and that was the difference. If it was a race, and it was, Anderson became the sprinter who just stumbled out of the starting blocks. Anderson looked at Bodmar's gun with his wide Yankee eyes. In a panic, his fingers scratched at the holster, still fumbling for his weapon.

"Stop and listen!" Bodmar pleaded.

He pulled out his 9mm, intent to use it, with no intention of listening.

She fired.

Rood lurched and stared at Liedberg. "Was that a shot?"

Liedberg looked terribly distressed. "I fear so."

"Christ Almighty!" Rood turned his back to Liedberg and took his walkie-talkie from his pocket. "Speak to me." He ate static. He lunged across the deck to the fore hatch.

The mate rushed to his captain. "We are finished!"

"I hope that it is not so," replied Liedberg, "and that Heaven has not deprived us of the best chance of survival which remains to us. We must now put our trust in the mercy of The Almighty and resort to the only remaining expedient. Have the crew armed immediately. We'll pay the villains off!" Liedberg's temper was at a full boil now, but he had to remain calm and to do so, he vented his anger by bestowing upon the soldiers the most vulgar names in his maritime vocabulary.

Bodmar freed Carina and she dropped into the hold. Seeing Rood leaving the main deck, Tom, Alvina-Kristina and Carina scrambled with their luggage and handed them to the sailors, including the navigator and the equipment Bodmar had given. Alvina-Kristina and Ralph went above to settle in the dinghy, while Carina continued to pass the luggage to the sailors and Tom watched the events on Silver's computer, waiting for the money and weapons.

Rood arrived at the office door. Locked. Not just the bolt, but all 12 which they only secured during an emergency. He swore with deep blasphemy when he took his master security key and released the bolts.

He lunged inside, his 9mm in hand.

The spit in Bodmar's mouth was gone. She froze with the handbag of cash and weapons. Anderson lay sprawled on his back, eyes wide open and his jaw slackened just enough to see his top teeth. His arms were spread evenly on each side like a crucifix, a river of blood slid on the slowly pitching deck like a seismograph registering a magnitude eight tremor.

Rood's face didn't change—maintaining the same odd look of pleasant interest.

"Before I blow your brains out, Sharon, would you mind telling me what exactly is going on?"

She dropped the bag of money and went for her pistol. Rood fired. Her dress exploded with cotton and blood splashing from her right leg. She grunted horribly yet continued to withdraw her nine. Rood fired twice more, one in the shoulder, the other in her right arm, still intent on keeping her alive long enough to interrogate her. Her shooting arm was all but crippled, but not quite. She rolled to her side. She put the gun to her face. The back of her skull exploded.

Rood said nothing. He stared dispassionately at Bodmar's body. Rood was neither surprised nor displeased. Under certain circumstances, suicide wasn't just acceptable, but noble. That would be the last respect he would have for her.

He glanced around the office. The security computer had been shut down. He turned it on and while it was booting up, found Jackson in his berth unconscious. He had a blissful little smile, sleeping deeply, far below the level of dreams. No Aunt Clarice tonight.

He anticipated the same when he found Rodriguez.

He gave a little huff of irritation. He went to the security computer and entered the password. His face paled. He went into his berth, booted up his laptop and entered his password. It took just seconds for him to realize just how badly screwed they were.

To prevent Rood from leaving the ship, Polman lowered the second dinghy and engine, still in their packing crates, to the inflated dinghy. Ralph sat at the nose while Alvina-Kristina fit the paddles in the oarlocks.

Tom and Carina appeared at the top of the bulwark. Tom's face was pale as wax. "Bodmar and Anderson are dead! Rood's on his way!"

"Jesus Christ, Tom, what the hell's going on?" Ralph asked. The stunning news shocked Alvina-Kristina into silence. Carina scrambled down the ladder two rungs at a time, illustrating the urgency.

"Rood's a traitor to the mission, that's what." Tom leapt over the rail and put his feet on the top rung of the ladder. "Thanks for everything, Captain."

"I thank you, Trasler. We are in your debt."

"We're all in Carina's debt. Make sure everyone understands that she saved us all."

"I hold a very different opinion of her from that which I had hitherto entertained. God grant that we may someday be permitted to prove to that courageous woman that she has not to deal with ungrateful people."

"Wish us luck."

"All great actions return to God, from whom they are derived, but you know I should see you set off to Long Island in that rubber boat with great uneasiness. Godspeed, Trasler." The captain gave Tom a bottle protected by a sheet of canvas and stuffed it in the same sack containing Silver's computer. Tom looked at Liedberg, his eyes questioning. "The bottle of vodka, Mr. Trasler, to celebrate once you have succeeded."

"God bless you, Captain!"

"Just a taste, Trasler. I have instructed Mr. Parker to chaperone your drinking." He pointed down at the dinghy. "I have installed your luggage as requested."

"Thank you." Tom scurried down the ladder.

"Hurry!" Carina shouted. "Rood will be here any moment."

"Did you get the money and guns?" Alvina-Kristina asked.

"No. Rood killed Sharon first," Carina said.

"We have no guns or money?" Alvina-Kristina yelled. The shock of Bodmar's death was brief, secondary at this point—the new crisis far more pressing.

"We'll have to make do without," Tom said as he settled into the dinghy.

"We cannot do without," Alvina-Kristina countered.

"You got a bottle of booze from Liedberg, but no cash, you moron?" Ralph said and chuckled.

Tom felt his head. The panic was instantaneous. "My baseball cap! I lost my Expos cap!"

"It is of no importance," Alvina-Kristina said. "Buy another."

"And where am I to buy another? At the local hatters?"

"I have a gun," Ralph smiled as he pulled the 9mm from his jacket pocket.

"See, and you didn't want me to bring him." Tom untied the dinghy's rope from the ladder.

"We need money." Alvina-Kristina was enraged. "How can we find a tolerable dwelling with no means of payment?"

"Yes," Carina added. "How do you propose we eat or hire travel?"

"What happened to all of your money?" Tom challenged Carina.

"It is buried in my trunk and I had no time to obtain it."

"So it's all my fault?"

"You have liquor and yet no money," Alvina-Kristina said. "Your priorities are revealed."

"We'll figure something out." He faced Carina. Hard.

Her mouth popped open. "How dare you even think something so wicked!"

"But it is what you do."

"Get on your knees and beg for my forgiveness!"

"I have a gun," Ralph repeated, raising his voice over Carina's.

"Guys, we really need to leave!"

"That is a wicked idea of yours, Thomas, and you distress me," Alvina-Kristina said.

"I have a gun!" Ralph shouted.

"Shut up, Ralph." Tom turned to Carina. "Just take one for the team."

"On—your—knees!"

"I'm sorry, I'm completely stressed out." He fell to his knees. "Forgive me."

She leaned with her back against the dinghy and crossed her arms. "No!"

"Goddamn bloody women! Let's get the hell out of here!"

"We will have nothing to eat, nor have a roof over our head, nor the means to travel," Alvina-Kristina shouted.

"For the last time, I have a goddamn gun!" Ralph was pointing it at Tom.

Tom realized that Ralph had a gun—*and it was pointed at him.* "You sonuvabitch! You said you were on our side!"

"Ya, and you believed me, dummy."

"Wretch! You are nothing but a traitor!" Alvina-Kristina shouted. "I told you he was not to be trusted." Alvina-Kristina sat there, shaking, balling her fists at Tom.

"I was also against him coming!" Carina shouted.

"He never listens!" Alvina-Kristina switched to Swedish and continued to yell at Tom. Carina joined in, twice a loud.

"You deliberately planned on taking us all back in time, you sonuvabitch!" Tom yelled at Ralph. The women were still yelling at him in Swedish. "Will you two shut the hell up!" They didn't shut up. In fact, it only throttled their tirade.

Ralph's shoulders shook while he released a low chuckle. "Rood thought using the Chinook was insane, and wanted the boat, and the plan was once the helicopter landed, you guys would be sent to shore with *The Salty Dog's* tender. Everything blowing up changed the game."

"Why, Ralph?"

"Rood and I have been buddies since before Afghanistan and I'm part of the mission. Not the official mission, of course, but his mission."

"To preserve the Confederacy?"

"I wish I was in Dixie, hooray! Hooray!" Ralph sung, finishing with a chuckle.

"Do the others know of your secret mission with Rood? Or do you just have a big mouth and forgot to keep it shut?"

Ralph's face went blank. "I think I might have to kill you."

Tom tapped his skull. "You need the computer passwords."

Ralph licked his lips. "It's the only thing that's going to keep you alive, but I can't promise anything for this bitch," he said, nodding at Carina.

"Thomas, you have brought ruin upon us all!" Carina shrieked.

Tom had it with Carina's rant but also saw an opportunity—assuming she and Alvina-Kristina would buy in. "Will you shut up, you . . . you goddamn bitch!"

"Bastard!"

She leapt for Tom. Her fists were swinging before she even got to him. *Yup, she bought in.*

Ralph chuckled while the two of them self-destructed. Carina had Tom in a headlock and pounded his face with one punch after another. The moment had become so sweet, so enjoyable, that Ralph took his attention off Alvina-Kristina to watch Tom get beaten up by a girl. Life couldn't be any better than this.

Alvina-Kristina sprang from her seat so fast Ralph never had time to react. Her arms stretched out, she struck Ralph's chest like a battering ram. He somersaulted backwards. He fired his first round. It missed Tom by two feet. The second round went vertical into the night sky. He tumbled into the water before he could even pull the trigger for a third shot.

Carina released Tom, not gently, and took the oar and swung it down hard, walloping Ralph's head with the sharp edge. A burst of bubbles broke the surface as he drifted back under. For a moment, Tom thought she was about to turn around and wallop him with the paddle, he knew her contemplations were all about doing just that, but she held off the impulse. Alvina-Kristina, stomach flat on the nose of the dinghy, waited for Ralph as he bobbed to the surface; blood poured off his skull and oozed into the water.

"Ass-hool!" She grabbed his hair and shoved him deep under water.

"Sonuvabitch!" Tom complained, staring at Carina while rubbing his cheek. "Did you have to be so goddamn convincing?"

Carina took the oar, shook it at Tom, and he knew if time wasn't so tight, she'd be beating him with it, instead, she shoved the side of the boat to push them away.

"I wasn't trying to be convincing. I was trying to hurt you. I wish I could have hurt you more, but, the night is still young."

Alvina-Kristina sat next to Tom while Carina took her place at the nose of the dinghy where Ralph had been just moments before. She looked down to see how he was doing. Ralph surfaced in a half-conscious daze and with only one good arm, splashed for the ladder.

"Rood," Ralph cried. He clung onto the ladder. A waterlogged cry, gurgled by water spilling from his mouth. "Rood . . . help!"

Rood slapped the banana clip into the carbine. *Payback is a bitch and what he had planned next will make the torching of the boy look like a folk dance*. He held the remote detonator in his hand, tossed it in the air a few inches, caught it then put it in his right pocket. He lunged out of the office.

The blackjack whacked him in the forehead.

Following the momentum of the swing, Rödin's body lunged from the right side. Rood lay on the floor, pretty as you please, taking a nap. Liedberg, waiting on the other side of the bulkhead, waved at his crew concealed within the berths.

"They are in our power!"

While Liedberg took the gun and detonator in Rood's pocket, the armed men rushed inside the office, greeted by the bloody mess and the two bodies. All of the secret equipment had been locked-up or shut down.

"Get the Negro and Mexican to forever vanquish the resistance of the ruffians. Quickly!" Liedberg ordered.

The captain stared down triumphantly at Rood, who slowly came to. He was groggy yet Liedberg had his full attention. "Colonel Rood, you and your blackguards will be paid for your troubles with the cat-o'-nine-tails and the chains. Then you will be delivered over to the justice of your country. When that blessed day comes to pass when your body hangs from the gallows, I shall have no further wants in life!"

Tom revved outboard engine to curl the dinghy away from the ship. He had a compass in his pocket, consulting it, headed due north to take them to Long Island. He turned the handle to full throttle.

"We have no money," Alvina-Kristina complained.

"I know, I know. We'll think of something. I wish I had my hat."

"I cannot believe you thought you could inveigle me into selling my body for your meal and travel." Carina was still in an ecstasy of rage.

"Yes, yes, Carina, I was wrong," replied Tom. "That's enough of this nonsense."

"You do not appear desirous to prolong a conversation which you were so very eager to begin."

"I apologise!"

"It was a wicked idea indeed that you had and nothing justifies it."

"Bodmar got killed and I'm still freaking out."

"You may not be in your senses, but you were lucid in thought when you said *it is what I do*."

"We have no money or guns," Alvina-Kristina persisted. "And I told you not to trust Ralph Parker and we almost got turned over to Rood, which would have been our deaths. I have never felt as excited as I do now and it is you who is solely responsible!"

Tom said nothing. He knew he was no match for two enraged women, and if he were alive fifty years from now, and was to meet them again, they would still not be finished with their tirade.

Liedberg rushed to the main deck. The sky had cleared and he could see the dinghy three hundred feet away, trailing a wake of bubbling white froth bright in the moonlight.

"Trasler, come back. We have the ship!" All he heard was the gruff roar of the engine, that and the voices of two enraged women peeling above the rumble. The dinghy buzzed up and down the swells, the engine fading into the backdrop of the waves, droning away into silence. The last he heard was the nagging of the women as they dwindled into the darkness.

Polman bent down, picked up Tom's Expos cap, and handed it to Liedberg.

"Mr. Trasler revered this strange cap," Liedberg said. "He will not be pleased."

"Do you despair of ever seeing him again?" Polman asked.

"Our enigmatic friend is a man who appears quite capable to get out of a scrape to which most others certainly would succumb. Regrettably, it is not a happy circumstance that he is suffering in much distress from the women whom he has thus agitated. I cannot think without great trepidation, my good man Polman, that the unfortunate Mr. Trasler, trapped in their company for perhaps days, will have no respite from their terrible fury. This is one scrape which appears truly hopeless!"

To be continued . . .

ABOUT THE AUTHOR

Born and raised in Montreal, Stephen H Garrity's passion has always been story telling. Having studied film production at Concordia University, the approach Steve takes to his writing is that every story must make a good film as well as a novel. In essence, every story he writes is adapted from a mental screenplay. A diverse writer, Steve's stories range from romantic thrillers, action adventures, to science fiction. Steve, an avid space, history, and military history enthusiast, applies a respectful scientific and historical basis as an integral foundation to his story telling. Even the phases of the moon are accurate for the date he describes.

In addition to his career in freight logistics, Steve assisted his wife Colette with her video production company, while becoming actively involved with Quebec politics during the height of the 1995 Quebec sovereignty referendum. Retiring from politics and turning back to writing after nearly a decade-long hiatus, Steve dusted off his time travel epic, and despite the efforts of an editor and agent, *The Wizard Blew his Horn* could not find a publisher.

In 2004, Steve, his wife Colette and their children, Carina and Matt, moved from Montreal to Kelowna, BC, for a lifestyle change. One of Steve's two new novels, the romantic thriller *Sweet Obsession*, won the 2007 Grand Prize of the Mount Arrowsmith Novel Writing Contest, beating over a hundred contestants; many of them published authors from North America, England and Australia.

In 2008, Steve decided that the time travel epic required a complete makeover and re-imagined it as *The Grandfather Paradox*, spanning five novels, with a lot more dynamics, plot twists and action. Three are complete and the fourth is approaching completion, with a planned release in 2018 for the fifth and final book. He will release *Sweet Obsession* in early 2017.

Steve currently resides in Edmonton, Alberta, as a transportation manager for a workforce accommodation company, with his wife of 36 years, Colette.

www.shgarrity.com

Made in the USA
Charleston, SC
19 July 2016